CHRYSANTHEMUM IN THE SNOW

CHRYSANTHEMUM IN THE SNOW

THE NOVEL OF THE KOREAN WAR

JAMES HICKEY

CROWN PUBLISHERS, INC., NEW YORK

Copyright © 1990 by James Richard Hickey
Map by Alan McKnight

Published by Crown Publishers, Inc., 201 East 50th Street, New York, New York 10022

CROWN is a trademark of Crown Publishers, Inc.
Manufactured in the United States of America
Library of Congress Cataloging-in-Publication Data

Hickey, James Richard.
    Chrysanthemum in the snow : the novel of the Korean War / James
Richard Hickey.
        p.   cm.
    1. Korean War, 1950–1953—Fiction.   I. Title.
PS3558.I228C47   1990
813'.54—dc20   89-38605
ISBN 0-517-57402-0

10 9 8 7 6 5 4 3 2 1
First Edition

For Colonel Charles R. Thomas, Armor, United States Army—

An honest soldier and dear friend of the long evenings, he waits across the river, his sword sheathed forever, hearing the sad bugle of the longest evening of them all.

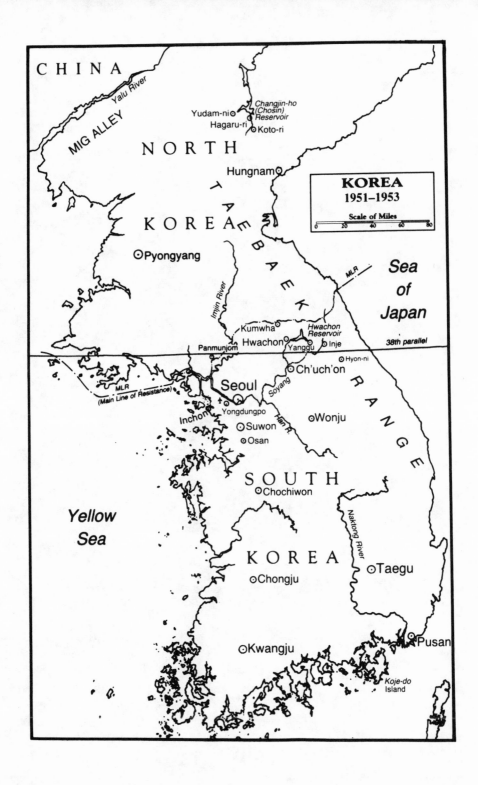

Author's Note

The few Americans who had slept awoke to a dismal rain. Anxiously, they stared down the road ahead of them. Here, three miles north of Osan, the motor road lifted gently to cross a saddle in the ridge that lay perpendicular to it. The ridge upon which the Americans had dug—puny by Korean standards—rose only three hundred feet above the low ground. Nevertheless, the railroad bent to the east, around the ridge. The two arterials rejoined in a few thousand yards and continued to Suwon, eight miles through the mist. Twenty miles beyond Suwon lay Seoul.

In a wry sense, it was only fair that this troubled day of July 5, 1950, announce itself by raining on the Americans; two hundred and forty hours earlier it had rained on the North Koreans whom the American soldiers atop the ridge now awaited. The earlier rain had wetted the invasion by North Korea of neighboring South Korea on Sunday, June 25: today's rain wetted the American response to that invasion. The conflagration that was about to ignite here on the Suwon-Osan road would rage for three years. It would earn a series of names. At first, it would be called the Korean Police Action. Then it would be labeled the Korean Conflict. Later yet, an exhausted world would admit that the conflagration had been, all along, the Korean War.

Lt. Col. Charles B. Smith, 21st U.S. Infantry, had positioned his thin battalion on a saddle in the ridge athwart the road. The command greeted the soggy military dawn by test-firing weapons. Almost at once a few rounds of 105-mm artillery burst on the road ahead. This signaled that the four howitzers spaded in two thousand yards rearward were registering for the day's work.

Smith's riflemen—389 enlisted and 17 officers—and the 134 artillerymen behind them breakfasted on cold rations. The C-ration menu included lima beans and ham, pinto beans and franks, and hamburger patties in gravy. The enlisted men were paid about eighty dollars a month, their officers not greatly more.

The officers stood together now, glancing often toward Suwon, talking in low tense tones. They were professionals, Regular Army and career reserve officers, stolid men who marched the methodical years between promotions. They weighed their prospects, which were not good. The force, newly yanked out of the occupation garrisons of Japan, had with it a hastily assembled collection of small-bore weapons. Among their twelve hundred rounds of artillery ammunition, they possessed exactly six rounds of HEAT—high-explosive antitank—all that could be found in Japan. Colonel Smith had issued that wealth to the howitzer sited just south of the saddle.

At about 0700 hours an American soldier pointed north. "There," he said. Others sighted in the same direction. They saw approaching a North Korean infantry-armor column spearheaded by eight Russian-manufacture T34 tanks, on that day likely the finest in the world. The initial sighting done, the men adjusted their testicles and rechecked weapons. A few made morbid jokes. They waited. Something was imminent, but the menace was yet unspecific.

An hour later, the lead T34s were about two thousand yards from the 21st Infantry's line of resistance. An officer shouted an order. The four howitzers supporting Task Force Smith engaged.

The Americans watched the conventional 105-mm rounds explode harmlessly on the thick frontal armor of the tanks. Even the densest understood the meaning.

Ignoring the firestorm, the tanks came on, followed by the North Korean infantrymen. If he knew he was fired upon by the American army, the North Korean commander clearly thought little of it—certainly no more than did the two hundred million Americans who had sent it there.

The morning accelerated. Within minutes, the combat range closed to fewer than a thousand yards. Smith's men opened with their 75-mm recoilless rifles. Shrugging that off easily, the T34s lunged up the road to the saddle, spewing fire and steel. An American second lieutenant, more mud on his clothing than on his courage, rose up out of the east road ditch and fired twenty-two 2.36-inch rockets into the rear of the tanks. There, claimed the training manual, the skin was thinner. It was not thin enough—boldly, the tanks came on.

PART

ONE

1

SNIPER RIDGE, NEAR KUMWHA, NORTH KOREA, JANUARY 4, 1952

The heavy wind from the Taebaek Mountains had howled for days. Tonight, at times Siberian-fierce, it snatched powdery spoondrift from the sharp edges of the prominent ridges and, keening angrily, hurled it at the sentinels in the American trenches.

Vision stunted by iced eyelids, hunched into hooded parkas and thick-pile caps, these men cowered in the darkness, backs submissively to the bitterly cold wind but ears strained to catch even more lethal rhythms. Occasionally one of them would ease the bolt of his rifle rearward a few millimeters, then ease it forward against the chambered cartridge, slowly, gently, so that the snick of steel on brass would not betray him to enemy ears. Having reassured himself the bolt was not frozen, he would breathe again.

Snow had drifted against the west side of the bunker, making it seem only another of the myriad snow-clad hummocks. Only viewing from the east could an observer have determined—and then with difficulty—that this white lump was a man-made structure, and that men did international business there.

About midnight, a returning patrol from the Third Platoon, shivering with cold and fatigue, had detoured past the bunker to report casually to the Second Platoon occupants there that the windblown snow had covered the dead man again.

The dead man had been there when G Company came onto the position. He lay about six hundred yards to the northeast, between the two lines, within sniper range of both. Because of this fact, no retrieval party could go to him in daylight. He could have been lugged in on any of the nights the company had been there, but the frozen corpse had been stripped and was so badly mutilated it was easy for the Americans to believe that the dead man was a North Korean and by that conviction not burden their own patrols with him. Whoever he was, the morning report of somebody's army carried him as missing in action.

Tentatively stateless dead men could wait until spring.

denies humanity

*   *   *

A vise squeezed Robertson's shoulder. Sergeant Carver's husky trench whisper clawed down into his sleep and pulled him up. Carver's words floated on an urgency that instantly effected the awakening.

"Lieutenant! George One on the line." Carver's voice dropped into a true whisper. "I think the Koreans are about to hit us."

Robertson nodded wearily, although it was so dark in the bunker Carver could not have seen it. The lieutenant had been dozing, head against the forestock of his carbine, in the corner of the log and sandbag shelter. The bunker, similar to a dozen others on the ridge, represented the solitary outpost the platoon maintained ahead of the George Company perimeter.

As Robertson shifted to put the receiver of the telephone to his ear, dirt loosened from the wall and insinuated itself into his collar to creep coldly down his back. Robertson arched away from the discomfort. Absently, he stroked his hair, feeling dampness there, although the temperature outside the bunker could not have been zero degrees Fahrenheit. He hawked to clear his throat. "Three," he said, identifying himself to his caller.

Robertson sniffed. The aroma of the stagnant winter line . . . bunker smell . . . man odors, tonight's damp exhalations tinged with the acid suggestion of yesterday's stale urine; over that the nagging presence of human feces.

Driven by a commanding firmness, Captain Hartung's broad Arkansas accent came across the telephone line. "George One here. What is your situation?"

Robertson hesitated before answering. "Quiet, Captain. We're on easy alert." Robertson waited out the silence that followed, stifling an urge to badger, knowing from experience that idle questions only cluttered tactical communications. Ideally, information went up; orders came down.

Clarification came quickly. "I've been trying to raise you on this goddamned line for five minutes, Robertson. I was about to send a runner to you. Lieutenant Noume reports he heard infiltrators down below his area. He thinks it's a raiding party." Hartung paused and added, "They must have brushed your position. Two of your Second Platoon people came in a few minutes ago like Chicken Little screaming that the goddamned sky is falling down."

Robertson evaluated. Noume was the plump, round-faced Hawaiian who ran the Third Platoon. That stolid officer rarely imagined goblins in the night. The Chicken Littles likely would be the two replacements who had joined the platoon the previous day. Men new to the Korean front did imagine goblins, but often quite validly.

Images of danger began to form in Robertson's mind. Knowing the others in the bunker would listen for threat, he disciplined his voice. Sergeant Carver would have cuffed them alert. Now they would dangle in impotent anxiety while the officers chatted on the telephone.

"How big a party, Captain?"

"Noume said he heard about a squad's worth, but thought that might be only the outguard of a larger force downslope from him." After a thoughtful pause, the company commander added, "A platoon. At least a platoon. Noume held his people in check so they wouldn't fire on them, but he thinks they'll either come back at him or go down your way. May be just a trench raid."

"That's a bunch for a trench raid," Robertson replied. At this point in the Korean War—a war now locked into the trenches on the red ridges—a platoon of North Koreans represented a large and determined body of enemy. An NKA squad might blow a steel-jacketed kiss or two and vanish into the frigid night. A platoon came to kill or be killed.

Hartung could only repeat, "A platoon, Robertson. I called battalion. They smell something larger than a raid. But then they always do."

Robertson's "yes sir" confirmed the sourness in Hartung's opinion of the Second Battalion headquarters. The battalion CP behind the ridge was notoriously nervous, a state of mind not always helpful to the companies on line.

After a pause, during which he began to visualize his tactical problem, Robertson asked, "What time is it? I can't look at my watch." Robertson's query certified his difficulty. He swam through chill velvet blackness toward unseen danger, deprived even of vision to read his watch. But to flare a light was to destroy night vision. To destroy night vision was to invite disaster.

"O-four-ten," Hartung replied. "What do you make of it?"

As Robertson factored in the clock, the picture began to develop, as the print emerges from the photographer's solution. But he decided to keep it from his men for a few moments, giving them those pitiful seconds to clear the cobwebs of sleep from their minds. Shortly, they'd need all their faculties. On the rifle line, better to scale upward from a graveyard whistle than to scale downward from a firehouse panic.

"I don't know, sir," Robertson answered. "If they work west from Noume's area and keep above us, they could pass well clear of my position."

Robertson nodded toward the shadow he assumed was Carver, wanting to enlist the black squad sergeant in the pathetic conspiracy against the other men in the bunker. But he knew from the tension in their respirations that his ruse was a weak one.

Hartung lashed back, "You know goddamned well better than that. They came up that goddamned gully. I should have mined that son of a bitch. I should—"

Robertson cut in. "Orders, Captain?"

Robertson could almost see Hartung shrug. "I'll keep a line to battalion," the captain said simply. "Sort it out and get back to me as soon as you can. You want flares?"

"Negative on illumination, sir. Not until I position my people."

The instant the receiver left Robertson's ear, Carver's hand reached through the ink to take it.

"Business for the stand," Robertson announced.

Someone growled, "Don't those bastards ever sleep?"

No one answered.

Robertson's slightest movement in the bunker brushed other flesh. He drew a deep breath to drown his own rising excitement and partitioned his mind while he thought it out. His outpost lay athwart any meaningful North Korean movement against the company. Less so at night, but in daylight a mere squad in the few yards of trench around it could cover any logical approach. If Lieutenant Noume's nocturnal prowlers intended to fight, they intended to fight here. It was only moments away from usable morning half-light. The North Koreans wanted darkness to achieve success, then daylight to exploit it. A mere raid would have come in much earlier.

Robertson had spent many hours weighing the host of potential threats on Sniper Ridge. He understood well the prelude of this one. The North Koreans had come up the gully, lightly brushing his own flank. Then the terrain had seduced them up toward Noume. Likely that movement was deliberate, but even if it was a blunder, it was one the NKA platoon leader would detect early. When he did, he would turn down the ridge again and crash into Robertson's trench and into George Three.

The men began to clamor half questions, each vowel muted with the anxiety of the prey hiding from the predator.

Robertson shushed them. He asked Carver, "Who's where?"

Carver obviously had his report prepared. "Solly and Kraut are outside where the trench curves. Sam Dougherty and the two replacements are out near the gully. The rest are here in the hole. I've been rotating them every thirty minutes. It's colder than a witch's tit out there." *emasculated*

Robertson did not answer. They were blind and naked, and they all knew it now. Because the two replacements had run up the hill—"bugged out," in Korean War parlance—he had suffered two casualties before the fight even began, leaving him with nine men. He felt a momentary anguish that the men with him tonight were principally his old squad, which he had relinquished to become platoon sergeant a few weeks earlier, then platoon officer only days earlier, his distance from them increasing with each promotion. He repressed that thought quickly. It was unfair to pursue it. [Always a lethal lottery, when the infantryman's wheel turned, it turned.

just infantry fodder

Wordlessly, Robertson groped for his carbine and helmet and went out through the narrow square of lesser darkness between the sandbags, sensing that Carver followed. The two leaders stood together in the trench. Eyes were useless. Robertson inhaled deeply, savoring briefly the cleansing effect of the bitterly cold air. The wind surged and lulled, as if it, too, had tired in the tedium of the long night's work. Listening to the corners of that wind, a man could detect the fitful sounds of the stalemate, as eerie in the interstitial silences as in the noises themselves. A mortar far to the west farted three quick rounds and a machine gun stuttered. Then frigid black silence again.

Robertson long had thought this night possible, and, in recent days, because the North Koreans across the broad valley from them had grown aggressive, likely. He had known from the outset, thirteen days earlier when George Company relieved a company of the 17th Regiment there, that he had an indefensible position. George Three, which the platoon called Robertson Forward, as distinct from Robertson Rear, the platoon CP about two hundred yards rearward, was literally only a wide spot in the trench. Robertson had improved it, building sandbag blast walls on the two exposed sides, solid on the west but leaving a small entryway in the east wall, but nothing could be done about the geography.

There lay the crucial flaw. The main George Company trenchworks snaked around the circumference of a steep-sided but round-topped hill with a deep gully slashed into its northeast face. The gully defined Robertson's right flank. Beyond, to the east and upslope, Lieutenant Noume's five clustered bunkers guarded the company's interests. In Robertson's sector of the company front, to the left of the gully, a crumbling trench that could not be improved in the winter frost meandered north and westward, sagging lazily downslope until it paused at George Three. From there, the trench struck directly westward across a puny rise, thence sharply southwest, curving strongly back toward the crest of the hill. There, at the turn, the trench came under observation of Lt. Max Shapiro, who did business out of two bunkers named Mutt and Jeff. Shapiro's defensive fires covered the communications trench and the mine field and the flesh-eating concertina and apron wire beyond.

Noume's front was also mined and wired, a fact the North Koreans soon would learn. Robertson's was not, which they might well have noticed. In any event, George Three was at the apex of a miniature salient anchored on the gully to its right and the right-angle turn in the trench to its left. The terrain contours channeled marauders to it; nothing except high-angle fire could support it.

Twice Robertson had discussed this weakness with Hartung.

Twice Hartung had refused to let him abandon the bunker.

Hartung even stabbed a dirty fingernail into his map to prove the rightness of his viewpoint.

Then reinforce me. Let me have some wire.

No wire. And reinforce with what? This goddamned hill can't be defended by the whole fucking battalion if the gooks get mean about it.

Then mine the gully.

I want the gully for a sallyport.

If we can sally out, the other side can sally in.

Keep a full squad out there and I'll give you an extra BAR.

An extra automatic rifle out there will be useless as tits on a boar hog.

I'm the goddamned commander!

Yessir.

Carver broke Robertson's reflections with a quiet "What are your orders, Lieutenant Robertson?"

Notwithstanding his situation, Robertson smiled at Carver's crisp competence. "I don't know where they'll hit, Tommy. String the men out along the trench to the east and tell them to cover the ground between here and the main wire. Keep them in hand so they don't fire into Lieutenant Noume's people."

Quickly, Robertson briefed Carver on what the company commander had told him via the telephone, adding to that his own appraisal.

"They came up the gully?"

"I'd guess that. As soon as they hit some resistance from Noume, they'll turn back down on us. Likely we are their main objective."

Carver turned away without comment and called a loud "Outside!" to the men in the bunker.

Robertson waited until the bustle issuing from the bunker assured him the men had complied with Carver's command, then stepped off along the trench toward the gully. He walked quickly for several yards, then clambered out of the trench onto the ground in front. Several times he paused to listen, but heard nothing he could not attribute to imagination. He chided himself. The signal would be indubitable when it came. He estimated he had ten minutes—a night firefight unfolded slowly.

Sensing the gully ahead of him, Robertson halted. Kneeling, he put his carbine down and removed his helmet, throwing it aside. Feeling a now-familiar inner excitation, he withdrew the hachimaki from the left breast pocket of his field jacket and fastened it around his head. As he fumbled at the knot, the thousand old negations cried in his mind, making him once again a man at war with himself. ← persona of war, inner conflict

A sliver of frosted moon punched through the cold clouds overhead. The linen of the hachimaki—if someone else had been there to see it in that moment—was as poignant in white as a fresh gunshot wound is poignant in red.

This done, he retrieved his carbine and went on. Soon a shadowy figure acknowledged his presence with, "I'm too goddamned frozen to shoot, but halt or I'll call my big brother."

Robertson laughed softly and dropped down into the trench beside Sam Dougherty. "Little humor never hurts, Sam. And I wish we had your big bud tonight and a hundred like him."

Dougherty snorted. "He's kind of an ass, to tell you the truth. Owns a liquor store in Portland. You got a brother like that?"

Robertson shook his head. "Sister," he said. "Haven't seen her in ten years."

Dougherty made no reply. Robertson knew he stared at the hachimaki. After a few seconds, Dougherty grunted, "When you put on your samurai's headband, Lieutenant, I smell trouble."

Robertson gestured up the hill. "Wish I had better news, Sam, but that's about it." Robertson quickly told Dougherty what he had told Carver minutes earlier. Dougherty, a tall, cleanly handsome thirty-two-year-old private first class, had fought as a platoon sergeant in World War II. With Dougherty, there was never profit in subterfuge.

Dougherty listened, then noted quietly, "The two new troopers bugged out on me before I could grab them."

"I know. They went in on the company CP. Maybe that is where they should be. Two more won't make any difference to us." Robertson scuffed his toe in the filthy, hard-packed snow in the bottom of the trench. "You'd better come back with me, Sam."

The two men stared at each other. Deliberately, Dougherty fished out his lighter and lit a cigarette. The unexpected light slammed into Robertson's pupils. "Goddamn it!" he hissed, although he knew Dougherty understood full well the error of revealing a night-fighting position by showing a light.

Dougherty chuckled loudly and waved the glowing coal toward the southeast. "That's the idea, Lieutenant. Two birds with one stone. A nervous man needs a smoke and the Koreans can find me here now. They'll be along shortly and I'll slow them up a bit for you."

"Come out, Sam. That's a direct order."

"You've never given me a direct order before."

"I've never had to. But I won't leave you out here alone."

Dougherty drew on his cigarette before answering. "I'd better stay, Lieutenant. They'll fall back to the trench line after Lieutenant Noume welcomes them. Then they'll regroup and fight along the trench toward the bunker. At least that's how I'd do it. They are going to whip our ass bad enough without you abandoning your flank." Dougherty stared up the hill. "They'll probably try to cut us off with artillery fire," he added calmly.

Robertson sighed. He knew Dougherty's assessment was correct. Suddenly, in his mind, he saw the North Korean officer's face, aloof, fierce, like the furtive Korean faces he had seen while riding past them in a truck—staring up, cold, alien, hard with hatred for Caucasians.

The North Korean would have studied the bunker on George Three through large, black binoculars. He would easily grasp the significance of the gully in relation to the salient. He would take out his contour map. His finger would be long and sensitive and it would ride the gully almost to Noume's obvious fire lanes. Perhaps he would pencil an X there for instant reference. Then he would let the finger go up a few yards farther—he'd want to test his luck there before turning right and downslope. Three or four flankers could screen all that movement on a black night. Detection would mean only a blind skirmish and a man or two down. Then? He'd drop off a squad to protect his rear from Noume and get down to business with George Three.

Robertson put it aside, knowing his time was limited. "It's a living," he said, "and better than the navy." When Dougherty made no response, he repeated his earlier order. "Come out with me. I can't leave you out here."

(margin annotation: racial stereotypes)

After a long hesitation, Dougherty said quietly, "Until I shit in my own mess kit, I was a pretty good NCO. I might have been stupid enough to get myself court-martialed and broken but I was never wrong-headed enough to give a man an order I knew he'd never obey."

"That's how it is then?" Robertson asked levelly.

"That's how it has to be." Dougherty threw down his cigarette and began to place grenades on the edge of the trench. "You'd better get back to the men. They'll be nervous as a virgin bride. I'll hold up this end for a while before I come out. Maybe the Koreans will get enough of it tonight out here at the gully."

Robertson assessed it. Finally, he said, "You are my best, Sam. I mean that."

Dougherty snorted playfully. "Thought you'd never admit it. Been that way from the first."

Robertson turned away. After a few paces he paused and looked back toward Dougherty, seeing only a vague shape over a rifle that pointed menacingly upslope, along the obvious recoil trajectory of the North Koreans. Robertson brought to mind Dougherty's face, proportioned strength under carefully combed wavy hair. Around his green eyes Dougherty was chiseled and sculpted. Robertson called back, "Did I ever tell you that you are the only man I've ever met I'd call handsome?"

Dougherty laughed. "Hell of a compliment, Lieutenant. If you were a woman, I'd invite you back."

Robertson turned away again. Dougherty called out, dropping all formality, "Robbie?"

Robertson halted. He sensed the finality in Dougherty's voice, as if Dougherty understood they might never talk again. But there also was an undertone of uncertainty and apology there.

As he waited for Dougherty to continue, the wind came and whipped the snow at Robertson's feet. He thought Dougherty had reconsidered and would now ask to return to the bunker with him. Surrendering the gully flank would leave them all dangling dangerously, since it would render the inevitable contact with the Koreans immediate and uncontrolled, but Sam Dougherty, any man on the ridge that night, was worth the exchange.

Suddenly Robertson angered. Ten months earlier on the Korea-bound troopship, in his ignorance he had fantasized that the war would contain for him grand charges of cheering immortal infantrymen, righteous Americans behind triumphant regimental colors surging to inexorable victory over some anonymous expendable enemy then identified to him as "gooks." But he had defrauded himself. Korea had been a game of blindman's bluff,

11

played out like this, on black nights, by minuscule units of gasping men frozen to the bone or steeped in their own sweat. When the missiles hit them, they screamed; often, as they died, they whimpered. If there was a grander issue involved, it was either shrouded in the summer dust or buried, like the dead man in the ravine northeast of them, under the winter snow.

He goaded Dougherty. "What is it, Sam?"

Now Dougherty's apology surfaced. "I . . . does our friendship permit . . ."

When Dougherty hesitated, Robertson stepped a few paces closer. "Best just to say it, Sam."

When it came, uncharacteristic for Doughtery, it came from around the corner of a clumsy preface.

"Hell, Robbie, you know who I am. And you know I slept with heavy thoughts enough long nights in a Leavenworth cell house to know when another man is hurting—"

"Sam, there isn't a lot of time—"

"Hear me out, Robbie. I need to get something said and you need to hear it. I know you wear that hachimaki on your head for more reasons than to keep your brain warm. Choi explained enough about it to me one night that I know it relates to something damned critical for you."

The breath went out of Robertson. When he filled his lungs again, the cold was sharp and vivid. <u>Now it was a rapier that pierced, not a frigid hand that crushed</u>.

"Am I common gossip?" Robertson asked bitterly.

After a silence, Dougherty spoke softly. "No. Choi thinks too much of you to gossip about you, even if he speculates. And if the others know anything, they've never mentioned it to me. They gossip, but it's the kind of gossip you'd want to hear to your face." Dougherty emitted an apologetic laugh and let it hang between them.

"Does Sam Dougherty gossip, then?"

"That's as unfair a question as you've ever asked me, Robbie."

Robertson bit his lip, feeling suddenly trapped and helpless, an emotion as overpowering as the anger of moments earlier.

"I know it is, Sam. I'm behaving like a green second lieutenant who is about to get his ass whipped good for the first time."

"You're better than that. And you know I don't gossip about buddies *or* officers, both of which you are to me. But I feel closer to you than to any other man I've known since I enlisted in '42. I'm bound to listen to what's gnawing away inside you—"

Robertson had interrupted with a sharp, warning sound. To that, he appended quietly, "Then you know it's ugly, Sam."

Dougherty's laugh was eerie. "I've heard ugly things before. A man hears about lots of ugly things in prison. And however ugly it is, I know it happened to you last June when you went down to Chunchon. Other than that one night, you haven't been out of my sight long enough since last April to get into the kind of trouble that eats a hole like the one eaten in you." He paused. "Little troubles a man talks about to his friends. Your trouble is a big one or you'd have spit it out before now to get a second opinion on it."

"Believe me, Sam, you don't want to give a second opinion on this one."

Dougherty spluttered helplessly. "Damn it, Robbie, you're making this hard for me. These kinds of conversations don't come around every day. I'm only trying to say for what it's worth to you right now that I wish I could have carried some of a buddy's load for him, and that whatever it is, I hope it heals for you."

Breathing now in short, labored gasps, Robertson inched closer, until he could see Dougherty clearly outlined. Perhaps *this* was the time to spit it out, share it with another, even for a few moments . . . if he could speak it publicly, stand it up for Dougherty's inspection, maybe Robertson could stand beside it and look fully into its face for the first time since it had come into his life that June night.

Unconsciously, he brushed the hachimaki on his forehead. Closing his eyes as he spoke, almost as if the tall private were no longer there, Robertson began quietly, "Sam, I did something worse in Chunchon than you ever heard about in jail. I—"

Upslope, a barely perceptible flash of dull red chemical light exploded across the snow, followed by a crushing noise. That would be an anti-personnel mine, signaling the initial collision between the blind North Koreans and the blind Americans on Sniper Ridge. A solitary human scream followed. Then came the customary shocked silence.

The black echo focused, demanding in its implications, as implacable as a falling away of the scaffold's door.

"They've hit Lieutenant Noume!" Dougherty called loudly. "I guess our conversation is over."

Robertson listened to it. At first it was only a few Garands, interlaced with the heavier reports of a Browning automatic rifle, answered by the quicker chatter of the North Korean weapons. Then all the noises merged into discord, the tit-for-tat of a night skirmish on the Korean ridges.

Robertson spun and began running west, toward the bunker. Even as he ran, the firing petered out.

Dougherty shouted, "So long, good buddy. Been a hell of a ride with you."

Robertson did not respond. After Lieutenant Noume, it was Sam Dougherty's turn at the gully flank. Next, that of Don Robertson and the rest of the men on George Three.

When the bunker rose out of the darkness, Robertson dropped into the trench. The only anger he had heard after the stilling of the brief firefight up the hill had been a few rounds, obviously from an American M-1, which had parted the air somewhere down around his knees. Sgt. Thomas Carver, one of the three draftees in the squad, waited there near the east portal, breathing audibly, but manifestly calm and alert. Ahead, Robertson knew, the rest of the squad would be staring into the night, safeties off, grenades clutched in nervous hands, nostrils flared and minds whirling.

Carver made a brief report and fell silent, adding that to the chilling lack of sound that followed the echoes of the brief fight up the hill and the nervous half clip someone had fired at Robertson. The sergeant stiffened when a weak flare, now somehow obscene in crimson and yellow, savaged the darkness upslope and east.

Robertson put his lips to Carver's ear. "That's the North Korean signal for isolating fires."

To the north, several howitzers made hollow cracks. The rounds whooshed over in seconds to impact in the general area of the George Company barrier wire, spitting up red-yellow flame. Robertson touched Carver's shoulder and Carver vanished, east toward the men.

In the tense pause between the Koreans' first artillery salvo and their second, Robertson detected automatic-rifle fire that had to be at the Dougherty position, and because the staccato rattling came from burp guns, it had to be hostile. Biting his lip, he listened for the answering, more measured reports of Dougherty's M-1 Garand. When he heard that, he breathed again. For a few dozen seconds, the exchange continued. Then two grenades exploded, intruding into the rifle sounds. Robertson listened again. He heard the burp guns but heard no answer.

Robertson cursed the world. Whatever its outcome, Sam Dougherty's fight was over.

Robertson swallowed instantly the bile of impotent rage and squelched an urge to go to the squad position to join his men. His responsibilities denied him this option. Besides, Tommy Carver could handle certain defeat as well as anyone could. The squad's fight would last only a few minutes longer than Dougherty's had.

Robertson crawled into the bunker. He found the telephone and carefully tugged enough slack in the cable to carry it out into the trench. Hartung waited on the other end.

"They've hit us, Captain. I'll do what I can."

"How many?"

"I'd buy your platoon estimate. I'll make my fight here and get my people out toward Lieutenant Shapiro's perimeter if we can't hold. I'd like that illuminating fire now."

"Keep me up to speed on it."

The tactical contact established, the line went silent.

The squad's confrontation with the Koreans was sharp. A single rifle cued the orchestra, then many joined in. The Koreans answered with grenades. Robertson detected two forward surges. He realized easily that the squad's response to the second surge was weaker than the scathing it had given the first. He put the telephone receiver on a sandbag and went east along the trench.

A pair of flare shells burst overhead. The earth around the trench became black on white, figure on background. In the brightness of the flare light, he felt as vulnerable as a rabbit feels when a fox gets between it and its burrow. The flares sizzled lazily earthward, dying in the fiery act of birth, maliciously neutral.

Before he had gone twenty feet, Robertson heard men stumbling toward him. The squad's fight had been briefer even than he had anticipated. He planted his feet to block the trench. He knew he'd have to deal with panic.

Someone—he thought Teasman—tried to shove him out of the way. Robertson grabbed the man's arm and held firmly. Several more flares flamed in the sky above, shimmering against the clouds. In this light, Robertson saw that two men supported Carver, but that the sergeant moved on his own legs. Carver held his right hand against his left side, as if he were trying to hold himself in. Robertson winced for him: a visceral wound was never a good one, if there were any good ones.

"Carver is hit," Teasman said testily, almost as if it were a personal affront.

Instantly, the others closed in. The men milled about and fidgeted. The count was difficult, and two short—three if he expected Dougherty to be with them. It was futile to expect the seconds necessary to examine Carver's wound.

"Anyone else hit?" Robertson demanded.

Kraut Klineschmidt, aflame with excited rage, lashed out. "These gutless sons of bitches made me leave Terry Cole. Cole was hit bad."

Wearily, Robertson added the need to determine the fate of Pvt. Terrence Cole to his growing list of obligations. "Is that it?" he insisted.

After an almost guilty pause, Zuckerman spoke. "Me. I'm hit. But only a little bit."

"Anybody see Sam Dougherty?"

"He probably got out and went up the hill like we should be doing. Nobody came in on us except a million fucking gooks."

"Catlin's right, Lieutenant Robertson. We'd better get out of here. Must be two hundred gooks out there—"

"Settle down!" Robertson commanded brusquely. The men fell back. When the artillery fire lulled again, Robertson called out, "Choi?"

There was no answer, but seconds later the Korean appeared. He carried something totally limp. That would be Cole, the squad's BAR-man.

Choi Min-soo let the reaching hands relieve him of Cole and stepped close to Robertson's face, saying quietly, in the awkward formality of his English, "Private Cole's wound is mortal. Our brief battle has impeded my countrymen of the north, but they are aggressive."

Robertson nodded. He stepped back a pace when the Korean lifted a hand to touch the hachimaki. Choi made a throaty disapproving sound. Everything stilled a moment, the stillness to be ended by the faraway cough of the company's light mortars. That provoked a renewed cacophony. Several more aerial flares exploded above them, and Robertson was certain he heard the engagement of the heavy 155-mm howitzers of the artillery battalion that supported them. Rifle and machine-gun fire erupted upslope, on the company perimeter. That fire could have no targets, but it would create a wall of steel to deny any enemy advance beyond Robertson's position.

The perimeter fire signaled to Robertson that he was on his own, but no more so than he had been from the first. The company commander had abandoned him to the mercies of his few options. Robertson did not resent that; Hartung had even fewer options than he had. While he pondered his next move, Robertson listened. What he heard was simply snapping and banging and hissing and whirring and snarling and crushing—sounds accompanied by dull light, but mainly sounds.

Who was to go? Who was to stay? The squad leader, Carver, was down. Zuckerman, the assistant squad leader, was hurt. If he, Robertson, stayed at the bunker, someone had to control the rest of the squad. Choi once had been a captain in the Japanese army. Would the Americans obey him?

The answers came. Robertson gave quick orders. "Cole, Zuckerman, and Sergeant Carver in the bunker. Choi, you take the others to where the trench turns back up toward Lieutenant Shapiro's bunkers. Hold there if you can. If you can't hold, get them out and report to Lieutenant Shapiro."

Choi Min-soo bowed and melted away. Whatever he thought about it, Choi would obey unquestioningly.

Zuckerman spoke up tiredly. "I can go with them, Lieutenant Robertson. I'm not hit bad."

Robertson felt the surge of the warmth he so often felt for the unobtrusive Zuckerman, one of the surviving originals in the squad, but he hardened his voice. "It's not a solicitation of preferences, Solly. *Move!*"

Robertson tapped the butt of the clip in his carbine and stepped off toward the North Koreans. Reasoning they'd never expect assault from the uphill side of the trench, he got out of the trench and walked there. After only a few dozen yards, a grenade exploded almost in his face, causing him to stagger. Shrapnel slammed into his shin. Gritting his teeth, he put his weight on the insulted leg. It held.

It was now grenade range. He unpinned one of his own and lobbed it toward the sound. When it burst, he threw a second, having closed the distance by about ten feet. The hollower *whump* of the second grenade suggested that it had exploded in the trench. The cries that followed it verified that. Lifting his carbine, Robertson fired a full clip in the general direction of the screaming.

The Koreans sent back fire and metal. The rifle and grenade exchange lasted several minutes before Robertson heard a flurry of retreating men. At the price of a throbbing leg and ringing ears, he had bought the American army perhaps five minutes.

As he limped back toward the sandbags and logs of George Three, the carbine dangling from his right hand, he reviewed the final decision. The North Korean officer had been forced to rally his men four times now. Each time they would be more difficult to inspire—four abrupt skirmishes on a dark night would tax even the fanatical courage of North Korean infantrymen. But rally them their officer would—and they would come on. Robertson had no doubt of that. Sam Dougherty, or Tommy Carver or Choi Min-soo, perhaps even Solly Zuckerman or Herman "Kraut" Klineschmidt, would have done it. Courage and military necessity spoke all the languages. Robertson smiled inwardly at his thoughts. Tough bastards as the North Koreans were, [he had killed enough of them since the previous spring to know they wore human skin.]—all humans, yet in human

Zuckerman called out from the bunker, "Lieutenant Robertson?"

"Get Carver on the north wall and stay there," Robertson answered harshly. "See to his bleeding."

He reached for the telephone. He did not shout. Field telephones either work or they don't. If the artillery and mortar fire had not cut the telephone line, it would work.

Hartung was breathless. "They're hitting Fox Company like a ton of shit, Robertson. Can you hold there?"

"All our hold is gone, Captain. I've got two wounded men in the bunker, one dead, one missing, and I sent the others toward Max Shapiro's turf."

"Goddamn." Hartung paused. "Robertson, I can't weaken the main perimeter. You've got to hold them at least until daylight."

"I need help, Captain."

"What can I do for you?" Hartung sounded helpless.

"We all could have used a three-day pass starting yesterday," Robertson replied lightly.

Hartung exploded. "This is no time for wiseass remarks, Lieutenant!"

Robertson chided absently, "A little wry humor never hurts." Suddenly he felt lighthearted, as he had on the other occasions when he had donned the hachimaki. Choi Min-soo had been absolutely correct—it went forward better with high spirit and good humor.

Hartung had not answered. When Robertson heard the noise in the trench at his back, a noise advancing, however cautiously, he asked quietly, hand cupped around the mouthpiece of the telephone to shield out the battle ruckus, "Have you got a patch to artillery?"

"That I can do. The forward observer is here in the CP with me."

"No time for a middleman, Captain. I'll adjust from here."

The line went stiff with the stubborn contest of wills so often carried on infantry telephone cables. A relay clicked and a new voice came on. It reeked of Texas, and of tension. "Redman here."

"Redman, George Three here. I need fire for effect on coordinates 214167. I've got enemy personnel overrunning me."

Redman paused. Robertson could imagine the tip of his pencil on a plotter, possibly a finger on a map under lantern light. When the seconds lengthened ominously, Robertson goaded with, "That's the bunker just left and forward of the gully."

Redman responded, "I see that. And I can't fire it for you."

"Why the hell can't you fire it? We are in deep kimchi here."

"That's got to be your position."

"I know it is my position. Goddamn you, Redman. Fire those rounds."

"What about your own people?" Redman's tone accused.

"My people are either evacuated or under cover. Fire it."

"You know I can't fire behind the danger-close line without authority. Damn it! You know SOP; you'll have me ass-deep in alligators if I cut those charges."

Robertson visualized the men on the howitzer line. The gun breeches would be open, drooling acrid smoke from earlier rounds, waiting to be fed. Gunners' hands would be on cranking levers and lanyards. Loaders would cradle shells and casings. They'd be nervous if told to fuse for airburst, even more so when they realized the meaning of the small powder charge they were to cut. Now it all hinged on mils and bubbles, and on his struggle with the cautious Fire Direction Center officer call-signed Redman.

Robertson felt the hairs rise on his neck. "Fire it, Redman. For God's sake—fire it."

A new voice came into Robertson's ear. Recognizing the voice, he understood. Many wires were plugged into the central thrust of the night, among them that of the regimental commander. Colonel Thompson's mellow Virginia cadence invited no disagreement from Redman.

"Lieutenant Robertson is protecting his men with his thin khaki shirt." A pause, then: "Fire his mission for him on my authority."

Redman yessired and said to Robertson, "Your rounds are on the way—high-explosive and proximity-fused."

Robertson dropped the telephone and inched forward. He pressed his body against the opening in the blast wall of the bunker, closing it. He heard Zuckerman cry out, "No! I heard. You're calling fire on us. That's insane."

Robertson shut his ears and stretched his arms to broaden the armor he had created for the men in the bunker.

A grenade exploded at his back. The concussion crushed him into the sandbags and stole his breath. Shrapnel tore into his right hip with the force of a razor-shod mule kick, burning even as it sliced. Steel pellets thudded into the wall of the bunker.

The HE rounds came with a hot whirring sound; he imagined he heard the click of a detonating fuse. Time suspended for him. Robertson put his face into the fabric of the sandbags to savor the cold gritty texture. A rifle butt struck his neck, then violent hands clutched.

Struggling free of the hands, he reviewed what he had done. His wounded were safe, the roof of George Three would withstand airbursting artillery, and his own body sealed the aperture. Had he sent Carver and Solly out, he would have encumbered Choi's already small force. And Choi surely would hold now against those of his countrymen of the north who survived the havoc the call to Redman would wreak.

Searing blast outraced tearing shrapnel. In the last writhing instant, his mind spoke to it all. An exhausted nonagenarian might speak that way to the angel of death. "You're late. . . . I've been waiting a long time for you."

2

Near Seoul, South Korea,
February 14, 1952

Along Route 18 this fresh, crisp morning a military ambulance crawled, a billowing cloud of exhaust steam in its wake. Riding in the right front seat of the boxy vehicle, First Lt. Wilmer A. Elwood, MC, USA, shifted the third time in as many minutes to relieve the ache in his left hip. Elwood and Corporal Odum beside him were heavily dressed in quartermaster woolens. Probably so attired was every American in Korea who was not making love at that particular moment. The hum of the heater fan along with the transmission noises sounded somehow pleasing to Elwood's ears.

Like all Korean roads, Route 18 was a poor track beaten poorer by the massive logistical outflow of the Seoul-Inchon-Yongdungpo base area. Even at this early hour, Odum pushed the ambulance against a throng of olive green trucks, six-wheeled vehicles Elwood had learned were called six-by-sixes or deuce-and-a-halfs, depending upon who spoke. Few called them trucks. For two hours these had been merely headlights and roaring noise. Now that the world was lighted again, Elwood noticed that few of the trucks had tops on the cabs. He did not need a medical degree to realize that the men in these would have frosted cheeks and dripping noses. Suddenly he felt guilty for his own comfort.

Elwood muttered, "The American army never sleeps." He began to muse on a speech he had read many months earlier when he had been yet Wilmer Elwood, M.D., a general practitioner in Tulsa. He recalled now how he had sighed relief—the Korean Police Action was over and he would escape it.

Odum, whom Elwood had discovered to be sociable and competent during the trip up to the mobile surgical hospital near Chunchon the previous afternoon, greeted Korea's brand-new day.

"Good morning, Mr. Sun. You made a bad mistake by coming here."

Elwood smiled and stared at the crinkled road ahead of them. The snow was thin and soiled. The exotic architecture of ancient Korea—irregular old structures randomly placed—came up into his world for a moment, then vanished behind him. The doctor did not comment on the driver's remark.

But, inviting conversation, Odum added, "Like the saying goes, Lieutenant Elwood, I had gonorrhea and I had diarrhea and now I got Ko-rea."

Elwood had heard that before, but he managed a polite snicker. He stretched and yawned. "When great marshals make mistakes, Corporal, they make great mistakes."

"What's that all about, sir?"

"I was thinking about a speech General MacArthur made in 1950 after the first recapture of Seoul. Old Doug flew over from his palace in Japan, strode into the National Assembly Hall in his customary pomposity and told Syngman Rhee, 'Mr. President, by the grace of a merciful Providence our forces fighting under the standard of that greatest hope and inspiration of mankind, the United Nations, have liberated this ancient capital city of Korea.' " Elwood imitated the public MacArthur, making the quotation appropriately sonorous.

Odum snorted. "Must have been a dull speech. Why are you thinking about it?"

Elwood scratched his chin, which was beginning to stubble. "Well, eighteen months have gone by and merciful Providence and the United Nations still struggle. The proof is in the back in the form of our patient."

Odum shifted down a gear to creep around a stalled jeep. After he had shifted up again, he said, "We could get shot for talking about a five-star general officer like that, sir." He laughed at his own remark.

"I won't tell if you won't tell." Elwood yawned again. "Anyway, Corporal, we are doing our providential duty this miserably cold morning by cooperating with these trucks we pass. They haul the ammunition up; we haul the results of the ammunition back. Efficient. And stupid."

Elwood's mission had begun the day before when Colonel Williams of the 107th Evacuation Hospital in Seoul called him away from morning rounds. "You are to go to the 1037th MASH and bring a casualty here," the white-haired colonel ordered stiffly. "I'm making you personally responsible for him."

Elwood had asked, "Isn't that unusual, sir? To send a physician, I mean?"

The colonel had snapped, "Everything in Korea is unusual. And I tell you this is also damned unusual, very damned unusual. This casualty should have been forwarded to Japan or to the States weeks ago, which is procedure. For some reason those idiots at the 1037 are sending him to us. Damned unusual, I say. I got a call yesterday from General Holloway—that is even more damned unusual."

"General Holloway is a corps commander, sir. How does a corps commander relate to it?" Elwood had been unpleasantly struck several times by the fact that senior army officers did not participate in the rest of the world's adulation of medical doctors; his query had been motivated by sheer self-preservation.

"He's concerned, Elwood. When a lieutenant general is concerned, everyone below that rank salutes and obeys."

"Yessir," Elwood had replied, remembering he was below the rank of lieutenant general.

Williams had added, "I hold you accountable, Elwood. I called the 1037 and the casualty is not long out of their critical facility. Make damned sure he is stabilized, and for God's sake drive carefully." The colonel then ordered sternly, "Take your steel helmet. The 1037 might be under shell fire."

But Elwood and Odum had found the staff at the 1037 unhelmeted and noncommittal, and clearly glad to shed the casualty and the overstuffed medical folder that went with him.

The 1037th MASH had been as securely rear-echelon as had been Elwood's office in Tulsa.

Odum interrupted Elwood's thoughts again. "Ain't it funny, sir? People we don't even know make a decision in Washington and here we are together driving down this shitty road in a country we never heard of before."

Although the corporal's observation was far from profound, Elwood shifted to address it. "I take it you were drafted?"

Odum shot back, "You bet your sweet—yes, sir, I was. Crappy part about it was that I was in line for a foreman's job at the mill. Now that son of a bitch Jerry Habling will get it. He's been sniffing around LuAnn, too. She was a gal I was just getting serious about when I got a greetings from a committee of my friends and neighbors."

"Welcome to the club," Elwood commiserated.

With a good head of steam up, Odum went on. "Just why in the hell are we over here, Lieutenant Elwood? My mom asks that in every letter she writes. I still haven't come up with an answer for her."

Elwood shrugged. "Tell your mother we got involved in a struggle between Marx and Mill."— *cold war (communism)*

"Never heard of those boys. Are they in this stupid war, too?"

"I think so. But they're both dead."

"If they're already dead, how come they're fighting? They fart around in this mess, they'll get deader."

Elwood laughed appreciatively. "They were philosophers. Marx would improve us by improving the state. Mill would improve the state by improving us."

"Why don't they just leave a man alone? You never impressed me as someone who needed a whole lot of improving on."

"Thank you, Corporal. I'll return the compliment to you."

Odum grinned, then shook his head. "I doubt Mom would understand things like you just told me. Don't understand them myself. I'd be more than happy just to go home to Idaho to kick the shit out of Jerry Habling and let the philosophers go take a flying you-know-what at a rolling donut."

"That's very normal," Elwood agreed. "And extremely sane."

Odum halted the ambulance at an MP checkpoint on the northeast corner of Seoul, just north of the bridge. An MP in creased ODs and parka bummed a Camel cigarette, saluted Elwood, and waved them on. Soon in the city, Elwood and Odum threaded decrepit passenger cars, officious-looking military vehicles, carts pulled by steaming horses, and early-morning pedestrians who scurried through the cold.

With his ambulance settled down on the broad thoroughfare that led through the city to the 107th Evacuation Hospital, a sprawl of permanent and temporary buildings located near the main supply road to the port of Inchon, the driver asked, "Who we got back there? They sure fussed over him."

"That's Lieutenant Robertson. He's the infantry officer who called American artillery fire onto his own position to save his wounded men. Sure to get the Medal of Honor for it."

"Him? For sure! I read about him in the *Stars and Stripes*." Odum removed a glove and chewed his right thumbnail for several blocks. Then he queried, "Is he going to die? I've been around the medical corps long enough to know when a man is hurt bad."

"He won't die if the Eighth Army can prevent it. He's very important to someone."

Odum's question set Elwood to thinking about the VIP casualty in the rear of the jouncing ambulance. He turned to Odum. "What would move an officer to risk virtually certain death in those meaningless fights up there?"

"Maybe he's just a brave man?"

Elwood shook his head. "People don't function that way. Or at least normal people don't. A man might sacrifice himself in the excitement of battle, but what this man did he did in sheer cold blood, probably with some forethought. It's crazy, but the opinion of the people at the MASH was that the wounded men were incidental—he could have sent them with his nonwounded men."

Elwood told Odum what he had learned over coffee at about 2:00 A.M. that morning of the fight on George Three.

Odum listened with a gaping jaw. "I don't agree that the wounded men were incidental, sir. As you tell it, he had a bitch of a fight on his hands. He probably did the right thing by not tying up his able men with their wounded. You said his orders were to hold that position if he could."

"Never thought of it that way," Elwood said. "God, it's almost as if he planned it. Extraordinary. I still don't think a normal man would contemplate what he did."

"Maybe he's not a normal man."

"In what sense?" Elwood demanded.

"Maybe he wanted to die. Then what he did was just a way to do it."

Elwood started. That exact thought had just entered his own mind. "Why would he want to die?"

Odum frowned thoughtfully, braking even then for the south portal gate of the 107th. "All I know about the infantry is that I don't want to be up there with it."

Before Elwood opened the ambulance door to get out, he turned to Odum. "You are a good driver, Corporal Odum, and good company. You'd also make a good psychiatrist."

In the rear of the ambulance, Second Lt. Donald A. Robertson, Infantry, USAR, had been awake for some time. He half listened to the hum and drone in the cab ahead of him. Unaccustomed to this much warmth, he sweated. He had awakened from the old hated dream, the one in which he stood under the glare of pitiless lights and scrubbed the ineradicable blood from his groin. When Odum greeted the dawn, Robertson glanced at the pale squares of window at his feet. He saw a weak sun, glazed over with late winter. The voices ahead were bodiless. He let them drone, familiar by now with the fact that army medical people discussed patients as if they weren't there.

Robertson let his mind drift back across the days—now almost six weeks—since the predawn events at George Three on Sniper Ridge.

He had first become conscious of the whine of a generator, a crass little engine that spun up more decibels than amperage. He realized slowly that he was plugged into tubes and bottles. Their shadows blended with others in the tent, moving about hushed and efficient.

The scene whirled and blurred. Robertson fixed his eyes on the overhead light bulb and struggled to free his mind. But when he did so, he discovered that the mind was the source of the whirling and blurring. Then he gave up. He had served a three-year enlistment, had been two years into a six-year reenlistment at commissioning and had long since learned that a soldier caught in army procedure was powerless over his own destiny. —politics/emasculated (a pawn)

The face of the battalion surgeon bent down. The surgeon was a captain, fair and slender. He wore round silver-rimmed army-issue glasses. Before Robertson could acknowledge him, the surgeon reared away and said, "Lift him up. I've got to do something about that bleeding."

Hands tugged Robertson's body until he was sitting. As the generator told him it was not yet full light, the bite of cold air told him he was naked. The surgeon applied a huge pressure bandage, scolding Robertson as he worked.

"You've got yourself in a hell of a mess, Lieutenant. You've got a chunk of shrapnel under your right scapula. Must have had yourself spread-eagled when the shell hit you. Hell of a place to have a piece of iron, believe me. I've only seen something like this once before—a Saturday-night knife fight when I interned in South Chicago." He smiled. "At that, I imagine you fared better than the North Koreans. Colonel Thompson said they pulled you out from under four of them. Good tactic, to use the enemy to cover yourself, but I don't recommend you try your luck there a second time."

The surgeon tugged manfully on the tails of the pressure bandage. Robertson could not suppress a groan. The captain continued. "The regimental commander was in here a few minutes ago and I told him he should give you guys some anatomy lessons. Make it better for everyone."

The doctor pulled again. Robertson swore aloud.

"That's a good sign. I like it when you guys cuss. I think I can do a paper for the journal on 'Voluntary Profanity as a Diagnostic Measure in Battlefield Medicine.' I've seen stupider articles."

A little while later, the bespectacled captain stood up. "Hell of a place to get shrapnel, believe me."

Robertson believed him. Deep inside, his visceral nervous cells examined the intruder and messaged to the command center of his brain that the alien that interrupted venous return from the right thoracic region was hostile and that preliminary field analysis yielded distinct traces of trinitrotoluene, red oxide of iron, and cordite. Robertson saw he had to get his mind off it, which is standard aid-station wisdom. Better to wait for the medics to report on how many ears you have left and whether the throbbing thing below your thigh is a limb or a phantom.

"My men?" Robertson croaked, finding it difficult to orient the nerves and muscles needed for speech.

"That, too, is a good sign." The doctor snapped to one of the figures at Robertson's side. "Get the lieutenant a report—he's George Company— then tag him for evac. I want him heli-lifted first thing. I don't think I got all the leakage." The captain fired an additional volley of medical orders and vanished from Robertson's narrow view.

After several minutes, a middle-aged medical sergeant came quietly to Robertson's stretcher. "Lieutenant Petersen is working on one of your men. I cleaned up a missile gouge in another of your troopers and he wanted to go back up on the hill to show off his bandages."

The sergeant hesitated, then whispered, "We have two outside. I can get the names if you want them."

Robertson brought fire on himself when he shook his head. He exhaled and closed his eyes.

Later, Robertson again sensed the silver eyeglasses. He felt a sharp stab in his arm. He drifted under the umbrella of the morphine with the misty awareness that masculine hands buoyed him and wafted him toward a monster dragonfly with a huge glass nose and drooping wings.

— When he became aware again, the hands were small and probing, and definitely feminine. All nurses in forward hospitals are gorgeous novelties for infantrymen. Some casualties report that their initial confrontation with nurses of any description was the supreme erotic experience of their lives. This one had a long strand of dark hair over her left eye and was so exhausted she could have been anywhere in age between sixteen and sixty. "He's conscious," she said.

One of the knot of consulting green gowns grouped around asked if anyone knew what the aid-station morphine dosage had been. "Damn those people anyway! They shouldn't knock these guys out. Soldiers can tolerate a little pain."

No one answered and the green speaker came over and pulled down the sheet to bare Robertson's torso. "He's iffy. We'll risk it; we got to get in there; he's leaking badly. Start him under."

Robertson felt another needle and went into poleaxed sleep to the words, plainly spoken to the other green gowns, "I'd watch this one. You won't see it often. I'm going to get under the shoulder blade and cut fiber until I can lift it away. That will expose the cavity—"

[At the last moment, Robertson felt, as did several thousand soldiers in Korea at one time or another, the reassuring squeeze of the small hand. If that therapy could be bottled, the bottler would be a wealthy man.]

The MASH surgeon, Capt. Herman Brinel, had red hair, a florid face, and appropriately long, delicate fingers. He came around shortly postop, trailed by a corpsman and a nurse, and studied Robertson's charts intently. In a competent New England voice, but one very concerned, he gave quiet firm orders and muttered about forty-eight critical hours.

During those hours the bed on Robertson's left turned over four times. Each time the corpsmen removed the transient occupants, they whispered together and worked swiftly to remove the linen. To Robertson's right, a part of the dark world his pain denied him, the bed was an aural entity. [The bed had been filled on his first day out of surgery and it cried frequently and once in that night screamed in rage. The scream brought a nurse with a syringe. After that, the nurses came frequently with syringes.] Other people came merely to look, or at least Robertson inferred this. When the ward got light in the morning and the nurse came with a thermometer, Robertson eased his head to indicate the whimpering bed beside him.

The nurse mouthed, "Amputations. Quadruple. Everything." The nurse whispered, apparently wanting to keep the amputations a secret from their owner.

When she left his bed, Robertson braved the fire within him to twist. On the bed he saw a blob too small, too white, too black, without the proper extensions. Somehow, he sensed that what he looked at related to tanks. The hand of death seemed to hover over the white blob on the bed, as if waiting for it to achieve full degradation before descending.

The cries and pleas stilled in the afternoon. People came to the bed and worked swiftly. They spoke in mortuarylike whispers. The river had been crossed.

Robertson did not weep. He spoke for the white blob: "Lucky bastard, you're out of it."

On the third morning, corpsmen wheeled Robertson into another tent. Captain Brinel came at once. His expression and manner indicated he was relieved.

Robertson lifted his head and the doctor asked, "How are you feeling?"

Robertson managed, "How soon can I get back to my regiment?"

The captain said blandly, "Your regimental commander said you were a tiger. But I don't think you should be in too much of a hurry. We took quite a pile of iron out of you."

Robertson renewed his attack by asking Captain Brinel again, "How long?"

The captain counterattacked with, "How would you like to go to Japan? Maybe even home to the Land of the Round-eyed Ladies?" *←Racism, sexuality*

Robertson shook his head. He felt flooded by exhaustion.

The captain shot him a frown; Robertson turned his head to deflect it.

Brinel asked, "Why? Most casualties nag me to go the other way. You've got the million-dollar wound. Home and pension for you."

Robertson whispered, "My regiment . . . short of officers."

The captain's rejoinder was as sharp as his scalpel. "If *you* are the reason, Lieutenant Robertson, the regiment is going to *remain* short of officers."

Late that evening, during rounds, Captain Brinel came alone to Robertson's bed. His right hand held a sheaf of records.

"I want to know exactly what my wounds are," Robertson greeted. "And I want to know when I can rejoin my regiment." *← dehumanising*

"Feeling sassy, I see." The doctor wrinkled his nose. "Your job is not to make angry demands, Lieutenant. Your job is to heal while we decide what to do with you."

"I need to know."

Captain Brinel sighed. He riffled quickly through the documents he had brought to the bed. "You've a terrible problem under your scapula, but you were somewhat lucky. The shrapnel tore a lot of muscle, but stayed out of your chest cavity. You have a bad missile laceration on your hip . . . your left neck is gouged. . . ." The captain paused to read documents. When he resumed, his voice rose, as if he were more caught up in his words than before. "Oh, yes. You have moderately severe powder or flash burns along your right side and you had a leg full of splinters until we took them out for you. Something banged hell out of your shin, but your X ray doesn't indicate a fracture. You've got me sitting up at night reading dull medical books on osteomyelitis and thrombophlebitis. Nurse Lieutenant Hickman thinks you're depressed and is nagging me to recommend a psychiatric work-up. Nurse Captain Anson says you don't eat enough." Brinel paused and smiled. "Other than these minor things, you are sound as a dollar. Better make that a South Korean dollar."

"Koreans use the won note," Robertson said quietly.

The doctor's smile warmed. "Well, here is the news from home and loved ones. Colonel Thompson of your regiment calls me every morning and demands to know how I'm treating you. He thinks a lot of you. I sent a man who said he was from your platoon to Japan the other day. He was grateful to go. Very intelligent man, I might point out to you. He tells me you wear Jesus shoes."

Before Robertson could ask for the patient's name, his instincts sent up red flags. He weighed it. No, he thought, better not to know. If he did not know, it could be as if they all made it. Perhaps he'd never need to ask.

Robertson found he could smile. "Nobody walks on water, Captain. Unless you can. You heal."

Brinel's eyes sparkled. "That's a high compliment which I wish were justified." He looked away and added, his voice lowered, "We just removed you from our . . . our guarded-prognosis unit. The turnover there indicates my failures."

"Heal me. I need to get back."

"My God, man! Why? Why not let me send you home? You can be done with combat."

Robertson paused to gather all his strength. He knew he was about to play a card that might get trumped. In his opinion, physicians shouldn't have been made officers. He knew they were usually drafted. Many he had encountered had a thinly concealed disdain for military life. Only a few hung around long enough to become soldiers and to grasp the rules that bound their patients.

He hoped he confronted a soldier.

"I appeal to you as a brother officer, Captain Brinel."

Brinel sighed heavily. He chewed his lip for almost a minute before countering with, "You think out your situation, Lieutenant, and I will think it out. We'll talk about it tomorrow after I make some telephone calls."

When Robertson ate his small supper, he feigned gusto. When Nurse Lieutenant Hickman came around to take her numbers, he winked lasciviously at her.

Captain Brinel returned shortly after breakfast the following morning. As Robertson watched carefully, the doctor paused to warm his hands over the diesel stove. When he came to the bed, he fastened his eyes somewhere above Robertson's head.

"The army drafted me, Robertson. I can't say that I'm ecstatic about that, but I have had a chance here to learn a few things about men I never learned in medical school. I'll also confess that I think about you a lot, and that you puzzle me. Many of our casualty patients here cry out in their sleep. You cry out a lot. I've heard enough of it to know you have something awesome on your mind. Share it with me. I'll help if I can."

Robertson's finger traced several crude circles on his blanket before he answered. "I wish I could share it, Captain. God knows I wish I could."

For several tense seconds, nothing more was said. Brinel backed away a step and looked down at Robertson. "You have a long convalescence facing you, Lieutenant Robertson. You came off that hill with enough wounds to kill most men. I'd be lying to you if I didn't tell you nobody in this MASH would have sold you a life-insurance policy. In the sense that I don't know what the course of your recovery will be, I still view you as critical. I'm going to keep you here awhile longer. Then I'm sending you to an evacuation hospital in Seoul. The issue went all the way to the desk of the corps commander. He rules you can stay in Korea, temporarily at least, if that is your wish. That is medically insane and I'm sure they'll recommend me for a psychiatric work-up when they realize what I've done to standard operating procedures."

Wilmer Elwood's nasal Oklahoma accent called Robertson back. "Here is the 107th, Lieutenant Robertson. You'll be just fine now."

Robertson sighed. Here was the new medical enemy.

3

107TH EVACUATION HOSPITAL,
FEBRUARY 14, 1952

Although different people asked different questions about Robertson, everyone was interested.

"What on earth goes on in the minds of those people at MASH? This patient should have gone to Japan."

"How much longer can we keep him immobile?"

"What does a jagged piece of red-hot iron do when it lodges under the scapula? What is the course of that kind of trauma? You ever see anything like it?"

"Is the trapezius involved? Damn it! Those people should be more careful with patient records."

"How about the infraspinatus? The teres major? Are they compromised?"

"Did they send his personnel records so we know where to forward him if he dies?"

One questioner sniffed perceptibly. "What interest do you suppose a three-star corps commander has in a second lieutenant? Looks like an ordinary second lieutenant to me."

 Finally, directly to Robertson: "Did you bring a toothbrush?"

Robertson shook his head negatively. Someone made a telephone call and someone else stuck a toothbrush into his hand. Two Korean male orderlies who stank of garlic hefted Robertson's canvas boat and an American corpsman wearing a balding head and a big red nose led off, saying gruffly, *"Bali-bali kapsuda!"* a horrible corruption many soldiers thought was Korean for "Hurry up!"

Robertson followed the journey by noting the world that floated over it.

32

His view of lofty papered ceilings was twice interrupted by the hazy winter blue of the open sky. The journey ended with a jarring trip up a flight of stairs, a sharp left turn, and the appearance of a large, solid wooden door. Robertson saw that he had been carried into a large room with a tall window, a metal hospital bed with several cranks attached, a chest of sorts, and, of course, the familiar hospital odors, at once antiseptic and musty.

Another corpsman had followed him into the room. The two corpsmen and the Korean orderlies rolled Robertson onto the bed. "You'll like it," the younger of the corpsmen said. "It's our best room."

The ceiling, a sickly ancient yellow, hovered above Robertson. He saw a single light bulb dangling at the end of a twisted cord. He saw no switch string. He searched the lime green walls and found the switch not far from the ornate molding of the door. The room was warm, but too large to be cozy. He got the impression it had once been an office.

The hour he had spent in receiving had left him drained. He dozed, to be awakened within minutes by a seductive voice. "Are you awake now, Lieutenant Robertson? My, we are a sleepyhead today, aren't we?" He heard a feminine rustling and a perfumed shadow fell across his OD blanket.

He stared at her, then turned his head away.

The woman came to the bed and waved her hand over his face. "Hello there! Are you home?"

Robertson looked up. He knew she'd have to be talked to. "I didn't see you," he lied.

The woman laughed and winked. "I'm Lieutenant Hardiman. I'm more accustomed to being seen than that."

Robertson appraised her. "I've no doubt of that."

"That's better. Will it be safe to be close to you?"

He shrugged. He knew she was toying with him.

Vivian Hardiman leaned forward and smiled; her lips were sensual looking, outrageously crimson. She was in her twenties, but she never told anyone where. Robertson's focus drifted to the bridge of her nose, where he saw a few faint freckles fetchingly placed between liquid brown eyes.

On an impulse, he lifted his fish-belly white left arm and compared it to Vivian's healthy tan. "How do you keep tan in the middle of a Korean winter?"

Vivian laughed again, a sound so uninhibited it rang faintly mascu-line. "I *work* on it, Lieutenant. And I'm a native Southern Californian. We are born with our beach tan and we don't lose it until sixty days post-mortem."

At the collar of her fatigue shirt, he noted a silver bar and the insignia of the Army Nurse Corps. A nurse . . . What else could she be but a nurse?

Vivian moved her head quickly, rustling the air over Robertson's bed with short brown hair. She stood erect and folded her arms, striking a no-nonsense pose beside his bed. "I'm supervisory nurse for this ward. You will meet others from the medical staff later."

"How long will I be here?" Robertson asked. "I have to be getting back to my regiment." If anything, that was reconnaissance by fire.

Vivian scolded with a toss of her head. "Already? The staff at the MASH warned us we'd have to keep you strapped into bed." Her eyes screwed up slightly as she became thoughtful. After studying him for a moment, she reached a hand to stroke his hair. Her fingers were long, with tapering red nails. "You need a haircut. I'll have to see about that." She let her fingers linger a moment; just a touch, almost an afterthought. She smiled again and her eyes were sparkling. "You're here for convalescence and physical evaluation, Lieutenant Robertson. The decision to keep you in Korea was not ours, but we'll make the best of it. In any case, you no longer belong to your regiment; now you belong to us." She smiled around beautiful even teeth and repeated, "To us." She nodded, as if everything had been said.

Deciding that prudence was a better course than aggressiveness, Robertson changed the subject. He was tiring rapidly. "Does everyone in this hospital get a room like this?"

"Only our special patients." Vivian spun and lifted a hand as if to display the austere room. "This is our VIP suite."

"What makes me special?"

"You are Lieutenant Robertson."

"The army has a million Lieutenant Robertsons."

"You are *the* Lieutenant Robertson." Vivian fluffed Robertson's pillow for him and began to edge toward the door. "General Holloway makes you special."

Robertson frowned. "The corps commander? He doesn't know I exist."

Vivian stood in the doorway and turned. "He seems to think he does. He ordered our commander that you were to be treated as a VIP. He's coming here tomorrow to see you."

"Damn!" Robertson said.

"Is that bad? I would think it good when a lieutenant general is interested in coming to see you."

"When a general officer pays attention to you, that's bad. He's probably coming to court-martial me for losing the fight on George Three."

"Hardly. He's coming to give you a medal."

Vivian Hardiman left the door open. Through it Robertson could see the corner of the nurses' station and two unoccupied beds in the ward. He explored his room again, suddenly feeling as if he had caught up with himself, at least for the moment. He knew he had forfeited the relative freedom he had gained so few weeks ago when he accepted his battlefield commission. But he hurt less, and in this room he would be alone. That would be good: he had not been alone since he joined the army. All things considered, the hospital was just another position; like a fold of ground or a rifle pit or a bunker, you took what you found and bent it to your purposes. With this thought, he vowed firmly to regard the 107th as a way station; once out of it, he would resume what he had set for himself.

Mildred Baumiller, from the nurses' station, had watched Vivian Hardiman leave Robertson's room. Mildred had read the medical folder, wondering with awe how the new patient could survive such wounds. "The Front," although everyone else called it either "The MLR" or "The Line," rarely touched Mildred's life. Most of her patients were the sick and injured from the base area around Seoul. Thus she shared in the Robertson excitement and listened avidly as Sergeant Darrow regaled the corpsmen with the man's story. It irritated her that Darrow, who often teased her, not only talked as if he owned Lieutenant Robertson, but as if he had been with him when the artillery shell hit.

When Dr. Kerns beckoned, Mildred grabbed her clipboard and followed, about five paces behind the doctors, as she normally did.

In the VIP room, she peered around Dr. Kerns, who always made her feel comfortable.

Kerns wore a white jacket and the ubiquitous stethoscope. He spoke to Robertson. "Hello, Lieutenant. I'm Major Walter Kerns." Kerns indicated the balding medical captain who had accompanied him into the room. "This is Captain Harrison." Kerns nodded to Mildred. "We have to begin somewhere; let's have a look at his leg and work up."

Mildred went to the bed and began removing dressings. She studied her patient. Younger than she expected; she guessed mid-twenties. Handsome? She didn't know, or perhaps, she told herself, she didn't have a right to ask herself that question about such an important person. He had blond hair and blue eyes, was of average size, but strong, even under the pallor. She winced inwardly at the scar that lanced across Robertson's right cheek, knowing it was another wound, long healed. Around the scar, the face told her nothing, seeming to hold secrets she could never know. That thought lingered as she worked gingerly at the bandages. She saw under her fingers that the MASH nurses had been lazy about shaving leg hairs.

The leg moved and she heard a sharp "Ouch!"

"I'm sorry, sir," she said quickly, "I'll be more careful."

"It's all right. Do what you have to do."

Something in the accent warmed; Mildred recognized it—Midwest, not much different from her own. Before she could analyze it, she felt herself pushed roughly aside.

Captain Harrison said, "Christ on a crutch, Mouse! Don't worry the patient to death. Let me show you."

Harrison cupped his hand around the end of the tape Mildred had loosened and spoke through gritted teeth. "Say 'Shit,' Lieutenant."

Before Robertson could say anything, the captain yanked. The room filled with the sound of tearing.

Mildred felt flushed. She looked at Robertson, pleased when he emitted a mighty "Ouch!" louder than the one he had emitted for her.

Harrison held the bandage under Mildred's nose. "See, Mouse. Shit, grab, and yank."

Mildred blushed deeply. Her nickname always made her blush. But she knew it fit her; she'd be the first to admit it; even her name was a mouse name.

Lieutenant Elwood came in and nodded. Mildred dropped back a step, gazing at Robertson, wondering about his secrets again while the doctors examined. She half listened, hearing chatter and comments such as "good color," "I'd leave jelly on it and expose it," and "something knocked hell out of his shin; shrapnel must have been ricocheting and flat when it hit," and, finally, after she had been called forward again to undress the shoulder, "that's a Harvard suture; worked with a chest cutter in Baltimore who did it that way."

Harrison ordered brusquely, "Dress him again, Mouse," and the three doctors turned toward the door.

Knowing her head was lowered, Mildred stepped forward. She froze when she heard a sharp, "Excuse me, gentlemen."

Robertson's face looked angry. The strength she had seen there had hardened. Mildred saw the doctors halt, then turn toward the bed.

Robertson's voice reminded Mildred of the senior sergeants correcting failures in discipline. Commanding, patient, but admitting no quarrel, ever.

"I'm Donald Robertson. The introductions aren't complete."

Mildred saw that Major Kerns had reddened, rare for him. Kerns's lips tautened, then he smiled sourly and nodded toward her. "Mildred Baumiller of our staff." Kerns jerked his head toward Elwood. "I believe you've met Dr. Elwood."

Robertson smiled generously. Mildred regretted that he had let the doctors off the hook so quickly. He turned to her and nodded slightly. "I'm very pleased to meet you, Lieutenant Baumiller."

Harrison frowned and lifted his hand helplessly.

Robertson glanced at Elwood, moved his chin, then glared at Captain Harrison. "Out where I come from," he said, as if he spoke to no one in particular, "we avoid using a nickname that embarrasses someone."

Harrison's lips moved, but he said nothing. Quickly, he lowered his eyes.

Kerns made a noise in his throat and went out. The other two doctors followed.

Alone with the patient now, Mildred worked to redress the injuries. She studied the huge surgical scars of his shoulder; never had she seen such an injury in that area. She caught herself swallowing heavily.

He said nothing, which both pleased and frightened her. When she finished, he smiled thinly and lay back.

Mildred paused in the doorway. Dare she turn and look? She had seen the possessive smile on Vivian's face as she emerged from that doorway earlier. Mildred went out, feeling she had cheated herself, an old feeling.

Toward midnight of that first day in the lime green room, a pale blonde woman in fatigues and boots came in. The unblinded window let in Seoul's February moon, enough to fill the east half of the room with a somber light. Robertson awakened the instant she entered, but decided to conceal this from her. If she realized, he would have to relate to her. She would apologize and he would have to explain the vigilance bred of eighteen hundred nights in a squad room and two hundred nights in a fighting hole.

But the woman edged into the shadows. She stood there, merely looking. He could hear her breathing, a sound that made him uneasy. After several minutes, he stirred and called out, "Come here, Lieutenant Baumiller."

Hesitantly, Mildred came to the bed. He studied her in the moonlight, but her face gave him nothing beyond the shyness it had given him in the afternoon. He felt a great urge to touch her.

"May I have your hand?"

"My hand, sir?"

Mildred's face registered momentary alarm, but then she lifted her right hand toward him, as if she obeyed an order she would not have dared disobey. He took her wrist and pulled her hand near his face. He examined the fingers; small, delicate, smelling faintly of medicine, but at the same time of woman, soft gentle scents. He touched a finger with his lips. He put the hand on his chest, pressing it firmly to indicate it was to remain there. Slowly, gently, he explored it.

After a long time, he felt Mildred stiffen. Reluctantly, he surrendered his prisoner. She withdrew her hand and put it behind her back.

"Why did you do that with my hand, sir?"

Robertson at first turned his head away, but he knew she deserved an explanation. "It's just been so long since I've touched anything like that."

"But it's an ordinary hand, sir. I have very ordinary hands."

"No. It's an extraordinary hand. It's an innocent hand."

After lowering her head silently for several seconds, Mildred lifted it. "Something terrible—more terrible than your wounds—has happened to you in Korea, sir."

"Why would you say that?" Robertson snapped. "You just can't know what's in other people's minds unless they tell you."

Mildred's lips quivered, but she thrust out her jaw. "Sometimes it's like I *do* know, sir. I don't know how I know, but I know."

Robertson stared at her, blankly. He saw an amorphous threat to himself there. Somehow, he sensed he would someday be forced to tell her about what he had done that night, now almost ancient history, when he had hunted in the misty streets of Chunchon and had opened a door he should never have opened. He closed his eyes. He couldn't divine when or in what tone of voice he would tell her about what had happened to him, but he understood that when the moment came, her claim to know it would be as honestly compelling as Sam Dougherty's claim that night on Sniper Ridge. He would be as trapped here as he had been trapped there.

When he opened his eyes again, the nurse was gone.

As he had not done in weeks, he set his mind free. He thought about those he had left on the ridges—how he had met them and what they had experienced together. Then, realizing it was as if he built the edifice before he built the foundation, he retreated further into himself. At last he came to the Tanner farm.

All the forces that brought him to a hospital bed in a country whose name he had not even heard until mid-1950 had issued from there.

4

SOUTHWESTERN KANSAS, JULY 23, 1943

The selling of the boy* occurred in front of the post office, next door to Mae's Café.

Donald Robertson stood patiently away from his father and Harvey Tanner as he had been taught to do when men talked business. He was dressed in a straw hat, chambray shirt, and faded jeans. He had rolled up his sleeves but not his trouser cuffs. To do so would have displayed his worn-out work shoes and he was ashamed of his shoes. When Mr. Tanner paid him—and surely it would be enough—he could buy cowboy boots—man's wear. That thought excited him.

The excitement paled quickly. He was growing uneasy now because he realized he was being sold. To escape, he stared into the street. Prairie had been cheap when the town had been young. The street seemed acres broad, the few cars parked at an angle to the curb. He identified Mr. Huffman's 1940 Lincoln, surely the best car in town. When he heard the rhythmic tinkling of harness bells and the raucous clatter of a chain, he glanced up the sunlit street toward the courthouse and saw a team of massive sorrels. Since the team pulled nothing but the trace chains, he easily inferred that Baldy Teeter was going after his dump scoop to dig another basement. It would be fun to go and watch that.

Then Robertson felt flooded with a sense of loss. If he understood the discussion correctly, they were taking from him the leisure to loll in the grass and witness a sorrel team scrape out a basement. He watched with longing when the team came past. The chains dragged behind the harness tugs, and scattered gravel. On another day, the dragging chains would have sent up puffs of dust.

The left sorrel tossed his head and snorted, sending ripples of muscle down his withers. Already the horses foamed around their collars. Listlessly, Robertson lifted his left arm and waved to them.

The summer of 1943 rained energetically on southwestern Kansas. The people there stood in the mud and listened anxiously to news of the war that lingered in Africa while outraged America sharpened its sword.

Robertson had experienced the hollow darkness of the Depression. He had seen the weary lines on his parents' faces and had heard the morbid poetry of their worry. At first the war had brought excitement and joy. The five-and-dime next to Dandy Miller's tire shop had been overflowing with cardboard soldiers, airplanes, and tanks. Robertson played with those precious artifacts until late in 1942, then went to the cemetery with his father and sister, Maggie, and a sprinkling of Robertsons and Pfeffers, to put his mother into the ground. Even then, he knew that events had simply eroded his mother away—she had died of heart-riving world pain, although Doc Feener had diagnosed a lung congestion.

The transaction between his father and Tanner was brief.

"He's big enough," Harvey Tanner admitted carefully. "But he's a town boy; they ain't all that strong."

"Oh, he's strong, Harvey. Just needs a little filling out."

Harvey weighed this while he rolled a Prince Albert cigarette, scowling when the hot wind blew some of the tobacco to the sidewalk. "He ain't got nothing wrong with him, has he? I don't want old Doc Feener to get his hand in my pocket caring for a hired man."

Robertson heard his father reply, "He's sound, Harvey."

"I don't know. Twenty a month and keep is a lot of money for a fifteen-year-old boy."

Charles Robertson looked away from his son and played his final card. "Well, Harvey, with the war taking all the grown men, guess you farmers will have to hire the boys . . . or do the work yourselves."

Harvey Tanner jerked a gnarled hand toward his old black Chevy pickup. "Get in the back, boy. In the back, hear?"

Robertson turned his eyes to his father. "When can I leave him?" he asked anxiously.

The father's eyes were lost under the brim of a gray felt hat. "When you're a man, I guess." The father took Maggie and went to California to see what the Pacific would wash into his life.

Tanner hauled Robertson to the farm to scoop chicken shit, much as he would have hauled a saddle horse home from the sales barn. Robertson had been spewed from the eight compulsory years of education Kansas law required. The same body of law required that he be an obedient chattel of his father, and of Tanner as the surrogate. Robertson's worldly goods that day consisted of two pairs of denim trousers, two cotton shirts, three pairs of socks, and four pairs of jockey shorts. In his pocket he had seventeen cents and a pocketknife with a broken blade.

The Tanner acres were south of the town, near a lake built by the CCC to drink the largess of the trickly creek that watered the parched valley when it was of a mind to trickle. Sometimes, the creek simply sank into its sandy bed and ran underground; this was nature's little practical joke. The Tanners bedded in a shingled bungalow with peeling white paint and two porches. A creaking windmill stood up near a well house and threw thin lines of shade upon the brown yard. The shed that garaged the rusting machinery shared a wall with an unpainted barn that penned a house cow and a horse. The Tanner range cattle shaded under barbed wire, and used their own shadows to deflect the biting Kansas winter winds.

Between the windmill and the clapboard chicken house was a dugout root cellar, closer to the chickens than to the water. Tanner told Robertson to put his things in there and come down to the barn. "Hurry now, I'm paying you twenty dollars a month."

Robertson threw back the horizontal door and found some dusty shelves and a sagging iron cot with musty quilts. He did not linger.

The old barn gave the illusion of coolness, as old barns do. Robertson found a buckskin horse there and stroked its muzzle. Shortly, a long shadow fell across him.

"Don't stand there and spoil my goddamned horse," Tanner growled. "You're here to work."

Robertson and Tanner looked around to find Robertson some work. Finding nothing better, Tanner commanded, "Pull weeds till supper. We eat when the Old Lady calls us."

Getting down on his knees, Robertson saw broad leaves and Russian thistle undulating in the wind as far as the wheat fields thousands of feet to the east. A man could spend a lifetime on his knees and never uproot all the Tanner weeds.

Robertson learned that Tanner got on in the world by preying on that sparse dryland wheat and by beating unthrifty calves out of bony-hipped cows. He milked whatever he could catch and sold the cream, feeding the separated milk to scabrous hogs. Lillian Tanner helped her husband by squeezing speckled eggs out of a horde of Plymouth hens. The hens ran at large, encrusting the farmyard, and often, Robertson, with excrement.

After he had cleared a fraction of an acre of weeds, Robertson heard Lillian call. He had not yet met her.

The back door was open and he walked in, having forgotten to remove his hat. "You march right back out of here, Mr. Donald Robertson. You remove your hat and knock. You do not enter until I bid you enter." That was about the friendliest exchange he had with her in the years he labored there. The Tanners were childless; Robertson understood why.

After supper on that first evening, he went to sit alone on the low knoll west of the buildings. The lower limb of the bloated sun brushed the horizon. Robertson could see miles to the west, and when he pivoted his head, he could see miles to the south and miles to the east. The earth sighed up in little rises, then sank tiredly into little valleys. The prairie seemed to drink vision, denying the eye direction and distance. Robertson knew southwestern Kansas as a grand land, but if he thought poetically he would have realized that the grand land was daughter to the sun and mistress to the wind. She was a hot-blown harridan who nurtured wheat and buffalo grass—but few dreams.

At the last of that evening's light, he looked into the darkening north. The north seemed to shimmer and to beckon. He knew the years would spin him into a man. Then, by all that was in him, he would escape Tanner.

The Tanners spoke little to each other, almost nothing to their hired man. His labor sufficed. Robertson befriended the buckskin horse and named it Buck. Tanner had given it no name, beyond "that goddamned knotheaded horse."

One day in the second year, after a man in a Model-A Ford had left the mail, Lillian Tanner wordlessly put a penny postcard into Robertson's hand. Tanner had gone to town to drink beer and Robertson went down to the barn to show his postcard to Buck. Charles Robertson had scrawled in pencil: "Your sister Maggie is marrying Mr. Thomas Walsh. I am working in a factory. The weather has been good."

That night, Robertson went down into his cellar. He fired the kerosene lamp and removed from his paper suitcase the picture of his father's family Aunt Celia had given him months earlier, before his contact with that windblown woman had ceased. Aunt Celia explained that the picture had been taken in 1917, the day Uncle John left for the army and a Flanders grave. The family in the photograph peered suspiciously into the camera. Robertson's father was so unrecognizably young, Aunt Celia had to point him out. Charles Robertson stood, one of the five children arrayed behind work-worn parents, between Uncle John and Aunt Celia. The grandfather, who had died long before Robertson could have known him, wore a neckerchief and held a wide-brimmed hat in his hand, the marks of a cattleman.

Robertson seized upon that. That night, he created an image, polishing it over the dark musty hours of many other nights, often when the wind howled over the root cellar. He came to believe that his ancestors had been the ones who had risen up in Virginia and had chased the homesteads across a century. They drove hell-bent through the blue valleys and the timber, across Ohio and Illinois and across the great river to stand upon the plains that thrust up the snow-spired mountains. It was the threat of the mountains, and the seduction of the grand land, that checked their progress, leaving them in an unwanted corner of Kansas. They "put down there" as the expression went, and plowed strips of land to provide sod for a shanty. They stood their ever-pregnant women in the narrow doorways, shielding their eyes against the sun while the wind stole their sanity and their men went to cohabit with the mistress land—millions of acres, there for the taking.

Once beyond the Mississippi, the Robertsons could feast only upon the land; the water and timber had given out. They loosened the lathered teams of hard-mouthed horses from the wagons that had brought them and hitched them to the plow. They lashed the sweating horses with the leather of their dreams until the horses lay dead in the traces. Someone said mules stood the heat better and they traded for mules. Some said a Kansas plow was an iron implement with a mule's brain on both ends. Kansans laughed at things like that, but they got up before light and at dawn cracked the leather and cried, "Ho, mule! Plow!"

In the end, they had plowed an empire. Then they put down cattle and saddled the spirited Morgans to herd them, interrupting that only with the wheat harvest.

A man could see forever on that prairie if his eyes had the strength.

Robertson kept his father always the age he was in Aunt Celia's picture. Because he could not remember that his father ever laughed, Robertson made his farm boy laugh gleefully. In his imagination, the boy-father romped through the golden Durham, mowing it down with a joyous heart. Robertson pretended it was the time of the reaping, when the wheat would be chest-high on a boy. The laughing boy ran on, arms out to feel the wind, under a cobalt prairie sky that draped over the ends of the world. Sometimes, when the Tanners goaded him until he cried out for release, Robertson scraped the chicken filth from his jeans with the good blade of the pocketknife and went down into his tomb and forced himself to reflect that his people had dreamed proudly, but not wisely. Drought, misjudgment, the New Deal, the Chicago grain brokers, bankers, implement dealers, cattle buyers, horse traders—all the dread host that overshadowed the grand land in the poor years—had chipped the Robertsons down into the header. The auger whirled them into the separator where the threshing knives flailed them. The Kansas wind blew away the shading clouds and sent the sun. When the sun was done with them, the wind came again and blew them away, casting them from the threshing floor and into pathetic human collages called towns. In the town, Robertson knew, his father had labored for a pittance, selling the ache of his muscles, all the dread host had let him keep.

The proud but foolish Robertsons had been victims of cold men who spurred black horses. A bright neckerchief and a wide-brimmed hat could not conceal that.

But even then, on the darkest and the loneliest and the windiest of the nights in the cellar, Robertson never gave up the idea that he carried the genes of one-hundred-and-fifty-pound men who threw themselves upon the backs of thousand-pound Kiowa ponies and shouted, "Let him buck! One or t'other of us'll have to give in; and it ain't gonna be me." Robertson grew fierce about that, and he vowed he would remember the passion of the race through the forests and not the barren disappointment of the faithless mistress.

When he got old enough to teach himself the meaning of time, Robertson also came to understand that to betray the past is to cuckold the future. Whatever he did when he escaped Tanner, he decided, he would never further dishonor the past with the jails and scandals and illegitimacies that had infected the Robertson children of Aunt Celia's photograph. His legacy had been corrupted; his future need not be.

He loved the quick horse Buck, a knobby-kneed nonentity of an animal who could show surprising dash under a firm saddle. One day, about a year from the end, Robertson rode Buck into the north under a sky that threatened rain it would never deliver. Huge black cumulonimbus spun up in Colorado shadowed Kansas. Robertson sought Tanner's cattle, who had found a weakness in the wire. He dismounted to rest Buck and to study the land before him. Buck refused his ground hitch and drifted on toward the slash of the creek. Robertson ran to catch him. "Not now, Buck. When I'm eighteen. Then I promise I'll set you free of him." They stared north toward escape and Buck nuzzled his ear.

The Tanner months had no Sundays and only two Saturdays. On those days they hauled Robertson to town in the black Chevy, along with the cream and eggs. After the wind had blown away the relatives, Robertson visited the library and read. One day, because the book had become unstitched, the librarian gave him Belloc's *Napoleon*, which he read many times under the kerosene lamp while the winter wind roared over his head. About a year later, Lillian Tanner gave him a ragged *Life* magazine. In it was a picture of soldiers in a barracks shining shoes, proud men, laughing at some joke the camera captured. Robertson studied the picture of the soldiers until he memorized each detail; he liked most the creased shirts and the neat piles of equipment on the sunlit shelves. Whoever the soldiers were, he ached to be with them.

Those two different documents, willy-nilly, hastened the end and cast the die. Shortly after his eighteenth birthday, on another Saturday, Tanner stood in the machine yard and informed Robertson he was not to be permitted the relief of the town: Lillian wanted her chicken house cleaned. Robertson balked.

"I'll send you to the industrial school in Hutchinson."

"Bullshit."

"What did you say, you spiteful son of a bitch?"

"I said bullshit."

Tanner's slap snapped Robertson's head and darted fire into his eyes. Heat assailed his ears. Robertson screamed in pain and rage. But he remembered his vows. He struck back, forgetting that Tanner owed him four months back wages. Buck may have watched; they were not far from the short day pasture near the barn.

When it was over, Harvey Tanner lay on the ground, at Robertson's feet, cursing. "Get off my farm," he croaked, "or I'll have Sheriff Danforth lock you up."

Robertson's chest heaved and his body ached. "I have been locked up, Harvey. Three years hard labor. But by God, no more!"

Harvey tried to get up butt-first. Robertson put his boot on the left hip pocket of Harvey's overalls and shoved. Harvey's face went down into the chicken droppings.

Robertson packed his cardboard suitcase and walked west about a mile. He hid in a plum thicket and smoked Bull Durham. His old antagonist the wind hectored the brush, but Robertson ignored it. When the Tanner pickup had gone past, and the Tanner dust had settled, Robertson walked back to the house.

Buck came in to a soft call. "Let's ride, Buck. I promised I'd help you."

He made an Indian bridle from a rope and mounted bareback. Buck was a quick horse. Long before night he had carried his rider into the narrow gullies at the foot of the town. When the darkness hardened, Robertson threw his suitcase, less one clean shirt, into a culvert where someone might make a lucky find. He had seventeen cents in his pocket; the knife with the broken blade was long lost.

Robertson caught Buck and rode him around the town to the cemetery where his mother slept. He smoked a cigarette while he said good-bye to his roots.

When Robertson rode beyond the cemetery, he let Buck choose the route because he did not fully understand where he trended. After several casual miles, the buckskin gelding reined himself in on a low hilltop. He whickered softly, as if he did not wish to sully the beauty of what they did. The night west wind drove toward the rising moon. That way lay Wichita, as good a place as any.

Robertson dismounted and removed the rope bridle and stroked Buck's muzzle as he had done on the first day. Buck whickered once or twice, tossing his head. Suddenly Robertson turned and struck with the rope. Buck reared and leaped forward. His unshod hooves bit the hard earth and he lunged down the hill. "Go, Buck! Run! We are free of it! Run forever!"

Buck stopped at the bottom of the hill and looked up, as if wanting Robertson to run with him under the windy moon. "Go!" Robertson shouted gleefully. "Never turn back!"

The horse spun and galloped into the night.

Robertson waved. He stood alone. He drew the rope he had used to his face and rubbed his chin thoughtfully against the coarse fibers. Then, angrily, he knotted the rope. He knotted until he held but a lump of hemp. He threw that into the wind that had taken his horse. He spat after it.

Robertson curled up in shiver and slept until near dawn. Then he set himself down on an east-trending highway which soon became a ribbon toward the new sun. After sunup, a shadow came to walk with him.

In Wichita, where his thumb had gotten him by Sunday night, he spent his estate on a cup of coffee and two fresh sacks of Bull Durham smoking tobacco. He slept behind a sign that advertised Packard automobiles. On Monday, the spiffy recruiting sergeant said cheerfully, "The army is a fine choice, son. Good place to learn a trade for when you get out."

Robertson talked more of getting in than of getting out.

He passed the recruiter's intelligence test with a near-perfect score. Notwithstanding this, and he puzzled over it only a moment, the spiffy sergeant marked Robertson for "Infantry, Basic Rifleman."

Robertson was not at all puzzled. Who cared? When he looked at the reflections in the windows of the train he rode to the induction station in Kansas City, he saw not Buck running free in the wind. He saw proud men in creased khaki shirts polishing fine shoes in a sunny barracks.

Wherever they were, those barracks were above the ground.

PART

TWO

5

CHUNCHON, SOUTH KOREA,
JUNE 21, 1951

They were formed up near the road and several Korean children clung to the wire, watching the *migook* soldiers. One boy, about ten years old, wearing a black jacket, short trousers, and rubber slippers over filthy bare feet, called loudly, "Hey GI! You like fuckee my virgin sister?"

An American in the last rank turned his head and snarled back: "I'd screw your virgin mama-san, you scabby little gook."

"How much money you pay, GI?"

The replacement depot first sergeant, a neckless man about as broad as he was tall, left his position in front of the formation and made two lumbering steps toward the children. "Go on now, you kids! The captain doesn't want you hanging around here." The children giggled and ran off.

Pfc. Solomon Zuckerman, viewing it from the first of the sloppy ranks, thought they would be back. He also thought, because the children had been so filthy and so obviously hungry, that such Korean children did not laugh often.

Beyond the wire he could see Chunchon, or what remained of Chunchon. Under the haze, the convalescing city—it recently had endured the artillery fire of two armies—was mysterious and aloof. Even if they had offered to let him, he'd not have wanted to go there. In the six days he had been in Korea his eyes and nose had conspired to teach him that the Land of the Morning Calm was something for an American to take in small doses, perhaps creeping up on it armored with an empty stomach.

Zuckerman thought the tentage of the division replacement depot reminiscent of the seedier sections of the Bronx. There was a suggestion of order to the compound, in the sense that the tents lined up to form rows around the muddy square where the noon shipping formation now stood, but the canvas itself was mud-crusted and baggy, held up slapdash by slouching posts and slack ropes.

Zuckerman had turned twenty-one on the troopship two weeks earlier. Under the obviously fresh-issue steel helmet perched squarely over his nose, his dark hair was GI-cropped. The high yellow sun, busy baking the mud of the previous evening's drenching rain into dust, tinted his eyes bluish green. If anything, he was faintly Baltic looking.

Thinking about it as he listened to the drone of formation business that hovered overhead, like flies around the garbage cans he had scrubbed so often on KP, he decided the replacement depot was slatternly because nobody cared about it. It was a transient station: since it belonged to all, it belonged to none.

Easily he detected two distinct types of soldiers in the ranks he shared with about forty other men. Most of the men wore shiny fatigue uniforms and new combat boots. These men, replacements all, had no weapons. The few men who did have weapons wore nondescript combinations of military garments. Patently, they already belonged to the infantry units north of them and were merely passing through the depot for various administrative reasons. Although two of them wore infantry blue neck scarves, they in the main presented Zuckerman's eye with a scruffiness identical to that of the tents of the depot. And, like the men who slung them, the weapons had a well-used look.

The first sergeant consulted his clipboard.

"Klineschmidt?"

The stocky Teutonic man next to Zuckerman filled his lungs and shouted, *"Yo, Sarge! Right here!"*

"You got orders for Company G."

Klineschmidt lifted a hand to acknowledge it.

"Zuckerman?"

"Here, Sergeant."

"Also George Company. You two men get with Sergeant Robertson. He's the sorry trooper over yonder leaning on the brace ropes of my orderly tent looking like he snuck over the fence from my repple-depple last night and got hisself clapped up and hung over. He's going back home to G this afternoon and he can nursemaid you." The first sergeant glowered at the man he had indicated. The man remained unmoving, as if the public accusation were beneath notice.

Zuckerman glanced over. The buck sergeant did look hung over. His helmet was pushed down over the bridge of his nose to deflect the sun. The condition of his uniform suggested that he was a man who measured his tenure in Korea in weeks or months rather than hours, as did Zuckerman. But, unlike the others who bore such manifest marks of being old hands, the sergeant had no rifle. Strangely, his only accouterment was a book, a vision rare in the army, certainly in the combat army.

Zuckerman did not understand whether or not he was to break ranks. He nudged the soldier who had answered to the name of Klineschmidt. Klineschmidt shrugged and frowned helplessly.

The first sergeant's breathy growl resolved the confusion. "You two get your butts over there with Sergeant Robertson like I told you. Next time you get in my formation, get the wax out of your ears."

Zuckerman slung his field pack on his shoulder and started over. As he walked, he heard the first sergeant shout: "Now the rest of you men sound off like Private Klineschmidt did when I call your name. Like you had a pair of balls. Don't make me strain my ear bones like Miss Zuckerman did." Zuckerman reddened. Klineschmidt beamed.

The two replacements halted in front of Robertson. "We were told to report to you," Zuckerman announced.

Almost a minute went by before Robertson looked up. At first he only stared blankly, but then he spoke. "Pay no attention to him. He's ticked off because I went AWOL on him last night and he can't prove it."

"Will he punish you?" Zuckerman whispered, slightly awed although absent-without-official-leave was by far the army's most common indiscipline.

Robertson shook his head.

Klineschmidt walked away a few feet and lit a cigarette. Robertson glanced at him and said nothing.

Zuckerman studied Robertson. Blond, midtwenties or slightly younger, clearly a Regular, accent mildly southern. Except for a long jagged scar under the right eye, the face was bronzed. The pale scar pulled the eye down, giving Robertson the air of a man in doubt. Zuckerman sensed that something had recently disquieted him. Surely not something as trivial as a hangover? Hangovers, Zuckerman had learned in the eleven months he had been a soldier, were as common in the hard-drinking American army as the reveille formations to which they were brought.

Uncomfortable that Robertson stared back at him, Zuckerman dismissed his speculations. It was none of his business if a sergeant was hung over. Zuckerman nodded toward the paperbound brown book in Robertson's left hand. It was obviously an academic book. "Strange to see a book here," he said fatuously.

Robertson remained blankly silent again before speaking, as if he debated whether or not to speak. He lifted the book for Zuckerman to see the title. Zuckerman recognized the genre—United States Armed Forces Institute, the army's correspondence school—and read the title: *English II, Poetry in Perspective.*

"Are you studying poetry?"

Robertson shrugged before saying, "I finished it. I came back yesterday from the company to take the final examination."

Intrigued, Zuckerman asked, "Why did you have to come back here? Couldn't they have given you the examination in the company?"

"That's the way the army does it over here. An officer at Division Rear administered it."

Warming, but warily so—a wide gulf separated career noncommissioned officers from green privates—Zuckerman smiled. "How did you do?"

Robertson shrugged again, as if he didn't care. "I won't know for weeks. Other times . . ." He paused, then explained offhandedly that English II gave him his sixty-third mail-order credit, making him roughly a college junior. "Other times it's taken weeks to get a grade back. The army never hurries."

When Robertson fell silent, Zuckerman spoke quickly, wanting to continue the exchange. "I'm engaged to a girl, Rachel Kahan, who's a student at Fordham." Zuckerman fished out his wallet and took out Rachel's picture.

Robertson studied it dutifully. "Pretty girl. Bet she's nice," he mumbled.

Before Zuckerman could respond, Robertson handed him the picture and turned away, going to stand by the wire. He stared dejectedly toward Chunchon, where undoubtedly his previous night's AWOL had taken him.

Zuckerman stood, holding Rachel's picture in one hand and the strap of his field pack in the other. As he watched Robertson, he got the sensation that whatever disquieted the scarred sergeant was recent, and that it had happened in the city.

Klineschmidt ambled over to join Zuckerman. Nothing more was said. It was almost five minutes before Robertson turned away from the wire.

"The trucks are coming," he announced quietly. He shook his head sadly. "In the army, it's always a coming-for."

Robertson began walking toward the gate of the depot, toward the sound of the trucks. Zuckerman was sure Robertson's shoulders slumped. He was equally certain that this was not the sergeant's usual condition.

The sun had done its work. If Degas had had an easel beside that road, he would have painted in grays. He'd have rendered the truck that thundered toward the regiment as a dusty chimera. Degas would have sketched gray-faced ghost men riding the back of his chimera.

Under the sun-lashed canvas, Zuckerman alternated his drowsy attention between Robertson, who rode on the hard, jolting bench across the bed of the truck from him, and the crenellated lime green terrain that presented itself through the aperture between the canvas and the tailgate.

Zuckerman realized he had only a weak notion of where he was. He had not positively known his location since he had left Seattle on the USNS *General John Pope* in May.

He had learned the names of the places, and certainly knew he had just left Chunchon, but the words had no meaning. As he pondered this, he slipped out his canteen and put it to his lips. The water was lukewarm, and tasted like chlorinated mud. He made a face.

He knew he was in the area of the world the army labeled FECOM— Far East Command. He also realized this punishingly hot ride represented the final leg of a long and exhausting journey across America from the Bronx to Seattle, across the Pacific in the crammed troopship to Yokohama, thence by train to Sasebo, thence by a small ferry ship named *Koana Maru* to Pusan, then more trains and more trucks.

At each of the stops there had been buses and marches and cursing sergeants and shouting officers. Not once on the trip had Zuckerman eaten two meals at the same table. Often, as at Chunchon, there had been no tables at all. On the ship he had eaten standing up.

Notwithstanding uncomfortable accommodations and meaningless destinations, it had been a busy time. Zuckerman had been measured, taken from, issued to, inoculated, certified, and corrected. In Seattle he had been insulted—this when a medical sergeant demanded that he, along with a thousand others, exhibit his penis to prove that he did not propose to export American venereal disease to Korea. The Koreans, the lectures reiterated often, had more than enough varieties of their own.

Other lectures warned Zuckerman not to touch buried ordnance, not to drink the women, not to eat the hand grenades, to keep the safety pins in the food, and not to have sexual intercourse with the whiskey. Or so it seemed to him. Except that the lectures were so ungrammatical, his own father could have written them.

The rationale for all this was the need to move massive numbers of replacements through a personnel pipeline and deliver them to the Korean front. Each time he was processed, Zuckerman's personal belongings decreased. He had departed from his leave in the Bronx with a full barracks bag. Now he owned only what was in the field pack. His only material gain had been in vaccine. His personal arsenal of antibodies could confront any known Asiatic disease.

The ultimate purpose of his trek had occurred in a tent in Pusan six days earlier. A chubby clerk had pointed a pencil at him and had growled, "Is Avram D. Zuckerman, Bronx, New York, relationship father, your correct insurance beneficiary?"

Zuckerman said yes.

"Better be right. When you get your ass shot off up there, your daddy gets ten grand from a grateful Uncle Sam."

The soldiers in the front of the truck groaned, but here near the tailgate, where Zuckerman and Robertson rode, the air was relatively breathable. Zuckerman adjusted his torso to the jolting of the truck and continued to muse on his status.

He dangled in time. The known world was behind him. Nothing ahead could be foreseen. Only a few personnel clerks knew his secret, and they'd likely never compare notes. The secret was that Solomon Zuckerman, who had angered his father by dropping out of Fordham and volunteering for the army, had outraged common sense by also volunteering for the infantry, compounding that outrage by volunteering for the Korean infantry. Any man on the truck, except perhaps Robertson, would have certified him insane for the last two of those; the draftees in the truck would have certified him for the first alone.

Well, it wasn't all that bad so far. He liked Sergeant Robertson and thought he might find a friend in Klineschmidt, although the young man from Wisconsin was as coarse as an issue blanket.

As if in tune to Zuckerman's thoughts, Klineschmidt spoke up for the first time in the journey, now almost three hours old. "Hey, Sergeant Robertson! Did you get any pussy in Chunchon last night when you went over the hill?"

Zuckerman jolted fully awake, eyes on Robertson.

For a few seconds, Robertson seemed not to have heard. Then he lifted his head and turned toward the others. His mouth worked long before he emitted words. "You serve your hitch, Klineschmidt, and I'll serve mine."

Zuckerman puzzled at this angry response. Rude though it was,

Klineschmidt's query was as common among soldiers as "Where are you from?" and "How long have you been in?"

But there was no mistaking Robertson's tone; Zuckerman had heard it often in squad rooms. Not a snarl, to be sure, and often rendered in a quiet voice, but such tones carried threat of personal violence. Clearly, whatever it was that had cast its pall on Robertson, he was in no mood for banter today.

Klineschmidt mumbled a few words of protest and settled back into morose silence.

Now Robertson did something else that puzzled Zuckerman. He had been holding the English textbook in his hands as a priest might hold a monstrance. Now he lifted the book to his eyes, looked at it blankly a moment, then threw it savagely out of the truck. Zuckerman followed the path of Robertson's eyes. After the wind blew the dust away, he could see the book. It lay in the middle of the macadamized road with the wind riffling its pages. The truck went around a curve, climbing steeply in first gear, and the book was out of sight.

Zuckerman sensed a finality to it. He caught Robertson's attention. "Whatever it is, I'm sorry," he said just loudly enough to lift his words above the noise of the truck.

Robertson stared back. He said nothing. After a while he put his head in his hands.

Shaken, Zuckerman looked back down the road, almost hoping that the sergeant might change his mind and demand that the truck return for his textbook.

But the road receded, a thin ribbon from the Bronx to the Korean summer front.

Now the truck began to pass military positions. The men were visibly armed and were bulwarked with sandbags. The units became scruffier and scruffier and ever more furtive.

A tremendous concussion rattled the canvas and slammed into their ears. Someone cried, "Cripes! That's eight-inch stuff. They told us in basic training it can fire a boxcar full of TNT all the way to the Yalu."

Zuckerman put his head out. A battery of monster howitzers sat in a field not far from the road. The men nearby had fingers in their ears. The tubes angled up sharply. One tube smoked. Zuckerman's heart raced. He was new to Korea, but he had been in the army long enough to know that this artillery must mark the rear of the combat zone. Ahead would be the 155-mm calibers, then the workhorse 105-mms. Then the mortars and machine guns and rifles. Then the bayonet, the range always shortening, sometimes, he had been told, to the range of the human arm.

Presently, the six-by-six slammed to a halt near a blue company guidon. The Hispanic assistant driver hopped down and came around to the rear, shouting, "G Company! Unload, amigos, before we change our mind. Next stop's the *working* companies."

Zuckerman understood the slur. It meant that George Company was in reserve. The American army in Korea tried to fight two-up-and-one-back, that is, theoretically, for each two units committed, one comparable unit would remain uncommitted, a reserve against trouble.

Robertson swung over the tailgate and dropped into the dirt. Zuckerman followed, then Klineschmidt. As they walked toward the guidon, lugging their field packs, Zuckerman heard someone in the truck behind him challenge the assistant driver: "Why don't you motor-pool guys ever roll the canvas? You could boil a friggin' egg with what's in my canteen."

"Yeah," chimed in another voice. "You bastards ain't got to sit back here frying your ass while you eat dust."

"That's easy for you infantry legs to say," the assistant driver replied hotly. "You don't got to put canvas back on again when our lieutenant gets on our ass."

Four northbound Sabrejets contrailed over high above the popcorn cumulus clouds of the central front. To the northwest, Zuckerman heard the distant dull *whomp* of a howitzer, followed shortly by a closer *whump*. Then he heard a closer *whomp* and a distant dull *whump*. He fought down unease and reasoned it out. The field artillery must be dueling over the uninvolved heads of the infantry. He approved of that, sure the other side's infantry approved also. As he listened, he speculated that afternoon cannonading, which seemed desultory, must have the purpose merely of a mischievous warning. Who'd attack in this heat?

William Manston, by any stretch of imagination George Company first sergeant, and the officious Reynolds, as clearly Manston's dog robber, or company clerk, waited near the dusty orderly-room tent. Robertson handed Manston the mimeographed orders that had brought them up from Chunchon and stepped back.

Manston gave the orders to Reynolds and regarded Zuckerman and Klineschmidt sourly. Then he folded his arms across his ample chest, as first sergeants did when they had business to do. He jerked his head toward Robertson. "You're going over to second platoon as squad leader, Robertson. We need to re-form the first squad. You can have these two you brought up with you, the two Weapons Platoon KATUSA, and some skimmings out of Third Platoon like you—"

Robertson's eyes narrowed under his helmet. "Hold on, Top, I don't want a squad."

Manston stiffened. "The army don't care what you want, Sergeant. It is what the army wants that counts."

Robertson scuffed the dirt. Manston glared. The air seemed thick with menace until Robertson said quietly, "Okay, Top. If you ask it, I'll try to do it."

Manston smiled broadly. "Good man. Couldn't ask for more than that." He turned to Zuckerman. "You two belong to Sergeant Robertson here. Maybe he can teach you enough between now and chowtime to keep you alive until reveille."

The beefy first sergeant turned and ducked through the flap into the orderly-room tent. Robertson walked away, leaving Zuckerman and Klineschmidt rooted under Reynolds's order for them to stand fast.

The clerk's speech was chock full of "bug-outs," "zaps," "gooks," and "Charley Chinks." Interspersed with such jargon, he gave the two replacements the rudiments of what they needed to know to function in G company.

Klineschmidt asked Reynolds, "Why does the first squad need to be re-formed?"

Reynolds grinned—maliciously, Zuckerman thought. "Last Monday we was on line. Two of the first squad, second, rotated out."

"What happened to the others?"

"They divided up a Chink one-fifty-two-round. What was left of them wouldn't fill your fucking mess kit."

Now Zuckerman was certain the clerk's grin held malice.

When Reynolds dismissed them, they walked down between the rows of filthy, almost-decrepit tents toward where Robertson had disappeared. The sides of the tents were rolled up, revealing only folding cots and carelessly strewn equipment. Zuckerman saw few men. He assumed the company must be out doing something.

In the tent to which Reynolds had directed them, they found Robertson waiting. He had gotten his equipment from somewhere and had thrown it on a cot. Most prominent among his equipment was a well-oiled M-1 rifle and several full bandoliers of ammunition. To Zuckerman the sight seemed wholly different from the neat locked rifle racks in the Stateside barracks, but also wholly typical of where he was. He pondered the abundance of ammunition, for in the States ammunition had been checked in and out, accounted for like Fort Knox gold bullion. But, of course . . . he chided himself for being naive.

"The bunks with field packs on them are in use," Robertson explained. "You can take anything else. Check the end sticks. It's a running prank in the company to unloosen the braces so the cots fold up when you sit on them."

Zuckerman glanced at the several empty cots and asked, "Isn't that dangerous?"

"Not as dangerous as some of the other pranks."

The replacements shrugged and threw their duffels onto the cots.

Zuckerman sat down and turned to Robertson, who had lain down beside his rifle. "The first sergeant said we'd have KATUSA in the squad, Sergeant Robertson. What are they?"

Robertson did not turn his head when he answered. "KATUSA— Korean Augmentation To United States Army—Korean enlisted men who soldier with us. The army got short of hands last year and dragooned a bunch of gooks—" He paused and corrected himself. "Bunch of Koreans to fill up the holes the Chinese shot in American units. They'll leave you alone if you leave them alone." He added, "I think the two Manston mentioned have been over in Weapons Platoon."

Klineschmidt had been bouncing on his cot. "This rack ain't the Sheraton," he complained.

This time Robertson lifted his head. "In a couple of weeks you'll think it's the Sheraton. Getting these cots for us was Captain Hartung's work. Normally in close reserve like this we sleep on the dirt."

His voice was again menacing. Klineschmidt muttered and fell silent.

Robertson added, "Hartung is the Old Man, and he's the best company commander you'll ever have. Bitching about what he does will not make you happy in George Company."

Klineschmidt whined, "I didn't mean to insult nobody. Just made a remark about my fucking rack."

Robertson's face twisted; he seemed frozen in some inner contradiction. Zuckerman nodded to himself, thinking he understood. Robertson had not impressed him as a peevish man; fully to the contrary. He was just hung over. Then the sergeant, as if he had corrected himself again, said pleasantly enough, "Forget it, then. Learn what you have to learn and keep your opinions to yourself until you get asked for them."

With that, he lay back, arms folded behind his head, staring at the canvas overhead.

Abandoned to himself by Robertson and Klineschmidt, Zuckerman glanced around the tent. The air droned. He felt as if he were drowning in the heat under the canvas. He understood that his old ideas of climate no longer applied. New York could be hot, down in the deep canyons between the bricks, and central California could be unbearable, but the heat here was somehow different, almost a living presence, murky and drenching, a predator waiting to pounce. Zuckerman had heard about it. Korean returnees *always* mentioned it, cursing both the sickening salt tablets and the bitter quinine horse capsules the army issued to combat the monsoon summer and the malarial mosquitoes it bred. He had also heard that men died in Korea from heat prostration. But how could he fight that?

Then he heard the sounds of marching men—cadence calls, the shuffle of boots as the columns went to half step to close up the formation. He glanced at his watch: 1600 hours, about the Stateside quitting hour. The sides of the tent were rolled and tied. To watch, he had but to turn his torso and look out.

He saw a platoon of men, backs to him. The men were obviously tired. The backs of their shirts were damp and he could see the sweat beaded on their necks. They were festooned with canteens, rifles, bayonets, and ammunition pouches. No two steel helmets cocked at the same angle. The ranks were ragged, but even in raggedness displayed a businesslike discipline, a certain cockiness that surprised him.

When the tall SFC who commanded them dismissed them, two squads came toward the tent. As they filtered in, Zuckerman sensed that they scarcely heeded him. Their clothing was ill-fitting and battered, like the attire of the infantry casuals he had seen in the replacement depot. He felt suddenly ashamed of his own crisp fatigues and new boots. That comparison made him feel more alone than he had felt earlier.

Zuckerman looked up when one of the sweaty newcomers rushed to Robertson and grabbed the toe of his boot to shake it.

This man, a sergeant like Robertson, shouted gleefully, "Heard you was in the good platoon now. I'll bet them mooses down in Chunchon town wore your pecker out."

Robertson lifted an arm defensively. "Let me alone, Brax. I'm not in the mood for it."

Braxton Fowlkes studied Robertson a moment, then frowned and said to Zuckerman, "What did you fellers do to my old buddy down there? He left here yesterday morning full of panther piss and happy like his usual self and you bring him back sadder'n a fresh-castrated billy goat."

"You'd have to ask Sergeant Robertson," Zuckerman answered quietly. That was the best way. Whoever these men were, they were important to him now. Don't risk offending.

That night Fowlkes and Robertson sat together in the road ditch about two hundred yards below the company. Robertson had not spoken for many minutes. Fowlkes chewed and spat streams of tobacco juice into the nearby wheatgrass. Busy field artillerymen flickered along the horizon and filled the air with *whumps* and *whomps*. A flare burst far to the north and floated downward, glowing long seconds before it winked out. Robertson pricked up an ear. Even at this distance, about six miles, he could hear the rattle of a heavy machine gun, knowing it sought a target in the flare light.

Fowlkes spoke. "Something eating you?"

For a moment, Robertson considered revealing to Fowlkes what had happened in Chunchon. But he saw he could not, knowing at once that it would put him on a dangerous path. He deflected with, "How did it go here while I was gone?"

Fowlkes spat. "We played Missy Blackthorne's cowboy and chink game like always in reserve. He's a silly peckerwood. Hear his old man is a four-star general."

Robertson didn't comment on the character and genealogy of the Second Platoon's officer leader. He stared at Fowlkes.

Fowlkes was twenty-six, sandy and tall and gawky and had a huge hooked nose and dull brown eyes that made him resemble a hung-over vulture. But of all the billions of humans who shared Robertson's planet, he most prized Sgt. Braxton Bragg Fowlkes of western North Carolina. Fowlkes had preceded Robertson into the Regular Army by almost two years, now he had Third Squad, Second.

"Us hillbillies don't sleep in beds," Fowlkes once had told Robertson. "We tie knots in our peckers and hang from nails in the walls." Fowlkes often sang in an excellent tenor voice, always weary songs that made Robertson choke. Once, about eight months earlier, in the Sunday-afternoon homesick stillness of an old wooden barracks at Camp Chaffee, Arkansas, Fowlkes, on the top bunk over Robertson, had broken out into a mountain song called "In the Pines." Robertson had put down the book he was reading. The bald notes of the unadorned music made him see in his mind a melancholy train on its way through the deep glades of the pines, moving toward what always lodged in a soldier's conscience, that vague thing called home.

At the end, Robertson hid his face, not wanting the others to see that his eyes were wet.

Each had come to Chaffee a corporal of infantry, Robertson from Fort Riley, Fowlkes from Fort Bragg, to mark time until the brand-new Korean police action could absorb them. The executive officer had ordered them to the gun sheds to help clean the .30-caliber light machine guns the trainees had fired that day.

Two-chevron soldiers among green recruits, they fell together at once, building lightheartedly on that. At one point, Robertson winked at Fowlkes and poked one of the trainees in the butt with a cleaning rod.

The trainee's yelp brought the husky paratroop sergeant who bossed the shed running. "All right, which one of you birds thinks horseplay gets machine guns cleaned?"

"I did it," Robertson admitted.

"Then you get your ass back here after chow, Corporal, and I'll give you a lesson in by God how to clean .30s."

As the sergeant turned away, Fowlkes took the rod, jabbing him sharply in the rump.

The paratrooper turned and glowered. "Another wiseass? You come back with this other wiseass. Don't plan on having a good time."

When the shadows were long across Chaffee's howitzer parks, Fowlkes and Robertson went to receive their punishment. Anticipating what awaited, they had eaten lightly at supper. Since the army was experimenting with horse meat at that time, to mollify the nation's ranchers, it was easy to dine lightly. Fowlkes and Robertson walked several feet apart, merely victims-to-be of an identical fate. Robertson knew little more about Fowlkes than his name.

The sergeant waited, shirt off, black chest hairs bristling with the afternoon's anger. Two .30-caliber M-1919 A-3s lay heavily across a table near the entrance of the shed.

"Pick 'em up and shoulder 'em, boys. Then double time and follow me." The paratrooper led them to the perimeter road around the sheds and into the gathering dusk.

The receiver group of the M-1919 machine gun is rectangular. The sharp edge of the metal began at once to bruise the flesh beneath the thin cotton of the corporals' fatigue jackets.

The guns jounced and the duo stumbled. Three miles and the dusk had long fallen before the sergeant led them back to the sheds and ordered them to halt.

"You two birds had enough?" he demanded.

Robertson and Fowlkes exchanged glances. Each shook his head. Each locked his lips.

"Heft 'em, then. Double time!"

They ran once more around the perimeter, about an additional two miles.

"You birds had enough *now?*"

"Shit no, Sarge. Me and this feller Corporal Robertson run like this every night. Keeps us in shape for coon hunting."

"Pick 'em up!"

Once more around the track, easier this time, because the sergeant, probably twenty years older, had slowed. When he halted them under the light again, Robertson saw the sweat on his chest hairs. The sergeant caught his breath and wheezed, "Enough, you shitheaded birds?" It was well after taps.

Fowlkes grinned at Robertson and turned on the paratrooper. "You is the dumb feller who is losing sleep, Sarge. Me and this other shitheaded bird here got a pass tomorrow. We can find a hole and sleep all day. You got to come back here and teach other birds how to clean machine guns, like you done taught us."

The sergeant ordered them to put the guns away and released them. He was cursing the night as they walked away. They were more than a mile from the barracks.

On the slow trek homeward, they walked side by side and Fowlkes sang about a great speckled bird. Chaffee was a training station, and the recruits on sentry were taught the formal challenge.

"Halt! Who goes there?"

The customary reply from an experienced soldier was something on the order of a snarled "Blow it out your ass, Mac," but Robertson's reply was a measured, pleasant "Friends go here."

Next day at noon, Fowlkes told the first sergeant how well they had done cleaning the machine guns for the paratrooper and the first sergeant—called "Top" or "First Shirt"—happily gave them an afternoon pass. They caught the bus into Fort Smith and went to the hotel that flew the Stars and Stripes. They drank Texas beer and caroused with the old whores. Having saluted the flag smartly on the way in, they saluted it smartly on the way out.

"What you thinking on, Robbie?" Fowlkes asked, bringing Robertson back to the present.

Robertson made a half smile. "That old bent-leg sergeant we ragged back at Chaffee shortly after we met."

"Wooee! That old rascal was a bear with a sore ball. You reckon he ever got his wind back?"

"Why did you get involved in it? He wanted my scalp, not yours."

Fowlkes shrugged. "Seemed like you needed a friend then, Robbie. Turned out dijobe and number one. Old sarge got his paratroop runnin' out of his system and I got a good buddy out of the deal. He could have run us around again a couple more times afore I'da give up."

Robertson fell silent for several minutes. He picked up a stone and skipped it across the road. He turned to Fowlkes. "What do you think about Koreans?"

"Gooks?" Fowlkes spat out his chaw and reached for a fresh plug of

Day's Work. Tobacco spittle dripped down under his lip. He wiped it with his hand, then wiped his hand on his trousers. Tobacco plug poised in midair near his mouth, he said, "I guess I don't think much about them at all. They don't count somehow like Americans count. But, except for getting us over here, Robbie, the gooks ain't done nothing to this old hillbilly."

Robertson came back almost immediately with, "They don't want us over here. I think we're hurting them more than we're helping them."

Fowlkes pondered this. "Well, Robbie, you call Truman on Cap'n Hartung's telephone and tell him that. I sure enough reckon he'll bring us home tomorrow."

Robertson ignored the gibe. He asked, "Have you ever heard the Korean word *seikse?*"

Fowlkes shifted and stared at Robertson. He had bitten his plug and worked his new chaw with his tongue to soften it. "Sounds like 'sexy.' Is that what you mean?"

Robertson shook his head, knowing it could lead nowhere. He shifted ground slightly. "Just a word I heard last night. Nothing important." He glanced meaningfully back toward the tents and got up, brushing himself off. Fowlkes remained seated, staring at the gun flashes on the horizon.

Suddenly he jerked his head and lifted a hand to point north. "I ain't against gooks, Robbie. That up there is what I'm prejudiced against. I was on Okinawa in '45 and we been here since March getting crap on our boots and I've had enough. When Missy Blackthorne and Cap'n Hartung blow the whistle, Braxton Bragg Fowlkes ain't going back up there with them and play cowboy no more."

"That's crazy talk, Brax."

Fowlkes got up and stalked past Robertson. "First fucking sense you've heard since we came here, Robbie," he muttered.

6

SANGYANG-NI RESERVE POSITION, JUNE 22, 1951

When the whistle blew them out of the tents, the Second Platoon men dawdled sleepily. They were taciturn and buttoned clothing as they walked. Presumably, they were beyond enemy artillery interest. Nevertheless, all wore steel helmets and carried weapons.

Waiting for them in the square of red dirt nearby, clipboard in hand, was SFC Milo Baker, a tall, lean reservist from San Antonio. Baker's helmet sat squarely on his head, officer-fashion; his trousers bloused out above his boots. Thus, vis-à-vis his platoon, the platoon sergeant was unique in military bearing.

Robertson stopped a few feet ahead and to the left of Baker, facing him. Sergeant Nelson, the florid man who led the Second Squad, stood behind him; then Braxton Fowlkes, who had Third Squad; then Sergeant Ollit, a nineteen-year-old who headed the weapons squad. Thus positioned in the geography of North Korea, the four squad leaders made anchors for the remainder of the platoon.

All the squads but Robertson's found places easily. Robertson's men screwed up faces and fumbled and jostled over the issue of who should stand next to whom. Soon enough they resolved it and lined up on Robertson's left.

Baker called them to attention, then demanded, "Reports!"

Reveille formation was the only occasion during the Korean War when enlisted men saluted each other. Robertson lifted his right hand, fingers rigid, palm flat. "First squad present!" Baker returned the salute. Nelson followed, "Second squad present!" then Fowlkes, then Ollit.

Baker gave "at ease" and rifled off some administrative instructions.

He paused a moment, then spoke again, his tone firmer. "Daily intelligence summary . . ." He glanced at his clipboard before going on. "Usual stuff, regimental companies on line tallied more than thirteen hundred rounds of incoming yesterday. Charley must have got some ammunition resupply since we left."

Someone called out of ranks, "The sonsabitches needed it; they used everything up on us before we hauled ass off line last week."

The ranks guffawed, to be shushed by Baker's frown.

At that moment, Robertson glanced to his left, across his new squad. In squad rank, noses line up. He sighted across them—red noses, pale noses, large, small and thin noses, straight noses and hooked noses. Carver was an Afro-American, Klineschmidt a German, surely Olson was a Norwegian. The two Koreans probably prayed to Buddha, and Zuckerman, if he prayed at all, prayed in Hebrew. Catholics, Protestants, maybe a heathen or two. If he examined the lettering on their dog tags, he could know, along with their serial numbers and blood types. But that knowledge was irrelevant, of use only to the chaplains and the medics, and the grim soldiers of the Graves Registration Office, those who disposed of the poncho-shrouded dead.

Robertson's thoughts began to assemble, ordering the jumble of ideas that had pummeled him during the night. A week earlier, he'd have leaped to command a squad; now he balked at it. To drown this reluctance, he examined the noses again. What had brought them there from out of the corners of the earth? Why, of the millions, these? To stand in the dawn dirt of the Kumwha Line to the left of Donald A. Robertson? To mingle the waters of their diverse manhoods? Did each have a personal crossroads, as Robertson now knew he had, a turn in the journey that brought one thing as opposed to another?

Then it came together. Robertson saw that if he completely filled his mind with these men, no other thoughts could get in. It would be like the reveille formation—once closed up, nothing else could enter.

Robertson said fiercely to himself: By God! You are here to be led. And I will lead you. Then the event in Chunchon released a few loathsome tentacles. Haunting as it was, it apparently was not inescapable.

Solomon Zuckerman waited until the Second Platoon had almost formed before leaving the security of the tent, which after fifteen hours was a known entity. Then he and Klineschmidt went to stand in the front rank to the left of two stone-faced Koreans. Shortly before SFC Baker called them to attention, a black corporal came to stand at the end of the rank, greeting them in a low voice as if to apologize for nudging them over.

Low fractured stratus clouds had formed in the night, but Zuckerman saw already that the sun would drive them higher, then away. He felt a momentary nostalgia for New York; he remembered how really low clouds there rode the shoulders of the taller buildings, and how once on Forty-second Street he had noticed this and knew then that the skyscrapers were the pillars of his world.

The previous day's truck trip had tired him, and he had slept well. Basic training and six additional months in garrison infantry had run off the adolescent plumpness he had brought into the recruiting station. Zuckerman knew he was hard and was proud. His eyes shifted toward the tall Korean on his right. He caught the profile of the squad leader, the sergeant who had brought them from the replacement depot at Chunchon.

He had realized by now that Robertson was as new to the Second Platoon as he and Klineschmidt were. Except for Sergeant Fowlkes and the few men who had come over during the evening with their equipment from the Third Platoon, few of the Second Platoon men had apparently known Robertson. Thinking about it, Zuckerman realized that what he saw here in Korea was no different from what he had seen almost from his first day in the army. A soldier's social world was defined by his daily associations. Friendships were determined by whether or not your cot in the squad room was on the east wall or the west wall, even, sometimes, by whether you had a top bunk or a bottom bunk. Here, however, the rule seemed more rigid. The squad was home, that was clear. The platoon was the neighborhood; beyond the platoon was the outer world.

Yet Robertson and the others from the Third Platoon had been accepted almost at once. Only he, Klineschmidt, and the two ghost-silent Koreans, were yet on the fringe. He thought he understood; the working infantry did not gush welcome, a place had to be earned. He winced. Could he earn his?

Turning his eyes to SFC Baker, who stood facing the ranks, one menacing the many, he thought he saw another strong man. That warmed him. Contrary to his father's tirades against military life, Zuckerman thought this morning that it was not wholly uncomfortable to be led by a strong man. Suddenly he felt eager and excited, fiercely manly to stand there with blooded infantrymen on his first day in a fighting rifle company.

But then his mind caught on the information Baker had given about the count of incoming artillery rounds and he felt uncomfortable. How large a front did a regiment occupy? Across how many linear yards had fallen those thirteen hundred units of high explosive and steel? He put that thought aside, knowing such ideas at this point were his enemy.

Once Zuckerman rotated his head and saw that Sergeant Robertson was staring down the ranks. Baker was talking. "Training problem this afternoon. This morning is clean and maintain equipment." Several men laughed. "Clean and maintain equipment" translated easily into "loaf out of the officers' sight until I call for you again." Then Baker said to Robertson, "Get your men fed and take them off somewhere and make a squad out of them."

After a breakfast of powdered eggs—sickly yellow globules floating in pea green slime—Robertson led them out of the tents of the company and a few dozen yards down the road to a grove of trees. Once in the trees, Zuckerman smelled a riveting odor. Klineschmidt pinched his nose and made a face, then drifted over to what obviously was a foxhole of some kind. As Zuckerman watched, Klineschmidt blanched and drew back. Zuckerman went over and looked down into the hole. Two partially buried dead men sprawled there, blackish green and showing weathered bone, teeth bared in a macabre greeting. Zuckerman wanted to vomit.

Dougherty, the tall, chiseled, thirtyish man who had stood second in ranks, laughed softly. "If the dead ones bother you, you're in for a hell of a ride with the live ones."

"Are they Chinese?" Zuckerman managed.

The tall man shook his head. "North Koreans. We saw them here the first day. We figure a mortar took them out. Just keep upwind of them."

Zuckerman was not sure naked death could be treated so casually. "Do the officers know about them?" he asked, sensing immediately that an officer would want the Koreans buried.

Dougherty shook his head and said sourly, "Officers don't dig holes to bury dead gooks; you know who that leaves to do it."

The early-morning shade was inviting; the men sat or lay on the ground, making a loose circle around the standing Robertson. Zuckerman sat next to the Koreans, Klineschmidt nearby.

Robertson ended his preface, which had been brief. He had asked, "Anyone want the BAR?" No one asked for it.

He nodded to Zuckerman, stared at him a moment, then shifted his eyes to Klineschmidt. "We have a rule in this company," Robertson said. "New men get the point. You keep it until a greener man comes in."

Zuckerman did not permit himself to flinch. But he had listened closely to the Korean War lore that had floated across the Pacific to Fort Ord. He understood "point." He and Klineschmidt, newest of the new, would be the squad's scouts. But they would not scout in the Boy Scout sense of the word. An infantry scout's unstated function was to draw enemy fire.

Whenever the squad moved through hostile terrain, the scouts took the point of movement. They walked with their head tucked, crouching, trying to reduce their size as a potential target. Those who were not scouts theorized that a lurking enemy would fire upon the scouts first, thereby alerting the main body to the danger. Those who were scouts embraced a countertheory. They fervently believed that America's battlefield enemies possessed trigger discipline. A disciplined ambusher would spare the scouts, holding his fire until the main body of the squad was on the killing ground.

Statistical evidence easily supported the first theory over the second. A Korean War scout's options were relief by a greener man, an honorable wound, or death.

Robertson's attention had moved on. The two Koreans sitting next to Zuckerman went as riflemen into the undifferentiated middle, as did Olson, the diffident dairyman from a Wisconsin farm.

Luke Plumber got the Browning automatic rifle. The BAR, with a rate of fire approaching five hundred rounds per minute, constituted the squad's fire support. Plumber got the assignment because he was a logger from Northern California. He smiled across huge stained teeth and said things like, "I can smash your butt like a bug, buddy," and obviously meant them. Long and weighing sixteen pounds, the BAR looked better on a big man.

Dougherty remained impassive when Robertson assigned him as assistant BAR man. Carver, the black man, a corporal, was named assistant squad leader.

These nine men conformed to the T, O, and E, that is, the table of organization and equipment, for a Korean War infantry company. Three such squads and an additional weapons squad constituted a platoon; three rifle platoons and a weapons platoon constituted a company; three rifle companies and a weapons company constituted a battalion. The weapons units, squad or company, carried recoilless rifles, heavy machine guns, mortars, and, indeed, anything soldierly theft and officer ingenuity could provide as support for the rifle units. A simple system, Zuckerman knew, easy to understand and to remember.

As it sat nine men in the trees this morning, the squad in a sense was the exception that proved the rule. Korean War infantry squads often had fewer than nine men, a result of casualty attrition and unreplaced rotation, and sometimes more than nine. This situation had resulted as the American army slowly understood the kind of enemy they faced.

Western armies preferred to field accurate, long-range weapons, means whereby they could fix the enemy in place at a distance while they

making themselves expendable

destroyed him with superior artillery and airpower. The Chinese and North Koreans, however, borrowing from the Russians who had trained many of them, took into the field short-range, rapid-fire, relatively inaccurate weapons. On the offensive, the strategy was to grip the United Nations forces closely with masses of expendable bodies, each body armed with grenades and a machine that hosed steel. Predominant in Oriental hands was the Russian-designed 7.62-mm PPSh-41 submachine gun. The ripping discharge of this weapon earned it immediately the sobriquet "burp gun."

As a poor answer, many infantry companies added an extra fire team to their squads, consisting of a BAR man and his assistant. A poor answer . . . that the Orientals had studied their enemy better than their enemy had studied them was evinced by the fact that some Communist weapons were chambered one thin millimeter larger than corresponding American weapons. Thus, the Chinese and North Koreans could use the copious quantities of ammunition they captured. The Americans could only have a bonfire.

The First Squad, Second Platoon was thus formed out of new cells and old, for all but Zuckerman and Klineschmidt had been grafted from other units in the company.

Robertson's final glance included all the men in a sweep. "We might as well loaf out here for a while," he suggested. "If we go back in, Milo Baker might find something for us to do." All the resident G Company men assembled at once near Robertson, leaving Zuckerman and Klineschmidt and the Koreans.

Zuckerman had been watching the taller of the two Koreans. He was sure of it: the Korean followed Robertson's remarks and translated them for his countryman. The Koreans wore American fatigue uniforms; the smaller Korean seemed to hide in his.

As if aware Zuckerman studied him, the tall Korean met his eyes. Zuckerman challenged timidly, "You speak English."

The Korean had a long face and a high brow, with even white teeth and a triangle of a nose. His black eyes were hooded slightly, but not slanted: a carpenter could have laid them on with a level. His skin was light brown, his hair ink black and string straight. Zuckerman had seen other Koreans in his few days in Korea but only briefly. A handsome face, he thought, intelligent and alert, but wary, as if it had seen much, like that of the old Irish cop who patrolled Zuckerman's neighborhood in size-14 brogans.

Seeming slightly embarrassed, the Korean smiled faintly. "One is fortunate," he said.

Zuckerman stuck out a hand. "I'm Solomon Zuckerman. I'm from the Bronx."

The Korean puzzled a second, then took the hand. "My name is Choi Min-soo. My associate is Kang Chul-ho. We are resident in the south in the vicinity of Kwangju, a very pleasant city at this season."

"But last night everyone in the tent called you Big Kim and your friend Little Kim?" Zuckerman protested.

Choi smiled patronizingly. "My associate Kang and I designate Officer Hartung and Officer Blackthorne as Big Honcho and Little Honcho."

Zuckerman nodded to the eavesdropping Klineschmidt. "Fair enough." Zuckerman made Choi repeat their names until his ear could hear them and his mouth could speak them. Choi spoke to Kang, and Kang nodded warmly to Zuckerman.

Kang's unworded warmth was Zuckerman's best welcome to the working infantry.

In the early afternoon, First Sergeant Manston sent runners down to the platoon tents to tell the platoon sergeants that the first sergeant, with admirable foresight, had managed to lift a quantity of delightful amber liquid. Immediately, the platoon sergeants sent runners to get the beer.

To placate American mothers, Congress forbade hard liquor to the lower three enlisted grades in Korea. They were, however, permitted to have rations of weak beer. Early on, beer had been free. But American civilians howled that the generals were getting the men drunk before sending them into battle. The army began to charge money for the beer. That seemed to solve the problem. Sergeants and officers could purchase small quantities of whiskey.

The Second Platoon leader, Lt. Roger D. Blackthorne, charged into Captain Hartung's conical tent. Blackthorne, who by collateral duty was also training officer, cried, "Sir, you can't cancel training and let the men drink beer!"

Hartung explained, "I did not cancel training. First Sergeant Manston canceled training."

"But," Blackthorne spluttered, "he's an *enlisted man*."

Hartung smiled patiently. As he reached into the locker near his cot to get the bottle of Scotch he kept there, he said, "Lieutenant, there are three things in the army you must never interfere with. And the wishes of first sergeants are two of them."

"The battalion commander will disapprove of your giving men in close reserve like this intoxicants—"

Hartung exploded. "Intoxicants? For Christ's sake, Lieutenant, it's 3.2 beer. Your grandmother could drink a case of it."

"But the NCOs have whiskey; they'll share that with the men."

Hartung set his jaw. "Damned right my NCOs will share their whiskey, if I've trained them properly."

He poured two drinks and lifted his to Blackthorne. "Health! Let the men relax. Day after tomorrow we go back on line." He lowered his voice. "We'll fight onto our new perimeter."

Few men from Zuckerman's tent went to supper. The mounds of crushed beer cans grew, and Zuckerman could see that the supply of moundable cans had diminished. In the middle of the tent, under hovering cigarette smoke, Fowlkes led a group of singers. The song had many verses, but often returned to the idea that "Way down yonder in Yongdungpo, sheeba-sheeba hava-no. Met a young nurse and to my surprise, she had la-aaa-aid forty GIs." Klineschmidt had insinuated himself among the singers. Zuckerman envied that, knowing he could not have intruded himself that way.

The two Koreans sat by themselves in the end of the tent. No one had offered them any of the beer; they had not asked. Robertson lay on his cot, staring at the canvas. Sam Dougherty sat on his cot, near the rear flap of the tent, cleaning his rifle.

Dougherty looked up when Zuckerman came hesitantly over.

"May I sit here?" Zuckerman asked quietly.

Dougherty nodded to the cot across from him and resumed his work. Zuckerman watched, noting the precision. He studied Dougherty. He was, excepting Baker and Nelson, the oldest man in the platoon. By far he was the handsomest. Carefully combed waves of hair stood above a strong, clean brow, the brow a pediment above strong green eyes. Zuckerman's nose told him that Dougherty had shaved recently, likely making him the best-shaved in the battalion.

Dougherty slipped the trigger housing into the Garand, locking up the assembly. He leaned down and slid the rifle between the legs of the folding cot.

"A soldier's bride, like the seminarian's breviary," he said absently to Zuckerman.

"Where are we?" Zuckerman asked shyly.

Dougherty smiled. "That village down the road—what's left of it—is metropolitan Sangyang-ni. Over the ridge to the east is the Hwachon Reservoir—"

Interrupting, Zuckerman said, "That's where the First Marine Division fought last year."

Dougherty shook his head. "No. The marines were at the Changjin Reservoir—that's northwest of Hungnam, up the coast." Dougherty's eyes closed a moment, and he turned his head in the direction he had named. After a while, he said quietly, "The marines got the credit, but the army was there." Then he added, even softer, "I was there."

Zuckerman sensed something awesome. After debating the wisdom of it a few seconds, he asked, "Would you tell me about it?"

When Dougherty started, Zuckerman added quickly, "I don't know whether I should ask things like that."

Dougherty lifted a hand. "You can't know things unless you ask about them."

With his eyes half-closed, as if he looked into himself, Dougherty told Zuckerman the story of Task Force Faith.

In late November of 1950 it all seemed so simple. The shattered North Korean army, that part of it not cut off far down the peninsula, fled in headlong retreat. All that remained was to chase them to the Yalu River, drown a few of them there, and go home. And it was time to go home. Not even the bounteous cloth of the U.S. Army Quartermaster Corps deflected the Siberian winds that screamed across the tortured terrain of North Korea. The war was a hundred and fifty days old.

MacArthur had divided his force, sending the Eighth Army to the west of the Taebaek mountain spine, sending the 10th Corps to the east. He waved them on with an imperious hand, ignoring the import of the increasing numbers of prisoners who wore brown quilted uniforms and spoke Mandarin Chinese. To anyone who would listen, and everyone would, MacArthur explained that peasant China was no threat to industrial America. In fact, he seemed to suggest, we might as well go beyond the Yalu . . . well, maybe.

Tenth Corps, flushed with the easy success of the Inchon invasion, was custered again near coastal Hungnam. Custering, as Dougherty explained to Zuckerman, was his own term for the folly a commander commits when he divides his forces in the face of an unknown but possibly superior enemy. The First Marine Division went up onto the Koto-ri plateau, faces turned into the stinging cold of late November. The mission was to advance to the Changjin-ho, a narrow water reservoir anchored to Hagaru-ri on the south and to Yudam-ni on the west.

The dirt road was tortuous and narrow. Along the road, winter waited.

Prisoner interrogation suggested that something else also waited, the latter as ominous as the former.

Tacked onto the marines was First Battalion, 32nd U.S. Infantry Regiment, Seventh Infantry Division. Lt. Col. Don Faith commanded the battalion, slightly more than a thousand men strong. He gave the force his name.

At Hagaru-ri, the road forked; an even poorer road went east of the reservoir. Faith left the marines at Hagaru-ri and led his men north on that road.

They vanished into the mountains; watching them go from Hagaru-ri, one saw men stamping on near-frozen feet. Vehicles emitted huge clouds of exhaust steam, giving the scene under the low pale sun a surrealistic quality. Faith winced when he saw what lay ahead of him. But he had orders; he led on.

Faith, and his officers, carried with them the intelligence gleaned from captured enemy soldiers that two Chinese armies were poised above the Changjin, waiting for the marines to spring the trap at Yudam-ni. That intelligence was incredible, but it was deadly accurate.

The Faith column shuffled. Dougherty walked with a dripping nose, fingers stiff where they gripped the sling of his M-1 rifle. Even under the parka he felt the below-zero wind. It cut like a dagger. Under his left armpit he carried a can of hamburger patties in gravy. That was the only way to guarantee a warm supper. The water in his canteen had frozen. Since he had fought as a platoon sergeant in Europe in World War II, Dougherty had more experience than many of his officers. His nostrils often flared as he lifted his eyes to examine the high rough terrain they threaded. When his eyes began to water and his lashes froze, he gave up on looking. And there was nothing to see, yet.

In the afternoon, Faith deployed his battalion into a rifle line, oriented toward Manchuria and the China that owned it. The frost had gone more than a foot deep. Dougherty and his platoon chipped out shallow holes with bayonets and entrenching shovels and got into them, to lie in frigid torture as the sun went down. The cold, below zero during the day, plummeted further with darkness.

Around 2100 hours, the Chinese patrols began to probe. These were kiss-and-run efforts, drawing sporadic rifle fire from the Americans. Dougherty hissed to the men within earshot of him, "Don't fire. That's what they want you to do. You only reveal our position to them."

Often, Dougherty heard bugles, at first distant, now close, at first in the north, then in the east. He removed his gloves and, for the third time, wiped his rifle with cloth from an ammunition bandolier. He wanted no oil on it; an oiled weapon would freeze out of action. He put some grenades on the ground in front of his hole.

The wind came up again and struck at them from across the icy face of the Changjin. The surviving officer of Dougherty's company stumbled in through the night. "Sergeant Taylor is dead, Dougherty. You are now acting leader of the Second and Third squads." The young lieutenant blew on his frozen fingers and then went away, leaving Dougherty with his meaningless promotion. He still was a private.

Dougherty went along the line of shallow rifle pits to inspect his new command. One man did not respond. His face was down; under Dougherty's probing hand, the man's neck was stiff and chill. Learning the belted machine-gun ammunition was used up, he set three men to disassembling rifle clips.

The Chinese struck at midnight. It was as if the dam of the Changjin had broken, unleashing fire and steel rather than brown water. Shouting encouragement to his men each time he reloaded, Dougherty fired until his rifle seized with heat. Then he took the cooler rifle of the dead man in the next hole and continued to fire.

Twice in the night, howling Chinese got onto a hill about seventy yards from Dougherty's position and fired down into it. Twice Dougherty badgered his exhausted, frozen men into a skirmish line. Both times fewer Americans came back. Dougherty winced at his losses, but he knew the action generated body warmth. That might save one or two.

The sun came up. That put the Asians in brown quilts at bay as effectively as the rifles and machine guns had done in the night. Dougherty had no food for his men, but he counted their noses and redistributed their ammunition and grenades. Then they lay down in the holes again. Dougherty saw that they were too cold to curse; each man was immersed to the neck in his private frigid misery.

Dougherty reasoned easily that there could be no rescue. He knew the battalion was adrift from its regiment. And he had no doubt the marines across the reservoir at Yudam-ni contended with their own flood. He kept such thoughts from his men.

The wind went east and brought sound to them. Dougherty heard cries issuing from the hill where he had fought his night skirmishes. For a few minutes, he tried to shun the screaming, although it rode down the wind and into his puffy ears with the thunder of a cavalry charge. He understood that it was a plea for quarter and exemption. At last, unable to endure it any longer, he got out of his hole and went up on the hill alone. The crier was

wounded and lay partly under two corpses. Dougherty thought the other two
had lived briefly and that the three had huddled together to share their final
warmth. He bit his lip. What should he do with a dying alien?

Squatting down, he removed his glove. His hand wanted to touch the
enemy's face. The Chinese's eyes widened in fear and he drew back.
"Christ," Dougherty muttered, "you're frightened of me—like an injured
animal." Dougherty stood and went down the hill. Cold and shock would
put the young Chinese out of it soon enough. Likely he'd join him.

Before Dougherty reached his hole, rifle fire began to churn the snow
at his feet. He ran headlong then.

When the sniper fire slackened, Dougherty could lift his head and see
thousands of brown man ants swarming over the distant hills. Some ground
had been retaken during the forenoon, but the Chinese effortlessly reclaimed it. That night, the bugles came again. This time the Chinese had
not only surrounded, but they had infiltrated. The bugles and the cymbals
and the chanting said it all.

Word came down to get out. Dougherty pummeled his men alert and
put them in column with the trucks. On the trucks they had loaded the
wounded.

The trucks started and the column began to crawl south, back down
the road to Hagaru-ri. To the west was the ice of the Changjin-ho; to
the east, on the high ridges above the road, were the Chinese. Fire
sleeted down on the column, into the marchers and into the wounded in
the backs of the trucks. A few men returned the fire, but it was a point-
less effort, ammunition better saved. The rewounded wounded began to
cry out. The column trudged on. Walking behind a truck, Dougherty saw
in flare light that icicles had formed under the tailgate. He knew that
tomorrow, if he were there tomorrow, he would see that the icicles were
pink red.

Word came back that Colonel Faith had been grenaded to death by the
Chinese. If command structure remained, it was concealed from Dougherty. He badgered his men on, repeatedly falling back to count them as they
passed, heads down, floating on their misery. He begged and cursed them,
slapping one sobbing face into reality.

When the defile narrowed, the Chinese were closer. The fire into the
wounded grew intense. There, Task Force Faith spent its last ounce of
spirit. At first wordlessly, the unhit men came out from behind and to the
west of the trucks and began to walk on the east side, inserting their own
bodies between their wounded comrades and the Chinese rifles. As they
walked into the steel, the men called out to each other, "Come on, let's

show the bastards." But lips were cracked and swollen; speech carried a high price.

Men began to fall. Headlights blacked out, the trucks started and stopped. The marchers beside them stumbled over crumpled bodies. Dougherty picked up one of the bodies and urged it on. "Stay here and you die here," he encouraged. "Keep putting one foot ahead of the other and you have a chance."

Then the trucks stopped, with a muted finality, engines idling aimless exhaust into the night. The battalion that had endured so long, so much of the brutal cold and the scalding fire, now in almost its hundredth hour of combat from the point of first contact below Hagaru-ri, could endure no more. The word was out: if you have any ideas about how to do it, try to save yourself.

Dougherty caught his remaining men under an arm. "Our best chance is across the ice," he said, "but do what you want." The men refused to chance the ice, preferring the false security of the column. Then, with the man he had urged along, he went out onto the frozen Changjin. Under the moon, the reservoir danced in a million lights. Chinese small-arms fire began to chip the ice. Dougherty heard screaming. He turned to see that the Chinese had set the laden trucks afire.

Dougherty did not tell Zuckerman this, or that out on the ice the other man had given up. "Please," the man had begged, "I can't go on."

Dougherty pulled him to his feet. "You'll die here."

"I know. I know."

Dougherty carried him a few yards. That was futile. He put him back down onto the ice. Between chattering teeth, Dougherty forced out, "Been a hell of a ride."

Dougherty managed a few more paces before he heard the man call out, "Please don't leave me here alone."

Dougherty went back. Only then did he realize that the man he had chivvied for so long was badly wounded. In the flame light of the burning trucks he saw the man's trousers were dark with crimson. "I can't stay," Dougherty said. "I'm freezing."

"I know. I know." The wounded man lifted an arm.

Dougherty ran his tongue across his cracked lips. He glanced up the moonlit path and across the Changjin. The flames roiled and he could hear the Chinese shouting excitedly. He heard the torment of the burning wounded. Closer, bodies littered the ice. The rifle in his hands mocked him.

Looking down at his companion, he said softly, "Turn your head. It will be easier for us then."

When the man looked away, Dougherty put the muzzle of the M-1 against his neck and squeezed the trigger.

Dougherty finished his story. "The Fifth Marines let me in over on the west side of the lake. I came back out with them."

Zuckerman let go his breath. "How many got out?"

Dougherty compressed his lips. "Fewer than two hundred."

"Why did the marines get all the glory?"

Dougherty smiled faintly. "You know how it rides. A marine platoon has had heavy casualties when it's down to three public-relations officers."

Zuckerman laughed. Dougherty added, "Don't take anything from the jungle bunnies; they had a hell of a fight at Yudam-ni, and a worse one getting back out."

"Well, you won't have to go through it again. You'll rotate."

Dougherty shook his head, saying only, "No."

Word came in through the warp and woof of the canvas that G Company would return to the line day after tomorrow. The more sober disentangled themselves from the singers and went to their cots. Some checked equipment; many began to write letters under the lantern light.

Zuckerman fished into his pack and got out the letter from his father, the last one, which had reached him the final day at Fort Ord before he shipped out. Avram Zuckerman had written:

Your mother is disturbed that you are to be sent away from California. You should tell your worried parents where you are to be sent. However, your Uncle Herman tells me it is common that the army censor movements of soldiers. You see why I disapproved when you enlisted to be a common soldier. I wrote to Congressman Santos that it is criminal for the government to permit a twenty-year-old to enlist without his father's consent. You at least should have been an officer as was your Uncle Herman. Now you may be sent into danger and you will pay for your error. You should have remained here and completed college, as I advised. Stephen Kahan came into the store on Thursday to buy a shirt and he told me that you gave his Rachel a ring when you were here on leave. You should have told your mother and me and I scold you for not doing so. However, Stephen Kahan is much respected in the community. Your mother instructs me that I am to write that she approves of your choice. You must not marry until you have completed college.

Avram Zuckerman had underlined *must* and had postscripted, "The anger over President Truman's dismissal of General MacArthur is no longer heard here. The general addressed Congress. He was on the television. He is an old man. I feel sorry for him. It is terrible to be old, as is your father."

Zuckerman smiled at the last sentence. His father, who left at 6:30 each morning for his clothing store on Fordham Road, was only forty-three, not much older than Platoon Sergeant Baker.

Taking up pencil and paper, Zuckerman got as far as "Dear Father and Mother" before he ran out of ideas.

He stared at the men in the tent. Except for a few remaining singers, they sat mutely hunched over the letters and equipment or held beer cans and stared without seeing. They seemed to listen. Zuckerman listened with them for several seconds. He realized they listened to the persistent *whump-whomp* that came over the ridges to the north and penetrated the canvas of the tent.

Zuckerman got up, squeezed past Kang Chul-ho, and went outside into the night. He stood at the platoon's piss-call tree and urinated. He let his ear catalog the sounds. Mixed with the hollow artillery sounds was the deep rattling stutter of a heavy machine gun. The gunner fired several short seeking bursts, then one long decisive burst. Although he had been an unblooded infantryman for almost a year, Zuckerman could not envision anything beyond a scenario in which a furtive yellow man ran from the seeking bursts, to crumple and fall, arms outthrust, when the killing burst caught him.

Back in the tent, he wrote his letter. "I am in Japan, where my company is to have permanent guard duty. The war is hundreds of miles away." Zuckerman went on for almost two pages about the beauty and joy of serving in peaceful Japan.

He looked up once to see that a drunken singer had thrown an arm around a grinning Klineschmidt.

The *whump-whomp* continued, an uncharacterizable rhapsody. Zuckerman experimented, and found, as he was certain others in the tent had found, that he could shut it out at will, letting it merely be background, as was the sound of the wind and the insects.

In the night, a sleepless Zuckerman remembered his thoughts at the piss-call tree when he had heard the searching fire of the machine gun. Was it not as reasonable that the gunner wore a brown uniform and that the victim was a Caucasian?

7

SANGYANG-NI RESERVE POSITION,
JUNE 23, 1951

Sam Dougherty's rage boomed through the early morning dust motes in the tent. Face twisted with anger, he towered over the seated Kang Chul-ho. "You swiped my watch when we were at the shower point," Dougherty accused.

Sitting on his cot a few feet away, Zuckerman flinched. Suddenly, he felt flooded with guilt. He was certain Dougherty's assault on the Korean had been seeded during Dougherty's recounting the previous evening of his horrible experience at the Changjin Reservoir, a recounting Zuckerman had instigated. In the night, Zuckerman had several times been aware that Dougherty thrashed and cried out in his sleep. At reveille, two hours earlier, Dougherty had appeared haggard and sullen.

Missing watches were irrelevant. Objects that represented the Korean experience to Sam Dougherty were not.

Zuckerman wadded his letter, the third attempt to enlist Rachel Kahan's support in the pathetic conspiracy he had erected the night before against his parents. He got up warily. The others in the tent also stood, tense, eyes on Dougherty and Kang. The air crackled. Zuckerman shot a glance toward Choi Min-soo. The tall Korean's eyes were slitted and watchful, but he remained seated.

"He wasn't even at the showers," Olson protested.

Someone else chimed in, "There's a stupid lost watch at the CP, Dougherty. Go over there and ask before you bring your hard-ass act in here."

Dougherty threw off Olson's arm and ignored the second speaker. He growled, "You bastards either get in it or get out of it."

Choi Min-soo had been reading a cheaply bound book, obviously Korean. Zuckerman caught his attention as he carefully put down his book, noticing that Choi's hand immediately went to the stock of his Garand, which protruded from the crosstrees of his bunk. Backpedaling out of the path of Dougherty's rage, Zuckerman stood beside him.

Dougherty raged again. "I'm talking to you, you gook son of a bitch!"

Kang glanced quickly at Choi, but said nothing. He froze his face and lowered it, looking at his feet.

Dougherty punched Kang on the shoulder. Kang rolled with the punch and sat erect again. Dougherty went on, his voice cold and harsh, "When I speak, you answer. I asked you what you had done with my watch."

Choi whispered to Zuckerman, "Kang will not respond. When the Japanese occupied our country, twice the Security Police beat Kang with cudgels and he did not yield to them."

The atmosphere deepened—puzzlement, anger, sympathy, even fright. Zuckerman thought Kang would have to respond. The custom of the Korean War Regular Army required a man to slay his own squad-room dragons or forever smell their breath.

But Kang did nothing; his face was as impassive as Dougherty's was contorted. Dougherty stood over him, glaring down. Zuckerman was drowning in emotion, fighting an urge to rush over and strike Dougherty. He darted his eyes, imploring someone to resolve it.

He heard Choi say, "My associate must not give offense to the Americans. He would be punished severely."

The sun broke in through the tent flap to bathe the tent in the heavy morning light; then the tented dusk returned. Robertson stood there, crouching slightly, fists knotted.

"That's enough, Dougherty." Robertson's voice stung the air. Like the artillery bursts on the northern horizon, it dripped danger.

Dougherty spun. "This isn't your affair, Robertson. Leave it alone."

"It is my affair," Robertson corrected. "Anything involving this squad is my affair."

Robertson went over to Dougherty and grabbed his arm. Dougherty threw it off. He put his palm out flat and pushed Robertson. Robertson pushed back.

Suddenly, so quickly Zuckerman ducked, Dougherty snaked his M-1 from under his cot. He hit the operating handle to chamber a round. The bolt snapped home; now the only sound in the tent. He turned slowly, holding the rifle in the ready-arms position, the muzzle pointed up toward the ridge beam of the tent.

Several men gasped. Zuckerman reeled. He could not believe what his eyes saw and what his ears heard. But he told himself that Dougherty would never truly point the rifle at Robertson. For an infantryman, that was the unpardonable sin, unstated, but always known.

Choi got up and removed his own rifle from the crosstrees, but did nothing except hold it casually by the forestock, as if he, too, understood what Zuckerman understood.

"Don't do that, Dougherty," Robertson said quietly. "Either I'll kill you or you'll hang. We'll need each other soon enough. Let's not get on each other back here."

Zuckerman, because he always let his infrequent angers run away with him, was amazed at the coolness in Robertson's tone. No one moved for almost a minute, then Dougherty hit the operating handle of his rifle and ejected the round. The bolt snicked and Zuckerman thought he heard the cartridge hit the packed dirt near Robertson's feet. Sneering, Dougherty thumbed down the clip's seven remaining cartridges and released the tension on the bolt. He threw the rifle on his cot. Stooping, he picked up the ejected cartridge. He held it under Robertson's nose. "You can have all of this one, Robertson. Screw me around again and you get only the tip of the next one."

Robertson struck him, a stinging slap that resounded in the tent. Dougherty never moved.

Baker swept in. Without breaking stride, he inserted himself between Robertson and Dougherty. The platoon sergeant caught Dougherty's raised right arm and forced it down brusquely. Baker's teeth were clenched. Dougherty and Robertson shot angry looks at each other across the bulk of Baker. Nothing was said. Zuckerman could hear his own heart.

Baker studied the fighters. He spoke loudly. "Everybody out of here except Robertson and Dougherty."

Choi barked Korean at Kang. Kang got up slowly and led the exodus. The men went to group silently around their piss-call tree, ears strained to listen. Several men lit cigarettes with shaking hands.

Choi and Kang stood together, aside, exchanging glances.

Hard voices came out of the tent, but the words were muffled. Zuckerman finally heard Robertson's voice rise to say, in the same cool harshness he had brought into the tent with him minutes earlier, "I'll see you after taps, Dougherty. Bring your goddamned rifle if you want."

Baker's voice rose, intervening as before. "I won't have it—" But the rest was lost. Dougherty came out of the tent. He brushed deliberately against Zuckerman and muttered, "Out of my way." He vanished in the direction of the stand of trees and the dead North Koreans.

Zuckerman felt cheated. The warmth he had felt for Robertson, Dougherty, and the Korean Kang had vanished. Suddenly he hated everything.

In the tent the men were morose and introspective. Robertson cleaned his rifle, not returning the glances he received. Fowlkes came in and tried to lighten the mood, failing. Zuckerman could not write his letter. Shortly after darkness fell, the men rustled quietly into their cots. Tomorrow afternoon they would go toward the cannons.

Dougherty had not returned to the tent.

Zuckerman did not undress. He lay in his trousers and boots; he did not want sleep. He watched Robertson across the tent for almost two hours, just drifting in aimless thought, as he assumed Robertson drifted. He knew that Choi Min-soo was awake; the Korean had smoked a cigarette twice. The tent still echoed with the anger of the morning, but most of the men slept. Zuckerman pondered this and decided the others were more accustomed than he to lethal rifles and violent assault. Even so, he did not understand it.

When Robertson rolled to a sitting position and began to lace his boots, Zuckerman felt a twinge of the anxiety he had felt when Dougherty had lifted his M-1. Without fully understanding why, he rose up silently and began inching his newly issued rifle from underneath the cot. He felt a hand on his and knew it was Choi's.

Zuckerman put his face into the Korean's and heard his own voice whisper, "This is American business. Keep out of it." His mind reverberated; perhaps those were his first adult sentences. Choi's hand withdrew.

Robertson had gone out the west flap. Zuckerman went out of the east flap and around the tent to follow. Robertson was unarmed. He walked briskly across the assembly ground to the kitchen tent. After he vanished behind the tent, Zuckerman crossed the ground, hesitated and listened, then inched along the side wall of the tent, trying to avoid the brace ropes. He melted into the shadows at the end of it.

Robertson and Dougherty stood face-to-face a few feet away. Robertson's chest was bare; Dougherty was fully dressed.

The moon was up. Zuckerman realized that for possibly the first time in his life he was watching killing anger in adult males. The affair had simmered, and had now reached full boil. Robertson and Dougherty did not speak: it was as if they were part of a ritual they both knew. Zuckerman shuddered. He felt as if each man saw in the other all his personal demons. The faces were locked into hatred. Dougherty's arm flashed in the moonlight.

They fought for almost thirty minutes, rolling in the filth behind the kitchen tent. Unlike the playground tussles of Zuckerman's childhood and the few barracks fights he had witnessed, there were no words, only grunts and curses and breathy cries, as animals might cry when they fought over territory or food.

Watching it, Zuckerman felt twisted again, not knowing fully how he felt toward the men who rolled in the dirt. He sensed the weight of the rifle in his hand and knew the rush of warm blood to his ears. He realized what he had done was foolish. Now the innocent rifle became the focus. Zuckerman thrust it against the side wall of the tent, pleased to hear it slither along the yielding canvas and fall heavily to the ground into the drainage trench. He thought he understood now: neither man really fought the other; both Dougherty and the squad sergeant fought a surrogate antagonist, as he had done as a child when he lashed out at his mother because his father had scolded him.

Zuckerman burrowed more deeply into the shadow of the kitchen tent, begging his heart to still.

Robertson sat astride Dougherty's chest and pinned his arms to the ground above his head. Dougherty surely could have resisted, but he did not. Robertson spoke the first meaningful words of the combat. "Bully another man of my squad again, Dougherty, and I'll whip you again."

Dougherty lay mute. Zuckerman tried to imagine his eyes. Robertson slowly got off and Dougherty got up. They faced each other, as they had before the fight. Their hands were open, no longer weapons.

"It was man-play, Robertson. Can't the gooks take it?"

"It *wasn't* man-play," Robertson hissed. "You knew he hadn't snitched your watch—" He paused before adding firmly, "We have two Koreans in the squad, and one of them speaks English. Let's find a better word for a buddy than 'gook.' "

Dougherty rubbed his nose. Finally he said, "I had it coming, Robertson." With that, he stalked off.

Robertson called after him, in a strangely apologetic voice, "Kang didn't put you in jail, Dougherty. Nobody in the squad put you in jail. Live it down and don't take it out on us."

Dougherty halted and mumbled something Zuckerman could not hear. Dougherty disappeared between the aisle of the rows of tents.

After a few moments, Robertson brushed himself and followed.

Zuckerman stood transfixed, long after Robertson and Dougherty had disappeared. He felt as if he had witnessed the most awesome event of his life. He waited until he was sure the assembly ground was empty and snuck back to the tent.

Choi moved, but said nothing.

In the morning, Robertson and Dougherty got up and dressed as if the fight had not occurred. A vicious welt lay across Dougherty's cheek and his lip was swollen and caked with dried blood. He did not look around, and went out of the tent almost at once. Robertson's right eye, over the scar, was discolored and puffed. He gave orders for morning cleanup in the tent. He said nothing else.

The whistle blew them out for reveille, just as the sun came fully up. In bad temper, they cursed and jostled their way into formation. The ranks hushed when Lieutenant Blackthorne stormed over from officer's country and confronted Baker, saying something to him in a whisper that could not be heard in the ranks. Baker gestured toward nothing and whispered back.

Blackthorne turned on the formation and called them to attention. He menaced them a second or two before calling to Dougherty, "Private Dougherty, what did you do to provoke Sergeant Robertson? That's an Article 91 offense."

The ranks stiffened and made low noises. The platoon leader had reduced them to children. It was the worst of form to punish individual transgression in front of the corporate body. To threaten court-martial was stupid.

Zuckerman kept his head rigidly forward, looking over the heads of the platoon sergeant and platoon leader. He heard Robertson say, just as loudly as Blackthorne had spoken, "Maybe I did the fucking provoking, Lieutenant."

The lieutenant's jaw dropped. The men tensed. Zuckerman wanted to run. In the few hours he had been in the company, he had learned that the Second Platoon barely related to its effeminate officer. Blackthorne was a West Pointer, the spoiled offspring of a military family, who had been further spoiled at the military academy, then given his rank as if by birthright. When the men spoke of him at all, they called him "Missy."

Blackthorne's voice came out a high squeal. "That's Article 89, Robertson, disrespect to a superior officer. I'll have you—"

Dougherty had stepped out of ranks. He half turned, so that his attention included both the officer and the men. "That's a crock of Class-A shit, Lieutenant." He inclined his head to the ranks of men and added, "I got out of line and Robertson did what any good NCO would do with a hard-ass."

Blackthorne's face darkened. His lips worked, but no sound came out. Baker stepped up quickly and nudged him aside, saying, "Well, it's settled then. We go back on line this evening. After chow, get your gear ready. Third Squad draw grenades for the platoon—four per man."

Fowlkes, at the head of the Third Squad, shouted out in a falsetto voice, clearly mocking Blackthorne, "Oh, dear me, Sergeant, not *them* terrible things. Us old boys in the Third are afeared of explosives."

After Blackthorne had spun and stalked off a few paces, someone whistled.

Baker shouted, "At ease! Goddamn you!"

Zuckerman quivered. He sensed that many of the others did so as well.

After breakfast, Robertson led them to the trees where they had organized as a squad. He carried an entrenching tool. He gave them a "smoke them if you got them," and began throwing dirt to bury the dead North Korean soldiers. After Robertson had thrown several spadefuls, Dougherty stepped up silently and took the shovel, continuing the burial. Everyone watched, saying nothing. Zuckerman shifted his awareness from the two South Koreans, who watched intently, to Robertson, then to Dougherty.

When the North Koreans were buried, Dougherty cleaned the entrenching tool by wiping it with his bare hand and handed it wordlessly to Robertson. Robertson nodded and Dougherty went to sit next to Kang Chul-ho, on the end of the arc that had formed around Robertson's feet.

It had been a simple drama, but Zuckerman felt something new, something he knew he could not explain to his father, or even to Rachel, who always listened to his most intimate revelations. He examined himself gingerly, not quite comfortable with feeling such warm affection for other males.

Robertson lifted his eyes and spoke. "I want you all to forget what happened yesterday. We go on line this evening and we don't want to carry anything with us we don't have to carry." He walked over to put his hand on Dougherty's shoulder. Dougherty stiffened. Robertson continued, looking at each of them individually and at all of them jointly. The wound scar under his inflamed right eye twitched. "And one more thing—every man in this squad is equal, *dead damned equal.*"

Robertson then made the first real smile Zuckerman had seen on him. "I also tell you that I am more dead damned equal than all of you."

The men roared. Plumber slapped Klineschmidt so hard he bent sideways.

Robertson waited until Klineschmidt had recovered. He said to him, "You can be 'Kraut.' " Then he turned to Zuckerman. "What did they call you back home; surely not Solomon?"

"Some of my friends called me 'Solly.' "

"Good name. Solly you are."

Robertson pointed to Choi Min-soo. "Big Kim is a terrible name," he said.

Choi clearly had followed it. He stood up. "Choi Min-soo."

"Choi then. And Little Kim?"

Dougherty answered. "Kang. Kang Chul-ho."

Choi spoke to Kang in Korean and Kang glanced between Dougherty and Robertson. Kang's black eyes sparkled.

Zuckerman felt truly comfortable for the first time since he had left the Bronx. He heard the *whump* of the morning cannons. He curled his lip and sneered at them. If he had to go on line, he knew he could go on line with these men. They were the First Squad of the Second Platoon.

8

The men looked down into the task before them and cursed. Opinion rendered, they grinned innocently at each other, then angelically toward Robertson. Clearly, no one wanted to be first among equals.

Robertson studied his leadership problem, which was to induce the First Squad, a body of reasonably normal men as far as Robertson knew, to bury the latrine in which almost two hundred men had relieved themselves for several days. Viewed objectively, the squad was to pay the company's due bill. This far forward, a formal latrine was a luxury. Captain Hartung had even mustered a canvas privacy screen, and the slit-trench toilets were drenched with lime . . . luxury, but foul-smelling luxury—very much so in muggy sun.

As Robertson had expected, Lt. Gen. Wilbur Blackthorne's son, Roger, exacted the first of what was probably many retributions for the humiliation of the morning's reveille formation. Although flogging the group for the crimes of the individual was expressly forbidden in the American army, mass punishments occurred routinely. A platoon leader might punish a squad if a sergeant had offended him; a regimental colonel might punish a company whose captain irritated him. It was merely a matter of echeloned human nature.

Robertson turned to his men. "Well, as we used to say in Kansas, the quicker we get the loafing out of the way, the quicker we'll get to go back to work."

Only Zuckerman made an effort to do the job. Seeing that, Robertson himself went to the mounds of fill dirt beside the long ranks of poorly interred feces, paper, and lime and began throwing spadefuls of red earth. The others, one by one, unlimbered entrenching spades and pitched in.

They warmed to the work, probably wanting to hurry it, even though a grueling route march and possibly lethal combat waited for them at the end.

They had been told that they would mount out at 1500 hours, but nothing beyond that. As he worked, Robertson mulled over the prospect of a midafternoon march. He doubted that the company merely would make a routine relief-in-place of another company on the line. Although this was normally done during the dark hours when enemy artillery and mortar observers were stymied, other facts bore on the situation now.

Hartung's command had been rested for a reason. Also, the officers had displayed a certain anxious fussiness with respect to ammunition issue and radio and equipment checks. There had been a late-morning visit of the small-arms artificers from an ordnance company. Weaponry had been examined. Those remotely defective had been replaced.

Sam Dougherty, who worked next to Robertson, must have been having similar thoughts. "Looks like Jimmy Hartung's merry men will fight onto a new position," he said quietly to the squad leader.

"I'd read it that way," Robertson agreed. "But I've been wrong a few times since I joined the army."

Dougherty worked in silence several moments before speaking again. "At least they left the tents standing. Maybe we'll be coming back here."

Robertson shook his head. "We're closing the latrine." He straightened up, adding, "I've also been in the army long enough to know that troops who have no place to shit are officially transient."

Dougherty chuckled. "Wise words. With insights like that, a man can make chief of staff."

Sergeant Fowlkes came over and hunkered down. After smiling for Robertson, he sliced off a chunk of Day's Work chewing tobacco with his bayonet. He worked his chaw around in his mouth a bit, then spat. He watched the work.

Presently, Fowlkes waved his hand, to indicate both the work and the men who did it. "You fellers that come over from the Third Platoon are getting acquainted with Missy Blackthorne," he said brightly. "Missy's mama must have been scared by an enlisted trooper when she was carrying him. Ain't ever seen a man so hostile to his betters."

The trenches were almost buried. Luke Plumber's biceps knotted as he used his entrenching shovel like a bulldozer, moving a fair fraction of a yard of dirt from the mound to the trenches with each thrust. He straightened and grinned at Fowlkes.

"You insulted Missy as much as Sergeant Robertson and Sam did. How come you ain't in the chain gang with us?"

Fowlkes waved his hand again. "Missy's saving me for something bigger than closing a shithouse. He's had an eye on me for a long spell now." He spat again, smiling to reveal tobacco-yellowed teeth. "Anyway, Luke, the army is keeping the promise it made you when you enlisted. Teaching you a useful civilian trade to use on the outside."

Plumber growled playfully, "We can dig it up again and give *you* some on-the-job training covering it up again."

Fowlkes chortled. "You're doing just fine for a BAR man, Luke. Don't spoil your good work by digging it up again."

When Robertson began to clean his entrenching tool, Fowlkes caught his attention. "Robbie, I got me an idea. Now that you boys are done, the officers will mark this spot on a map and deliver it to headquarters and they'll file it away. If me and you can G-2 around and find the Eighth Army shithouse file, we can steal the maps for after the war. Then we can come back and make a billion of them wons digging up the latrines and selling the shit to the gooks for fertilizer."

Robertson glanced quickly toward Choi and Kang. Kang sat back smoking a cigarette. Choi's face had darkened as he stared at Fowlkes.

Fowlkes's head was back and he went on lightheartedly with his fantasy. He lifted his hands to indicate the breadth of something and said, "I can see our sign; we'd do her in neon: 'Fowlkes and Robertson, Latrine Dealers.' We'd have a motto, like businesses have: 'Our shit is your bread and butter.' "

Robertson's voice was sharp: "That's enough, Brax."

Fowlkes frowned lightly and went on, "Like I done said, we'd make a billion wons. We'd get old Syngman Rhee to line up all the mooses in Korea and we'd buy the purtiest two hundred of 'em. Then we'd stick one ever morning and put two on notice for the afternoon—"

Robertson stepped toward Fowlkes, face contorted. "Knock it off, Fowlkes. Get the hell back with your own people."

Fowlkes's jaw dropped. Choi pulled on Kang's arm and they walked off, back toward the sleeping tents. The others in the First Squad, after glancing between Fowlkes and Robertson, followed. This was a quarrel-to-be between known buddies, a private matter.

"What did I say to rile you?" Fowlkes asked after the others were out of earshot.

"What the hell do you suppose the Koreans are thinking when we say stupid things like that?" Robertson gestured toward the receding back of Choi Min-soo. "That tall Korean speaks English better than we do."

"I didn't say nothing to hurt no gooks," Fowlkes replied testily. "Anyhow, it wasn't nothing but a joke. They can take a joke."

Robertson shook his head. "Maybe they can. But why insult their mothers and sisters?"

Fowlkes put his face into Robertson's. "I ain't insulted nobody's mothers and sisters."

"What do you think 'gook mooses' are? Fathers and brothers?"

Face frozen in puzzle, Fowlkes stepped back and lifted his hands helplessly. "You ain't ever wolf-snarled me before, Robbie. Kind of hard for a feller to take."

Robertson stalked off to report to Baker that the First Squad had tidied the offal of Korea and was ready to move out.

At about 1500 hours, under a muggy sun, the company began the march up. One long column snaked along each side of the dirt supply road, on the berm above the ruts. Even here, forward of the combat support companies, the military police had erected a thicket of road signs proscribing everything from venereal disease to debasing the currency of Korea.

Early in the march, when jeeps and an occasional weapons carrier came rearward against them, the men catcalled the drivers. Later they became grimly silent. Where earlier they had marched, and later they walked, now they trudged. Equipment jangled and jostled, galling shoulders and hips. Finally, into the fifth sweated mile, the equipment became nothing more than oppressive weight.

Even here in its north, monsoonal Korea spat malice on laden soldiers. Sweat could not evaporate in air as soggy as itself: Robertson felt like a man stewing in his own juices. And, as if dissatisfied with the current misery index, the sky called up its reserves, black cumulonimbus from the sea to the east, clouds that would tease, then drench, then resimmer.

Robertson's squad carried as additional punishment the platoon's machine-gun ammunition. His squad alone was so encumbered with metal canisters and it obviously was another of Blackthorne's petty punishments. Chewing on this, Robertson decided to let it stand. Although Captain Hartung would have angrily rectified this situation, Blackthorne's childish ire, like Robertson's fight with Sam Dougherty, could be used to help unite the squad. The more spitefully the officer behaved, the closer they would grip each other.

Baker claimed Robertson's attention. As platoon sergeant, he had sent his own equipment in the communications jeep. Now he went along the platoon, carrying for each man in turn. So relieved, the man was freed for a few delightfully buoyant paces. Then Baker would resaddle him and go on to the next. Thinking on it, Robertson realized Baker would carry as much as any man, and, because he went both forward and back, would hike farther. Robertson saw then a new dimension to duty.

He smiled affectionately when Baker came alongside and puffed out, "Lucky we aren't in the cavalry, Sergeant Robertson. They'd make us carry the horses."

The Third Squad was across the road. That file inched ahead for a few yards and brought Fowlkes abreast of Robertson. Fowlkes called over, "Saw a yeller dog chase a bunny rabbit on a day like this one, Robbie. Damned if both of them wasn't walking."

Robertson said, neutrally, "You are a born infantryman, Brax." Then he managed a forgiving grin.

Fowlkes forged on. Staring across the road at his back, Robertson pondered Fowlkes's remark that he would not return to the line. Surely just depression talking. Depression was common enough in line soldiers.

The towering clouds thickened and darkened. Without warning, they crackled and boomed. Initially, large drops puffed the dust of the road like plunging rifle bullets. Then a hard sheet of rain came down and enveloped the columns. Visibility diminished to misty yards. The rain was warm, so warm the protesting mind sensed it as hot. Such rain was new to many of them; this was the meaning of "monsoon."

Behind Robertson, someone called out, "It always rains on the infantry. Why can't it rain on the artillery for a change?"

Someone else answered. "You know damned well it always rains during an approach march. God's way of getting you cleaned up for the Graves Registration boys. Don't want the army hauling a bunch of dirty bodies around."

"Blow it out your barracks bag, you ghoulish bastard."

"I'll whip the son of a bitch that said that."

"You couldn't whip your little sister."

Soaked boots squished in the red mud and a rearward-flowing weapons carrier with four .50-caliber machine guns mounted on it splashed the hikers as it passed. As if no one wanted to tackle quad .50s, one of the American army's most-feared weapons, the insult went unchallenged.

Word came down and the company halted. In soggy clothing, under stifling helmets, they ate C-rations. When the march resumed, they trudged through the mud, one foot ahead of the other. Robertson played an old game with himself, one he'd taught himself in basic training.

Wearily but craftily, he'd start a count toward five hundred paces, knowing he could make those if he promised himself to quit after five hundred. But then he'd pretend to himself at about the three-hundredth pace that he'd lost count. Then he'd start a new count, knowing he could fool himself into making five hundred more if he promised himself a rest. No doubt others played similar self-deception games.

They halted and closed up in full darkness, stumbling and cursing. The assembly area lay immediately to the rear of Easy Company, near an abandoned cluster of mud-and-wattle houses, some roofless and eyeless in the faint moon that came up and punched through the residual of the afternoon nimbus clouds. Robertson got his orders from Baker and paired his men on a narrow squad perimeter anchored on the yard of one of the houses. "Fifty-percent alert," he told them. And to Zuckerman and Klineschmidt, "No firing unless you get the order. Friendly folks ahead of us."

Zuckerman asked anxiously, "Should we dig a foxhole?"

"No need," Robertson reassured.

"But what happens if they attack us?"

Robertson brushed Zuckerman's shoulder. "They won't; they'd have to get through the rifle line ahead of us to do that."

"Then if we aren't on line, why are we here?"

Robertson sighed. The present disposition of the company confirmed his morning speculation that they would attack rather than simply relieve another unit. Were it a simple relief in place, they'd already have moved up.

He lowered his voice to make it casual and said, "I think we will lay out the dark hours here and jump off through Easy Company in the morning."

"Jump off?"

"Attack."

Robertson could sense Zuckerman's drawn breath. He patted the shoulder under his hand. "Worry about tomorrow when tomorrow comes, Solly. Thinking ahead makes it worse."

They ate more C-rations and sagged into the sucking wet ground. Paired off, one man of each pair alternately watched the night while the second dozed fitfully, damp and uncomfortable, buttocks screaming. Legs numbed and slept when the man could not. Robertson trioed with Carver and Olson, next to the abandoned house. They speculated briefly on who might have lived there, then fell silent. Confused orders came along the line, armed sounds interspersed with "Dago" and "Red," which were the sign and countersign. Almost immediately those orders were rescinded and superseded by other confused orders. Men coughed and rustled and pissed upon the ground. Someone farted loudly. It was not a recruiting-poster night.

Some men dismantled pieces of the village, which obviously had undergone heavy air attack, to make contrivances to keep themselves out of the mud. A few men put down unfolded ponchos for ground sheets. Most didn't; water would squeeze out of the mud and up onto the rubber, carrying grit with it. Better to try to doze on soft mud than on rubber sandpaper.

Robertson put his face to Carver's. "They taught me in basic training that an experienced field soldier would always find a way to sleep warm and dry."

After laughing sourly, Carver replied, "My recommendation is that we go to my much-missed hometown of Cleveland, Ohio, and rent suites in a hotel. Let me be the first to know if you come up with something more practical."

Robertson was struck again with Carver. He had known him only casually in the Third Platoon, but he knew Carver had graduated from Ohio State and that he had been drafted. Black men were a novelty. Having begun integration only as recently as 1948, the army still had de facto Jim Crow units.

"Why aren't you an officer, Carver? You're the only enlisted man in the company who talks like one."

"Brass on black? No thanks. Most of my white brothers aren't quite prepared to salute a Pullman porter."

Yielding to an instinct, Robertson said, "I'm sorry it's that way." And it was that way. He knew of one black soldier sentenced to two years in the disciplinary barracks for merely sassing a white officer.

Carver stiffened and muttered a cautious thank you.

Robertson named him then. "It'll get better, Tommy. Maybe even better for the Koreans before this mess is over."

Blackthorne, Baker, and the platoon runners and medic were in the house, where Blackthorne had set the platoon CP. The wall of the house nearest Robertson had been blown down, permitting the thatched roof to hang crazily, letting out a faint barnlike odor of what once must have been contained there. It was a familiar odor, one he had smelled in Chunchon that night he went AWOL—musty straw, unwashed Koreans, long-dead odors of alien food. It made him uneasy.

Often in the early night Robertson overheard the intrusive crackle of the backpack radio. Whenever the radio broke the squelch with the platoon call sign, Amber Two, Robertson would hear Sergeant Baker's voice. The radio exchanges consisted almost entirely of "What's your situation, Second?" and Baker's drawled "Amber Two's fine." He realized that Baker would not sleep. Knowing that, he decided he would not sleep. He went repeatedly along his line, encouraging, sometimes merely visiting to kill a few empty minutes of the empty hours. At each position, although one man could have slept, often both were awake.

The rifle line ahead slept as fitfully. The usual flares and booms and spurts of noise, then long nothings. A heavy machine gun directly ahead, probably Easy Company, fired several short chatters, then a long sustained rattle, then the doubtful bursts again. Robertson had gone to check on his replacements.

"Are they fighting?" Klineschmidt asked. He had his nose in the mud next to Zuckerman's.

"No. He doesn't have a target. Just having a little fun to pass the time."

Zuckerman's strained grunting indicated that he doubted that.

Robertson stood erect. Heavy firing broke out. The fire built up, halted, and built again, obviously orchestrated. He could hear no answering fire. Zuckerman got up on his knees and asked, "What is *that*, Sergeant Robertson?"

"That's our battalion commander at work. He wants to keep the Chinese awake." It was a signature Robertson had witnessed before. Lt. Col. Raymond D. Burton would fire sporadically. Never daring to doubt that the Americans would violate practice and attack at night, the Chinese could not rest. In the morning, they would be tired and careless.

But then, neither would the Americans rest; E Company would pull triggers; G Company would listen, wondering anxiously about their own involvement in it. A few secretly wished E Company would not irritate the Chinese; almost all knew by now G Company would reap the harvest of that anger with the advent of a new sun.

Robertson decided not to explain it. His replacements were alert, which was sufficient for the moment. They would learn officially before morning what was to happen.

Shortly after Robertson returned to the bombed-out house, he heard the radio squawk, "Amber Two. Officers to the CP."

Blackthorne slid across the yard and vanished. Robertson lit a cigarette and puffed it into a red-hot coal. With that light, he read his watch. The long day had begun. It was 0330. He had no doubt in his mind that Blackthorne would put the First Squad at the head of the assault.

The sky pinked and faces had noses again and standing figures cast honest shadows. Word passed down the column for squad leaders to assemble on Blackthorne.

The platoon leader crouched on the ground near an E Company fighting hole. The careful movement forward to that point had begun about twenty minutes earlier.

The sergeants grouped around the officer. He, too, showed fatigue. "We will advance through here where Easy and Able Company tie in. There is a ridge ahead of us, and a finger goes up onto the ridge. Second Platoon will assault up it." Blackthorne stared heavily at Robertson, then added, "Robertson's squad takes the point."

Robertson stared back. Blackthorne averted his eyes and went on. "We go in on the right as one claw of the pincer." He gave a long series of instructions, some of which were needed, many of which were not. All the sergeants were more experienced than he. During the briefing, Robertson often glanced at Fowlkes. The North Carolinian seemed lost within himself, but perhaps that was fatigue. When Blackthorne began to talk about casualty procedures, Fowlkes turned his head away, as if he didn't want to listen.

Robertson occupied himself then with studying Blackthorne. The lieutenant was dark-haired and well built. He was a military aristocrat, with an overt contempt for enlisted men. That was something Robertson had seen in few officers, although the caste line was sharply drawn. He doubted that Blackthorne, if he survived Korea, would have a happy career. Robertson found himself thinking about Blackthorne's reputation in the company and envied his old Third Platoon, which Captain Hartung would take up on the ridge. Hartung led from the front; officers like Blackthorne stayed with their radiomen in the rear, cheering the fighting on.

Robertson understood clearly that the burden of battle leadership in the Second Platoon fell upon its sergeants.

Blackthorne finished his briefing and dismissed the sergeants. As Robertson started back, one of the Easy Company men in the fighting hole nearby called over. "Give them hell, buddy. They been pounding the billy piss out of us."

Robertson flicked his hand. He knew the caller enjoyed the morning. Nothing in an infantryman's day is better than watching somebody else attack an enemy who has shot at him for days.

Robertson briefed his squad, trying for the replacements' sake to make it seem routine. He noticed Zuckerman's eyes were on Dougherty, obviously seeking reassurance. As if he understood, Dougherty spat on the ground and muttered, "Looks like an easy ride to me. I'd expect to see more combat in the barracks on payday night."

They had a moment to eat now, before they moved up to the line of departure. Robertson pooled their rations and let them choose. They chose to the last olive drab can, pinto beans and franks, Robertson's best-of-a-bad-lot favorite. The Koreans had not chosen. Robertson threw the beans to Choi, who held only a B-unit, the companion condiment can. "Here, you share this with Kang."

Choi examined the can a moment and said, "You have nothing, Squad Sergeant Robertson."

"I've eaten. Share with Kang."

"One thinks to the contrary, but thank you for your immense kindness."

Carver and Plumber put opened cans into Robertson's face. He smiled his thanks but shook his head.

The men waited. The sun got all the way up over the low mountains to the east. Six silver F-51 airplanes roared over, shaking the ground. They flew far to the east, then banked around and came back parallel to the front, dipping and firing and napalming before pulling up and away. This was repeated twice, then one of the airplanes waggled its wings and the flight climbed away toward the southwest. Black oily smoke was their legacy.

When the order came down, the men saddled up and in a long puffing file followed Baker and Blackthorne up into a notch in the near ridge. Beyond, floating in the morning haze, they could see the enemy ridge, somewhat higher, silent, yet so far noncommittal. The men glanced self-consciously at each other and assumed various degrees of crouching. Most of them grinned foolishly and straightened when they realized that E Company had a fighting hole there.

One of the two gritty helmeted occupants of the hole called to Robertson. "If you guys are going up the finger over yonder, keep your ass tucked in when you cross the low ground between here and there. Charley fires on it. We lost a man out there the other night."

Robertson waved a hand and glanced at the ground they would cover. He saw they must cross a swale, about four hundred yards of dipping open ground, before they reached the relative security of the finger. The finger itself—in effect a smaller, inclined, ridge—formed a long causeway to the top. If his appraisal of the contours was accurate, the finger would be defilade to fire until they reached the point where it shelved decisively to join the parent ridge. Then they would again come under fire.

He saw a smaller shelving in the finger about halfway up. He noted that carefully. The assault would likely halt there while support fires were adjusted. Once halted, it would be difficult to break loose. By that juncture, the men would be drenched with exertion and sweat. If they had in fact taken fire on the swale, they would be double-gunshy and the shelf would be a restful haven, one a sane man would be loath to depart.

Noting that, he glanced grimly at Baker and Blackthorne, then away. It would be their problem.

Easily, Robertson understood Captain Hartung's plan of action. The captain would take the main assault up the larger finger to their west. The Blackthorne mission was twofold. Even if its effort failed, Blackthorne's platoon would create a diversion for Hartung. If Blackthorne succeeded, the Chinese would be, at the point of closure, bullied on both sides by the company's killing cross fire.

Any other maneuver against that ridge would have been suicidal.

Robertson heard someone behind inquire, "Where is Sergeant Fowlkes?" He checked an impulse to act on that. He knew there was nothing he could do about it. Likely the query was an innocent part of the routine milling confusion of the preparations.

He made a final survey of the finger and the ridge. He blotted the sweat from his upper lip and rubbed his left eye, leaving it stinging from salt. He knew that initially the men would love the steepness of that climb, for it would shield their minds from the fire. But before they got all the way up, they would begin to love the fire: it would shield their minds from the steepness.

Faces were blotched with red dampness and dark spots had formed in crotches and under armpits. The night's mud was drying on boots and clothing. The men made murmurs and sighs and chewed on their lips. Occasionally, a man would drink from his canteen and wipe his mouth carefully while he looked around to see what the others were doing.

Robertson turned to study his two replacements. Solomon Zuckerman stared at the ridge and his lips quivered, subtly, but discernibly, if a man knew what to look for.

"Hang in there, Solly." Feeling what he had felt in the night with Carver, Robertson reached for the rifleman's shoulder. Robertson heard himself saying, "I'll take the point with you this time."

Robertson went down on one knee and waited, rifle on safety. The older hands of the squads adjusted the clothing around their testicles and fingered rifles nervously. The two Koreans stared at Robertson, mutely, faces devoid of expression.

From the unseen west, where Hartung would go up, came the sound of rifles. Robertson fitted that into his pictures; the Third Platoon had started up, trying to lay down a moving wall of fire ahead of themselves. Somewhere behind, Robertson heard Blackthorne's radio. It crackled, "Amber Two. Go!"

Robertson stood and shouted, "Keep an interval!" Then he ran onto the swale, turning back after about thirty yards to verify that the others followed. Satisfied, he turned and ran on, measuring the yards to safety. Once he glanced up at the ridge, hazy in the north, but surprisingly close, considering E Company lived across the alley from it. He saw he had misled himself about the danger of the swale. Only the last one or two hundred yards could be under direct fire. He reached this area, paused, and half turned to glance back again. Zuckerman and Klineschmidt were hunched over, but were coming on. Light fire began to fall on the truly enfiladed area of the swale. He examined it, ruling it rifle fire, and ruling it sparse. That was Charley's mistake. A Chinese machine gun would have denied them the swale, hence denying them the finger.

Robertson shouted, "Let's go!" He lifted his rifle overhead in a jerking motion and plunged on. He heard the rifle fire from the ridge build up, but sensed it was randomly aimed. Soon across, at the base of the finger he exhaled gratefully and turned to look back. He counted aloud the figures of the First Squad men who were crossing. All were safe.

Heads down, grunting, they began the climb. When they reached the first shelf, they went down on their knees and drew at the damp air with gaping mouths.

The howitzers that had intermittently bombarded the ridge during the night now began to fire the final preparations. The shells whirred over to pound mindlessly, lifting a pall of smoke up into the morning haze. The G Company mortars joined in. Mixed in with it all was the rage of gunfire on the platoon's west.

The fall line of the mortars was ear-punishing and eyebrow-raising close. This, Robertson knew, was Captain Hartung's battle signature, one it was understood he had learned to write in World War II Europe, where he had commanded a company as a first lieutenant. Left to his own authority, he once had told a group of awed men, he'd march up a hill enveloped in his own support fire, rather than behind it. He'd expect to lose fewer men to friendly artillery than to the dazed but unimpeded resistance that got up out of the ground when the suppressing fires lifted, he had explained all too casually.

Down on his knees beside Robertson, Zuckerman had lifted his canteen to his mouth. He gulped so avidly that the chlorinated water ran in two streams down his chin. Robertson saw that Zuckerman's hand shook. After he had let him drink a few swallows, Robertson tapped Zuckerman's helmet. "We might have a long day, Solly. You'll be better off with water in your canteen than in your belly."

Zuckerman shakily capped the canteen and returned it to the canteen carrier on his rump. "I'm sorry, Sergeant Robertson."

Robertson squeezed the scout's shoulder and said nothing.

He realized he had trifled with his own knowledge of combat by not explaining to Zuckerman the real reason he forbade him to drink heavily. A combat medic once had argued to him that a visceral wound was more dangerous if the belly the missile hit was full of water. Robertson didn't know whether this was so, but he did know that a stomach full of food and a colon full of feces were bad baggage at a firefight. Few who had seen a bad stomach wound could doubt that, and Robertson had seen several. He also knew that Zuckerman, as did all of them, stood a demonstrable chance of being hit somewhere between the shelf and the top of the ridge, and risked odds of about one in seven that any hit would be the big one. That was not theory; that was reality.

Robertson squeezed the shoulder under his hand again and dismissed such thoughts. He adjusted the bandoliers of ammunition that crisscrossed his chest and reoccupied his mind by evaluating the turmoil on the ridge. Twice, he himself had cowered over his own thick buttons on the incoming end of preparatory fires. He pitied the Chinese on the ridge. Their problem was to keep eyes above ground sufficiently to deal with the oncoming attackers. That was a hard thing when the air overhead spat shards of red-hot jagged steel.

Sensing Zuckerman's searching eyes on him, Robertson deliberately lit a cigarette. He wiped his upper lip again.

Blackthorne and the platoon headquarters party closed up. The platoon leader stood by the radioman. Behind, down at the base of the finger, the other two rifle squads waited. Robertson prayed that Braxton Fowlkes was with them.

The radio blatted again and Blackthorne lifted an arm to point up the finger.

Robertson jabbed Zuckerman's leg and began the second phase of the climb.

The howitzer firing stopped, leaving only the crisper booming of heavy mortars, which could range closer to the assault line. The mortars walked along the ridge top, throwing up spurts of loud black fire. Robertson knew that would lift shortly. As he climbed, betting the point must eventually come under directed fire, Robertson was flooded with the feeling that an irresistible mechanism put blinders on his eyes and dragged him with narrowed vision into thundering, acrid, resolute danger. His heart pulsed excited blood into screaming ears, but he forced himself to breathe evenly. He had learned that was the best of the possible responses. When they reached the terminal shelf, he motioned for the scouts to go to ground. He glanced back, to receive Blackthorne's signal to continue.

Even before they rose, fire began to lance down, hesitant at first, then determined, building into a strong warning. Time began to slow down. Robertson disciplined his mind. He saw that the longer they waited, the more difficult it would be. They had easily broken loose from the first shelf, for there had been no fire. Here, because the danger was undeniable, the others would demand a motivator, and likely one wearing chevrons.

Rolling onto his back, he unpinned a grenade. He vowed to himself he could stand and throw it on the count of three.

He counted aloud for Zuckerman. When he stood, he stepped vigorously to his right and threw. He shouted for the others; then, with the butt of his rifle against his right hip, he started forward. The others got up quickly and emulated him. Now it was the familiar fire-and-climb. As wisdom went, if a man was around next morning to think about it, it must have been done right.

The Chinese fire slackened. Robertson sensed the enemy was assessing his own prospects. As if to hasten the decision, the two Koreans and Olson dropped down on one knee off to Robertson's left and continued firing in the general direction of ahead. Luke Plumber and Dougherty came up.

Robertson pointed right. "Get in those scrub trees and work up," he ordered breathlessly. "If Charley was dumb enough not to cover that swale any better than he did, he might not expect fire from those trees."

Plumber glanced at the ground up to the trees, then lumbered heavily toward them, Dougherty following, both men crouched over.

Robertson gestured to Zuckerman. They went up. Twice Robertson grenaded the smoke ahead of him. Then they reached the top. A hail of fire came from behind. Robertson heard Sergeant Nelson's enraged cease-fire order. That was wise, the upper finger presented opportunity only for the narrowest of fronts; fire from behind was dangerous to the point. Friendly fire kills cruelest.

The ridge top unfolded before them, allowing small bits of information to reach through Robertson's blinders. He advanced deliberately now, forcing himself to study the situation carefully, disciplining himself to make the necessary decisions. He saw no men, but he heard the savage hammering reports of Plumber's BAR. He waited, alert, ready to react. A flurry spat out of the trees; Plumber fired from the hip as he advanced. Abruptly, Plumber stopped firing. He turned to face Robertson, as if to ask, "What do we do now?"

Before Robertson could communicate with his BAR team, Klineschmidt, near him, opened up. Robertson went across the finger a few paces to see that Klineschmidt shot into a human body, one likely dead for minutes. Klineschmidt's bucking Garand picked at the dead Chinese. Robertson stopped him with a sharp, "Save your ammunition for the live ones."

Although he could also hear scattered small-arms fire and grenading up the ridge, where Hartung would be climbing, Robertson sensed that the Second Platoon's part in Hartung's breakfast battle was over. He glanced at his watch. Fourteen hours from the beginning of the march, twenty-eight minutes from the jump-off line; nineteen minutes from the point of first fire.

The ridge was crater and debris, shattered trees standing stark against an even higher ridge to the north. Robertson shook his head lightly. This was to be home now.

Korea was in the era of stalemated ridge battles—King of the Hill. The only way up was up. Sergeants directed the fragments of the battles, each piece a battle entire.

Now the Americans had the ridge, which was like a thousand ridges between Kumwha and the Yalu. Now the Chinese would regroup and rethink. They'd mortar and shell heavily for a few days, then begin to pick at the ridge with foot patrols, wanting revenge as much as real estate. King of the Hill, a child's game.

And the ridge fights were either less bloody or more bloody. When Nelson got up to tell him that only one man was hit crossing the swale, even after the Chinese realized their error and began to mortar it, Robertson decided this one was less bloody.

"Who got hit?" Robertson asked, somehow certain it was not Braxton Fowlkes.

One of Nelson's men; just a name to Robertson. Even so, he was relieved when Nelson said the casualty was under cover, screaming for morphine, a Purple Heart, and evacuation, in that order. The chief price had been paid in sweat and adrenaline.

Sergeant Nelson asked, "Have you seen that peckerwood Fowlkes?" Nelson looked back down the finger and added sourly, "I brought up his people."

Robertson shook his head. Together, the two sergeants formed the three squads into a defensive perimeter and redistributed ammunition and grenades and encouragement. They tallied up; except for Nelson's man down on the swale, the Second Platoon had gotten away with it. The Chinese commander must have misread Hartung's intentions, shifting to his right at the fatal expense of his left. Neither Robertson nor Nelson mentioned Fowlkes again.

There was a breeze on the ridge. The sweat dried on the men, leaving deposits of salt on their clammy fatigues. Everyone breathed in gasps and gulped water.

Sam Dougherty was jubilant. He called over to Zuckerman, "See, Solly, told you we'd have a good ride. Your grandmother could have done it."

Zuckerman replied grimly, "Next time, I'll let her go in my place."

Blackthorne's headquarters team trotted up. The lieutenant glanced at the men in the holes and went along the ridge toward where Hartung's chunk of the company would be. One of the runners hung back to say that the radio had told them G Company had the ridge. Then the runner puffed off after the platoon leader and radioman.

SFC Baker came up alone. He halted a few feet away from Robertson and Nelson and beckoned Robertson over.

Robertson bit his lip.

He knew what the platoon sergeant wanted to discuss. Robertson and Fowlkes were known buddies. By the logic of things, each was responsible for the other.

9

HILL 874,
JUNE 24, 1951

T he platoon sergeant repeated his angry question. "Where the hell is Sergeant Fowlkes?"

Robertson replied quickly, "Maybe he got hit. I could go back and check on him."

Baker's head shook vigorously. "He's not hit. Charley *gave* us the ridge. That hillbilly dogged it on us."

Mind wild with possibilities, Robertson floundered. "Let me go back for him," he pleaded.

"No. A firm goddamned negative. He hangs."

"Dammit, Baker. Brax is fighting something in his head."

The two sergeants stared at each other. When one moved his eyes, the other followed the movement.

Baker softened. He stammered a moment. "It's no good, Robertson. We can't hide it. His squad knows. Blackthorne will find out about it, if he doesn't already know."

"Blackthorne will be tied up at the company CP for a few minutes," Robertson suggested. "Turn your back to this for twenty minutes. That's all I'm asking for."

Baker shook his head again, but hesitantly this time. "Running away before the enemy is a capital offense, Robertson, and you know it. You might as well ask for a year. We are consolidating an objective. Charley may well counterattack yet this morning. What will I tell Blackthorne?"

"I'll take my hits there. Maybe he won't come looking for me."

The platoon sergeant cursed at nothing for a second. "Christ, Robertson. Next time some bastard asks me to sign up for the Ready Reserve, I'll strangle him. I went through this shit all the way from Normandy to the Rhine. I didn't like it then, and I don't like it now." He motioned back down the finger. "Maybe you'll meet him coming up. Turn your squad over to Carver. I'll think of something for Blackthorne."

Carver nodded and glanced down the finger when Robertson told him he was going back. The black soldier mouthed, "Fowlkes?"

Robertson nodded. Carver would know anyway.

Robertson dashed down the finger and across the exposed yards they had bought so fearfully minutes earlier. He remembered a deep cut in the swale, just before the enfilade ground. Fowlkes would probably be there.

Fowlkes sat, rifle at his side, helmet off, knees drawn up, head on his arms. In the slanting sunlight, even his shadow cowered. Robertson glanced at his watch; seven of his precious minutes were gone.

He forced himself to act calmly. "Get up, Brax. You have to come with me."

Fowlkes looked up. His eyes were red. "I can't. I tried to cross over yonder . . ." He faltered. "I was catching up with you, thinking I could do her . . . the Chinks was firing . . . I just can't do it anymore."

Robertson pulled Fowlkes to his feet. Fowlkes stood unmoving. Robertson put Fowlkes's helmet on and seated it with a pat. Putting Fowlkes's M-1 in his hand, he murmured, "You've got to come, Brax. This is very serious."

Fowlkes's face showed his inner troubles. "I ain't going up. I'd sooner lay out my twenty years in Leavenworth. Let them college boys come over here and do their panty raids. I'm veteran enough for one lifetime. It ain't fair that some fellers got to do it all."

Sensing that Fowlkes was rational, Robertson readied himself to deal with him. He knew nothing about combat fatigue, except that some men broke. He doubted that the psychiatrists knew much more. Watching Fowlkes now, he felt awash in emotion. Chief of the emotions was fear— already events had chipped away at the armor he had put around his mind only a hundred hours earlier. Fowlkes had gotten in easily.

"They might shoot you, Brax," Robertson said carefully, watching its effect.

"The army growls like a bear with a sore ball, but it don't shoot nobody."

"Eisenhower shot a man for desertion under fire."

"That was only one feller, out of thousands."

"One was enough for the guy who got the firing squad." Robertson breathed easier. Fowlkes was making sense.

"I'll take my fucking twenty years, Robbie." Fowlkes began to cry and rubbed his nose with his bare arm.

Robertson glanced at his watch. Fighting panic, he grabbed Fowlkes's shoulders and shook him. Fowlkes's helmet flew off. Robertson winced and put it back on before he spoke. "Time is eating us," he said angrily. "Let's knock off this shit and get back up there before Blackthorne comes looking for us. You can go back and start clean. Stay here and you'll come out of prison an old man with nothing but a sackful of shame."

Robertson felt the vehemence of his own words. Of all the dangers in the army, none was worse than official disgrace. This was a thought he had weighed several times in recent days.

Fowlkes sobbed louder, his body racked.

Robertson stood back, feeling himself choke. He had seen men break under fire, but the ruptures had been obvious and decisive. A man screamed or beat the air with his fists or ran mindlessly into the flames. Never this before; never this close.

Fowlkes lifted his hand, removed his steel helmet, and threw it on the ground. He turned to Robertson, mouth opening and closing, eyes unfocused. He drooled brown spittle.

Robertson closed his eyes a moment, not wanting to see, merely hanging on to space and time. Then slowly, instinctively, he embraced Braxton Fowlkes, realizing he was surrendering more of his own armor. He had never embraced another man. He felt self-conscious at first, but then it seemed right and natural. When Fowlkes put his face into his shoulder, Robertson spoke into the matted hair. "Let's go, Brax." The hair tickled his lips.

Fowlkes choked out a muffled, "Don't hate me, Robbie. I can't stand it when you're against me like you was yesterday morning."

"I don't hate you," Robertson whispered. "But you've got to come back with me." He thought wildly and was able to add, "Captain Hartung will let you evacuate. I'll go and talk to him for you."

Fowlkes's crying stilled. He said brokenly, sadly, "I—don't—want—that. If I have to face the other fellers, I don't want them to know."

"If you come, Brax, I'll guarantee it for you." He knew that his promise was foolish. In the combat infantry, no man could guarantee another man supper.

Foolish or not, Fowlkes responded, although the response was odd. "Maybe we *could* stick together. Maybe if'n I'd been with you, I could have done her. I could have run 'cross that fucking ground dodging them Chinks' bullets like you and the other fellers done. Been like an old quail, Robbie.

107

Can't hit me on the ground 'cause that's agin the law and can't hit me flyin' 'cause I'll fly sideways." He laughed. "Like I always said, them Charleys can't shoot straight 'cause they eat rice and their mamas didn't have no tits—"

Fowlkes eased out of Robertson's arms and stepped back, searching Robertson's face. "Like at Chaffee when we outrun that old bentleg. Didn't even know you then, but I saw you was a tough one. Long as you was with me I'da run that old sergeant's legs off clean up to his pecker."

"I'll stick with you," Robertson promised.

Fowlkes began to giggle. It was shrill and girlish and it tore into Robertson like a scream in a graveyard.

With jerking motions, Fowlkes picked up his helmet and put it on, still giggling. "Come on, Robbie. When it gets so fucking tough the IG and the chaplain go over the fucking hill, it is about right for us old hillbillies."

Robertson tugged and they ran up the finger together.

Baker and Blackthorne stood waiting at the top. Robertson looked up at them, knowing he had used more than Baker's grant of twenty minutes. Fowlkes, a few paces behind, slowed to a cautious walk. Robertson halted and waited for him. They went on up, side by side.

"Where have you men been?" Blackthorne demanded immediately. "We might have been counterattacked."

Robertson glanced imploringly at Baker. Baker spoke to Blackthorne. "I told you, sir. I sent them back down the finger to see if the men had abandoned any equipment."

The officer spun on Baker and retorted, "And I told you that you were stupid. You can't send off two of your junior leaders at a time like this."

Blackthorne accepted Baker's noncommittal stare and turned on Fowlkes. "Article 99. Misbehavior before the enemy . . . any member of the armed forces who before or in the presence of the enemy runs away"—his lips took on a suggestion of smile—"shall be punished by death." He screamed, "*Death*, Fowlkes, do you understand me?"

Robertson lifted a clenched fist, but before he could speak, Baker snatched Blackthorne's attention. At first the platoon sergeant only spluttered, but then he forced out, "You little fart! You're actually enjoying this. The Uniform Code of Military Justice has been in effect for only two months and you've memorized every goddamned punitive article of it. Are you going to spend the next thirty years threatening every man you command with a court-martial?"

Blackthorne flinched from Baker's anger, but reasserted himself. "I'll also court-martial *you*, Sergeant."

Baker laughed. "Draw up your charges, Lieutenant. But get me first. If I'm around to testify at Sergeant Fowlkes's court-martial, I intend to say I couldn't go down and give him orders because I was too busy wet-titting you while you hid behind your radioman."

Blackthorne implored Robertson shrilly, "You heard Sergeant Baker threaten me—"

Interrupting, Robertson answered pleasantly, "I heard him tell you why Brax and I were down on the finger. Then I heard you tell him he was stupid." He paused, gauging the effect. When the officer blanched, he added firmly, "Must be an article in UCMJ against verbal abuse of subordinates. It has everything else covered." He smiled. But he knew it was the thinnest of defenses for Fowlkes; an officer stronger than Missy Blackthorne could puncture it in an instant.

Blackthorne sagged, then backed up. Finally he said, "We'll forget this incident . . . this particular incident."

"That's reasonable," Baker said softly.

Blackthorne drew himself up. He glanced at Fowlkes, then at Robertson. With some of his normal arrogance, he lifted a finger and pointed to Fowlkes. "Break this man. Now." The finger went to Robertson. "This man's squad is to be positioned on the right flank of the platoon. They are to patrol every night until I rescind the order." He turned to Baker. "Is that clear?"

"Clear enough," Baker replied levelly.

Blackthorne walked off, head down. After he was gone, Baker shook his head at Robertson and told Fowlkes, "I'll have to break you. I'll tell the Old Man you asked for a voluntary reduction in grade." When Fowlkes nodded, Baker added, "Get on up with your squad. Tell Corporal Sinterman to come and see me."

Robertson stepped forward. "Don't leave him in the Third Squad."

"Who else wants him? All the platoon knows by now what he did."

"I want him. I'll trade a man for him."

Olson went to the Third Squad. Fowlkes came into the First.

On the perimeter, when Robertson told the squad about the change, Klineschmidt piped up. "Why do we have to take the gutless shit?"

"Fire off a few more clips at *live* Chinese before you get cute about combat, Kraut," Robertson snapped.

Dougherty had been listening. "It could have been any one of us. It takes a bunch of firefight to earn thirty-six rotation points. Fowlkes has had his fair share."

Sensing the absolution, Zuckerman added, "If I'd have known what it would be like, I'd have stayed back with Sergeant Fowlkes."

Dougherty and Robertson both smiled at Zuckerman. "That's the spirit," Dougherty said approvingly.

Fowlkes came over diffidently. At first no one spoke to him. Robertson decided to let it work itself out. Fowlkes sat dejectedly under a broken tree behind the crest of the ridge for about half an hour. Then Dougherty got out of his hole, stretched, and went back. Shortly, Robertson heard Dougherty's loud, "Come on, Peckerwood. The First Squad is okay when Robertson isn't kicking hell out of you."

Sighing relief, Robertson thanked the hypothetical Chinese for not having decimated the G Company assault. Had anyone in the Second Platoon joined hands with the two dead men in the platoon Captain Hartung had taken up, Fowlkes's sentence in the platoon would have been more cruel than a stint at Fort Leavenworth.

Fowlkes had made sergeant weeks before Robertson. The North Carolinian had worn on his helmet a decal of his rank insignia—three superior chevrons and one inferior arc. Robertson turned his eyes away and bit his lip when he saw Fowlkes had already scraped off the decal, leaving a brighter bare spot as obvious as the chevrons had been—a sad echo.

At the last light of the day, after a robust but futile mortar attack had raked the ridge, leaving the men cringing in their holes, Robertson, now on the threshold of a second night without sleep, surveyed his perimeter. The counterattack had not come, which squared more with Chinese practice than with North Korean. The North Koreans would have tried to come back up immediately. China was more patient. China would wait for the night.

The men had minimized their exposure during the day. Now, all around was the sound of labored breathing and digging. That would be the first night's work, unless the Chinese struck. In the morning, the holes would be deep, roofed over with sandbags and logs. Fields of fire would have been chosen and cleared; telephone lines would have been strung. Within days, the ridge would blossom into a community—sleeping bunkers, fighting holes, connecting trenchworks. They'd put down concertina and apron wire and mines and trip flares and site listening posts.

All that while George Company would leak maimed and dead men rearward. China and North Korea had hardy men to carry artillery shells across the mountains through the UN air interdiction. Ridges such as Hill 874 would be the ultimate focus of that labor.

As Blackthorne had ordered, the squad had holes around a short arc at the most exposed top of the finger. The ridge immediately to their east was unoccupied, since both sides could fire on it easily, at least until the Chinese commander realized the meaning of G Company's possession of

874 and adjusted his own position. Then the ridge to the east became more tenable for the UN. But for now, viewed in a straight line, nothing amicable obtruded between First Squad and the Sea of Japan. E Company had gone back, leaving an almost three-thousand-yard gap through which China could flow before it hit the blocking line the regiment had thrown up. That area would require constant patrolling, at least until Item Company moved forward, which might not happen for days.

In the meantime, that three-thousand-yard hiatus in the MLR would serve the UN artillerymen as a bowling alley. And the enemy went into it with the obvious danger of G Company poised above his line of march. Thus, the company was there to do two things. It would direct the traffic to its east. It also would be bait for the trap.

Each echelon owned a chunk of the problem. As he studied his chunk, Robertson drafted patrol rosters in his head. On each one of them, whenever the name Braxton Fowlkes came up, he deleted it and substituted the name Robertson.

10

NEAR HILL 874,
JULY 19, 1951

The night was a pit, so blackly silent Zuckerman heard insects, yet in his ears thrummed also the tread of dragons. It was eerie and insane—insane that he had been ordered here. Zuckerman wriggled for the third time in seconds to ease his discomfort—his shoulder ached where it pressed against the butt of Plumber's on-loan BAR; his hip ached and his right leg tingled. He let his finger caress the trigger of the automatic rifle; he wanted that reassurance.

Zuckerman felt stranded and alone, although Robertson, Klineschmidt, and the gentle Korean Kang Chul-ho were only a few feet away.

Item Company had come up after Company G had been six exposed days on 874, to occupy the low ridge to their east. That had been nineteen days earlier. Yet the First Squad patrolled. Tonight they aimed to ambush any random passing party of Chinese, hopefully assassinate all but one of them, and capture the survivor. God willing, the survivor would know high state secrets, or at least the Chinese Communist Forces' plan of maneuver for the coming year. Straightforward as that, but dicey, as Zuckerman had learned that most things in his new life as line infantryman were dicey.

From the second day, the Chinese had shelled the ridge so indefatigably that Plumber had growled, "If Charley doesn't stop to clean his tubes purty damned soon, I'm going over and smash his unneighborly butt." The shellfire attrition had gone on; apparently, the CCF was unaware of Plumber's threat.

A threat the Chinese were aware of had been the work of Robertson. The CCF had been shown this one several nights ago.

On the third full day on 874, Robertson had emplaced a .30-caliber light machine gun down in the tree line of the woods Plumber and Dougherty had climbed up through. He had put Carver and Klineschmidt together on the gun, with a sound-powered telephone connecting them with himself. Zuckerman had held his breath when he heard Carver's alerting whistle in the telephone. He heard Robertson give his order. "Lie low and let them come on up. Wait until we fire, then cut loose on them. Sustained fire, about knee high, right across the finger."

On the two other occasions the Chinese had brushed contact on them, Robertson had grimly forbidden his squad to return the fire. Now, surely thinking the east flank soft, the Chinese had returned. Suddenly they were there.

Dougherty had engaged then. Other rifles spoke. Zuckerman had pointed his own rifle down the slope and had pulled the trigger. When the empty clip twanged out, he reloaded and fired again. Then he heard the machine gun, and sensed he was in a maelstrom of stabbing lights, cries, and small-arms noise. He felt his rifle heating. He realized later he had remembered little else of it; he did not remember that he had been afraid, but surely he was, as he was afraid now.

Robertson's brief ambuscade on the finger that night had awakened the company. Throughout most of the darkness flares burst overhead, each time to cue raking gunfire from the American line. After that the Chinese had not molested the finger.

Just that day, the mail had come up. Zuckerman's mail indicated his first letters had winged home to New York and had fetched answers. He got a fresh letter from his father and two from Rachel. His father had typed a long account of the business and had remarked how fortunate Solomon was to have been given duty in Japan, instead of in Korea, where, according to both the *New York Times* and the *Wall Street Journal,* the Eighth Army continued to attack despite the earlier promise of settlement. "I think Truman will find," he wrote, "that the North Koreans and Chinese will strike a hard bargain before they give it up. I don't know what Truman is doing over there anyway. Why can't those Asian boys fight their own war? Mark my words, the business restrictions now will get worse unless they get it settled. There is even some talk of rationing, as in the last war." Zuckerman's mother was well and reminded him not to do something foolish such as volunteering for Korean service as he had volunteered so foolishly for the army.

Zuckerman was pleased that his ruse had worked. His father would not realize that not all San Francisco APOs ended up in Japan. After reading his father's letter, Zuckerman had sat back against the sandbag walls of the bunker and nursed a feeling of satisfaction. If he soldiered in Korea, at least he soldiered unmolested by demanding fathers and protective mothers, on his own terms as a man. The worst of it was that he could not write about Robertson and Dougherty and Choi and the others without exposing the lie. The descriptions of Japan came from Luke Plumber, who had served on Sendai. The only difficulty there was that Luke tended to remember Japan chiefly as an Elysian saloon where beautiful brown-eyed maidens slept with enlisted soldiers for a dollar and a half; Luke Plumber had not been a Kodak-carrying sightseer on Sendai.

Rachel's two letters, written over a period of three days, gushed on about the lovely summer and what courses she would sign up for in the fall. She helped in her father's law office and enthused about buying a new wardrobe, mostly in tans and yellows, both of which were nice colors for her, didn't Solomon think? Zuckerman blushed because one of the crumpled envelopes—it had survived many handlers and eighty-five hundred miles—was marked SWAK. But that was not as bad as the envelopes the others got, which had hearts drawn on them and contained admonitions to the letter handlers such as "Love Letter, Rush Like Hell."

Zuckerman put the butt of the BAR more tightly against his shoulder and flexed, seeking comfort, knowing he'd not find it. For the hundredth time he let his finger check that the safety lever was off. His thoughts returned briefly to Rachel. He tried to picture her face, and couldn't. Rachel Kahan and college semesters and yellow wardrobes seemed irrelevant to a man who lay in fear on the back of the moon, pledged to kill in the coldest of blood the first innocent unsuspecting anonymous Chinese who happened along.

Two weeks onto the line, Zuckerman realized that his original sharp anxiety had modulated into a vague apprehensiveness, which he assumed everyone suffered. He adjusted to sleepless nights. Warm food came up at least once each day, sometimes twice. They lived.

Zuckerman knew that the First Squad of the Second Platoon carried more than its share of the patrols. He also realized, because Klineschmidt called it to his attention, that Sergeant Robertson went on all the patrols, even when Carver went. Klineschmidt also insisted that Fowlkes never went, but Zuckerman could not remember well enough to agree to that. The twenty-four-hour days blurred, one blending into the other without benefit of numbers or names. Some men were carried down the hill, some men walked down the hill; new men came in to replace them. The new men had faces and voices exactly like the old, so the change barely registered. In fact, Zuckerman had begun to wonder if he had lost his own face.

Zuckerman tried to recapture the featureless days, but they seemed to stretch back to infinity. All he grasped was that the men got more dirty, more weary, and more irritable. One day Zuckerman had been sent down to one of the Fourth Platoon bunkers on an errand. The startled solitary occupant, a pudgy blond-headed man, buttoned his trousers too quickly and made apologetic sounds out of a bright red face. Rumors, and the carefully controlled press accounts in *Stars and Stripes*, hinted at violent action west of them. That was all they knew of the war except what they could see and hear and smell and taste and feel.

The ambush patrol he was embarked upon at the moment was clearer.

Robertson had made his patrol divest themselves of anything that shined or jingled. They poured canteens into the dirt and made mud to rub on cheekbones and noses, despite the fact that the night promised to be, as Fowlkes noted sourly, "darker than a sackful of black kittycats." Zuckerman was ordered to carry Plumber's BAR, and Klineschmidt to carry some of the heavy ammunition clips for it.

Robertson made contact with the Item Company position at the turn point and they eased through the wire, trying beyond that point to stifle their own breathing, begging not even to hear it in their own ears. Under Robertson's tutelage, Zuckerman had learned to put his foot down carefully, step by methodical step, crushing the grass slowly, anchoring each boot before its companion lifted. Now he lay where Robertson had put him, bound by the orders Robertson had given him.

Zuckerman's bladder was full, but he decided to try to ignore it, wishing he were like the others who could halt even a solemn combat patrol to piss. Zuckerman concentrated on hating the grass and the lieutenant and the recruiting sergeant. His side ached from the pressure of his urine.

Ahead, the night rustled as Robertson stood up. "Might as well go back in," he said quietly.

Then it happened; the Chinese had been waiting for them to rise.

Zuckerman learned, as had thousands before him, that nothing prepares a soldier for the stark terror of night ambush fire. The rifles exploded in their faces, crushing in their loudness, spouting dull flames. Initially Zuckerman froze into mouth-gaping helplessness, but when a round heated his ear, signaling an indubitable miss, he crouched and triggered the BAR. When the hostile fire was reduced to an echo, either in the ridges or in his mind, Zuckerman heard someone gurgling loudly as if to clear his throat. The sound shocked him. He saw Kang or Robertson go to ground. Then his leg was drenched in wet warmth. From the grass next to his feet, Klineschmidt shouted at him, "It's the Chinks! They were waiting for us!"

Robertson was at Zuckerman's side, down on one knee. His voice rose sharply. "Four or five of them, about a hundred feet ahead and slightly to the right; fire at the muzzle flashes." He fired rapidly. A hot cartridge case ejecting from his M-1 singed Zuckerman's left cheek.

Zuckerman pointed the BAR again and pulled the trigger. It kicked brutally—he had not pressed the butt firmly to his shoulder—spat out a few rounds, then froze.

Robertson was into his third clip before Zuckerman realized the BAR had jammed. Fighting panic, he went fully to ground and pulled the BAR back under his body to get at the breech. He begged his mind to recall his training, but it gave back nothing except a stern order to flee back across the valley to the safety of Item Company. He cried out hoarsely, "The BAR is jammed. I don't know what to do."

Zuckerman felt the BAR wrench from his hands and Robertson's M-1 come in to replace it. A silence, almost as terrible for Zuckerman as the ambush fire, lay on them. His ears begged for sound, then he thought he heard running men, a sound mingled with Robertson's labored muttering as he tried to curse the jammed round out of the BAR . . . and the horrible gurgling.

Klineschmidt struck Zuckerman on the leg. "Let's bug!" he shouted. Feeling wet fabric rub his leg near the crotch, Zuckerman fled into the night after the running shape ahead of him. He felt his most crushing fear then.

The Item Company outguard accepted their stuttered password and let them in. They waited there, grateful for unfearsome company, for several minutes. Then Zuckerman became violently angry.

"Kraut! You shouldn't have told me to bug out. Sergeant Robertson is out there with only Kang and the jammed BAR. We've got to go back."

Klineschmidt crowded closer to the two watching Item Company soldiers and did not reply. Zuckerman was trying to order himself to return alone when they heard Robertson call out that he was coming in.

Robertson had left the BAR that had betrayed them. He carried instead Kang Chul-ho, in a fireman's hold, struggling up the dewing grass to the sandbagged outpost hole. He was war's beast with two backs.

Zuckerman rushed to help. Robertson let him take Kang. The Korean slipped out of Zuckerman's hands and struck the ground limply. Before Zuckerman could react to the anguish that flooded his ears, Robertson said quietly, "It's all right. He can't be hurt now."

Robertson said tiredly to the Item Company sentinels, "Call your CP on your sound power and ask them to notify George One that I've got a man down. I need stretcher bearers." After a heavy pause, Robertson added, "Tell them he's KIA."

Zuckerman sat down near Kang's body, trying to read Robertson's voice. Suddenly he felt drained, as near to exhaustion as he had ever been, much more so than after the thirty-mile hike of basic training, which, in retrospect, seemed trivial. His legs twitched and his mouth was dry. He knew the most important act of his life would be to get Sergeant Robertson alone, to try to explain what had happened. But Robertson stayed near the Item Company men, smoking a cigarette in cupped hands, ominously wordless.

Some strangers rustled out of the night with a poncho and a stretcher. One of them, clearly a corpsman, examined Kang, feeling rapidly around his body. After a long minute, the corpsman's torso straightened, outlining him against the faint sky above the horizon; Zuckerman sensed the man's pain. The corpsman wiped his hands on Kang's trousers, making whishing sounds, before he spoke. "Went in his mouth and out the back of his neck," he said. The hush that greeted his words was followed by the additional opinion, "Likely your man never knew what hit him."

Zuckerman recalled the horrible gurgling sounds.

The Item Company men covered Kang for them and carried him back over the ridge to the defilade area and then laterally along the path until they met a party from Second Platoon, G Company. Several hands, affectionate and concerned, touched Zuckerman, then the Item Company neighbors vanished back up the path. The George Company men whispered brusque questions, which Klineschmidt answered. Robertson went on ahead, toward the CP. Beyond the request to I Company, he had said nothing.

Zuckerman reported to Corporal Carver, who had already heard the news. "The BAR jammed and when Kraut shouted I ran," he explained, waiting then with his lip in his teeth for Carver's anger. Carver only said, "Work it out with Robertson." Then Zuckerman crawled into the narrow bunker he shared with Klineschmidt and pulled his sleeping bag up over his waist, wanting heat to dry his trousers. Klineschmidt sat silently in the trench outside, staring north.

Zuckerman dozed, thinking dully about the ambush, just letting the ideas fill his mind. The firefight had lasted probably no longer than forty-five seconds. The Chinese had fired only the initial fusillade. He found himself wondering if he had drawn blood with the few rounds he got off before the BAR fouled; then he felt insinuating fear, knowing it was silly, but thinking the Chinese might hold him accountable and come again through the night.

At morning twilight, Zuckerman slipped from his sleeping bag, wincing at the rancid odor that followed him out. Although it was understood to be forbidden to leave the perimeter without permission, he went directly to the company CP, a large bunker on the reverse slope of the ridge. They had left Kang under the poncho and Robertson sat beside him. Outlined against the dawn, they were an eerie sight. The two bodies merged in the faint light, as if the living man were connected by some loathsome tissue to the dead man. The exhaustion in Robertson's posture suggested that he had been long beside Kang.

Robertson looked up and stared at him blankly. Zuckerman blurted out, "I'm sorry, Sergeant Robertson, when Kraut said to bug out, I thought it was your order."

Robertson did not seem to acknowledge his words.

Zuckerman forced his right hand to touch Kang, hard and cold now under the rubber fabric of the poncho. "Am I responsible?" he whispered anxiously. When Robertson shook his head, he asked, "Is Kraut responsible?"

The head moved again and turned to face Zuckerman. Zuckerman knew that if he lived a thousand years, he'd never forget the pain he saw there. Robertson's eyes were hollow, half-closed in a tortured face. The lips moved helplessly before they made words. Zuckerman strained to hear them.

"I alone am responsible, Solly." Robertson said no more.

The .30-caliber machine gun down in the tree line, known in the squad now as "Robertson's Charley-whacker," was attended in daylight by only one man. As he had been there when his countryman Kang Chul-ho lay dying, Choi was there when Robertson went to him.

After a moment of guilty silence, Robertson sat down wearily and lit a cigarette. "They've taken him away," he said, referring to Kang's corpse and to the Korean Service Corps bearers who had come for him.

Choi said nothing. Robertson said, his tone accusing, "You could have gone to see his body."

Choi turned his head and spoke harshly. "I have seen many dead men, Squad Sergeant. I have *created* many dead men."

"But you were Kang's friend."

Choi said fiercely, " 'Were' is in the past tense. Do not labor in the tenses of your clumsy language."

"I didn't mean it that way."

Choi smiled faintly and lit another cigarette. "I, too, am in apology. One knows you came to console." Choi sighed out some smoke. "He was a superlative man who much cherished the simple life he had." He paused then and looked south, toward Kwangju. "Kang resided not far from my mother's house. He made things to grow, loving life and hating death. We had met but once before our fortunes brought us together here with you Americans."

When the Korean fell silent, Robertson prodded with, "I'd like to hear about it, if you'd tell me."

Choi stared a moment, drew on his cigarette, and went on. "That was in 1946. I had returned from Okinawa, where I had been a prisoner of the Americans. My father had died while I was away. . . ." He seemed to struggle to arrange his ideas. "I had served the Japanese as a soldier, which was not approved of by all Koreans, as the Japanese were hated when they occupied my country. My mother's neighbors scorned me and I must confess I walked the paddy dikes around my village in great self-sorrow." He paused, asking, "Is in English such a concept?"

"I understand," Robertson said softly.

"Kang accosted me one day when I walked. He bowed formally to me and said, 'Captain Choi Min-soo, one is personally happy that kind fortune has returned you safely to us.' I thanked him for his words, and he begged my permission to say, 'Nothing is so important in the dark mists of yesterday that we must forfeit our bright todays to it.' That is a very old Korean idea, Squad Sergeant, and a wise one."

Robertson nodded and Choi continued. "That was all, but I felt that Kang Chul-ho understood my situation, which was pitiable at that time. I remember that I went afterward to a shrine and asked the stones why I had not been made of the simple fabric of Kang, whom all admired."

"What will happen to him now?" Robertson asked.

Smiling faintly, Choi explained, "His children will make a memorial to mark the passing of his life so that those whose lives Kang touched will remember the man that he was. Another man will be born to walk where Kang walked and the river of reality will flow on. What else can there be?"

Robertson said nothing, and Choi added, "Koreans believe that river runs swiftly; tears cannot catch it."

"Americans cry," Robertson said lamely.

"I will not mock those beliefs, Squad Sergeant. Thank you for your concern. I am told you risked the enemy to rush to the fallen Kang."

Robertson shook his head negatively. "Once they fired, it was all over."

They sat in silence until Choi reached to touch Robertson's arm, saying, "May I make bold to tell you something, Squad Sergeant?"

On Robertson's nod, Choi said, "One is aware that you came to him because you have implicated yourself in guilt for the death of my countryman—"

Robertson held up a hand, which Choi ignored. "Private Solly has explained your sentiment to me. I wish to say to you that when I was a young officer of the Imperial Japanese Army in China in 1941, one of my corporals came to me to accuse an old Chinese woman of stealing our rice. 'You may beat her with sticks,' I said. The corporal returned several minutes later to report that the old woman was dead—she had died under the sticks of my soldiers."

Choi seemed to wait then for Robertson's response. Robertson only made a noise and Choi went on.

"I did not lament the old woman's death, Squad Sergeant."

Robertson shifted. "Why not? You caused it."

Choi smiled broadly now. "Not at all, Squad Sergeant. It was the order I gave which caused the old woman's death, but when I gave the order, I did not contemplate that death. I contemplated only a logistical matter of the Imperial Japanese Army, to which I owed my fealty through the commission I had taken as a cadet."

The Korean stared pointedly, through obsidian eyes. "The old woman's death had no more moral significance than a whirlwind which destroys a man's children. Do not sorrow for Kang Chul-ho. He honored you with great esteem in the few days he knew you. If he would have had your language, he would have told you that, for he was a man of great passion."

"But he seemed so quiet . . . so . . . gentle."

Choi flicked a hand dismissively. "You saw him only in your world. Koreans dislike to display emotion to foreigners." He hesitated, and added, "That is why you think us brutish."

Robertson let his words sink in and lifted his hands helplessly. "I want to say I'm responsible. We got the patrols because I offended Blackthorne, and I offended Blackthorne because I fought with Sam Dougherty and I fought with Sam because of something I did in Chunchon—" Robertson locked his lips and shut his eyes for several seconds before continuing, "because of something else I did."

Choi shrugged, although the Korean shrug seemed to Robertson to be more related to embarrassment than to indifference. Choi said only, "What is applauded in Seoul will be scorned in Washington; that is something you Americans must realize."

Robertson got up to go. Glancing down at Choi and the machine gun, he said, "I'm sorry I killed Kang."

Some of the Korean's earlier anger returned. "Then sorrow if you wish that, Squad Sergeant. But do not inflict your American guilt on a nation you cannot understand."

Stunned, Robertson drew back, as if from an unexpected flame. Choi Min-soo had struck at the essence of it. Even so, he wanted to possess it on his own terms.

Robertson turned and started up through the trees. The trees had been shredded by artillery fire. They were denuded of the green of summer; like Robertson's first KIA, they dwelt now in perpetual winter. Once Robertson paused and looked back. Choi Min-soo stared morosely along the barrel of the Charley-whacker.

11

INJE RESERVE POSITION, AUGUST 2, 1951

Line time is measured grossly. At the turn of the month, Sam Dougherty stood beside Robertson. Together, they watched the French company's long climb up the ridge to relieve them of the burdens of Hill 874. The Frenchmen were lean and hard and many of them were bearded. Because someone somewhere somehow thought beards attracted trench lice, they were forbidden to the Americans.

The Frenchmen had red sweating faces by the time they reached Robertson and Dougherty. Even so, most of them were full of bows, muttering breathlessly, *"Bonjour, mes amis."*

A huge blond noncom, sleeves rolled up, began to bark French. The language of the orders quickly lapsed into German. Dougherty had served in Germany. "I hear something distinctly guttural there," he noted for Robertson. "Probably *Légion Étrangère.* Werhmacht types from WW the Two, still soldiering. Likely volunteered from Indochina."

The foreign legionnaires were aloof and suspicious. They wore white kepis instead of helmets. Robertson thought this not good. Desultory Chinese mortar fire twice this morning had acknowledged the activity on 874.

Robertson was thinking about Kang as he noted sourly, "If they volunteered out of Indochina to come to Korea, they'll learn about what my grandmother called 'out of the frying pan into the fire.' "

Dougherty watched the Frenchmen for a few moments before saying, "They know what it's like. All those bastards want to do is fight and make babies."

"They'll get half of that on *this* hill," Robertson said.

The Americans' remarks were occasioned by the fact that in support of America, which carried the largest of the non-Korean UN efforts in Korea, thirteen other nations had sent infantrymen. England, Canada, and Turkey sent one or more brigade-sized formations; Australia sent a mix of services—air, navy, and infantry. Thailand and the Philippines sent regiments of tough brown men who carried rifles as long as they were. Ethiopia, Belgium, Colombia, the Netherlands, Greece, and France sent battalions. Tiny Luxembourg managed an infantry company. Other countries furnished ships and airplanes and hospitals, and the folks to man or woman them.

But, as Robertson and Dougherty knew full well, the Americans contributed as ten is to the one.

The relief accomplished, the Americans walked down the hill, taking what they had brought up, less the wastage, less the expenditure. To compensate for what G Company had endured on 874, they did not have to hike far. A column of trucks awaited them not far from the ridge. The men mounted and the trucks clutched. At Hwachon the convoy turned east, along the south shore of the reservoir, then through Yanggu and Chang-ni. At nightfall, the first truck of the column rolled into a flat area of the earth near Inje. None of the men in the trucks, excepting perhaps Captain Hartung or the Transportation Corps officer, had the faintest notion where they had been during the day; only a handful knew where they were now. Inje was desolate rubble.

Lieutenant Blackthorne celebrated their return from the line by insisting that the squad tents be pitched and aligned at once. Later, after inflicting on the exhausted platoon almost two hours of stumbling and fumbling in the darkness, when the tents were up, he called the sergeants aside to remind them that in reserve, he expected a higher standard of military courtesy than they had observed on the line.

Toward the end of Blackthorne's speech, Robertson reached a hand to restrain Sergeant Nelson. Nelson had come through the ranks to command an infantry company in the Pacific, before reverting to enlisted man in 1947.

On the first morning, the post exchange trinkets came, along with Hartung's first beer issue.

Platoon Sergeant Baker brought around the handful of post exchange supplies. Since the army furnished toothpaste, cigarettes, candy, and chewing tobacco, the formal post exchange service provided only a few geegaws, artifacts presumably marketable to young, healthy males. Sometimes, these were greeted by a heady demand. Except for bootlegging and gambling, infantrymen had little use for money; even postage was free.

Luke Plumber, once a logger, kept his bayonet, as he explained, "Douglas-fir sharp." He was granted the honor of cutting the lottery straws. As the others watched, he carved slivers from a plank torn from an ammunition crate.

Plumber deftly slivered seven, the first one much shorter than the others. He had started on the eighth when Robertson caught his eye. When Robertson shook his head, Plumber reddened. His hand hesitated, then he sliced the eighth sliver and put it in his mouth, as if he had intended it for a toothpick all along.

Klineschmidt had been counting. "That isn't enough, Luke. You won't need one, since you hold them, but there's nine—"

Dougherty cleared his throat and Klineschmidt shut up.

As was the custom, the men drew lots for the right to purchase any particular post exchange item. They chortled and encouraged and jeered, laughing for the first time in days.

Robertson drew the short sliver from Plumber's massive hand and won the right to purchase the gold-plated seventeen-jewel Bulova watch for nineteen dollars. He removed his old square-faced Elgin and looked around for some way to dispose of it. He saw Choi.

"Here, Choi. You can have my old watch. I don't need it." He put the watch in the Korean's hand.

The tall Korean stiffened. Before Robertson could figure out this reaction, Fowlkes's angry voice cut in. "You shouldn't give your old watch to a gook, Robbie. You should give it to an American."

Robertson spun. "It's none of your goddamned business, Fowlkes. It's my watch. I can give it to anyone I want to give it to."

Under the hush of the squad, Choi Min-soo reached down and put the Elgin on Fowlkes's cot. He stalked out of the tent. Robertson scowled at Fowlkes and followed.

In the afternoon, Robertson searched out Fowlkes. He found him sitting alone, back against one of the communications jeeps, an open can of beer beside him. Fowlkes's head was down on his knees and Robertson realized he had been crying.

"It's okay, Brax," he said helplessly. "It's just one of these silly quarrels friends have."

Fowlkes offered nothing in reply. Feeling trapped in the aftermath of his own earlier anger, Robertson went away. They were near the Soyang-gang River, although no one knew the name. Robertson went there. He had given his beer to the others.

Choi Min-soo looked up as Robertson approached. Robertson saw that

Choi, too, had come to wash clothing. Choi stood politely, then silently resumed his laundry.

After a while, uncomfortable with the silence, Robertson asked Choi about himself.

"I am a soldier, Squad Sergeant Robertson. After I graduated from the university in Seoul in 1937, my father bought me a fine sword and I attended the academy for officers of the Imperial Japanese Army." Choi paused and smiled for himself, dimpling the skin around his nose. "My father was reluctant to purchase that sword, Squad Sergeant. He said to me, 'If you insist to be a soldier, I wish for you to be a soldier of the nation of Korea.' And I replied, 'Father, there is no meaningful nation of Korea. Japan is the star in the sky of Korea—if I am to rise, I must rise to the star of Japan.' I served Japan, Squad Sergeant, not the proud Tungusic people of Korea." He added matter-of-factly, "I fought the Americans on the island of Okinawa." He smiled. "Does that distress you, Squad Sergeant?"

Robertson shook his head.

Choi went on, gesturing magnanimously, "Politics are as the wind. The wind blows first from the land, then from the sea." He fell silent and sloshed his clothing in the river.

Robertson smiled faintly. "If you had that experience, why aren't you an officer in the Korean army?"

Choi stiffened and looked southwest toward Kwangju, hundreds of miles away. "One's father was identified with the socialists, which so distress your countrymen."

To verify something he was beginning to understand, Robertson said, "You were offended when I gave you my watch, weren't you? You saw it as American charity."

Choi blushed deeply, but did not look up.

Robertson stared a moment, then attended to his own laundry.

After a while, Robertson straightened his back and looked around. Several Koreans had come to the river. One of them, an old woman with wrinkles shooting from her eyes and a black tooth in her mouth, caught his attention and came over. She spoke to Choi, who seemed to listen with impatience.

Choi translated. "This old mother is by profession a washerwoman. She seeks employment with our clothing."

Robertson stepped back and handed the old Korean woman his dripping fatigue jacket. Choi shrugged and gave the woman his laundry.

The woman produced a short smooth club from the folds of her white dress, a stiff garment that ended in a high bodice under a short white jacket. She alternately soaked the clothing in the river and pounded it against a rock with the club. She seemed to Robertson, because her head was so erect and her lips so firm, to drive the dirt out of the cloth by the main force of her will.

Shortly, Choi said in near whisper, "She tells me her name is Soon Ok."

The laundress began to sweat, beads that glistened on her brow while her arms flailed the EUSAK cloth. Suddenly Robertson knew he had seen it before. He remembered as a small boy watching his mother sweat as she worked over the scrubbing board.

"Ask Soon Ok to tell me about herself," he commanded Choi.

"She is but an old washerwoman, Squad Sergeant. She would have no interest for you."

"Ask her. I order it."

"As you wish," Choi muttered.

Choi questioned Soon Ok in sharp and staccato phrases. Soon Ok's answers sounded mellifluous. Once she glanced at Robertson and gave him a timid grin as if something Choi had asked amused her.

Choi summed it up. "She is a resident of Chochiwon—that is far south of here, near Chongju—and her husband was employed by the railway."

"Then why is she here? This is close to the line."

Choi addressed Soon Ok. This time, the woman's smile was sad, showing the blackened tooth.

"She lived in a stone house with a small garden near the railway station. Her husband often entertained gentlemen from the railway there. She has two sons who are now in their manhood."

After a second or two, as if it were beneath him, Choi grunted, "She possessed a bright tapestry of a bird with a long, plumed tail."

"But why is she *here?*" Robertson demanded impatiently. He was beginning to understand the Korean way of rendering ideas, a flood of detail that often postponed the conversational essence.

Choi spoke to Soon Ok sharply. Soon Ok waved her hand in front of her face when she answered. She spoke briefly, looking at Robertson.

Choi translated. "My countrymen of the north came last year and took her husband and sons. She followed them here, but they are gone now. The Americans will not let her continue her quest."

Robertson looked away toward the river.

Soon Ok straightened her back and put her dripping hands on her knees, which were folded under her, as Korean women sit along a river. She narrowed her eyes and spoke again.

"My countrymen of the north executed her neighbor, Mr. Paik Yung, because he would not give them his son."

Robertson shook his head sadly. "Tell Soon Ok I'm very sorry."

Soon Ok folded into neat wet squares the clothing she had washed, smoothing the damp wrinkles as she folded. She stood expectantly.

Robertson gave her an American five-dollar military scrip note and sixty thousand Korean won, about eight dollars and fifty cents.

Soon Ok immediately gave the money to Choi and waved her hand vigorously in front of her mouth. From behind the hand came burp-gun Korean.

Robertson's brow furrowed. "Does she want more money, Choi?"

Choi shook his head. "She wants less. She insists you compensate her too greatly for her laboring."

"Doesn't everyone want more?"

Choi shook his head again.

"Make her take it. And ask her why she wants less."

After some exchange, Soon Ok smiled sadly for Robertson and took the money from Choi's hand.

Choi said, "She will accept, because she fears to offend Americans. She wanted less because she wishes some old washerwoman will help to wash the clothing of her husband and sons."

Robertson choked back some emotion and ordered, "Tell Soon Ok she is beautiful."

Choi blushed and hissed, "One must not say things like that to an old washerwoman, Squad Sergeant."

Robertson stood and bowed, knowing that was a foolish thing for an American to do. He watched Soon Ok's back until she had disappeared up the river. When he sat down again, he lit two cigarettes—it was called the soldier's kiss—and handed one of the Lucky Strikes to Choi. The Korean shrugged and sat down beside Robertson, striking a Buddha pose.

They smoked in silence until Choi said, "I explained to the old woman that you were my military leader. She asked me to beg you not to fight with the"—Choi hesitated, as if the idea was distasteful—"the North Koreans, as her husband and sons are in that force."

Robertson said nothing until he turned to Choi and asked, "Is it hard for *you* to fight against Soon Ok's husband and sons?"

"Hard?"

"Difficult. Is it more difficult for you to fight with the North Koreans?"

Choi spoke after a long silence. "As I explained it before, politics are as the wind."

They finished the cigarettes and sat in silence until the Koreans upriver had vanished.

At last, Robertson sighed heavily and asked, "Tell me about Korean girls, Choi. What are they like?"

Choi's frown revealed his puzzlement. "What does the squad sergeant wish to know? Korean girls are young females who are taught to be Korean women. Little girls often play at games. They chatter and dream of the things of little girls. What else can there be?"

"Not little girls. Older girls."

Choi answered carefully. "Korean maiden girls are meant to marry. Their prayer is to be married to a strong man and serve him and give him children. Is that not true of your American girls?" He smiled wryly. "From your films and magazines I detect that American girls are quite forward."

"Are Korean girls . . . as you say, 'forward'?" Robertson asked quickly.

"Sexually forward? Is that your query?"

Robertson nodded, still not looking into Choi's face.

Choi blushed deeply. "One thinks that a preoccupation of your countrymen, Squad Sergeant. But one hoped it was not true of you."

Robertson blushed then. "It was just a question, Choi," he insisted firmly.

"Of course," Choi said at once. "Merely a question for answer. How does one answer? Korean maidens are instructed to be suspicious of the intentions of foreigners, particularly Americans. We have harsh customs. A maiden girl would be punished severely if she permitted an Occidental soldier to make sexual advances on her."

Robertson took a deep breath, to still his pulse. He caught Choi's eyes and asked, "Translate the word *seikse*."

Choi stared hard before replying. And before he replied, he corrected Robertson's pronunciation, to make the word sound less like "sexy." That done, Choi explained, "The word describes a young maiden, as we have been discussing." The Korean looked suspicious now.

Robertson forced himself to ask, "And a *seikse* is a virgin?"

Choi blushed again. "A *Korean* gentleman would presume that."

Robertson blanched, feeling something writhing in his stomach, something he wished to escape. He heard a birdcall and listened intently, realizing suddenly that the Korean beside him listened also. When the bird stilled, Choi, face expressionless, stood, bowed slightly, and walked away toward the tents of the company.

Robertson watched him go, catching on the breeze the sounds of laughter and quarreling. The tents had been erected on an old riverbed. The tents seemed to sigh dejection, as if G Company had been abandoned there, in an unlovely place, because it had been used up and had no more purpose.

In that somber mood, Robertson lay back with his arms behind his neck and gazed into the sky overhead. Shredded cumulus, with flat bottoms and churning tops, scampered in sun-washed blue. He remembered how often he had lain thus in Kansas. After a bit of study, he realized a new thing. The prairie of Kansas kept its horizon at a distance, this way making large things small, but the corrugations of North Korea pulled in the horizon and made small things large. In this artificial largeness, the cumulus clouds looked sullen and menacing.

Mulling over the meaning of this, alone and undriven for the first time in weeks, Robertson dozed. In his mind, put there by the contrast he just had discovered, rang the word "America" and the word *seikse*. His mind was suspended between a yin and a yang, between the hammer and the anvil of the contradictions he saw in those words.

Now his carefully constructed defenses also slept. Without warning, she leaped into his mind and he saw her again. How many times had she used her word? And the more she spoke it, because it was a Korean word caught without understanding by an American ear, it had only propelled him on.

She had yanked him awake. Sitting up, he closed his eyes tightly and massaged his forehead with angry fingers, wanting to force her out.

12

Patrol to Hyon-ni, August 27, 1951

Sergeant Red Nelson yawned and shook Robertson's foot. "Reveille, Robertson. Get 'em up. Missy Blackthorne volunteered your legs again. To beautiful Hyon-ni, I hear."

It was barely light, but it did no good to curse reveille. Robertson muttered that he was awake and swung his legs over the edge of the cot. He groped for his sweat-soaked boots, calling resignedly, "First Squad go to the head of the chow line. We go out again today."

Another day had begun. At the end of it, assuming he still lived, Robertson would be six dollars and eleven cents richer. Also, he'd be one turn of the sun closer to the last bugle. Little else.

Grumpy men shook awake other grumpy men. Throats hacked phlegm. Cigarettes flared. Outside, urine splattered. The air stank— canvas mold and sour salt—a high summer's day already ruined. The First Squad was booted and armed within seconds. Most had slept clothed.

Because the Second Platoon contained highly experienced soldiers such as Red Nelson and Sam Dougherty, who could explain the news, the others in the platoon were able at Inje to grasp the dimensions of the broader war beyond their immediate horizon.

The platoon had learned that the events they had endured on Hill 874 had been part of a grand master plan. The Eighth Army really hadn't told itself what it was doing, but it had been engaged in the business of drawing blood from the other side, perhaps to probe its willingness to remain in the field, perhaps to pressure it to negotiate harder at Panmunjom, perhaps to tidy the line against future contingency, perhaps just to tweak its nose.

As Dougherty had pointed out just the previous evening, once in firm contact along reasonably linear defense lines, one side inevitably would lean on the other. No less true in 1951 Korea than in 1916 France. The Amerians and ROKs leaned first.

They leaned into a new military reality. The other side had dug, hollowing out entire mountains to shelter themselves against the possibility that someday one of the shiny B-29s spraying contrails above them would open its bomb-bay doors and lay Hiroshima or Nagasaki on their heads.

As the men of the Second Platoon read it, even the army newspaper, *Stars and Stripes*, admitted carefully that there was a fight going on. The ROKs, since it was their country, were sent to lean first. They went up onto a peak they called Taeu-san. This prominence thrust up on the west of the area the Americans had named the Punchbowl, a deep arable valley nature had carved out of the helter-skelter rocks of east central Korea. On American operational maps, Taeu-san was Hill 1179, a tall one. Taeu-san's summit was an inverted bowl, but the finger ridges reaching to its summit were razor sharp and were covered with tall grass and shrubs and hardwood trees.

On Taeu-san, a regiment of North Koreans waited in bombproofs for their countrymen of the south. They sent the ROKs down after exacting the tariff of a thousand men. The Americans went up. Hand-over-hand, they climbed for four days, pushing against a wall of red-hot steel. Aid stations set up on the slopes overflowed. In some places it was a casualty to the yard; in others it was a casualty to the bitter inch. Damn you, gooks! And damn you back.

Suddenly, almost inexplicably, the NKPA gave it up and went down. The Americans stood on the summit of Hill 1179. All around them they could see other forbidding ridges. Not far, under the blue-gray haze of artillery smoke, lazed one which in a few days the Americans would name Bloody Ridge, whatever the Koreans called it.

The First Squad had been lolling near the river while Dougherty explained all this. At the end of it, they turned wordlessly to Choi Min-soo. Surely he must understand.

Choi smiled thoughtfully. Then he lifted a hand to gesture to the northwest and said, "This is now to be a war of statements because no longer can it be a war of maneuver. Our colleagues of the UN are stating they will claim the earth and remain forever."

"What are the go—" The speaker checked himself: both Robertson and Dougherty now punished anyone using the word "gook." "What are the North Koreans saying?"

Choi smiled again, then pursed his lips. "Our associates of the north? My dear late father often reminded me that good rice roots deeply."

It was left that way, with the patrolling, in intellectual limbo. The reality of the patrols had emerged slowly, but even the least-interested saw that the business of the Inje reserve was not to train and to refit, but to hunt. They patrolled constantly, driving the hideaway Koreans around Inje into the net of the unsmiling ROK army. The ROKs threw the civilians onto trucks and hauled them away, so the Americans hoped. Known guerrillas were shot.

And Inje was not all beer and skittles. Many survivors of the 1950 North Korean army, cut off by General MacArthur's breakout at Inchon and his sweep across the peninsula, lived in the wasteland behind the MLR. Frequently, they came out of the mountains with blood in their eyes to snipe away at the UN communications lines, which stretched now to Pusan and Taegu in the south, and to Seoul and Inchon in the west.

The straggler North Korean soldiers were aided and abetted by many South Koreans who did not necessarily subscribe to Western political thought. By day, as America would learn in Asia, they all looked very much like peaceful rustics tilling in the fields. By night, they looked like frothing tigers.

In any event, if things were to go forward properly, nothing could remain in the combat zone except organized armies. And because they were there, the organized armies must tunnel. Because they tunneled, one fellow had to dig the other fellow out.

The Americans had the machines and the diesel fuel. They bulldozed roads and dragged eight-inch artillery and tanks up to the tops of the ridges. They bore-sighted for pinpoint accuracy; they yanked a lanyard and blew things up. "There, you sons a bitches. That's American ingenuity."

The Communists waited until darkness. Then they muscled up 152-mm artillery—even if it crushed men under the wheels—and yanked their own lanyards, stuffing explosive and jagged shrapnel into the throats on the lower ground south of them. "There, honorable Occidental enemies and Korean lapdogs. That is *Asian* ingenuity."

Robertson sparked up his men. "Come on, lads. Move it! Full canteens and basic ammo load. Today we go to Hyon-ni." Robertson caught Solly Zuckerman's friendly stare and smiled affectionately at him, adding, "Wherever the hell that is, good buddy."

For the dozenth time that day, Robertson went ahead of the patrol to reconnoiter. Behind him, the First Squad fell into a half-serious perimeter, rifles primed, but safeties on. After a few vertical feet, Robertson dropped off the scouts, Zuckerman and Klineschmidt, and went up alone. At the top of the slope, out of breath, he scrutinized what was before him. Sweat dripped from his chin onto his map.

Korea here was raging. The brilliant sun bore down on dull grass and weary life. Water in a canteen seemed warmer than the mouth that gulped it. The patrol had begun that morning at a bridge near Hyon-ni, where they had been hauled in two jeeps. The route took them over high wooded ridges and through the grayish shrubs of clefted valleys, in a long circuitous route that eventually would return them to the bridge. By early afternoon, the livid humidity had found the men and steeped them in their own juices. Plumber, who was heavy, and who carried the BAR, puffed out of a red face; sweat dripped from his broad chin. Little was said, or needed saying—this was routine infantry work. They had done nothing else for days, so much of it that the other squads had begun to tease them, calling them "Missy's Commandos."

Now, five hours into the patrol, Robertson saw that his next task would be to lead the weary line of men up onto what the map promised was the final ridge. He came back down from the knoll, pointing up there, saying tiredly, "Let's get it over with."

Of all the patrols G Company had thrown out from the Inje position, Robertson's men had flushed the least game. That was because, under Choi Min-soo's approving eyes, Robertson had not tried to hunt hard.

The climb steepened near the top, and the men had to find handholds to keep from falling. But, as the map the staff captain had given Robertson had predicted, a tan ribbon of gravel rewarded their toil of fifteen minutes up the slope. That constituted the first formal road of the patrol. They walked along for a few hundred yards, enjoying something level.

Robertson halted them. "Take a break. We have almost two hours to kill." The men smiled at each other and sat or lay down in place. All knew—a soldier's time is the army's least valued weapon.

Robertson made them stack rifles and let them drink. He sat against the sheer edge of the dropoff to the valley they just had escaped. His helmet lay upturned on the ground beside him. He pulled up his knees, folded his arms across them, and stared, lost in himself.

The glaring sun made the men drowsy. They watched languidly as Fowlkes and Plumber played Bayonet. The wager was Fowlkes's two cans of C-rations against Plumber's dollar, a wager that vastly favored Fowlkes. The game had simple rules. Two soldiers stood facing each other a few feet apart. In turn, each threw his bayonet at the other's left foot. Each player's object was to stick his bayonet in the ground within a bayonet length of his opponent's foot. If he succeeded, the opponent moved his foot outward to the bayonet. Bayonets were retrieved and thrown again. The contestants' legs spread ever farther apart. The player won who still was on his feet after his opponent no longer could stand. Although less lethal than many other Korean War soldier games, Bayonet did sometimes produce punctured boots and lacerated feet. The precise rules governing this contingency were never set down.

Plumber spraddled on the threshold of victory. Fowlkes, cursing playfully, had his legs spread so far apart that his upper body was parallel to the ground. Plumber got a good throw; the final trump. When Fowlkes tried to reach the bayonet with his left foot, he fell on Robertson, striking Robertson's helmet.

The helmet bounded away, gathering momentum, down the slope.

Initially, Robertson felt the grief that comes when men lose important possessions to accident. But that was immediately replaced by a raging anger. He got up and pushed Fowlkes away. "Goddamn it, Brax! Watch what the hell you're doing."

The squad got to its feet. Heads turned to Fowlkes and Robertson.

Robertson pushed Fowlkes toward the slope. "Go get it," he ordered fiercely.

Fowlkes threw off Robertson's arm. "I ain't going after the son of a bitch, Robbie. You should have had your pot on your head, like a helmet ought to be."

As the men watched, the runaway helmet went all the way to the bottom. It fetched up there, spinning upside down in a clump of tall brown grass. Klineschmidt pointed to it. "See, by the grass there." Zuckerman strained his neck to see.

Carver admonished Fowlkes. "You knocked the sarge's pot galley west, Peckerwood. You go down and get it for him."

"I ain't going to do nothing a nigger tells me," Fowlkes sneered. "Me and Luke got a right to play Bayonet anyplace we want." Carver's face froze as Fowlkes turned to Plumber. "Ain't that right, Luke?"

Carver said nothing. Plumber growled. "No, it ain't, Peckerwood. If you knock a guy's pot down the hill, you ought to go get it for him. A guy who wasn't doing nothing shouldn't have to climb this ridge again. If you knocked my helmet off the hill, I'd smash your butt like a bug."

Fowlkes's eyes appealed to Dougherty, who merely threw up his hands. Zuckerman turned away, as if he wanted to avoid involvement. Klineschmidt spoke for him. "If I was Sergeant Robertson, I'd throw your hillbilly ass down the hill." He looked around for support before adding, nastily, "You want to keep in mind how you came into First Squad."

Fowlkes's face took on the expression of a poleaxed steer. Zuckerman shushed Klineschmidt. No one spoke for a moment. Eyes turned to the Korean. Since the death of Kang, the squad had closed around Choi Min-soo; tacitly he had become the mediator of the American quarrels. Choi Min-soo stepped forward to stand near Fowlkes. "You are obligated to retrieve the squad sergeant's property. You were the cause of the accident."

Fowlkes bared his teeth. "You gooks keep the hell out of it. This here ain't Korean business."

Losing a helmet was not a trifle, even in Korea, where the loss of an M4A3E8 Sherman tank could be written off as battle attrition. Two facts were essential. To begin with, the helmet did not belong to Robertson, but to the quartermaster general of the United States. Secondly, being helmetless in a combat area was a military crime. All the men gaping down into the valley had seen this emphasized by bullet- or shrapnel-perforated helmets stuck on stakes beside the supply roads leading to the line. The fractured helmets sat forlorn and contrite over crudely lettered signs that sang out, "Wear Your Helmet. This Soldier Did."

The first time they had seen such a sign, early in the spring, Fowlkes had observed pointedly for Robertson, "Seems to me that feller would have been better off not to be wearing that thing when the round went through it. Bet you a nickel on payday he's deader'n hell and the generals just use his helmet to scare us."

Choi Min-soo slipped up behind Robertson. He whispered, "You are the commander, Squad Sergeant. Send your clumsy subordinate."

"To hell with it. Let it rot."

Then Carver started down the slope. "I'll get it for you."

Robertson stepped forward to check Carver. "No! I said let the damned thing rot down there."

Carver's face showed his awareness of the impasse. He nodded in the direction of Zuckerman and shouted, "I've got five bucks says I can beat you all to the bottom." He turned and lunged down, headlong, taking huge strides.

The tension broke. Zuckerman whooped gleefully and charged after Carver. Soon they all ran; Robertson and Fowlkes, the former solemn, the latter giggling, brought up the rear.

Carver won easily. He stood grinning, dangling Robertson's helmet by its chinstrap. "See, white boys. Everyone knows we're natural athletes."

They closed in. Fowlkes slapped Carver on the back, then opened his mouth to speak, but froze. The others turned to him.

Slowly, Fowlkes's right arm stiffened behind a pointing finger. Eyes turned to follow.

"Jumping Jehosophy, look in them trees!"

Robertson shouted for them to take cover, but the men only stood helplessly. The rifles and the BAR were back up on the ridge. But, as they stared into the trees, faces relaxed.

Several Koreans were sheltered from the sun in a copse of trees nearby. They stared back mutely at first, but then two of them moved and came slowly toward the Americans. Everyone but Klineschmidt, Choi, Robertson, and Dougherty stepped backward. Klineschmidt got behind Robertson, as if to hide.

The unclouded sun still hung high in the west, glaring down on the earth of Korea, as if to say, "Damn your eyes! All of you."

The two Koreans from the copse shuffled to within about four feet of Robertson and halted. They made sad sounds. "Pop. Gohung. Mizzou. Suk. Mizzou." They begged in two languages, neither of which the Americans understood.

One of the Koreans was tall. His jaw was bound with a spittle-wet, olive green bandage made out of an ammunition bandolier. The man's nose melted into a shapeless discoloration. Slowly, almost fearfully, he cupped his hands together and lifted them, to create an invisible bowl. One hand was thumbless; the other had just a stump for a thumb. The second Korean's face bore huge diseased-looking pustules, giving him the appearance of a seed potato that had been boiled by mistake.

Robertson saw that the tall Korean led his companion by the arm; he realized then the second man was blind.

Choi Min-soo spoke. "They are lepers. They seek food and water of us."

Robertson stared, not knowing immediately what to do. The tall Korean wore a filthy American field jacket, buttoned to the collar, despite the heat. The left shoulder strap had torn away from its button and flopped like a broken chicken wing over the Seventh Division patch sewn there.

Sam Dougherty acted first. He turned in place and snatched off Klineschmidt's helmet. This action caused the leper to turn. Lettered on the back of the jacket, with black laundry marker, were the words "Fuck Doug MacArthur."

Dougherty went to the other men. "Give me all you got," he growled. Klineschmidt's helmet filled with C-ration chocolate and chewing gum, cigarettes and matches, three cans of C-rations, a can opener, and a plug of Fowlkes's Day's Work chewing tobacco. Dougherty made them relinquish the field dressings from the first-aid pouches at their waist. Then he demanded their money. "All of it, men; all of it."

Wordlessly, the soldiers fished out scrip notes and Korean won notes, the latter always in thousand-won denominations.

When the apologetic voices and shrugging shoulders indicated the men had nothing left to give, Dougherty went over to the lepers and dumped the helmet at their feet.

"They seek also water," Choi reminded.

Dougherty smiled a thank you and returned to the squad. "Your canteens. You won't need another drink today."

The canteens also went to the feet of the leper.

Dougherty stood back, arms folded across his chest, a noncommittal expression on his face.

Robertson pulled his eyes away from the lepers in front of him and looked into the trees. He saw that the trees, too, were diseased, with many decayed limbs. Yet, he noticed, the few limbs that flourished cast shadows, not deep, but benevolent, for those who sheltered there. Perhaps the trees, too, were lepers, and had a pity the sun did not. The lepers there simply watched, possessed with their own alien thoughts.

Then it struck him. Robertson realized that a young girl was there. She had been hiding behind the others, but something brought her forward. She dressed much as the washerwoman, Soon Ok, had dressed, in a high-bodiced dress and rubber slippers. Her legs were bare and dirty. She had an angular face, soft and leached, with thin lips. But her eyes were dark and deep and penetrating. Her hair was braided into a single strand. She looked eighteen or so, but she could have been older.

Anyone could have seen she stunned Robertson. It was as if he had been shocked into a recognition, and as if drawn by a rope around his neck, he went to her. At first, under the eyes of the others, he merely stood, beholding her, clearly wary.

He studied her. Instantly, guilt flooded him. He realized he wanted her to be hideous and decayed and blind and corrupted, like the leper men near him. He also realized that was the most unfair wish of his life, but he could no more escape it than he could escape her eyes when she raised them to capture his own.

But he saw she was unblemished, except for a weariness that lived in her eyes, and even that vanished the instant she arced her lips into a thin smile.

With jerky, uncertain motions, he took her hands and formed them into a container. Into that he gave all he had to give that was material, even the new nineteen-dollar Bulova watch. He stepped back and lowered his eyes.

"I'm sorry," he told her quietly. "I'm so terribly sorry."

Then Fowlkes brushed him. Grinning heavily, Fowlkes said loudly, "Bet you ain't ever looked that horny at no American gal, Robbie." The North Carolinian gestured toward a deep shadow east of them. "If you want to fuck her, take her over there into that ravine yonder. Us fellers will wait for you."

Robertson spun and lashed out, "You've got a stupid mouth, Fowlkes."

Obviously stunned, Fowlkes reeled backward. "But you and me is friends. A feller don't dog-snarl a friend."

"Don't count on that, Fowlkes."

Cautiously, the girl backed away. Robertson slumped.

Klineschmidt jabbed Fowlkes on the shoulder and said loudly, "You dumb hillbilly. She has *leprosy*."

Fowlkes stared, through wild, searching eyes. Robertson turned his back.

"Saddle up," Robertson shouted angrily. He stalked away to lead his men back up the slope to the gravel. The men followed meekly. They were self-consciously solicitous of each other. It was as if they wanted to apologize to themselves for something, but did not know how they had offended themselves. On the road again, they put on their weapons and equipment. Robertson marched away swiftly toward the far-distant bridge. No one spoke to Fowlkes. He stood to the last, then brought up the rear by several dozen feet.

At the bridge, shadeless in the orange sun, Dougherty and Robertson sat together. Zuckerman sat near them, off to the side. Robertson pushed his helmet forward to shield his eyes. Zuckerman pushed his also.

Fowlkes had disappeared down the bank where the bridge abutted the edge of the river.

Kraut Klineschmidt, kneeling in the dirt a few feet away, called over to Dougherty, "I'm going to tell Lieutenant Blackthorne you took all my water. And my cigarettes, too. You won't even let a guy smoke."

Plumber's angry voice snaked over. "I'll smash your silly ass like a bug, Kraut."

Robertson lifted his helmet to see. Dougherty had merely looked away. Klineschmidt sat back, more relaxed, as if the BAR man's anger had drained a boil for him.

Robertson nodded tiredly. "Korea. Some of them are seeing it for the first time."

Dougherty picked at the ground with his bayonet. "It was worse when we went north against the refugees last year. Poor bastards . . ." Dougherty seemed to be on the verge of inarticulateness, as a man often is when he relates his worst memories. "Sometimes the North Korean infantrymen got into the refugee columns. Then we had to fire into them. . . ." He fell silent.

Robertson lifted an arm, to point toward where they had left the lepers in the trees. "Are those people better off if we report them to the ROKs?"

"My fellow lepers?" Dougherty pondered the unanswerable, then said only, "You are the patrol leader."

"Then I say negative. We don't report them. They know what they want without Americans deciding it for them."

Dougherty grinned. "What people are we discussing? I saw no people on this patrol."

Zuckerman nodded toward Klineschmidt and the others. Then they nodded. Choi Min-soo smiled toward Robertson.

Robertson turned to Dougherty. "I'd shake Sam Dougherty's hand," he said quietly.

Dougherty's hand went out. "Don Robertson is the best man who'll shake it today."

When Dougherty resumed picking at Korean soil with the point of his bayonet, Zuckerman got out his and began picking also. Nothing more was said, and when the sounds of approaching vehicles came up the road, Robertson stood up.

"It's the coming-for," he announced to no one in particular. "Always it's the coming-for that changes things in the army."

He ordered the men to assemble on the far side of the bridge. Dougherty stood and glanced pointedly down toward the river where Fowlkes had gone.

"He's my casualty," Robertson said sadly, but loudly enough for the others to hear. "I'll go get him."

Fowlkes, red-eyed, lay on the bank of the river and stared morosely into the sky.

"Come on, Brax. The jeeps are coming."

Fowlkes got up onto his knees. Head bowed, he reached his hand until it rested on the toe of Robertson's boot.

"Don't touch my foot like that," Robertson whispered. "You surrender yourself. Don't give up that way."

Fowlkes shuddered, and when Robertson reached down to remove the hand, he grabbed Robertson's wrist.

Fowlkes lifted his face. "Was it just that she was a leper gal? I didn't know she was no leper gal, Robbie. I swear that to you. But it was like she was more to you than to the rest of us fellers."

"It was just the wrong thing to say."

"But we talk like that all the time. Us soldiers talk like that," Fowlkes protested.

"It's just wrong." Robertson stiffened to the realization that the leper girl had been the ghost from Chunchon. How easily she had gotten in where he had promised himself she would not.

He pulled his wrist free and tugged Fowlkes to his feet, facing him. Moisture had cut a thin river in the dust under Fowlkes's right eye.

"And I swear to you, Brax, that you had nothing to do with it." He paused, then, as if speaking to himself, said in a whisper, "I know you don't understand it, but you're innocent of it."

They went up onto the bridge together and stood on a broken creosoted plank near a crude sign that read "Tanks Keep the Hell Off." Under that advice, lettered smaller, was "Courtesy of 318th Engr. Const. Bn."

Fowlkes sniffed loudly and looked around. As Robertson had done earlier, he gestured toward the space and time behind them that contained the lepers. "I shouldn't have said what I said. They was just people gettin' on in spite of things. Like we're all trying to get on."

When Robertson made no comment, Fowlkes added, "I'm like them leper people. I'm dead. I just ain't laid down yet."

The jeeps halted and the others began to find seats. Robertson touched Fowlkes's shoulder, whispering, "You've got to talk to the captain. He'll send you back—"

Fowlkes interrupted vehemently. "That's Section Eight. They'd lock me in a nuthouse. I'd sooner be like them lepers than be locked in a nuthouse."

Lieutenant Maren, the assistant battalion surgeon, wore horn-rim army-issue glasses under cropped sandy hair. Robertson was third on the sick-call list.

Maren sat at a rickety field desk. The tent was cooler, much cooler than it had been beside the river at Hyon-ni the previous afternoon during the patrol. He challenged Robertson with, "You indicated to Sergeant D'Amato that you wanted to talk with me, but that you weren't sick?"

"Yes, sir."

"That's more interesting than my usual reserve run of sniffling noses and suspected venereal infections. What can I do for you, Sergeant?"

After considering carefully, Robertson lifted his eyes and began. "It's about one of my men, sir. I need to know something . . . well . . ." Robertson shrugged helplessly.

The doctor toyed with a pencil a few seconds, then suggested, "Why not just tell me in whatever words come to you?"

Robertson described Fowlkes's behavior, ending with "He doesn't want our commander to know, sir."

Maren smiled. "You guys set a needlessly hard code for yourselves, Sergeant. I know Captain Hartung; he's got a reputation for mothering his men—"

"I *know* Braxton Fowlkes, sir."

"I see."

"Can you help me, sir?"

Sighing so heavily his exhalation whistled in his teeth, Lieutenant Maren began, warming to it as he talked. "I think combat stress has several components. Fear of death and wounding, which is normal in any man, and an anxiety over showing that fear to your friends—as I said, you guys have hard rules. And I think a third anxiety, the fear of paralysis from the other fears."

Maren nodded thoughtfully. "A sane man under enemy fire has an instinct to flee, and a sensible and strong instinct it is. If he can't do that . . . well, sometimes he gets sick. I think that's what you see in the man you describe. Couple all that to the fact that you infantry types function on the ragged edge of malnourishment and exhaustion most of the time, mix in the obsession to survive until the hagglers at Panmunjom come to terms, and the need to perform in spite of that. It is a wonder anyone comes out of it intact." His voice became apologetic. "You'd know more about it than I would."

Shaking his head, Robertson said, "It's never talked about. People . . . well, people handle it different ways."

"People react in different ways," Maren agreed. "Combat fatigue used to be called shell shock, but the medical literature I've seen on it doesn't seem to lay down classical symptoms." Lieutenant Maren opened his hands in protest. "I'm not a psychiatrist, Robertson. And I'm not sure *they* know all that much about it. We know that combat stress overloads the psyche, almost like an electrical circuit—"

"You mentioned paralysis."

"As I said, nothing seems to be paradigmatic in combat neurosis. But

I've read that paralysis is often present. Sometimes a severely anxious soldier surrenders even the ability to take the protective measures available to him. Or else he carries his paralysis of the will into other irrational behaviors such as running toward the enemy or just baring his breast to the fire. I imagine it must be like a nightmare, where we dream we are in great danger but we can't take action to escape."

Robertson responded with a long silence.

Finally, the doctor cleared his throat softly. "Let me treat *you*, Sergeant."

Robertson lifted his eyes, puzzled.

"Take this to your officer and wash your hands of it. You can't carry another man on your back, not when they're shooting at you, too."

When Robertson shook his head, Maren smiled sadly. "There comes a point, Sergeant Robertson, when it is ethical to follow the dictum 'Every man for himself.' Please accept that."

"Thank you for your time, sir." Robertson stood up.

Back at G Company's tent city, the men prepared for the return to the line. Fowlkes showed his other side. Jumpy now, he walked over to Zuckerman. "Solly, do you New York fellers know the difference a-twixt you Yankees and us Johnny Rebs?"

Warily, Zuckerman confessed he didn't know.

Fowlkes chortled in advance and spat a stream of brown juice. "You Yanks just walk up to an old gal and stick it in. Us Rebs stick it in and *then* walk up."

Robertson did not join in the general laughter.

13

NEAR HEARTBREAK RIDGE, AUGUST 31, 1951

Pfc. Solomon Zuckerman crouched behind the out-cropping of rock that formed the western demarcation of the meadow they had just crossed with a leap-and-bound maneuver right out of the basic training manual. With Captain Hartung and Sergeant Robertson, he stared upward through the August haze. He let his eyes glide carefully up to the top of the rounded hill above them, then downward. Zuckerman realized he was embarked on another dicey one. This was the first serious infantry business since the return from reserve.

For the company commander to lead a reconnaissance patrol was novel. Notwithstanding this fact, they had seen nothing. Zuckerman had learned that this was typical when patrolling against longtime residents of any combat position. But he assumed hostile men were somewhere on the hill, or else the captain would not have brought a patrol there.

Zuckerman wiped sweat from his face and breathed deeply, forcing himself to relax. Nearby, the First Squad, less Braxton Fowlkes, had formed themselves into a casual perimeter, focused partly on the ridge about seven hundred yards to their northeast, and partly on the hill above them. Fowlkes's absence today was poignant. There was no denying it. Fowlkes, for some reason unknown to Zuckerman, had been excluded from the patrol by Robertson, as he had been excused from outpost duty the previous night at the turn of the roster. Zuckerman did know that Fowlkes's behavior was erratic and unpredictable. Perhaps Robertson excluded him as a matter of military safety.

Luke Plumber and Sam Dougherty seemed to Zuckerman to be most interested in the distant ridge. Zuckerman assumed that the current threat to military safety lay in that direction.

Pressed into the ground at Zuckerman's feet was the anxious form of John NMI Johnson, NRP, lately of Joplin, Missouri, now in Korea to replace Kang Chul-ho. Still slightly miffed, blaming the replacement for the fact that he had lost the coin toss the previous day, Zuckerman shifted his thoughts to Johnson. Kraut had correctly called Robertson's coin toss to win relief from scouting duty. Zuckerman now shared the onus with Johnson, who was greenest of the green.

Johnson had come in high good humor, freely introducing himself as John NMI Johnson, NRP. Zuckerman understood the meaning of the letters NMI. If a soldier's parents had given him no middle name, the orderly clerks recorded him as NMI—no middle initial—thus triply compensating for the parental oversight.

"What is NRP?" Zuckerman had asked.

"No religious preference," Johnson had answered proudly.

Slightly scandalized at that, Zuckerman asked, "How on earth did you get *that?*"

Johnson screwed up his face. "I dunno. The corporal in the personnel tent at the replacement depot asked what my religious preference was and I just thought about it a minute and answered, 'God.' You don't suppose that pissed him off, do you?"

Zuckerman had shaken his head.

Now, under the hill, Captain Hartung spoke. With a warm smile that included everyone, the commander explained their tactical situation. He gestured first to the ridge mass to the northeast. "He didn't shoot our asses off when we crossed the meadow back there, so we have to assume he doesn't cover the meadow, which is stupid." He gestured toward the hill that rose above them. "We do have to assume he occupies this knob. He's observing us from up there; that's why he can put his goddamned mortar rounds in our mess kits at chowtime." Hartung turned to Robertson. "What do you think?"

Zuckerman watched Robertson's face closely, having learned to read as much into his expression as into his words. After a thoughtful moment, Robertson answered. "That knob sticks up like a sore thumb between the ridges, Captain. If the NKA has an OP up there, and if they didn't read us as an assault party, they may have held fire in the hopes we wouldn't go up."

"But what if we do go up?" Hartung asked, clearly rhetorically.

"We are a small enough force that their OP could handle us."

Hartung, an OCS officer who had graduated from the University of Arkansas in 1942, beamed on Robertson, as he often beamed on all his sergeants. "Very good, Sergeant Robertson. It occurs to me the other guy is making a fool of himself."

"How is that, Captain?"

The men stared at Hartung. The captain had wide-set eyes under a broad brow. He wore his helmet cocked at an angle as sergeants did, not squarely on his head as other officers wore their helmets. He gestured toward the ridge again. "If he had driven us off the meadow with fire, we wouldn't know anything we didn't know when we got out of bed this morning. If his OP cuts hell out of us now, we know he observes us from the knob and we only got fired on once in the process of learning that." Hartung smiled around again. "Pretty good deal for our side."

Zuckerman doubted that. He had long since concluded that being fired on once was enough.

Robertson smiled thinly. "Look at it from his point of view, sir. If we don't go up, we don't know anything and his OP is undetected. If we go up and the OP cuts down on us, he's got as good a target on us coming out as he had going in." Robertson returned Sam Dougherty's grin, adding, "Maybe a better target, sir. Going back across the meadow, we'll be disorganized and running like hell."

Hartung frowned, an expression melting easily into a mischievous grin. "Well, that's good, too, Sergeant. We have days like that in the army."

Hartung resumed his study of the knob. After a few moments, he beckoned for his radioman. Studying his map as he talked, he spoke to the battalion CP. After giving some coordinates, he requested, "I'd like division artillery and anybody else who wants to blow the soot out of his tubes this morning to prepare a mission on that ridge northeast of me. Make it on call—if I have to come down in a hurry—but don't fire it unless I call." Hartung added pointedly, "Artillery ammunition costs money."

Zuckerman had crowded in. "Are they really up there, sir?"

Hartung unslung his carbine. "We are here to determine that, soldier."

Zuckerman glanced nervously at Robertson. The sergeant stepped off first, wordlessly taking the point. Hartung swung off and Zuckerman followed with Johnson, then the squad. Hartung's radioman remained at the outcrop. A few dozen yards up the hill, Hartung and Robertson simultaneously made a down-sweeping motion of the hand, ordering the men to ground.

Ahead, Zuckerman could see fresh earth only poorly camouflaged. He held his breath, wondering what they would do now.

Hartung and Robertson were up on one knee.

"Fire a few rounds in there, Sergeant Robertson," Hartung ordered.

Robertson motioned for the BAR team. When Plumber and Dougherty came up, followed closely by Choi, Robertson said, "Luke, put a couple of rounds on them. Try to graze just over the yellow dirt you can see."

Plumber stood erect, holding the heavy BAR as steadily as another man would hold the much-lighter Garand. The reports reverberated, drawing Zuckerman's heart into his mouth. This was the commitment.

Nothing came back at them. The echos of the BAR died away. Robertson stared at Hartung.

The captain said, "Son of a bitch is going to make us do it the hard way." He started forward alone.

Zuckerman's jaw dropped when he saw Robertson grip the company commander's arm firmly, draw him back, then go ahead himself. That was mutiny, however gentle.

Before Robertson had climbed twenty feet, fire sleeted down from the area of the spoil dirt they had seen. Robertson fired a clip from his M-1, then slid down to stare at Hartung as before.

Hartung scowled. "Touchy bastards, aren't they? But trigger-happy. The Germans would have let us go on up, then they'd have dropped us."

Back at the outcropping, Hartung radioed again. "You boys might as well let the gooks know they've pissed off an old razorback."

Within seconds, artillery and mortar fire began to fall on the ridge to the northeast. Hartung's suppression mission was apparently successful; if they were fired upon as they ran across the meadow, Zuckerman was too scared to realize it.

When they had returned to the company CP, Hartung dismissed them. "Thank you," he said. "Now we know."

After a few paces of the trudge toward the Second Platoon perimeter, Zuckerman felt an urge to turn and look behind him. He met Hartung's eyes. The captain nodded fraternally. Zuckerman's heart warmed. He felt that if he could have one wish, it would be to relate to that rawboned man as Sergeant Robertson related to him. How casually, and how literally, Robertson had risked his life for the captain; how casually each had accepted it.

At the perimeter, John NMI Johnson asked timidly, "Is it always like that, Solly?"

Zuckerman let himself grin with self-assurance. "NMI, some days it's worse. A lookee-Charley patrol is a piece of bagel. I'd . . . I'd expect to see more combat in the barracks on payday night." Then, having spoken Sam Dougherty's lines, Zuckerman spat upon the ground and loosened the cloth around his testicles as the old hands did it.

Johnson paled. His expression indicated doubt.

But Zuckerman felt elated. He had been around long enough to name a replacement. And if the others let Johnson's name stick, he'd have his acceptance at last.

For reasons he never explained to anyone, Robertson had moved Choi Min-soo into his bunker. Long after darkness that night, Choi stared at the hill they had visited in the morning.

"What are you thinking about, Choi?" Robertson asked.

Choi rustled the darkness. "I shall name that hill 'Konsi.' "

Robertson grew thoughtful. The official army numbered hills, the numerals describing the height in meters above sea level. The men who related to the hills gave them names, for mere numbers are cold. Among the dozens, Jane Russell Hill, Tessie, Iron Horse, Baldy, Luke the Gook's Castle, Bloody Ridge. The names, Robertson knew, described what the men saw and felt. Gloster Hill, near the Imjin, would forever speak for the First Battalion, Glouchestershire Regiment. Robertson spoke aloud.

"Brave Brits, the Glosters, they stood six hundred and twenty-two, all ranks, against fifty thousand Chinese for three days. The battalion commander, the sergeant major, and the doctor stayed with the wounded. Probably died there."

Choi asked, "How many Englishmen survived that terrible battle? We Koreans were not told."

Robertson said softly, "Thirty-nine, Choi. Thirty-nine."

They fell silent. To the northwest an artillery duel raged. Robertson listened, knowing a fight pulsed there. Rumors had reached the company of the Second Division's now-two-week-old struggle on a north–south-trending ridge complex not far from Bloody Ridge. This probably was a continuation of the events at Bloody Ridge. At Bloody, Robertson had learned, one company had been decimated three days running, three full turns of replacements. A half-million artillery shells had been fired by the Americans alone. At Bloody Ridge, the Americans also had expended three thousand of the Second Division; the ROKs had spent a thousand. Listening now, Robertson had no doubt he heard a battle building toward those proportions. He wondered vaguely if his regiment would get involved.

But such thoughts violated a rule; better to deal with Korea one day at a time. After a while, Robertson stirred and asked, "What does the name you gave the knob mean, Choi?"

"One fabricated the word, Robbie-san."

"Then it means nothing?"

"It means 'Virgin's Tit.' "

"Why that name?"

"The hill tempts our benevolent officer Hartung."

"I get your meaning." Robertson caught something. "You've named me, too, Choi."

The Korean laughed, as he rarely did. "One sees his inner thoughts have escaped. 'Robbie-san' you shall be."

"Why that name? Everyone else calls me Robbie."

Choi smiled, broadly, which Robertson had learned to interpret as a hint of teasing. "One begs to make bold, Squad Sergeant?"

Robertson nodded. Choi lit two Chesterfields and handed one to Robertson. He explained, "That is a Japanese custom. 'San' is a suffix of affection."

Robertson went to check his outguards. He savored his new nickname. He alone in the squad was a "san," and a Korean had named him. That made up a minuscule fraction for some other things. He thought often of Choi Min-soo. If he offered friendship, Robertson accepted it.

14

AHEAD OF HILL 973, KOREA MAP E-66,
SEPTEMBER 4, 1951

Choi Min-soo had been accurate. Captain Hartung had been seduced by the Virgin's Tit. The fight for Konsi ensued as did so many of the battles that characterized the stalemated war. Small fights, not the stuff of a general's memoirs, they were fought by squads and platoons, led by sergeants and lieutenants, under the galling punishment of the heaviest artillery concentrations the world has ever known.

Already, every feasible air target in North Korea had been bombed to rubble. Yet the enemy resisted, valiantly, asking no quarter and giving none. If the combats now had a clearer rationale, it was the rationale of pride. Large battles were fought for small reasons. Conversely, large reasons were found to justify small battles.

As he was a human, the G Company commander was not exempt from this doleful dialectic.

In many ways, James Arthur Hartung represented a better man than the world credited. A reserve officer, as were twenty thousand other officers in Korea, many of them recalled from unpaid inactive status to reiterate their World War II experience, Hartung had simple goals. He wished to remain in the army until he had served twenty years; then he wanted to return to Arkansas and buy a service station. If possible, he would like to be a major.

Hartung had two moods, a genial one and an angry one, although he exhibited the former far more often than the latter. He cursed habitually when he was angry, but his fits of temper never lasted long.

Hartung instinctively gave more than he took. No one in the company ever recalled seeing him eat, sleep, or eliminate, but they were aware that

149

he thought about these things because he strove continually to make them possible for his subordinates to enjoy, in spite of the grip of the enemy.

His men accorded him an honor few officers earn: they'd not have dared to disobey him, but they genuinely loved him, although they'd never have admitted it. If any one of them had thought about it, he would have realized that Captain Hartung was a very dangerous man. Inactivity bored him, and if he was capable of fear, he concealed it well. In the collective memory of the company was the story about the day Hartung held a North Korean to the ground with his foot and shot him with a pistol. The North Korean had sniped Sergeant Booker to death and had failed to gauge the swiftness of Hartung's personal vengeance.

The day after the Konsi reconnaissance, Hartung took his map, a U.S. Army Corps of Engineers copy of one drawn by the Imperial Japanese Army in 1927, down to the Battalion S-3 and called the hill to the attention of that officer, a maturing captain much like himself. Hartung swept his hand across the map. "If we had 973, we could fire on them and unhinge them here, forcing them back to there. That would take some pressure off the 23rd Infantry on Heartbreak."

S-3's eyes lighted. He swept his own hand. "And here and there. It might help a little."

Hartung straightened. "It's a winner, isn't it?"

S-3 said he'd call it to the attention of Lt. Col. Raymond D. Burton, who commanded the battalion.

Ray Burton called down next morning. "You've got a winner, Jimmy. I'll make some overlays and write an endorsement and send it to regiment."

The regimental S-3 took it to Col. Byron Thompson. The colonel had doubts, but he instructed S-3 to make overlays and addenda, ordered S-2 to gather intelligence, and ordered S-4 to prepare a logistical annex. S-1 was instructed to write a cover letter. S-3 called Ray Burton. "You've got a winner, Ray. The colonel will take it to division."

The division commander, who wore a bright scarf and buckled tanker boots, smiled. "You've got a winner, Byron. I'll send it up to corps to see how the flag flies for it." At division and above, the staff functions are *G*'s, rather than *S*'s. G-3 made new overlays and wrote addenda to the addenda. G-2 and G-4 examined the document and wrote endorsements and recommendations. G-1 had a sergeant write a new cover letter.

The corps commander shared the excitement. He called down to division. "You've got a winner, Harry. I'm going to EUSAK tomorrow. I'll hand-carry it."

The corps officers stamped Konsi "Top Secret" and "Eyes Only."

They added new addenda, suffixes, endorsements, recommendations, and overlays.

The stellar EUSAK officers in Seoul examined it. "Go ahead, General, if you aren't doing anything else." EUSAK did not have to send the documents forward; Konsi had soared to the ultimate heights. Hartung's meager plan to attack the North Koreans on Konsi had become part of the Army Plan of Maneuver.

The corps commander read the EUSAK endorsements with pleasure and took Konsi with him back to his compound, where all the stones were whitewashed and many flags flew in the Korean breeze. At lunch—they had Jell-O salad, split-pea soup, braised calf's liver, and peach halves—he hinted at an operation to come. The press representatives made some notes.

The corps staff generated directives and maneuver plans, with wordy annexes for intelligence and logistics. The thick packet hit the divisional G-3 as he was having his after-dinner brandy and cigar. The division staff worked late into the night, subparting the schematum, adding new directives and plans, annexing wildly.

Colonel Thompson was breakfasting on steak and eggs when his adjutant brought him the documents, now annotated with elegant signature blocks and date-and-time stamps. He counted. The pages had multiplied not arithmetically, as he would have expected, but geometrically. He sighed and handed Konsi to his adjutant. "Send it down to Ray Burton." After a pause, he added, "Better endorse it."

Later in the morning, the colonel growled the opinion that on Normandy he'd have sent a corporal's guard to take the hill and wouldn't have mentioned it in his after-action report. But he was aware of the problem. Congress had discovered the war it had funded for so many months. It had called in some generals and had chewed them out. The word floated across the Pacific to Korea: "Kill the Commie Orientals, but for God's sake don't make any noise and don't get any one killed." Generals now interested themselves in companies, colonels in squads. To engage a platoon was a courageous military act; except in extremity, to commit a company was unthinkable.

Battalion got the Konsi plan at coffee time. Burton discussed it briefly with his elderly sergeant major and ordered, "Endorse it and send the damn thing down to Captain Hartung; maybe he knows what to do with it."

Hartung had been eating a can of C-ration beans and franks when the battalion courier reached him with Konsi. He admired the stamps and signatures, yawned, and scratched his nose. On his yellow legal-sized tablet he had two days earlier drafted his own maneuver plan. It read:

"Blackthorne send up two squads; Brady support." Below that he had scribbled, "Write Old Lady today." He asked his first sergeant to send runners for Blackthorne and Brady.

His briefing was brief. "Lieutenant Brady, we'll position your people to provide weapons' fire on 973, then Lieutenant Blackthorne will go up with his people and do the job."

Blackthorne twisted his West Point class ring. "Why me?"

"You've got Sergeant Robertson and his cutthroats; they've been partway up there."

Then Captain Hartung added his only addendum. "Flamethrower," he said firmly. "Must be one or two in battalion somewhere."

Brady, the heavy-weapons officer, raised his eyes. "Flamethrower, sir?"

"Flamethrower," Captain Hartung answered pleasantly.

The Flamethrower, US, Model 1, was a sixty-pound weapon that shot out a billowing stream of pressurized petroleum mixture, with an effective range of about 70 feet.

. Brady grinned. "I see it, sir. We button them up with fire, then we advance a brave man with the flamethrower to roast the Koreans like a suckling pig at a luau." His eyes widened. "We got any brave men like that in the company, sir?"

Hartung nodded, adding, "But if we shoot them or bayonet them or blow them up with hand grenades, that's okay, too."

All in all, a pleasing plan to go to sleep on and to wake up to.

The plan went—up with respect to terrain elevation, down with respect to military echelon—verbally to the Second Platoon that evening. Despite the fact that the idea was now contained in a dossier the size of the Chicago telephone directory, and despite the fact that the Konsi operation had been studied by a body of men who owned ten stars, fourteen silver eagles, sixteen silver oak leaves, seven gold oak leaves, ninety-two silver or brass bars and included a sergeant major with thirty-two years of service, no one had considered the plan's obvious flaw.

Braxton Bragg Fowlkes detected the flaw at once. He gestured help-lessly toward Konsi. "Them stupid officers should know the North Koreans wouldn't send men up there unless they could support them from their ridge over yonder. They let you up the other day figuring you'd not go up far enough to find out their OP." He spat a brown stream. "It was hidey-seek the other day; now they know we know where their moonshine is hid, and it ain't going to be hidey-seek if we fuck around up there again."

Robertson heard it, but said nothing. He knew Fowlkes was correct.

No one but Fowlkes had mentioned the fact that anyone crossing the meadow at Konsi's feet would be naked to fire from the opposing ridge line. And Konsi had no other door.

NMI Johnson fidgeted in Fowlkes's angry shadow a few moments before asking, "What's up there, Sergeant Robertson? I was too scared the other day to pay much attention."

Although he had been exempted from the patrol, Fowlkes answered for Robertson. "Probably ten old Koreans laughing like hell at us and talking about an old gal one of them diddled in Pyongyang."

The matter was referred to Dougherty and Robertson. Dougherty shrugged, saying quietly, "You don't get your forty-five dollars a month combat pay for playing marbles." Robertson glanced at Konsi, but said nothing.

The outguards were set and the company went to sleep. Konsi brooded over its meadow.

15

THE VIRGIN'S TIT,
SEPTEMBER 19, 1951

To the surprise of no one in the First Squad, they were ordered to lead the Eighth Army's assault on the hill Choi Min-soo had named Konsi. A corporal came from the battalion pioneer platoon with a flamethrower. Solomon Zuckerman kneeled on one knee and listened to the pioneer corporal's ungrammatical instructions on how to use the weapon. Overhead, fracto-stratus clouds rode on the back of an unfelt wind, yellow pink across an infant sun. It was unseasonal, but the air was cold enough to have forced the assaulters into field jackets. To the west, Zuckerman could hear the morning cannonades. He listened a moment, then put the noise out of his mind.

Zuckerman did not smoke, but he accepted a Camel when Dougherty offered it. He forbade his hand to shake as he held it for Dougherty's Zippo. Trying to inhale, as the others did, Zuckerman hacked violently. Surreptitiously discarding the cigarette, he glanced at Robertson. He saw again, around the shrapnel scar, a troubled, yet reassuring face. He pondered the scar. Luke Plumber had told him about the evening Robertson had come back from the aid station with a huge bandage across his face. "Robertson was hit bad, but he came back that same night. Said the damned medics just wrote him up for the Purple Heart and advised us all to keep our heads down," Plumber had said, chuckling as if it were funny, adding, "That was easier to do then; we was all in Third Platoon where we didn't have Missy Blackthorne."

Zuckerman nursed a little guilt because he had, about an hour earlier, eavesdropped on a sharp business conversation between Robertson and the platoon sergeant.

"Find something for Fowlkes to do here in the area," Robertson had demanded of Baker.

"You know I can't do that," Baker said coldly. "If the platoon goes, Peckerwood goes with it."

"You weren't out there, Baker. It's dicey as hell. If the Koreans contest that low ground east of the knob, we'll be hip deep in kimchi from the start line. Even if they are asleep when we cross there, on the knob it will be a frontal assault over open ground."

"So what is that supposed to mean?" Baker replied.

"He's not up to it, that is what it is supposed to mean."

Baker said, "I'm not up to it either, my gut is burning again this morning, but *I'm* going."

The conversation had ended unresolved. When two squads of the Third Platoon came to take over the Second Platoon perimeter, and the First Squad had moved out to the assembly area, a morbid Fowlkes went with them.

The pioneer corporal ended his instructions on flame weapons with a ringing, "Hold your body into this baby, fire the igniter match, and squeeze the trigger. You'll char old Joe Gook's gonads for him."

The squad stood up, brushed off their knees, and turned to face Robertson.

A yellow passerine bird came to perch on a twig of a little bush near Zuckerman, chirping out some morning glee. Zuckerman inched closer, listening to its innocent reveille. He had not before much noticed birds, but he remembered what he once had read: even at Verdun, where the shells buried the dead in layers four thick, the birds came to sing. He reached a hand to touch the twig, but the bird flew away instantly, leaving him alone and hollow.

Robertson evaluated the flamethrower. "You carry it, Luke. You're the biggest of us."

Plumber handed his BAR to Dougherty and grinned. "I'll roast their unneighborly butts like a bug. Teach them to spy on George Company."

The men stepped off behind Lieutenant Blackthorne. The ammunition belts at their waists were full, and they had cloth bandoliers slung across their chests. Pockets bulged with hand grenades. The three rifle squads opened out to increase the mortar interval, leaving each man, like Zuckerman, alone in a piece of hostile space and rushing time. Seen from the small L-19 spotter aircraft that droned overhead at about three thousand feet, they were simply men going to work early in the morning.

They made contact with the left flank of Fox Company, as they had done the day of the reconnaissance to Konsi. Somehow, to Zuckerman, the scruffy Fox soldiers seemed wary of the intruders. Then he remembered Blackthorne's briefing: if the platoon got into serious trouble, Fox Company was poised to commit to the extrication. If Fox Company had to fight, Zuckerman's platoon would be blamed.

The regimental and battalion commanders and some strange officers waited. These officers conferred with the G Company officers while the men stood waiting. When Blackthorne came back, he announced, "We'll go up without preparatory fires—"

"That's fucking stupid, sir," someone protested.

Blackthorne shot a withering glance and went on. "Lieutenant Brady's platoon will come behind us and set up near the outcropping of rock you will see up there. You First Squad men know where that is." He paused and looked around. "Then we go up."

He nodded to Robertson and Robertson strode toward the meadow, saying, "Keep your interval. They'll likely shoot."

Zuckerman understood at once, although he had not doubted it would happen. As he always and so casually did, Robertson would take the point. Again, inside, he felt the glow he so often felt now for Robertson—for all of them.

After several paces, Robertson turned and frowned. "Where the hell is NMI?"

A quavering voice called from behind Zuckerman. "Just lacing my boot, sarge. Be right with you."

"You aren't going to kick them, Johnson. You got to shoot them."

No one laughed. They prodded Johnson to get him up with Robertson and Zuckerman and the file went up onto the meadow. Huge Luke Plumber and the flame weapon brought up the rear of First Squad. Blackthorne and Sergeant Nelson's squad followed. Fowlkes's old Third Squad waited with the officers, a puny reserve against contingency.

The men hunched and tried not to disturb the grass, even though the chilly sun had now fully risen and the sound of a crushed stem would make little difference.

When the point was still about thirty yards from the rocks that shielded the face of Konsi, machine-gun and rifle fire began to scorch the meadow. Zuckerman froze momentarily, thinking insanely that he also could freeze the meters and the microseconds, holding the killing fire in harmless suspension. Seeing that Robertson turned to look, Zuckerman glanced back. The meadow grass seemed to ripple, like rainfall on a quiet pond.

The men behind had inclined their bodies forward, as if they walked in sleet. Blackthorne pointed excitedly to the North Korean ridge before turning to run back off the meadow.

In a corner of his narrowed vision, Zuckerman saw Plumber go down. He fell first to his knees, then leaned forward and rolled; the flamethrower pulsated, as if it were a hump on Plumber's broad back.

Robertson shouted, "Go for the rocks!" Dougherty and Choi Min-soo grabbed Robertson and dragged him forward, although Zuckerman understood that Robertson had intended to go to Plumber.

Nelson's men, far back, had gone to ground. They got up in ones and twos and ran weaving across the meadow to the safety of the jump-off line. Two fell. One got to his feet and ran limping after the others. Three men dragged the second man across the meadow, his arms flailing wildly.

The First Squad was alone at the outcropping, which spat granite shrapnel when the Korean fire pelted it. Many of the rounds ricocheted, whining insanely. Zuckerman pressed his body against the rocks and fought down his stomach while he looked back at Plumber. Surely he was dead; the body twitched as fire picked at it.

Zuckerman put that in the rear of his mind and responded when Carver yanked his arm to take him a few feet up Konsi to cover the slope.

Robertson crouched, studying the meadow. Artillery fire began to pummel the Korean ridge. The L-19 churned the air, weaving and banking, adjusting for the artillerymen. The Fourth Platoon's heavy machine guns began to umbrella the meadow with hot steel. Mortar fire—the frisky pop of 60-mm—began to fall on Konsi, but Zuckerman could see that the rounds impacted far from where they had seen the rifle pit the day they had gone up with Hartung. Zuckerman darted a glance at Carver, seeing a grim black jaw under a helmet. Zuckerman forced himself to take several deep breaths. Surely, he thought, the officers, and there had been so comforting many of them, will come now and get us out.

As Zuckerman had learned, a firefight is an event unto itself, anchored but weakly to antecedents and consequences, a thing with a life of its own. He knew he was trapped, but it was out of his hands. He was thankful for that.

In mortal danger, the clock is a trickster. Events plunged swiftly, even as the long-range small-arms fire plunged onto the outcropping and the meadow below it.

Zuckerman heard Fowlkes shout, "The old hillbilly will fetch Luke's bug-roaster for you, Robbie, and we'll go up and fry their balls like that battalion feller told us."

Robertson returned a loud, "No!" But when Zuckerman twisted around to look, he saw Fowlkes walking slowly across to Plumber's body. Zuckerman held his next inhalation and mouthed his first prayer in years. He gripped his rifle and gritted his teeth. His mind shouted, "Run, Fowlkes, don't walk!"

But Fowlkes walked. The grass around his feet undulated, as if the wind had come to earth, but Fowlkes was not hit. He kneeled over Plumber and turned him, releasing the straps. He took the flamethrower in his arms, as a fireman would carry a sooty child, and walked back, as slowly as before. Robertson ran out a few yards and dragged him roughly. The brown grass writhed again as the North Koreans tried to hit their suddenly increased target. Robertson stumbled before lunging toward the rocks. Fowlkes hugged the flamethrower to his chest and gabbled excitedly.

Zuckerman turned his face away. From the voices in the rocks, he understood that a round had clipped the heel off Robertson's combat boot.

Robertson gave orders and the rest of the squad came up to Carver's improvised defense line, which had consisted only of Carver and the two scouts. "We'll go up as a line of skirmishers," Robertson announced. "We might drive them out and we can use their holes."

Zuckerman got to his feet and kept mindlessly in line with Carver. They lowered their heads and leaned forward as they had done on the meadow. Fire rose up out of the hill above them and drove them back. Robertson encouraged and ordered them up again. This time Dougherty held the BAR at his waist and fired as they ran. When they reached the point of the first advance, the fire from up the hill increased, burning the air, but obviously off to their left and high. Zuckerman sensed that the others, one by one, fell back and found protective ground. He dropped in place; he knew he could not go on. His spirit ached, and he was dead tired.

Nearby, Choi, the Korean, was saying calmly, "We cannot advance, Private Solly. We have done all we can do."

The firing stilled, as if it awaited the decision.

"Back to the rocks," Robertson called. Men began to slither down the hill.

Fowlkes stood erect then, under the heavy flamethrower. He started forward, passing near Zuckerman. Zuckerman sensed his nearness and reached a hand to catch Fowlkes's leg. Fowlkes smiled down. "Let me go. I got to go up there." His eyes were glazed and his lips dribbled brown juice.

Fowlkes walked on. Zuckerman gestured helplessly. Choi Min-soo rushed toward Fowlkes, Robertson and Dougherty following.

A rifle fired twice. Fowlkes halted, as if paralyzed. He stared ahead and did nothing. Before the others reached him, the rifle fired again, a single sound, louder than any that had been fired that morning. Fowlkes stood a moment longer, then sat down wearily. The flamethrower hose dropped to the ground.

Robertson and Choi grabbed Fowlkes's field jacket and began to drag him down the hill. Dougherty stood erect and fired the BAR up the slope, screaming obscenities to the rhythm of his automatic rifle. Several black grenades came through the air and exploded not far from Zuckerman, filling his ears with concussion and his nostrils with dirt. He relaxed his body and let it roll down the hill.

Then the beginning of the events on Konsi ended and the long day began.

At the rocks, Carver formed them into a pathetic perimeter, generally focused on the slope above them. Choi and Robertson removed Fowlkes's trousers. His legs were stark white, thickly covered with black hairs; the legs worked convulsively, folding up, then straightening. Choi forced his wound dressing against Fowlkes's groin, but Zuckerman could see that bright red blood flowed around it, coloring Choi's hand. Choi's head shook slowly, as if he wanted to explain something to Robertson. Robertson only held Fowlkes, as a man might hold a reclining lover.

Zuckerman crawled over and kneeled while he removed his bandoliers and field jacket. He put his jacket over Fowlkes's legs. Robertson looked up and nodded. Zuckerman turned on his knees to face up the hill, wanting to escape what was at his back.

He heard Fowlkes speak, hesitantly and with effort. "Did I do okay for you, Robbie? Didn't old hillbilly fetch Luke's bug-roaster for you and go up that hill like an old grizzled bear with a sore ball? Did I please you, Robbie? Say I did and tell the other fellers I did."

Zuckerman turned to see that Robertson had pressed his cheek against Fowlkes's forehead to whisper something that Zuckerman realized he was not meant to hear. Fowlkes answered weakly, "Hold me. I'm so cold."

Then Choi sat back with the bloody dressing in his hand. The field jacket slipped off Fowlkes's legs. The legs were red-shot, more naked now than before. The boot, which Zuckerman could see, was deadly still. Choi replaced the jacket. He touched Robertson on the shoulder and went to stand where the rock parapet was chest high. He rested his rifle there and stared defiantly at the North Korean ridge.

Zuckerman, jacketless, was also cold. As on the day they had run into the lepers, the sun was pitiless. Where it had punished that day with brutal heat, today, when warmth was needed, it provided none. That was the soldier's sun.

And he became violently angry, more angry than at the loss of Kang or Plumber. It had been unfair to destroy Fowlkes, who had been defenseless.

Zuckerman hoped Robertson would order them up again. He knew he could go. He'd welcome it.

On the meadow where Plumber lay crumpled, a stalemate developed within the broader stalemate. Three times Captain Hartung threw his unblooded riflemen onto the meadow. Three times fire sleeted across from the ridge to the north and drove them back. Fox Company tried to help. The force they sent around to the south of Konsi, not far from the gray slivers that formed the glacis, pulled back, more in awe of the impossible steepness there than in awe of the few aimless rounds that spat down at them.

The sun was higher, sucking up the stratus clouds of dawn. On the artillery line, a 105-mm howitzer failed to respond to the lanyard. The section sergeant cursed and scattered his gunners to the protection of their sandbags. Deciding he would not wait the requisite safety minutes, he cranked the tube down, opened the breech, and went around to the bore end of it with the rammer. The portion of his face nearest the gun was crimson in the light that radiated from the tube. As he worked, he tried not to think about what would happen if he had a cook-off, rather than a simple hang-fire. A flight of four 122-mm counterbattery rounds impacted nearby, buckling him with their concussion. One ear oozing blood, the section sergeant regained his feet. Crazily, he shouted to his loaders, "Catch that baby when she comes out—either that shell is going south or I'm going north with it." He rammed hard. The howitzer gave birth to its dud and the Konsi struggle resumed.

The officers assembled near the meadow that led up to the approach to Konsi. "It'll take them a few minutes to get set up for effective high-angle fire on those rocks," one observed hopefully. Then they all looked at the colonel, standing around him in order of rank. Since Hartung was parent to the problem, he stood closest.

"I've got men up there, Colonel. I've got to do something damned soon."

The colonel stood with folded arms. He smiled paternally at Hartung. "Who is your leadership up there, Jimmy?"

"Sergeant Robertson, if he's still on his feet."

"Steady man?"

"Yes, sir. One of my goddamned best."

"Then they are all right for the moment."

The colonel turned away, brows knit with thought. Hartung badgered, speaking to his back. "You've got the Third Battalion, Colonel. A battalion could lean on that goddamned ridge while I went up and got them out."

Colonel Thompson answered patiently. "You know better than that, Captain."

Several suggestions were offered. All were rejected in the tense air. Hartung stood glaring at Thompson's back.

Finally, the colonel turned. He nodded to Hartung and called to the field-artillery forward observer who stood with the other officers. Gesturing toward the North Korean ridge across the valley, he said, "Tell your people I want a time-on-target concentration on that ridge—every tube that will range it."

"Everything, sir?"

"Everything, and on my call."

"That's a lot of fire, sir. Corps directives require that intra-echelon fire missions be—"

"Don't make me repeat myself, Lieutenant."

"Yes, sir."

A reregistration round burst on the North Korean ridge. This one was white phosphorus; it flowered like a prom carnation, easily seen. The first fall was too far right and short. An airborne FO corrected and the next fall was more to the left and longer, right on the ridge. That done, for miles along the front, the tubes stilled. Fire direction centers coordinated. Azimuths and charges were calculated and the results were sent to the guns—105s, 155s, eight-inchers. Elevations and deflections were cranked in and shells and casings went into the breeches. Then the gunners slowly took slack from the lanyards until they were taut. They waited, eyes on the sergeants who held the telephones.

Back at the meadow, Colonel Thompson said to Captain Hartung, "Make a demonstration up there. Let's see what they do."

Hartung sent Nelson's squad. As soon as the squad exposed itself, the Koreans fired. The Americans went to ground and began crawling back to safety.

Thompson spoke to the FO. "Fire my TOT now. And prepare another."

Time-on-target—the artilleryman's most intricate dance—involved synchronizing the lanyard pulls of many guns, massing fires within space and time in a violence calculated to deliver many rounds simultaneously on the target. Properly achieved—and this required a bit of luck—TOT at the receiving end was a foretaste of hell.

Today the American artillery was lucky. Experienced from near the meadow, it was pregnant silence, then an ominous whirring, then almost a single savage concussion as the rounds exploded along a quarter mile of the North Korean ridge line that had dared to fire on the United States Army.

The ridge erupted into a storm of debris and smoke and fire.

Then silence, like a volcano spent.

When the smoke and dust cleared, the colonel nodded grimly to Captain Hartung. "Another demonstration, Captain."

Nelson went again. This time the denying fire was longer in coming, more hesitant in the buildup and clearly was less determined than minutes earlier. Nelson sent his men to ground and turned to look back. Thompson motioned for him to come back.

Pointing a forefinger at the FO, the colonel ordered, "Fire me another TOT. Better prepare a fourth one."

The devastation was reiterated.

Nelson went back onto the meadow. The North Korean fire was ragged and reluctant. Nelson came back on the colonel's signal.

"Fire it!" Thompson ordered.

Again, the Korean ridge exploded.

"And yet another demonstration, Captain."

This time there was no hostile fire. The colonel motioned for Nelson to return and smiled at Hartung. "Went to school with several Oriental officers at Benning. Eminently sensible men when you communicate with them. We'll wait three minutes and then risk it. Send only a squad or so. More than that might provoke the Koreans into demanding an encore from our cannon-cocking colleagues." Thompson turned to the FO. "Tell your people thank you for some of the finest TOTs I've seen since I left Virginia Military Institute."

When Nelson came back, Hartung told the colonel, "I'll go up now."

Colonel Thompson shook his head. "Thanks, Jimmy, but I believe I had better go. It's my idea."

Red Nelson volunteered at once and all his men gathered around him. The medic Blandings shouldered three stretchers and went to stand with Nelson and his men. Many others offered to go. Hartung thanked them and ordered them to remain.

Thompson went to Nelson. "Understand you commanded a company before you were riffed back to the ranks?"

"Yes, sir. O-3," Sergeant Nelson replied, indicating he had reached the grade of captain.

"Well, among the stupider things the American army does, it savages its loyal reserve officers every time Congress pinches a penny." Stressing the now purely honorary title, for Nelson's reserve commission effectively had been revoked, Thompson said, "If I am wrong, *Captain* Nelson, we are going to have a short day. The North Korean commander may have read me differently than I hope he read me. He may have decided to hold his fire only until we put a force up on that meadow and then trump my ace. You've done more than your share this morning; I'll let you and your men off now if you ask it."

Nelson replied firmly, "No, sir. I'll go. Sergeant Robertson would help me if I had a tit in the wringer."

Thompson smiled. He addressed them all. "Thank you in advance, gentlemen." Then he stepped off.

The NKPA did not fire.

Luke Plumber was dead. Four men put him on a stretcher and came back with him. The others went on.

A military lull, almost expectant in its heaviness, descended over the MLR in that sector. An AT-6 spotter aircraft weaved between the ridges, flying at only a few hundred feet. The pilot had throttled back; nevertheless the Pratt & Whitney engine snarled a threat to the North Koreans that Colonel Thompson expected they would heed.

At the gun lines behind Konsi, loaders hustled ammunition forward to stack it beside the trails. The tubes crinkled as they contracted. Four Sabrejets reported on station. They began a lazy series of three-hundred-and-sixty-degree turns, waiting. Except for the sounds of the air force and the muted, distant sounds of the battle raging on Heartbreak Ridge to the west, the meadow was picnic-peaceful. Waiting.

Choi Min-soo went to stand over Robertson when they saw the approaching men. Then Zuckerman went over. The others in the squad, as silently, went to complete the protective shield around Robertson and Fowlkes.

Understanding it, Robertson whispered to Choi, "I should never have quarreled with Brax. It was"—Robertson dropped his face into Fowlkes's hair again before he completed his idea—"just something he didn't understand. It was a trap that caught both of us."

Choi's face was pained. He said gently, "Your sentiment toward Private Fowlkes has never been at question."

When the medic Blandings reached for Fowlkes, Robertson refused to let him go. "Brax is cold," he explained. "He wants me to hold him."

Blandings hesitated a moment, then lifted the field jacket Zuckerman had placed over Fowlkes's legs. He winced at what he saw, then gently nudged Robertson's jaw out of the way to feel for a pulse in Fowlkes's neck. Nobody breathed until Blandings stood erect.

"He's had it, Robertson. Let me take him."

Robertson resisted. Blandings glanced helplessly at the colonel. Thompson kneeled, saying, "Let your corpsman help you, Sergeant." Then he looked around into the other faces, seizing finally on Zuckerman, who alone was without a jacket. He nodded thoughtfully, then said for the benefit of everyone, "Let's assemble. We need to be getting back down before the North Korean commander changes his mind."

Robertson let Choi and Zuckerman deliver Fowlkes's corpse to Blandings.

On the return trek, Robertson walked beside the litter. Choi followed by several paces, carrying Robertson's helmet and rifle.

The regimental commander interrogated Carver. Carver said at one point, "Fowlkes froze, sir. It was like he was paralyzed. It was like murder; Fowlkes just—"

The men nearest could have heard the colonel's interruption. "We are in a cruel business, Corporal. It's wise not to dwell on our errors."

When they regained the area below the meadow, Thompson said brusquely to the assembled officers, "I want no fire on that meadow. If the North Koreans try to get out, let them go."

They put Fowlkes down near Plumber, on the berm of the raw trail the engineers had cut almost to the Fox Company CP. Soon, an ambulance jeep came and the litters were belted to the racks over the driver's head. The driver was an Oriental. He backed up too far and hung up his jeep. Several men leaped to push him. One snarled nastily, "They should never teach gooks to drive."

Robertson had stood, staring emptily toward Konsi, with his hand resting on Fowlkes. When the jeep began tracting forward, he walked along several paces. Dougherty trotted to check him.

16

SHADOW OF KONSI,
NIGHT OF SEPTEMBER 19–20, 1951

In the early evening, the war there resumed. Artillery and mortars began to duel across the meadow. The battalion companies on line scrubbed night patrols and listening posts. The North Koreans particularly punished the terrain around Fox Company with concentrated mortar fire.

The Fox Company commander telephoned Captain Hartung. "Damn it, Jimmy, you people stir up the Koreans and my outfit catches hell for it. Do your mischief ahead of your own wire from now on."

Hartung could only offer, "What he shoots at you tonight he can't shoot at you tomorrow."

On the rifle perimeter at about 2100 hours, the exchange between Private Dougherty and Second Lieutenant Blackthorne was as sharp as the cannonading.

The Second Platoon rested from the Konsi fight. Those who had not been involved shared in the general morbidity of those who had been. Dougherty and Nelson had been conversing in soft voices when Blackthorne intruded. Choi sat nearby, silently, stone-faced, watching.

"Where is Sergeant Robertson?" Blackthorne demanded. "I want him. And now." The officer folded his arms, adding sarcastically, "I suppose he's off hiding somewhere."

The two enlisted men said nothing at first. Finally, Dougherty answered, "Get off Robertson's neck for a few hours, Lieutenant. He's had a rough ride today."

After an offended silence, Blackthorne spoke angrily, "That was a *poor* effort today. You could have taken that position."

Dougherty straightened. "Likely could have if we'd had the leadership of an officer," he answered pointedly, looking knowingly at Nelson as he spoke.

Blackthorne stiffened, but recovered quickly. "Well, where is Sergeant Robertson? Sergeant Baker has gone out and Robertson is to be platoon sergeant." Blackthorne went on to explain that Baker had been evacuated with bleeding ulcers, which Dougherty and Nelson already knew. The lieutenant's tone indicated he approved neither of evacuating nonwounded enlisted men nor of Robertson as platoon sergeant, despite Hartung's insistence on both.

Nelson, who was senior to Robertson, said nothing, as if he understood that Robertson's advancement was both reward and compensation.

"I'll tell Robertson when I see him, Lieutenant," Dougherty said. "In the meantime, be man enough to let him lick his hurts. Fowlkes and Plumber meant a lot to him."

Blackthorne screeched, "Are you belittling an officer's masculinity, Private Dougherty?"

Dougherty advanced until his face was in Blackthorne's, motioning at the same time for Nelson to remove himself beyond hearing range. After Nelson had sidled away, Dougherty said firmly, "We had an officer like you in my company in World War II. One night he was blundering around the perimeter and his own men cut him down." He paused before adding, "It was a moonlit night, Lieutenant, any man could have seen the difference between an American helmet and a Kraut's coal scuttle."

Blackthorne backed up a few steps and hissed, "Is that a threat? I can have you court-martialed for that."

Dougherty smiled in the darkness. "That, Lieutenant, is not a threat. Unless you get off our ass, that is a fucking promise."

Warily, the officer backed up a few more paces and turned to trot down the hill toward the CP.

Then Choi Min-soo drifted up the hill toward the bunker he shared with Robertson.

Robertson was sitting with his head on his knees, bent to his private grief. After listening to the night wind around Konsi for a few moments, the Korean said offhandedly, "My Konsi sorrows. One can feel the hairs of his neck rise when he hears such a thing."

Robertson lifted his head to acknowledge Choi and leaned his back against the crumbling wall of the trench outside the bunker and said abruptly, in a tone heavy as lead, cold as ice water, "I'd like a piper at my funeral, Choi. And six friends to fire three good volleys. Luke and Brax should get that."

Choi made puzzled sounds, finally remarking, "One does not know 'piper.' "

"Bagpipers, Choi. The Brits and the Canadians have them." He elaborated briefly.

"Scotsmen," Choi said, understanding. "The men who wear skirts." Robertson nodded.

Choi busied himself opening a can of franks and beans, which he offered to Robertson.

Robertson shook his head. Choi threw the can downslope, hearing it strike the barbed wire with a dull twang. Turning to Robertson, he asked, "May one touch your person?"

When Robertson nodded, Choi reached until his hand rested on Robertson's wrist. "We humans have frail connections, Robbie-san. A touch of flesh, a few puffs of air . . . beyond those, each of us is alone."

Robertson said, "Braxton Fowlkes always spoke of it as crossing the river. He had a lot of mountain wisdom."

"Very apt, Robbie-san. And pleasing to the ear and heart. Let us remember it together of your comrade." After a moment, Choi added quietly, "It is not good in our situation to dwell upon death. That was a pathetic habit of the Japanese soldiers with whom I served."

For several silent minutes they listened to Konsi's somber dirge, a sound that intruded in the lulls of the mortar fire onto Fox Company's position. To the west of them, the fight that had raged for days still flared in the night, sending back dull echoes. Choi had to order his mind even to hear it, so long had Heartbreak gone on.

Then Robertson spoke in a voice so soft Choi had to strain to hear. "I'm unclean, Choi. I'm flooding with death. Why shouldn't I dwell on it?"

Choi squeezed the wrist under his hand. "One makes bold to observe that you have carried some sorrow for many weeks, Robbie-san, even before the death of my associate Kang. If it relates to death, I must tell you that you are a novice at death. Choi Min-soo is the master."

Robertson looked into Choi's face a moment, searching, then looked away as Choi went on.

"I came to tell you what I have told no man, Robbie-san. Then you may judge both of us." Choi lit two cigarettes, not bothering to shield the flame, and handed one to Robertson.

"On Okinawa in 1945, Robbie-san, I was a captain with the 13th Independent Brigade, under Colonel Tanaka, a haughty Japanese officer.

Only in the final days of the battle there did Colonel Tanaka permit me, a despised Korean, to command soldiers. When the relentless energy of the invading Americans carried to our nostrils the smell of our own defeat, the colonel sent for me.

"The colonel said, 'Our supreme commander, the high person of Lieutenant General Mitsuru Ushijima has told us that General Kuribayashi on Iwo Jima made the detested invaders pay death in the ratio as ten is to one. On Okinawa we will make them die as twenty is to one. You have a fine sword, Captain Choi. I shall give you to command the soldiers of Captain Ikichi, who has committed suicide with his officers. You must with those Japanese soldiers and your less-efficient Koreans make the Americans pay as twenty is to one.'

"What was one to do? I had sworn a blood oath to Japan. I obeyed. The Americans were skillful. They forced me south across the island. I fought every day for almost four weeks; each time your countrymen encircled me, I attacked them and killed many of them in order that my men could escape to fight again." Choi paused thoughtfully. "This does not disturb you, Robbie-san? As I have said, politics are as the wind; then from the land, now from the sea."

"No," Robertson answered. "I understand."

Choi made a little sound and continued, "In my extremity, I began the terrible barter. I traded men for time, ever retreating south. I fought mindlessly, thinking that General Ushijima perhaps saw in the smoke of battle some vision of victory which I did not. Then one day I learned that the general himself had suicided. By then, we had reached the area around Mabuni and Kiyamu. We who had survived found caves there and I decided we would stand in the caves to the end.

"The Americans waited down below to kill us if we came down. We had little food, and it was this aspect of our condition which dictated events." Choi paused before going on, puffing at his cigarette.

"I rationed our rice and barley most stringently. At first, I issued a handful to the man each day. Then it became a handful of grain each second day. Finally, I could issue only a handful each fourth day. My soldiers lost spirit."

Choi shifted to face Robertson more closely. "Then the men reproached me because I had so little for them. Such indiscipline was unheard of in the Japanese army, but I did not punish them. I sent a patrol to steal food. The Americans fired heartily on them and killed them, reminding me they had closed that avenue to us. One evening, the Japanese remaining in my command came to me, Robbie-san, with a request."

"What did they want, Choi?"

"They wished the commander's permission to *seppuku*. Their leader, a corporal who had served me honorably, said, 'I speak only for my countrymen, sir. Not for your Koreans.' "

"What is *seppuku?*"

"Ritual suicide, Robbie-san. It was a custom of the Japanese soldiers, drawn from the samurai's Code of Bushido—the Way of the Warrior—which the Japanese army practiced. Under this concept, in certain circumstances a soldier was required to die by his own hand. Corporal Saito asked permission for his men to perform *setsujoku*, which is the informal suicide to evade capture by the enemy. There also is *teppo-bara*, suicide by gun, and, of course, *ji-jin*."

"What is *ji-jin?*" Robertson asked.

"*Ji-jin* is the *seppuku* of the man who wishes to escape dishonor."

"*Ji-jin*," Robertson repeated, faint awe in his voice. "Go on, Choi. What did you tell Corporal Saito?"

"One lied," Choi replied firmly. "I said, 'Corporal Saito, a great army will come from Japan and destroy your enemies. You must continue to fight with brave spirits and uplifted hearts.' The Japanese admire those foolish sentiments, and I wanted to provide a time for them to reconsider. But I knew they would disobey me."

Robertson interrupted to ask, "Did the Koreans also want to commit suicide?"

"Of course not," Choi retorted. "*Seppuku* is a Japanese idea, one not compatible with the Korean mind, which honors the acceptance of fortune, however cruel. Some of my Koreans tried to go down the cliff, but the Americans killed them."

"Did all the Japanese commit suicide at once?"

Choi sounded annoyed. "No, Robbie-san. One day, Sergeant Han, who had served me so long, reported to me that a Japanese soldier had taken *seppuku*. Sergeant Han's face barely covered his skull then, for we were starving.

" 'Are we to lament the suicider?' Sergeant Han asked me.

" 'That is their custom,' I said. 'Provide the Japanese soldier a burial. Do not lament him.'

" 'The men are too weak to dig,' Sergeant Han protested. 'They have barely strength for their duty as sentries.'

"I became angry at myself and shouted, 'Then do as you will! Do not bring such triviality to your officer!'

"That terrible night my belly awakened me. I smelled the odor of roasting meat. I arose and went naked to the fire near the mouth of the cave.

"Lee Kwang-ku, my senior sergeant, stood before the fire, which played light upon us. I demanded to know, 'Lee Kwang-ku, where did you procure the meat you devour? Have you been able to steal from the Americans?'

"But he did not need to answer my question. 'Try the meat, Captain,' Sergeant Lee begged."

After a long pause in his storytelling, Choi blew out smoke and said, "As a scientist, one saw such a wonderful symmetry. So long as the foolish Japanese insisted on *seppuku*, we Koreans would eat. I mentioned that aspect to Sergeant Han. He remarked upon the irony. 'I remind my officer that Japan has feasted upon Korea for decades.' "

"And then?" Robertson asked softly.

"After several days, the remaining Koreans came to me on the cliff one evening. Lee Kwang-ku, as their senior, spoke for them. 'We wish your permission to surrender to the Americans.'

" 'Of course,' I said at once. 'That is a sensible action at this time.' I gave Sergeant Lee my ring from the university, all the property I had remaining to me except my tattered uniform and the sword my father had given me.

"I watched the surrender from the rocks near our cave. The Americans killed them all. One stuck Lee Kwang-ku in the body with a bayonet. I had known fully the Americans would kill them."

"They had a chance with surrender," Robertson said quickly. "They had no chance in the caves."

Choi did not reply to that. After finishing his cigarette, he said brusquely, "I was not alone then, as you might infer from my narrative. Two Japanese remained—Corporal Saito and Private Ibitsubo. The latter had often cried out at night for his parents. They came to me that evening. 'What do you seek?' I inquired.

"Corporal Saito bowed deeply and replied, 'We confess our shame to our officer. We beg his assistance in *seppuku*, for which we lack the manly courage to act.'

"I commanded that the matter wait until the next sun. In the night they prayed to their gods and the corporal made from his shirt some hachimakis for them. For his own hachimaki, the corporal created a haiku—a small poem, as the Japanese often composed—but it was a clumsy haiku."

"What are hachimakis?" Robertson asked.

"The headbands which the Japanese samurais fixed upon their brows. Once, one is certain, the intent merely was to protect the eyes from the sweat of battle. Now the hachimaki is a symbol of the acceptance of death and the pain it brings."

Robertson nodded in the darkness.

Choi continued. "In the morning, in the new light, I went to them with my sword, which I had honed against the leather of my boot. I had repaired my uniform with the pitiful resources available to me. Corporal Saito seemed quite gay, but Private Ibitsubo was sorrowful and drew me aside. I was impatient with him when he asked, 'Kind Captain, do you not think the Americans might accept the surrender of a single humble man if he went down to them, and permit that humble man to see again the faces of his dear father and mother?' I scoffed. 'Heed the wisdom of your corporal,' I said coldly. 'None of us can survive these terrible events. The surrender action you propose is unthinkable for a Japanese soldier.'

"Private Ibitsubo kissed my hand and apologized for his weakness. He asked to touch the blade of my sword, which I permitted. We then went to the top of the cliff, near some small trees. We listened a few seconds to the chirping of the little brown birds who sought their morning food. I remember that I glanced to the east above the mists and commented to Corporal Saito, 'Your gods have provided you a beautiful red sun, Corporal Saito. That is the very symbol of your homeland.' I commanded them to kneel."

Choi looked through the night for some time. When he resumed, his voice had muted, the words coming slowly, mired in his reluctance. "I had seen beheadings, twice in the Philippines when I was there and once in China when Colonel Tanaka executed a prisoner. But I had a personal horror of the act. I knew the sword would attempt to waver in flight, and that I must discipline my will and hands, which would rebel—"

Robertson interrupted. "Why didn't you refuse them?"

Choi grunted. "Even a common soldier must own his death."

"Go on."

"Since Corporal Saito was the more composed, I selected Private Ibitsubo for my first stroke. Private Ibitsubo flinched at the last instant, but my sword anticipated."

Choi spoke more firmly now, rushing on to finish his account of the events in the caves near Kiyamu. "The birds called again. One curious little bird came to light near us. I said to Corporal Saito, who kneeled at my feet, 'It is done with Private Ibitsubo. Tell me your desire now.' Corporal Saito cried loudly, 'Strike!' "

Choi stiffened in the coils of his own recollections and fell silent. Robertson took a deep breath. "I'm sorry, Choi, it must have been horrible for you."

Choi said harshly, with a tinge of regret in his voice, "There, you now know Choi Min-soo is a master of death. You also know his horrible crime.

The corporal was the last of the one hundred and seven men Colonel Tanaka had entrusted to me."

"Where is the crime? The Japanese wanted to die."

Choi Min-so hissed, a kind of "ahso." He explained, "My crime was not in *that* I beheaded them, but in *why* I beheaded them, Robbie-san. With Corporal Saito, because I was so weak from hunger and had spent one hard blow, I was required to strike twice. My first blow merely wounded him and made him cry out with pain, screaming at me, 'No! No! Please, Captain, no!' " After a long pause, Choi added, "Even immersed in his screams, I struck a second blow as eagerly as I had struck the first."

Robertson tried to interrupt, but Choi said quickly, "Then I destroyed the fine sword my father had given me when I became a cadet at the Japanese academy. I was pleased then that my father had died in 1943. I would never have to account."

Choi ended, "Private Ibitsubo's query regarding the willingness of the Americans to accept the surrender of a single enemy was quite insightful. I waited until their flag ceremony that evening, knowing they would be in good humor at their release from duty, and went down. One American slapped my face and a second pulled my hair, but that was only to be expected. I had long resisted them."

"I still don't see the crime, Choi. I just don't understand."

Choi edged closer, until his nose brushed Robertson's. He whispered, "You *must* see, Robbie-san. On the cliff above Kiyamu under my sword died the last two men on earth who could reveal that proud Choi Min-soo had crouched naked to eat the flesh of his own pitiful soldiers."

Robertson buried his head again. Choi stared away and said nothing more.

At last, Robertson straightened and turned to Choi. "You mentioned *ji-jin*. Explain that to me."

"*Ji-jin* is the suicide of dishonor." The Korean shrugged helplessly. "My conception of *ji-jin* is perhaps more Korean than Japanese—"

"Explain it," Robertson demanded.

Choi inhaled sharply, then exhaled slowly. "As I conceive it, the dishonored soldier must *force* the enemy to kill him. He must go forward to it freely and in good humor. In effect, he must say, 'Here, enemy, my hated self has defected to you; join it in destroying me.' " Choi shook his head slowly. "It is an idea alien to the Western mind; even a Korean has difficulty with such a concept."

"But that is just suicide by another name," Robertson commented.

Choi challenged at once. "No. One disagrees, Robbie-san. As an answer to dishonor, mere suicide is a coward's act. If he commits suicide by his own hand, the suicider is a man in full retreat from his own shame. In the case of *ji-jin*, the thrust is forward—" Choi gestured broadly, as if lecturing, and added forcefully, "In *ji-jin*, by a positive act, the dishonored man *ransoms* his shame with his greatest possession." Choi fell silent.

Robertson nodded thoughtfully. "And there is his redemption," he said softly.

The mortar fire that earlier had plunged into the Fox Company area now shifted right, from the North Korean gunners' point of view, to fall onto the George Company perimeter. For several minutes the ridge around Robertson and Choi was an outrage of dull flame and dusty explosions. Neither flinched, nor acknowledged the fire.

Then the mortaring lifted, as if everything had been said.

Robertson gripped Choi's arm fiercely. "Make me a hachimaki, as you said Cpl. Saito made a hachimaki, and write me a haiku for it."

Choi blanched. "No! You cannot ask that of me!"

But Robertson's glare had a core of steel. "Who else could I ask, Choi?"

17

Near Hwachon-chosuji, North Korea, October 7, 1951

Choi knew he no longer could procrastinate over the hachimaki. He gazed at the darkness around him, then flicked his eyes north before pulling his thoughts in.

Although few of the Americans ever told him anything, Choi understood better than all of them where they were and why they were there. Relative to Choi, the blazing fight, now twenty-four days old, which the Americans called Heartbreak, had moved. From Konsi, the fight had been in the west; now, since the company had moved to this position near the reservoir, it was in the north. Much closer.

Choi's principal informants were in the Korean Service Corps. These were his countrymen who carried the UN matériel up the ridges on A-frame packs buckled to sturdy backs. The KSC bearers were older men, hence exempt from the stringent conscription regulations of the Republic of Korea. Choi knew the Americans regarded these men no differently than they regarded their many trucks. Perhaps, Choi mused, the Americans thought the KSC rested between labors in a motor pool, hoods up, awaiting new American trip tickets. But Choi knew better. Many of the KSC had served in the Imperial Japanese Army. Many of them understood the events of autumn in both military and political contexts.

The elderly gentleman from whom Choi had bought the cloth for the hachimaki he had been commanded to create had spoken very well. The gentleman had been reluctant to accept the seven dollars Choi insisted he accept.

"That is far too much to pay for a piece of linen cloth," he had argued.

"Not at all," Choi had asserted. "The value of a thing is relative to its purpose. One would pay more, but this money is all one possesses at this time."

The old gentleman had smiled sadly. "It is but a cloth we removed from the pocket of a dead American officer whom we carried. I think the Americans use such trivial cloths to evacuate mucus. I shall give you the cloth."

Choi had held up a denying hand, wanting to hear no more of it.

As he had tucked away the material for Robertson's hachimaki, the old gentleman had inquired, "As one who lives intimately with the *migooks*, does the gentleman Min-soo speculate upon their motives?"

"What opinion does one wish?"

Then they had discussed the fact that the Americans might stalemate on Heartbreak Ridge, then accept terms from the Chinese and North Koreans and sail away, leaving Korea divided as before.

"This battle will convince them," the KSC noted.

The Korean bearer then impugned the Americans, bringing a sharp retort from Choi. "The Americans *are* political children," he said angrily, knowing it was rude to rebuke an elder. "But one must recognize their courage and energy. Also are *they* not instructing us Orientals that we do not monopolize the world's courage? I fought Americans on Okinawa. They are valiant and skillful in battle, as our countryman Kim Il-sung is discovering."

And the rebuke had offended. The old gentleman stiffened and slitted his eyes. Choi had blushed and bowed away.

Now, stationed in the listening post, Choi reflected vaguely that "Heartbreak" translated poorly into Tungusic Korean, and made no sense at all there. Reality was a river words could never capture.

Next to Choi, Zuckerman stirred to complain that he was cold. Choi grunted sympathetically and sniffed the night. The air suggested subtly that the biting winter of North Korea was at the door. He did not mention it. One could not change weather; one could but endure it.

Choi had learned to address his companion as "Solly," knowing that as a diminutive of his given name, which was biblical. Of all the English he had read, Choi liked most the archaic cadences of the King James Bible. Notwithstanding, he regarded the document itself as the repository of primitive superstition.

In his mind, Choi's fingers drummed.

Zuckerman settled down again and soon became still. Choi smiled. The Americans said "good buddy."

Choi placed Solly second only to Robertson among the Americans. And, excepting those two, and perhaps Dougherty, Choi regarded Americans as a vastly inferior race, given to scatology and strange eating habits, crude in manner, vulgar in culture, ignorant to a fault.

As he understood them, they had come to Korea armored in their own superiority to correct the political situation of a nation older than their own god. This amused, rather than angered, although it did anger that so many of the Americans regarded him and his countrymen as barbaric subhumans. The Tungusic Koreans, a people who had invented movable type and the phonetic alphabet, who had devised the suspension bridge and astronomical instruments to fix the stars in their courses, and the compass and the armored ship. Barbarians? Ha!

To correct Korean politics . . . not one in a thousand of them could explain his own political system. Choi could not fathom why a nation with so many fine schools and so many fine books permitted its children to grow up in such slothful ignorance. Perhaps it was genetic.

The hole embracing Choi and Solly functioned as a listening post. They had come there shortly after darkness descended onto the hills of Korea, erasing the false warmth of the sun, bringing down with it the crisp bitter stillness that can be understood only by anxious men who sat out the dark hours in the embrace of frigid rocks, numb ears cocked against stalking enemies.

The two soldiers had with them three flares and four fragmentation hand grenades, two rifles, one hundred and fifty-three rounds of ball ammunition, and a sound-powered telephone that linked them to the wired and mined world behind them. Sentinels on listening posts are human barbed wire, breathing land mines. They cannot stay, but they can impede and warn.

Zuckerman had offered to take the first watch.

"No," Choi had said pleasantly. "One is not pressed with sleep. One would be pleased if his comrade took the first rest of this night."

Zuckerman had settled in his sleeping bag, drawing the zipper carefully only to the waist, as Robertson and company policy demanded. To bag fully was to invite comfort; comfort would induce deep sleep; and deep sleep could mean death at the hands of enemy patrols. Many sentries in Korea were found in the morning bayoneted to death in sleeping bags.

Zuckerman did not doze at once. He fidgeted for several minutes, then whispered to Choi, "Is something bothering you? You seem sort of distracted."

Choi smiled disarmingly. "You are kind to ask that, my dear young friend, but one hastens to reassure you to the contrary."

Soon Zuckerman slept trench sleep. There is no greater form of human trust than that of a soldier who has slept on a forward listening post in Korea while his friend watched over their lives. They will remember that to the last. With love.

Choi smiled paternally on Zuckerman and slowly zipped his sleeping bag fully closed. He looked around and sniffed the wind. Sound would carry north that night, and the next day would be warmer. The rhythm of nature never changed.

Choi put his rifle down carefully with the operating handle up. He gauged the sky and decided he would have a peaceful sentinel. His countrymen of the north, perhaps the world's most superior night soldiers, would shun a golden autumn moon.

It seemed hours later when, yielding to an impulse that had been driving at him, Choi touched Zuckerman, letting his hand rest on him, lifting and falling with Zuckerman's vitality. Zuckerman awakened, whispering, "What is it? Do you hear something?"

Choi sighed aloud. "One regrets to awaken a sleeping comrade, but one seeks information."

"Sure," Zuckerman said agreeably. "What do you want to know?"

"Koreans consider it rude to discuss a third party, Corporal Solly, but I will make bold to inquire of you regarding Sergeant Robertson."

Zuckerman hesitated, then said, "I don't know much about him myself, Choi. Sometimes I think about him. I don't think I've ever met anyone before I admired so much. He's one of the old-line interwar regulars—lifers—they came into the army to get out of the rain. He's a gutsy guy, kind of Asiatic."

"Asiatic? But he is a Caucasian, as white a Caucasian as Private Kraut."

Zuckerman sat more erect and cleared his throat. "Maybe that's a stupid term. All we mean by it is that someone acts . . . well . . . different than Americans normally act."

Choi chewed on that information. He turned the idea of "Asiatic" in his mind. He was Asiatic, yet he did not act differently than other men acted. Then he saw it clearly. "Asiatic" must mean in context "aberrant," with a strong suggestion that the aberration was unnatural because it was infected with the culture of the Orient. Interesting, and insulting, as the Americans were so often unconsciously insulting.

He sighed. How easily he could escape them. He was here only because his records in the ROK army had been lost in battle and his countrymen, officially, had forgotten he had been dispatched to the Americans. The KATUSA program had been abolished months ago— as unworkable.

Choi put that aside and let his mind gambol. He dredged up old scenes that came always with new meanings.

Reminding himself that Solly was now assistant squad leader, hence a figure of, at the least, petty authority, Choi nudged him deferentially.

"Corporal Solly, one asks, why do Americans suicide?"

Zuckerman sat bolt upright. "God, Choi! That is a strange question." He hesitated. "You *can't* be still thinking about Sergeant Robertson?"

"Can you respond to my question?" Choi demanded.

Zuckerman fidgeted before getting out an answer. "People get depressed over things. When the depression gets so bad they don't want to live with it any longer, they blow their brains out or jump off the bridge. Is it any different with Koreans?"

"Not at all," Choi hastened to say. "But it is a cultural matter. What in your culture makes Americans yield to self-destruction?"

"I don't know."

Choi realized that Zuckerman was uncomfortable. But he waited. Finally, Zuckerman offered, "Different things depress different people. I get depressed sometimes over how my father treats me, but I don't intend to blow my brains out about it. He'd disapprove of that, too."

Taking a deep breath, Choi asked softly, "What depresses Sergeant Robertson?"

"Choi!"

"Please answer. You must know. I have watched you become the very shadow of Sergeant Robertson."

"Well, I *have* thought about it, maybe. But whatever it is, it's his private business. In the American army, whatever the other guy has in his footlocker is none of your concern."

Choi discounted Zuckerman's disclaimer. He knew the Americans loved to gossip about each other, even their closest friends. He sighed again. Perhaps he should not speculate upon the motives of a man who asked this favor.

Zuckerman thumped Choi's leg. "My turn, Choi," he said sleepily. "And you're wrong about Sergeant Robertson. He's solid."

Choi brought his thoughts home and turned to his companion. "One is not sleepy, Corporal Solly. I would be honored to continue our sentinel."

Zuckerman settled into his own warmth again and Choi stared at the orange moon. Zuckerman slept longer than an hour. When he awoke again, he asked, "What are you thinking about, Choi?"

Choi smiled. "One was thinking of an event of his life."

"There is a lot of time for that out here," Zuckerman agreed. "Tell me what it was."

"Are you familiar with chrysanthemums?" Choi asked.

"Naw. I don't think so. My mom raised flowers in our window box, but I didn't know the names of any of them."

Choi nodded, then said, "Once, in the autumn of the year the Americans released me from the prison on Okinawa and returned me to Korea, as I sat on the porch of the house of my late father, an early snow came, huge flakes on a warm wind. Snows are pleasant in my region and my mother came to watch with me. She had grown old in the years I had been away, but not until that moment did I realize her age. She said to me, 'The snow is so lovely; you must let it mask now the things which torture you.' "

He added, after a moment of private silence, "I kissed my mother's lips then, Corporal Solly. In all my life I had kissed only two women on the lips. Then I went to stand by the river. Soon, as my mother had promised, the snow covered the earth. There was a mist above the river, and it welcomed the snow, as if to say to it, 'Come, together we will soften the world of Choi Min-soo.' That was the loveliest snow of my life."

Zuckerman started to speak, but Choi gripped him firmly, demanding silence.

"When I returned up the snow-blanketed path to my late father's house, something caught my eye. A single white chrysanthemum—they are an autumn flower—in my mother's tiny garden thrust up from the snow. I ran to it, for its beauty compelled. The snow cradled it, even as the mist cradled the snow. Lovely, Corporal Solly, but I knew the snow would kill." Choi added softly, "Nature gives nothing without price. It was as if what the snow had given me, it would rob from the chrysanthemum."

When he fell silent, Zuckerman prodded. "What happened then, Choi?"

Choi stared blankly for several moments before he responded. Then he spoke softly, almost a murmur, as if he were a man speaking only to himself. "I could not accept the thought that the chrysanthemum would linger in that icy embrace until it had surrendered all its radiance. I plucked the chrysanthemum so that its death would be clean and swift." Choi sighed. "During the horrible events of the Pacific War with America, a Japanese kamikaze pilot wrote: Like the cherry blossom from the branch, let us fall clean and radiant."

"Gee, Choi, that's kind of sad."

"Thank you for sharing my sentiments, comrade Solly. Now I must tell you that I took the blossom to the river. The wind had turned. No longer was it the warm wind that had brought the snow; now the wind was cold and hard."

Choi fell silent and Zuckerman demanded: "What did you do with the chrysanthemum at the river?"

Staring east, toward the promised dawn, toward his own mists, Choi responded, "You will think me foolish, but I kissed the brow of that flower. Then I threw it aloft so that the wind could take it to the river. I sensed the chrysanthemum needed to begin a journey."

"I don't think you are foolish, Choi, but where did the chrysanthemum need to go?"

Choi shrugged. "Perhaps to Okinawa." He sighed. "The current was bold, and crossed to the far bank not far from where I stood. I saw no more of the chrysanthemum, except in my foolish heart, perhaps."

The stars had moved across the sky and dawn was a thin pink line, ordering the sentinels and the outguards of the outpost line of the war to evacuate those dangerous holes and return to safer holes. Zuckerman unzipped the sleeping bag to permit the cold air to wake him up. He stared long at Choi. At last he spoke. "Where is the chrysanthemum for you now?"

Choi lifted his eyes. "Perhaps the river cheated the sea of the chrysanthemum, Corporal Solly. But, notwithstanding, neither the snow nor the wind nor the river could defraud it of the radiance it had in the garden." He thrust his face into Zuckerman's. "Radiance cannot be destroyed."

Then, so quickly it almost staggered him, Choi had the haiku Robertson had demanded. It came whole and in Japanese, which is the true language of haiku. Choi resisted an urge to translate it immediately. Better, he decided, that it remain in Japanese until he presented it.

Across the valley, the enemy fired a long, sustained burst of small arms. Choi muttered angrily, for they had profaned his beauty, "You fools. You think you do that to disconcert any possible dawn attack. You only reveal your vulnerability." He frowned at himself before adding, scolding in Korean, "My associate, Solly, will think you Asiatic."

The firing had fully awakened Zuckerman. He snorted out of his sleeping bag, shivering at the change from warm night to cold dawn. "Give me the sound power."

Choi handed Zuckerman the telephone. Zuckerman whistled into it to alert his auditor.

"George Seven. Nothing happened and we're coming in now. Any chance of a hot breakfast?"

Sergeant Carver, who had been put in charge of the squad as Robertson put up SFC chevrons and echeloned up to platoon sergeant, told Choi to get some sleep. "Tomorrow," Carver said grimly, "we'll go up onto Heartbreak."

Choi nodded agreeably. He had expected no less.

Dougherty, with whom Choi now lived, had gone back to the CP with a working party. Alone in the bunker, Choi whetted his bayonet against his boot, as once he had whetted his sword. He chewed patiently on a twig he had snatched from an already broken tree. As his saliva softened the cellulose, his tongue separated the lignin fibers. Soon, he had transmuted the twig into a brush.

With his bayonet he carefully severed the threads along the diagonal of the dead officer's handkerchief and cut a three-inch strip from the mother linen. He felt as if he was present in a human birthing, well aware that death begins with the act of birth. He held the strip of linen before his narrowed eyes and saw immediately the essence of the hachimaki. He put it down gently and removed his upper garments, exposing a hairless chest.

Lifting the bayonet, he cut the flesh over his heart. Then he placed the bayonet edge under the incision to collect the blood. The blood pooled and quivered.

Thinking now inescapably in new metaphors, he beheaded a cartridge that he gripped in his teeth with such force that his jaw hurt. He poured the gunpowder into the blood to create ink.

He brushed the haiku he had created during the night sentinel onto the cloth of Robertson's hachimaki.

Except for one hearty exchange of mortar fire, the immediate line was quiet that day. It was as if the inferno on Heartbreak drew all the fuel. Choi slept, but he worked even as he dreamed. He had placed the hachimaki between two slats he had pulled from an ammunition crate, and he slept conscious of the rudeness of the slats under his back. A small discomfort, and it would press the hachimaki.

In the afternoon, he went to Robertson. "One has the thing you requested," he said simply.

They stared at each other until Robertson said, "Let's go somewhere else to talk."

Down at the logs the KSC had piled for reinforcing bunkers, Robertson halted. He sat down and lighted two cigarettes, handing one to Choi. At first nothing was exchanged except the cigarette. Robertson smoked under half-closed eyes. Once the scar under his eye twitched.

Choi cleared his throat softly. "Do you think Asiatics capable of romance, Robbie-san?" he asked quietly, turning his face to get directly at Robertson's reply.

Robertson lifted a hand in protest. "Of course I do. Why wouldn't I think that?"

Choi nodded approvingly. He stared southeast before going on. "When I served on Okinawa for the Japanese, shortly before the Americans came, I met in the village a young Japanese woman. She was lovely. Her name was Kyoko Michishita. Her father was an official of the Japanese administration."

Choi paused and smoked in silence. Then, as if he had never lapsed, he resumed. "One night Kyoko permitted me to touch her cheek and to kiss her lips. We were both very shy, but she laughed gaily when I told her that was as the Europeans did. The next evening I put on my best uniform and went to her father, as custom required."

Robertson had looked up, but Choi held out a hand to check him. "Her father was a haughty Japanese, much like Colonel Tanaka. He scoffed at me because I was a lowly Korean and drove me from his house."

Robertson reflected on it before answering. "Six years have gone by," he said. "Maybe it would be different if you went back."

Choi's face had become a mask. He said, "That would be to no avail, Robbie-san. Almost the first naval gunfire of the Okinawa invasion destroyed Kyoko's house."

"I'm sorry, Choi."

Choi's eyes closed. "I tell you of Kyoko because you are at this moment linked with her in my thoughts." With that, Choi placed the hachimaki in Robertson's hand.

Robertson unfolded it and placed it across his knees.

Choi pointed to the first of the characters. "You must infer the verb. Is that not permitted in English?"

"Yes."

"And be aware that your haiku has the requisite number of syllables in the Japanese language, but lamentably it lacks that constraint in translation."

"You are teasing me," Robertson said.

Choi shivered. "One is not teasing. But one sees he tears the fragile petals from a chrysanthemum."

"Translate, Choi."

Tracing the formal characters—he had employed the squarish characters of the *katakana*—Choi translated:

Alone in the cold embrace,
A chrysanthemum in the snow.

18

HEARTBREAK RIDGE,
OCTOBER 9, 1951

The earth shook under him. Impressions flew in at him, striking his mind with freight-train force, then, before he could grasp them, ricocheting away to merge with the shrapnel whine. Dust and smoke, fire and noise, a fury so implacable a human brain could not relate to it. Zuckerman struggled with himself, feeling that a great machine had made him naked and timeless and had dragged him here to grovel helplessly before a firestorm that hated him.

Because the air was heavy, concussions seemed to cling to the face of the earth and roll down on them, as if the North Koreans on the peak above had been able to forge the very atmosphere into a weapon. He had been told that the Second Division gunners already had fired a quarter of a million rounds onto this long ridge—double that to include the North Korean fire. One man—was it hours or seconds earlier?—had buckled. Throwing down his rifle, he had run screaming down the spine, as mindlessly headlong in retreat as the assault was in advance. That must have been one of Sergeant Nelson's replacements, for it was Nelson's calm, patient voice that had acknowledged it with a firm "Steady. Steady now. Steady" addressed to everyone and to no one.

Nelson's admonition helped. Zuckerman decided to build on it and his eyes sought out Robertson, who was down on one knee only a few feet away. Zuckerman focused on the platoon sergeant's upper lip. He had learned to read that lip. Sweat there adumbrated danger. And today it sweated, although out of the mouth under it the words came as businesslike as they were when Robertson gave orders to clean up the tent, or when he announced who had guard duty.

Several anonymous holes had been shot into the platoon, but they were defilade to the fight there. Zuckerman understood that they waited. The discussion between Robertson and Lieutenant Correlli clearly had to do with whether or not they should request an uphill shift in the fall line—the ragged zone of American artillery bursts that had moved up the hill with them.

Robertson was opposed. "It's the devil you know versus the devil you don't," he shouted at Correlli. "We've got a hard climb on up from here. Lift the suppression fires and let them out of their holes and it could get damned interesting."

Correlli shouted back something, but Zuckerman did not hear it. The lieutenant did not beckon for his radioman: apparently Robertson's view had prevailed.

Zuckerman didn't know whether he approved of that. He doubted anything could pave the platoon's way to the top. The North Koreans had honeycombed the hill with deep entrenchments. A few minutes earlier, on the way to this point, he and Johnson had stared into a cavelike fortification that was now a jumble of logs and dirt, and into the face of a dead Asian who greeted them with a rictus smile. The death smile had seemed so earnest Zuckerman was sure he had returned it. Johnson had drawn back, gasping profanity. On that, Zuckerman had blurted, "If the dead ones bother you, NMI, you're in for a hell of a ride with the live ones." The moment he said that, he felt cheapened by his own mouth. Those were Sam Dougherty's words: no one else deserved to speak them.

Robertson was shouting, "Red, when we move out, you take your squad and go with Lieutenant Correlli. I'll take the other two rifle squads up with me."

Realizing he was helplessly included under the rubric "the other two rifle squads," Zuckerman took a deep breath and shut out the future. Robertson got up and moved out of his view and his eyes sought out Dougherty. With Dougherty the necessary message was in the eyes— slitted, wary, searching, weighing. Watching that now, Zuckerman fielded a train of ideas, irrational to be sure, but no more irrational than the environment itself.

Why not just refuse the invitation? If Sam or Robertson would lead him, he could go back down the spine and tell whoever had ordered him up here, very politely, "No, thank you, sir. I can't participate today. Please try me some other time."

Or why not do what Nelson's man had done? He could yield to the panic that gnawed at him and panic would give him wings to fly away. He'd be punished, but he'd survive.

More nobly, why not just surrender to the fire? With Robertson or

Dougherty nearby, he thought he could do that. Perhaps it would be as it had been for Fowlkes, except for the convulsions of the stark white legs, so calm, so effortless, so innocent. Perhaps he would go cold with shock and Robertson would hold him as Robertson had held Fowlkes. That had been an awesome moment, washed with an unspeakable tenderness. Zuckerman was certain it could be reexperienced. This thought comforted, but it was insane, and Zuckerman knew it. He shook it out of his head. Reality was here, in the writhing morning, in the crushing concussions, and in the dangerous climb ahead of them.

But before he let it go, Zuckerman mouthed the infantryman's prayer. "Lord, if you've decided to hit me, please hit me with a little one."

Second Platoon, less its weapons squad, under Lieutenant Correlli, a dark quiet officer who had come in to replace Blackthorne when Blackthorne went to battalion staff to escape what rumor claimed was an assassination threat, cringed in a depression on the flank of the lofty mass the press now called Heartbreak Ridge. The ridge, almost seven miles long, tended in a north–south direction, somewhat perpendicular to Bloody Ridge. It pointed toward the North Korean supply base at Mundung-ni, farther to the north.

As the American Ninth Infantry had gone up onto Bloody Ridge earlier to decimate or be decimated, the American 23rd had attacked Heartbreak twenty-six days before. The latter fight had gone no better than the former. Only a few days ago, Captain Montfort's company had climbed up through a wall of automatic weapons and artillery fire, taking their objective at nightfall. Montfort had counted his survivors and had placed them to meet the inevitable counterattack. All night, heating their tubes crimson, the American artillerymen had ringed Montfort with protective fires. But the Koreans had attacked through it. In the morning, another assault force found Montfort's men crumpled on the slopes. Montfort sprawled in death across a dry machine gun. Not a single round of ammunition remained in the command.

That had been the story of Heartbreak. Intact companies started up, the thirty or forty survivors who succeeded clung to the roof of the world by their fingernails until other companies could get thirty or forty survivors up to relieve them.

Robertson and Correlli could not be heard above the roaring, but Zuckerman saw them gesture and shake their heads, stare blankly at each other, then gesture again. Excited instructions frequently crackled out of the radio on the back of the timid little runner near the lieutenant.

The company was in deep trouble. The majority of Captain Hartung's command was pinned down on their left, held to ground under a galling fire from the spire above them. The noise of this came obliquely across the ridge. Zuckerman could sense the building and fading of fire. The buildups would correlate with each upward surge of the company. The fadings would signal the company had gone again to ground. Zuckerman had also learned to interpret the magnitude of fire. This particular fire suggested that at least a company of North Koreans stood above them.

Second Platoon was isolated. Nothing but a radio signal could cross the fire-swept ridge between it and Captain Hartung. The only options, as Zuckerman had learned in this vertical war, were up or down.

Robertson slid back down to close the few feet that had separated them. After speaking a few words to Choi Min-soo, he stood erect and discarded his helmet. Then, as Zuckerman watched, he put on his brow a white headband with Oriental writing on it. The act seemed strange, in that context, but Zuckerman sensed that Choi understood the meaning of it. The Korean's face revealed both alarm and acceptance.

Zuckerman's mind flew back to Choi's interrogation at the listening post. He grasped the fact that Robertson's headband was meaningful, but he could not interpret it. He shook his head. He did not want those thoughts now. Without Robertson, he would perish there, as surely as the hazy sun had risen.

Despite their situation, Robertson seemed in good humor. He flicked a grin toward Zuckerman and sidled over to stand near Teasman and Catlin, greenest of the green.

Zuckerman was shocked to realize that he was joking with them. "I'll stroll up with you," he told them. "And I'll give you the G Company wisdom: Charley can kill you, and he can skin you and he can boil you in his pot. But, by God, he has bad teeth. If you are a tough enough son of a bitch, Charley can't eat you."

Correlli's radio spat out a stiff: "Second Platoon. Jump!"

Robertson's next words stabbed Zuckerman in the stomach, whirling all other thoughts out of his head. "We'd better fix bayonets. They won't give us the hill without a close fight."

Bayonets rattled onto rifles. Zuckerman took several deep breaths. He unsnapped the ammunition pouches on his web belt and gripped his Garand. Keep eyes on Robertson and Correlli now. Try not to think at all. Have no past and no future. In a few minutes it will be over, one way or the other.

As if he had been aware that Zuckerman was looking at him, Lieutenant Correlli nodded pleasantly, although distantly.

Suddenly an eerie calmness came to Zuckerman. In the wake of that, he had the most irrational thought of the day. He realized that were Lieutenant Correlli to say to him, "Your father would disapprove if he knew you were here, Solomon Zuckerman from the Bronx, consequently we will excuse you," Solomon Zuckerman would have pleaded to remain.

On the wings of that thought, Zuckerman tensed his leg muscles. He tested the point of his bayonet with his finger. He knew he could go.

Robertson and Correlli stepped off, walking near each other for a few feet. Then the lieutenant and Nelson's squad peeled off and started laterally across the sharp crest of the spine. Now that they were up out of the depression, rifle and automatic-weapons fire began to seek them out. The rounds rattled like hailstones. Like men walking in hail, they inclined their heads. Men began to scream, but Zuckerman locked his lips. He had seen the climb that confronted him: he knew he'd need his wind.

Someone stepped on Zuckerman's heel, making him stumble and almost fall. The man who had unwittingly tripped him apologized. Just as crazily, Zuckerman heard his own mouth saying, "It's all right—I walk on it myself."

After several dozen yards, the assault halted. Several men went to ground. A new sensation came. Zuckerman remembered from basic training when he had worked in the target butts of the firing range, listening to the crack and whistle of the rounds that came from the firing line. He recalled his thoughts of that afternoon, how he wondered what it would be like to be aboveground and plod into it. Now, he knew.

Robertson, his face aflame with exertion under the white headband, turned to break loose his attack. "You'll die here on the slope," he shouted angrily. "Better to die on the hill up there."

The men got up and began to move again, heads inclined as before. Fire came in sheets, like the first rain of a storm.

Blinders came onto Zuckerman's eyes and he went forward with the familiar narrowed vision. He was aware when the slope widened, because the assault fanned out into a more pronounced line. He was aware when the final shelving of the top came; he could lift his feet again without pain.

The final awarenesses came when they closed the top. Zuckerman had the fleeting sensation that they had dangerous animals at bay. He loaded and fired, walking forward, conscious of it when empty clips twanged out of his rifle. Each time he reloaded, he was a few feet closer. The screaming continued, enraged and mindless now, venting all that had been pent up. Zuckerman joined in. He sensed it would help: it would be more difficult for the Koreans to kill men who screamed. Even animals knew that.

The machine had become animate, taking on a life of its own. Nothing could have stopped it then. The violent closure was inevitable. Zuckerman quit looking; he merely fired and walked on.

Between clips, something in brown reared up out of the earth and lunged at him. Zuckerman instinctively braced for it, right leg ahead, left leg flexed behind him, rifle butt held against his left hip, right arm locked to hold the bayonet forward at the proper angle. He shut his eyes.

The impact was hard, then yielding, then hard again. He locked up his left leg and it held him. Flesh brushed against his and he smelled garlic and sweat. Dougherty screamed at him, "Duck your head, Solly!"

When he ducked, he felt a whistling above his head. Dougherty's rifle butt caught the Korean squarely in the face. Then the bayonet was free. Some bile tried to get out and Zuckerman choked it back. Just as the assaulters who had come up behind him closed and swept him along, Zuckerman dared a furtive glimpse at the dead man. Arms out, he lay on his back. Dougherty's rifle butt had crushed his face, leaving his nose askew. He was either young or old, tall or short. Zuckerman looked away from him.

It was over. Beside him, Dougherty shouted excitedly, "Nobody in the squad down, Solly, and we got their fucking hill. Robbie pulled it off. Never lifted the fire."

Dougherty vanished, and although a quarter of a hundred men milled around him, Zuckerman was alone. The spire, Hill 936, was taller than the surrounding peaks and a breeze came across it. In his evaporating sweat, Zuckerman began to shiver.

Carver gave orders and the squad went into position facing downslope. Fire laced up at them, but it was random and passed overhead. Then Klineschmidt pointed. "They're down in that ravine! Christ, the lieutenant and Sergeant Nelson will be coming that way."

Zuckerman turned to see that Robertson was there. Zuckerman would have sworn to it, Robertson was disappointed. His face carried an expression Zuckerman had seen in high-stakes dice games on payday, when the shooter stared morosely at craps, in disbelief that his luck had been that bad.

Downslope, heavy firing broke out.

The Koreans in the ravine below 936 waited until Lieutenant Correlli and Nelson's squad were only about a hundred feet away. Then they volleyed and threw hand grenades. The Americans went down as if scythed.

Red Nelson worked his face in the shale until he could see ahead of him. He could see nothing in the mouth of the ravine except shadow. Beside him, Correlli was speaking. "Just like that," he said disgustedly. "Just like that the sonsabitching bastards shot my ear off. My ear, Sergeant Nelson. They just shot the damned thing off. How bad does it look? Will I be deformed and ugly?"

New fire from the ravine sleeted over them and Nelson had to wait before he could examine the ear. He saw then that it hung down from Correlli's head, dangling from a bloody ribbon. He winced, but said aloud, "You'll be all right, Lieutenant. I've seen men hit worse and still not look all that bad."

"Thank you, Sergeant." Correlli's mouth worked convulsively for several seconds before he managed a strained, "You're sure about what you said? I think a man would look funny with only one ear."

Nelson squeezed his arm. "Sure I'm sure. They'll sew it back on for you and you'll never know it happened."

The fire came again, then slackened. Nelson squirmed around until he could see behind him. Three of his squad lay crumpled. The other four had faces turned away from him, staring behind themselves, obviously hoping for rescue.

Exhausted, Nelson began to sort the problem out. It would be his. The ravine was not a natural defensive position for the Koreans. They'd fight out of it. From sounds on the ridge above him, he realized Robertson had gotten up. If Robertson had gotten up, the Koreans were dislodged and the way was open for Hartung to come up. Extrapolating from that, Nelson understood that the North Koreans had erred. They were caught now with G Company at their backs and what was left of his own squad at their throats. They had trapped themselves in the ravine as surely as if Hartung had planned it that way.

Correlli must have worked it out also. He brushed at his severed ear, as if to flick away a mosquito bite. He spat out some blood and croaked, "Why the hell are they fighting, Sergeant Nelson? They're beaten."

Before Nelson could answer, the ravine exploded again. He could sense steel only inches from his head. "They're fighting because we're fighting. We've got them trapped." Nelson found himself grinning. "And the shitty part about it, Lieutenant, is that they also have us trapped."

Seconds later, the Koreans boiled out of the earth, brown flashes behind the fire they put down ahead of them. Nelson rose up onto his knees and threw his two hand grenades; he fired his rifle dry, then fell back. When he reached the bodies of his squad, he was able to turn one man over and take a bandolier. Heedless now, he reloaded and fired, sitting back on his rump as if he were on the five-hundred-yard firing range. Two of his squad had come up behind to join him. Dazed, they drove the Koreans back into the ravine. One of the joiners, Tercell, picked up a rock and threw it at the Koreans. Nelson saw that Tercell's back had been torn open.

Lieutenant Correlli was dead, his face turned so that the ear rested on his neck. Nelson reached and pulled it free, putting it into his pocket. Suddenly Tercell collapsed. He spoke, plaintive but not whining, "Red, I can't move my arms and legs. Do you suppose something is wrong with me?"

"Hang in there," Nelson advised softly.

As Nelson surmised they would do, the Koreans had regrouped; they volleyed again. Nelson's remaining rifleman went down. The sergeant was alone.

The Koreans did not emerge from the ravine, but a solitary rifleman began to snipe. Nelson could not see into the ravine well enough to spot him. He listened to several rounds, then ruled that the Korean was a poor marksman. Nelson wryly decided not to expend the effort on him. If he killed him, they might post a better sniper.

The two riflemen who had joined him were either unconscious or dead. Nelson collected their rifles and waited, eyes never far from the mouth of the ravine. Suddenly exhausted, he pressed against Correlli's body, using it as comfort more than as shield.

Nelson glanced at the sky, finding it blue and peaceful, dotted with autumn cumulus. He studied the cratered ridges, so shorn of life they were like a moonscape. A neutral moonscape, he decided, despite the muted battle sounds around him. As good a place as any, and it had to be somewhere.

Nelson lectured himself. Soon, one way or the other, it would be over; then he could rest. As for the work? Whatever the tactical significance of fifteen or twenty Koreans trapped in a ravine, it was his tactical significance. Whatever had brought him there, he was there. They had destroyed his squad and they would answer for it. He smiled at that; nine years a soldier, once all the way to captain, then to sergeant, and finally pissed off at the other side.

Three or four minutes passed. From the sounds, Nelson knew for certain that Hartung was securely on the hill. That in mind, he continued to stare into the ravine, waiting. They'd come out, or they'd be driven out. He'd fire until they were on him, then he'd club with his rifle. They'd pay.

Robertson watched Nelson's fight and came to Nelson's conclusions. When the firing dwindled to the single sniper, he formed his own picture. Nelson's squad had drawn the purse string; the Koreans were trying to keep them at bay. On that, he walked wordlessly to Dougherty and took the BAR from his hands.

"I'll go with you," Dougherty offered at once.

"Stay," Robertson said. "It'll either be a cakewalk or a hornet's nest. One more man won't make any difference, either to the cake or to the hornets."

Choi Min-soo reached for Robertson's arm. Robertson shook it off and started down toward the ravine.

Two days later, the atmosphere at the G Company command post was formal.

Capt. James Hartung handed First Sergeant Manston the paper on which he had been writing. "See anything that needs to be changed?"

While Manston read, Hartung wearily stretched his back. His company, forty-three men fewer than two days earlier, still held the spine they had captured. The first night's counterattack had been robust, but was repulsed after about twenty minutes of blind night fight organized and orchestrated by Robertson. The North Korean attempt of last night had been halfhearted. Still, the NKA had drawn blood, destroying the First Platoon's weapons squad.

Hartung had pulled the truncated First Platoon back behind the ridge as a reserve. Robertson, now acting platoon leader, held on the spine with the three intact squads of the Second Platoon, spread thinly, as was the Third Platoon that held an elevated position about seven hundred yards up the ridge.

The telephone rang. "For you, sir."

Hartung thought about the field phone; his commo men had strung the wire rearward almost a mile. With a telephone installed, the army was business as usual.

Lt. Col. Ray Burton told him word had come up that the 72nd Tank Battalion, after lethal days of running along the Mundung-ni Valley, had reached a point several thousand yards north of Mundung-ni. Both sides now accepted that the North Korean stranglehold on Heartbreak Ridge was broken.

Hartung noted, "It's over then. How bad are we hurt?"

"Still digging our corpses out of the caves and bunkers, Jimmy, but I'm getting a figure of about fifty-five hundred."

Hartung gave out a weary whistle.

The battalion commander went on. "EUSAK and Department of the Army are mad as hell about it. Congress is screaming."

"Can't the head sheds get it?" Hartung demanded fiercely. "They refuse to let the Eighth Army fight with both hands. We send piecemeal units to duke it out on a mountain with some top-drawer Oriental infantry in artillery fire thicker than fleas on a junkyard dog. God, Colonel, can't have been fights like Heartbreak since Grant and Johnston slugged it out at Shiloh."

"What would *you* do, Captain?" Burton retorted.

Hartung snorted. "I'd damned well go back home to Arkansas and see if the catfish are biting."

After chuckling sourly, Burton said, "A soldier salutes and obeys. What do you need?"

"A platoon and a half of tough replacements, Colonel, and a long rest for my people. How many replacements is Kim Il-sung going to need?"

"Counting his losses on Bloody Ridge, about thirty-five thousand."

"Well, we stung them. Did it do any good?"

"They're back at the negotiating table with fright in their Machiavellian eyes. Maybe we've made our point."

"What was our point?" Hartung demanded.

Burton seemed offended that the wisdom of the field-grade intellect had not been manifest at the company level. "Damn, Captain, it's simple enough. We showed them the American army can muster men who can swallow their worst fire and still kill them seven to one. Should make them think about something."

Hartung growled, "If it had been left to me, I'd just have sent them that information in a registered letter." Before the battalion commander could react to that, Hartung added, "I'm sending down a Silver Star recommendation for SFC Robertson. I also want him promoted to master sergeant."

"I hear he's a good one," Burton observed. "Why not give him a battlefield commission? The sergeant major says he has completed a couple of years of correspondence college."

"I don't want to lose him," Hartung said quickly. "If they commission him, they'll take him out of here. They'd never let him officer where he had been an enlisted man."

"Maybe, maybe not. If you'd like, I'll take it to the regimental commander. Colonel Thompson has a way of tempering army policy with good sense."

"I'd like, sir, but don't get him taken away from me. With Lieutenant Correlli dead, I need Robertson for platoon leader."

The line was silent for several seconds. Then the battalion commander cleared his throat pointedly. "Do you want Roger Blackthorne back? That would give you a platoon leader and it would also help erase a mark against you."

"A goddamn mark against *me?* I'd think it would be a mark against Lieutenant Blackthorne. I sent him down to be your supply officer to get him the hell out of my company and thus keep his scalp on his head for him." Hartung hesitated before adding bitterly, "If there is to be a negative comment on my own efficiency report, I think it should be for letting him blunder around in a line company as long as I did, not for sending him out."

"Who threatened him, Jimmy? I heard of a few cases of threatened officer assassination in World War II, but none in Korea before this."

Hartung laughed harshly. "The official view in the company, Colonel Burton, is that Lieutenant Blackthorne was not threatened. As I see it, a young officer was merely getting wise advice from a very experienced combat soldier. That soldier's name, incidentally, I have totally forgotten. I'd like to leave it at that, but if Lieutenant Blackthorne insists on pressing it officially, I'll lay out his entire record up here."

"His father is very senior in the army," Burton warned.

"And I'm very senior in this company, Colonel. When Roger Blackthorne gets the picture of what combat leadership is all about, give him a fresh start somewhere."

"Well, it's over then, Jimmy, all of it. We're all sadder but wiser. I'll work up your replacement request and get it off to regiment." After a silence, Burton added softly, "You know, Captain, there may be no reunions of Korean War outfits. We've been replaced so many times over, we're strangers to each other."

"We get acquainted quickly," Hartung said as softly.

Burton hung up. Hartung stared at the telephone receiver in his hand and sighed heavily. He doubted the Korean War would offer another fight of the magnitude of Heartbreak Ridge, but he also knew the final pattern had been set there. Now it would be march up the hill, then march down the hill, for both sides. Lieutenant Correlli's ear, which had been found on Sergeant Nelson's body, said it all.

Hartung turned his attention to his first sergeant.

Manston handed him the document they had drafted. "You end 'intrepid' with a 'd,' not a 't.' "

"Well, goddamn it, change it. What the hell are first sergeants for?"

When Manston made the correction, Hartung took the paper and read what they had written:

Recommendation for Award of Silver Star: On the afternoon of 9

October 1951, during offensive action near Mundung-ni, North Korea, Sergeant First Class Donald A. Robertson led against fierce resistance an assault that succeeded in forcing the enemy from a commanding position that had blocked the advance of his company. On the objective, seeing that the platoon leader and a squad of his platoon was under heavy fire, SFC Robertson single-handedly threw himself upon several enemy soldiers entrenched in a ravine to his front, killing four and capturing the remainder. Although SFC Robertson was unable to rescue his platoon officer, it is felt his intrepid action is in the highest tradition of the United States Army. Entered the military service from Kansas.

"I think it should be 'platoon leader and squad *were.*' "

"How about Sergeant Nelson?" Manston asked.

"We don't know what he did. Only Gilmore and Corporal Puller survived it, and they never got as far as the ravine."

"But we know Red Nelson, sir."

"We damned well do know Red Nelson. Make something up and I'll sign it. Ask for the posthumous Silver Star."

"Happy to do that, Captain. Did you know he had five children?"

Hartung choked and turned away. Then, sensing that Manston stared at his back, he turned. "First Sergeant, could I have done better?"

"Man-to-man, sir?"

"You know it is always goddamned man-to-man with me."

Manston drew his shoulders back. "Captain, there isn't a trooper in this company who feels you failed him. They'd walk through hell for you and ask the devil for a light."

Hartung winced.

"That's what I asked them to do day before yesterday."

19

KUMWHA RESERVE POSITION, NOVEMBER 19, 1951

In another context, the three soldiers would have looked down upon as benign a scene as they had been presented in Korea. The mountain hut and the snowscape in which it nestled was a Currier and Ives print, a Vermont postcard, as innocent as a mother's smile.

Small, mud and wattle in the poorest tradition of Korea, the dwelling should have been saying, "Admire me from a distance, but let me alone: I have no part in your loud affairs."

But the hut's forlorn appearance told the Americans something else altogether. The winds had turned. And the new wind brought Korea its winter, its most ferocious tiger, frothing far more viciously than the war's mechanical tigers.

Dougherty, who had survived the winter of 1950–51, Korea's coldest in decades, could have explained what they would experience. The cold would be driven against flesh by the bitter energy of Siberian air, which had replaced the dripping tropical air of the Korean summer. At first, it would be sensed as visceral chill, perhaps a tingling finger or a numbness on an exposed cheek. That could be fought with another layer of cloth, or a second glove drawn over the first. But, later, as the calendar deepened into December and January, all the layers of cloth a man could bear could not conquer it. Then winter would be sensed as perhaps a tomb is sensed, an implacable icy envelopment from which there is no escape. Then it would be time for the surgeon's nippers on too-white toes and the rasp of his saw on frozen bone.

All the extremities of man—feet, hands, ears, noses, weapons, and the human spirit—froze unless carefully protected.

Looking down upon the hut, seeing that it probably had only the one door that now presented itself as merely a dark shadow under the overhang of the roof, Lieutenant Robertson evaluated their prospects. He betrayed his thoughts when he remarked quietly, having gestured toward the thatch of the roof, "I read once that Napoleon's horses had to try to survive on the thatch from the Russian roofs when the Grand Army attacked Russia in 1812. War is hell on good horses."

Sgt. Thomas Carver agreed silently.

Pfc. Sam Dougherty made the verbal reply, noting firmly, "And nobody remembers the lesson. Here we are a century and a half later with snot frozen in our noses still offering to campaign in the Siberian winter."

Robertson nodded thoughtfully and continued his appraisal of the problem before them, namely, the hut, which the regiment had sent them to investigate. The snow between them and the hut was devoid of cover. He'd be risking someone's life in a wager that the hut was really as benign as it appeared. If he erred, fire would burst somewhere out on that innocent whiteness.

He removed a glove and reached to test the snow. It had crackled underfoot when the patrol had left that morning. Now, because the air had relented slightly, the snow had softened. Letting his hand linger, he said to Dougherty, who was on one knee beside him, "Well, Sam, you can cover us from here with the BAR. Then I suppose it'll just be a matter of going down and knocking."

Dougherty shifted. "I'd recommend we scout out the back first, Lieutenant." He grinned and exhaled, making steam. "But I don't want to be telling the regiment's brand-new second lieutenant how to conduct his patrols."

Robertson chuckled softly. Dougherty's remark was his first formal acknowledgment of the brown bars Robertson had put on his collar six days earlier. The ceremony, in the tent of the regimental commander, had been brief. Colonel Thompson and Major Trowner, the adjutant, had been there. Robertson had not at first known why they had sent for him. In fact, he had gone to regimental headquarters with a vague apprehensiveness. To be asked to accept a battlefield commission was not one of the possibilities he had considered.

The colonel had been surprised that Robertson didn't know. He had turned to Trowner. "How on earth did Captain Hartung keep a commissioning secret?"

"There's more to Jimmy Hartung than many realize, sir. He said he wanted to make it a pleasant surprise. I saw no reason not to go along with it. Hartung would make every day Christmas for his men if he could get away with it." The adjutant smiled on Robertson. "Hartung exhausted his nonprofane vocabulary with praise for the sergeant."

Then the colonel had turned to Robertson. "Is it a pleasant surprise for you, Sergeant?"

"It's a surprise, sir, but I can't accept it."

Thompson frowned. "Could you tell us why?"

Fidgeting, Robertson managed, "It's a personal situation, sir."

The colonel nodded. "I'd have to respect that. But before I accept your decision as final, I'd like to try to sell you on it."

Thompson put both hands on his desk and went on. "This thing might not end for months. Until it does end, it's going to be a war fought by platoon leaders. EUSAK might as well pack up all the field-grade officers and send us home. That's how it will be, Robertson. Young officers and noncommissioned officers will have to take green men up against some damned tough opposition and try to keep them alive until the political world comes to its senses again. The NKA doesn't rotate; the fittest have survived. The problem now is to select superlative platoon officers." The colonel glanced sourly at his major. "We can't halt the waste, but we can minimize it with good junior leaders."

"Then why me, sir?" Robertson asked.

Thompson threw back his shoulders and laughed. "Why you? Sergeant, you are a legend in this regiment. Is it fear of responsibility? Can't be that; you're already acting platoon leader. I'm only giving you a grade commensurate with your present responsibility."

Robertson realized he had reddened. He straightened his back and said, "I'm sorry, sir. It's not the responsibility; I'm just not officer material."

The tent was warmed by a potbellied diesel stove. Under his field jacket, Robertson sweated, suddenly wanting to get away from this situation. This tent was for officers, a strange world of formalities Robertson had never permitted himself to trust. But when he lifted his eyes to meet Thompson's, the colonel made no sign of releasing him. Robertson dropped his eyes to the colonel's hand, which drummed on the desk.

The colonel's tone now was that of a lecturer. "Military leadership, Sergeant Robertson, is when one frightened young man persuades six terrified young men to cross a fire-swept field. Your battalion officers tell me you can do that."

When Robertson opened his mouth to speak, the colonel held up a hand to stop him. "Before I continue my recruiting pitch, I want to tell you that what I'm offering has a catch in it."

"A catch, sir?"

Thompson nodded to his adjutant. "Tell him, Major."

Trowner indicated with the sheaf of documents he held in his hand. "You have enough points to rotate at the end of next month. If you're commissioned, EUSAK directives require you to extend your tour an additional six months."

Thompson spoke again. "I know that's more than I have a right to ask, Sergeant Robertson. But I want to add to it that I *need* you." The colonel indicated a pile of letters on his desk. "These are condolence letters; the more men like you I have in charge of my troops, the fewer of them I have to write."

Robertson stiffened, realizing he had to surrender. "You know I can't refuse an appeal like that, sir."

Thompson sighed audibly. "No, I knew you wouldn't and I'm apologizing immediately for having used it on you."

The new oath of office was brief, administered by the colonel himself.

That done, Thompson jerked his head toward the flap of his tent, speaking to the adjutant. "Let me have Lieutenant Robertson for a few minutes of Officers' Candidate School, Major. You get busy and get him a new field jacket; the one he's wearing makes him look like a platoon sergeant."

When the major was gone, Thompson turned to Robertson. "Now I'll tell you about another catch. Your battalion commander insists that I leave you in G Company. That's unusual, and it's asking a lot of a young officer to put him into that situation. If you want another company, I'll override Colonel Burton. . . ."

"No, sir, I'd like to stay in G Company."

Thompson smiled. "You can handle it. Just remember that it's quite a shift in perception for your men to see you walk away a sergeant and come back an officer. Might be hard for you. Now, I've got two rules for my officers, although all don't obey them. First, the order of privilege—follow the old army precept. Feed the horses first, the men second, the sergeants third, and the officers last. Captain Hartung assures me you already know that rule. My second rule is that in my command, an officer is expected to protect his men with his thin khaki shirt. His officer's shirt is all the armor an infantryman has. I think you already understand that rule, too."

Robertson stared and said nothing.

Thompson's jaw firmed. He waved toward the condolence letters he had mentioned earlier. "We have no choice but to grip the other side, and he has no choice but to remain in contact with us. That means attrition, no matter how careful we are."

The colonel stood. Robertson saw him suddenly, as if for the first time. The colonel was short, like a barrel with legs. Close-cropped brown hair, starting to gray, certified his seniority. He wore an infantryman's blue scarf at his neck. Robertson met his eyes, knowing he carried the sobriquet "Battling Byron."

"Accept the attrition and do your crying in private, Lieutenant. Lose more than attrition and you'd better be able to show me a few holes in your shirt."

"I understand, sir."

"And while I'm on that baleful subject, I want to tell you about the one reservation I have. Aren't you afraid of fire?"

"Yes sir," Robertson said slowly. "Everyone is."

When the colonel met Robertson's eyes again, he smiled broadly, "You'll make a fine officer, Lieutenant Robertson. Keep my men alive, and I include you in that group. Your OCS is over. I've done in five minutes what the stone college on the Hudson often can't do in four years. Salute me and get back to your company and get to work."

Robertson saluted, holding the salute an extra moment.

Thompson's return salute snapped. "And remember to make the adjutant get you that field jacket, Lieutenant. Dress well. One of an infantry company second lieutenant's principal functions is to lend elegance to what otherwise would be a vulgar brawl."

Back at the company, which was drinking the welcome beer of its first day in safe reserve in ten weeks, the change from platoon sergeant to second lieutenant made barely a ripple beyond Manston's first careful "sir."

Robertson stared down at the hut again, tested the snow, and weighed it all up a second time. He turned to Sergeant Carver.

"You are our real-estate expert, Tommy. What do you think?"

Carver gestured toward the hut. "They wouldn't have sent an armed patrol unless somebody up the line expected it to be occupied. I'd agree with Sam. We ought to get a look at the back side before we try to cross that open ground between here and there."

Robertson stood up abruptly. "Sam, you take Teasman and Catlin and scout around the back. Keep below the crest and you'll get around unobserved. Tommy, you put a couple of riflemen here. Tell Choi I'll need him to go down with me in case I want to do some explaining to what probably are very peaceful noncombatant Korean peasants."

Carver jerked an arm toward the hut. "They'll be damned cold noncombatant peasants this morning. I don't see smoke coming out anywhere."

As Robertson waited for his orders to take effect, he reviewed his mission. He understood from Hartung that the hut had been found by an observation pilot. He also understood that it was close enough to the MLR, only about six miles, that it would have to be neutralized. Hartung had suggested taking a mortar; Robertson had refused, saying, "Probably just an empty house, Captain. Why blow it up?" Hartung agreed with that wisdom. Robertson took his old squad, ordering them to take a day's rations.

Catlin returned from Dougherty to say the back of the house was as devoid of threat as the front. Choi Min-soo came forward silently and waited.

Robertson smiled and asked, "What's in there, Choi? I don't see any tracks in the snow. The place looks empty to me."

Choi's eyes narrowed in thought. "One associates a dwelling with persons," he said at last. "But we will not ascertain unless we inquire."

"How could anyone live there now that the lines are here?"

Choi shrugged, answering, "My countrymen are resourceful."

Carver posted Zuckerman and Klineschmidt where they could cover the hut with fire. Klineschmidt chortled to a wary Zuckerman, "We'll kill the Charleys in there and eat their rice and fuck their women."

Robertson reflected that Klineschmidt's idea for the hut was as good as any regiment had in mind. For this reason he decided anew that the operation could best be accomplished by simply going down and knocking.

"Well, Choi, bad guys are either in there or they aren't. Want to walk down with me?"

Choi smiled faintly and nodded.

They went down, slipping at first on the snow, but walking quickly once they reached the level ground that led up to the house. As he approached, Robertson flicked his eyes between the door and the window that punctured the wall not far from it. The snow swallowed the sounds of their approach. When they reached the south wall, Choi chambered a round and slid off to stand to the right of the door, rifle barrel laid on a line to focus on the head of any adult who happened to answer the door. Robertson rattled the crude wooden door with a balled fist and stepped to the left.

The man who answered the door was ancient.

Choi spoke in Korean while Robertson studied. The old Korean was small, as wrinkled as a seed potato. His scraggly goatee bobbled as he answered Choi. He wore a black robelike garment, shredded with time, grimed with his condition.

Choi spoke again, easing around to confront the man fully. But the old man watched Robertson, and when Robertson stepped away from the wall, he closed the door partially, blocking the remaining opening with his body.

Seeing that he threatened the old man, Robertson lowered his rifle and backed up several steps. As he did, his nose caught a decadent, crushing odor. He pondered that while Choi and the old man conversed. Choi Min-soo had inclined his torso to a near bow. They talked for several minutes, their voices assuming and dropping nuances incomprehensible to Robertson.

Choi turned and explained blandly, "This gentleman is a hermit. He has lived here alone in these mountains for many years. He is not political and has no interest for us. Perhaps we should not molest him in his house."

Choi had not met Robertson's eyes. Robertson protested, "There's more to it than that, Choi. What are you not telling me?" Choi blushed deeply and looked away.

Robertson went forward until his nose rested a few inches from the hermit's. The hermit widened an eye and stiffened.

The hut moaned. The odor came out again, sandwiched in defeated chill, and Robertson knew now what it was. He thrust his shoulder forward to signal his intention and said to Choi, "Tell him I'm sorry, Choi, but I'm going in, either around him or through him."

Face flushed with alarm, Choi lifted a hand to protest. "No, Robbie-san, that cannot be, one—"

Robertson shouldered aside the hermit and went in. A second man lay beside a firepit. Staring down, Robertson sensed the old hermit at his back.

If anything, the air in the little hut was chillier than the air that played outside over the fresh snow. Robertson got down on one knee to study the new element in his patrol. The prostrate man moaned once more, but his eyes were closed and he breathed shallowly through bloodless, gaping lips. A Korean, Robertson saw, and from his uniform jacket, a North Korean. He was naked below the waist, thrusting into Robertson's awareness an obscene penis and some hair between malnourished legs that had black toes. The legs were motionless, not twitching as Fowlkes's naked legs had twitched on Konsi that day. Someone, Robertson assumed it was the hermit, had put a yellowed dressing on the Korean soldier's left thigh. The dressing oozed blood and pus. Robertson reached. Suddenly he felt a grip on his wrist, feeble, but afire with denial.

Robertson turned his head to meet the angry face of the hermit.

They stared, in a contest of wills, until the hermit yielded with a quick bob of the goatee.

"Tell him I have to look, Choi."

Choi spoke hesitantly. Warily, the hermit released Robertson's wrist and kneeled; his angry eye relaxed into simple anxiety. Choi kneeled also, hovering protectively over something Robertson didn't yet understand. Robertson removed the stained dressing, wincing at what he saw and smelled.

The gunshot thigh swam in gangrene. The stench of fluid-filled blebs laced with black and green filled Robertson's nose and caused him to turn his eyes away. Below the knees, the legs were frozen. Robertson asked Choi, "Is this man a North Korean?"

Choi answered at once. "This hermit gentleman insists that my countryman of the north who came seeking his aid at this hut is no longer political. Perhaps we should remove our intrusion from his house."

Robertson muttered, "You are resisting me, Choi. Ask the hermit if he understands that this man has an infected gunshot wound and that his legs are frozen. He's dying."

Choi spoke in the hesitant, deferential tones he had used since they had entered the house. Robertson glanced around. He saw sour death, mustiness and cold air, some rags, a low table, and many books, which were piled in careless heaps. He put his hand into the firepit; the coals were as dead as the North Korean's chances. He fixed his eyes then on the hermit, who listened to Choi with bowed head. Robertson realized that whatever they discussed had already gone beyond a simple acknowledgment of the fact that the North Korean was dying.

The hermit seemed confused, shifting his eyes rapidly between Robertson and Choi. Then a pleading tone came into his responses. Robertson turned his face away. He felt horror, facing it squarely for the first time since the night in June when he had gone AWOL from the replacement compound. He knew this was the ultimate face of the war—an old Korean hermit on a mountain standing beside armed Americans who understood him no more than they understood Sanskrit. As the war touched everything in Korea, now it had come into a hermit's hut—as if that were the final place—as implacably as the first shovel of dirt strikes a coffin. What did the old man see? What did he think? Could such an intrusion ever be forgiven?

Suddenly the hermit made an angry sound. He lifted his right arm and began striking Robertson. But the blows were weak. Robertson accepted several of them, then reached to stop them. Under his hand, he felt the hermit's muscles relax. He let his hand linger, hoping his touch was reassuring.

The hermit sat down, folding his knees under him. He linked his hands in his lap and began to rock on his legs, head down.

Robertson quieted him now. "It's all right . . . it's all right. Tell him it's all right, Choi."

The hermit raised his head as Choi spoke and Robertson turned to Choi.

Choi said sadly, "The old gentleman is aware of his guest's condition. The man came to him several days ago to flee the battle."

Robertson pondered it. "We can take both of them back with us. Can you make him understand?"

Choi shook his head. "He does not wish for us to do that. In any case, Chong-il will not survive many hours."

Robertson nodded to the wounded soldier. "Chong-il?"

"Of course he has a name," Choi answered. "He is a peasant boy who once resided near Ch'ongjin. That is in the far north, on the sea. The hermit tells me that when he was conscious, he spoke fondly of his black ducks."

Robertson stared at the wounded soldier a few seconds before speaking. "The old man can't stay here. How will he survive?"

Choi shook his head again, saying, "Many of my countrymen live in these mountains. They refuse to go away."

Robertson ordered softly, "Go and call in the men. Tell Sergeant Carver to leave Sam Dougherty with the BAR to watch the hut from outside."

Choi went out. Robertson turned to the hermit. "I know you don't understand me, old-timer, but I understand myself. I'll not track mud into another Korean house. I did that once in your country." He added vehemently, "By God I'll not do it again."

The hermit lifted his eyes, but made no sound.

They waited together. Several times Robertson put his hand into the firepit, reconfirming.

A flurry of men came in through the door, accompanied by the rattle of rifles and equipment. They eyed the hermit and the soldier on the floor, made pained faces, and eased back carefully to stand against the walls near the door. They filled the room, warming it with their own heat.

Klineschmidt spoke first. "Jesus, Lieutenant Robertson! What—"

Robertson stood up and raised a hand to stem the questions. He said, "The wounded man is dying and they have no wood to keep the hut warm."

"What's that to us?" Klineschmidt answered. "The guy on the floor looks like a North Korean and the old guy is probably a North Korean, too. We should kill them or take them back and let battalion kill them."

Robertson fixed him in a steel gaze. He said quietly, "I'm not taking them back."

He stared pointedly, into each face.

Klineschmidt shook his head. "Even if you are an officer now, Lieutenant Robertson, you can't make me get wood for enemies."

Carver muttered angrily. Robertson checked him, then addressed Klineschmidt. "You go up and relieve Sam on the BAR."

Klineschmidt's face darkened. Robertson snapped, "That's an order, Kraut. I'm exempting you."

Klineschmidt huffed out. The others shifted toward the door, but waited for a catalyst.

The men fidgeted. Then, clearly disgusted, Tom Carver said, "Should be a lot of downed trees back up the canyon behind the house."

Solomon Zuckerman stepped out the door, saying, "I'll help get some wood."

Teasman and Catlin smiled guiltily and followed Zuckerman out. Robertson grinned at Carver and gestured to Choi, "You stay and keep your countryman company, Choi."

NMI Johnson was the last out of the hut, because he had stopped to stare at the dying soldier. He ran to catch the others, calling, "Hey, wait for me, I'm an old woodchopper from the hills of Missouri."

It began to snow again, quiet neutral flakes that floated down, spinning out all the best that was in nature. The men stacked rifles a few hundred feet up the canyon from the hut, hooking them at the swivels, leaving them to rust a little bit in the falling wet crystals. Sam Dougherty came to join them.

"Get only dry wood," Johnson cautioned Dougherty. "Wet wood makes smoke and will just attract attention to the old guy."

The ancient canyon rang with the activity of the young and vital. The men gathered the wood, cursing playfully. The mound of wood grew, hacked into orderliness with bayonets and broken over knees. Carver organized the chore. Robertson broke branches and said nothing, lost in himself.

To the north, several cannons fired, monsters, probably earth-churning 152-mm, but the muzzle noise and the bursts of the impacts were smothered in distance and snow. A rooster pheasant flew up when Johnson wrested a branch from a downed tree. The bird whirred off in startled excitement and landed a few feet away. Johnson put his hands on his hips and studied the pheasant. "Back home, I used to hunt pheasants," he said to no one in particular. "Why the hell did I do a stupid thing like shoot a pretty bird?"

Several stared at the pheasant, but no one answered Johnson. They carried and made a new wall against the south face of the hut, piling wood up to the eaves.

When they went in, Robertson saw that Choi and the hermit sat beside the wounded soldier. Choi had replaced the filthy dressing.

He greeted Robertson. "I can do no more for Private Chong-il." Choi's face spoke it well. He sat in the presence of foreigners, keeping watch on a countryman.

The hermit smiled, gazing possessively on Chong-il. Robertson understood; the Koreans were singing their own anthems.

He dropped his armload of wood and built a fire, the Korean way, beginning with a small patient flame that he nursed slowly into the requisite dimensions. As he worked, he sensed that Zuckerman hovered close by.

Looking up, Robertson saw the same emotion in Zuckerman's face that he had seen the day on Konsi as Zuckerman had looked at Fowlkes. Zuckerman whispered, gesturing toward the soldier.

"Can't we do something for him?"

"His name is Chong-il. He'll be out of it before long."

Zuckerman's face twisted. "I'm sorry for Chong-il."

"He's the enemy," Robertson said.

"Not my enemy," Zuckerman answered gently.

Robertson squeezed his arm. "Thanks, Solly."

Wordlessly, Zuckerman removed his field jacket and placed it over the North Korean's legs, as he had done for Fowlkes.

Robertson bit his lip and looked away. He wished the entire world could see it, and put it in a glass case and keep it inviolate forever.

20

RETURN FROM THE HERMIT'S HUT, NIGHT OF NOVEMBER 19–20, 1951

Robertson led them through the snow in a single, silent file. In fact, no one had spoken since they had left the hut where they had met the old hermit and Chong-il.

Although he should have been weary beyond thought—it had been a long day and he had been duty officer the previous night—Robertson's mind was racing. He sensed that the day's events had some special meaning he couldn't grasp. This notion nagged at him, to the exclusion of all other thoughts.

Yet it refused to come clear.

To their north as they walked, the rifle line was as silent and distant as the stars they could see when the clouds finally broke up and dispersed. An unblinking moon bore down on them, glancing light from the snow crystals the men kicked up and casting thoughtful shadow-soldiers to hike along with them. Breaths were sharp. Robertson knew the night cold was punishing. Soon, the Siberian winter would arrive.

Siberian winds howl—there is no other verb. The company had been issued thermoboots, clumsy thick-toed footwear immediately dubbed Mickey Mouse shoes. The idea, born of the thousands of amputated toes of the winter of 1950–51, the worst Korea had experienced in decades, was to encase the American foot in insulated rubber. For Carver and the other sergeants, the thermoboot brought with it a dreaded chore. Each night, the sergeants inspected their men's reeking bare feet for signs of frostbite and trenchfoot.

Wearily, Robertson looked ahead to their somber winter. They would live wrapped in as many layers of cloth as the spirit could bear. In the bunkers, if the lines didn't move, they would cling to charcoal-burning devices constructed from tin cans, contrivances that punished eyes and throats and scorched a careless finger. The only escape would be into a damp sleeping bag and, hopefully, into dreamless time-drowning sleep. Outside the bunkers, and sometimes inside, would lurk a dragon named Freezing.

This dragon thickened the air until it was fluid ice, then wrapped the mixture around the spirit, leaving it in chill exhaustion. The spirit writhed, as the red rocks of Korea writhed—in fire and ice and steel. None of the poets Robertson had read, and he had read many, could slay that dragon with words, or even tame it with syntax.

The dragon Freezing would manifest himself in many ways. Carelessly oiled weapons would freeze—in an emergency, they were best thawed by a stream of warm urine. Mortar and artillery tubes would contract. The metal would whine when the gunners ran them into battery. Chemical actions would slow. What in the summer had been an explosion would in the winter be a puny fart. It was no warmer on the artillery line. Numb hands on numb shells invited error. The error, when fired, dribbled short, onto the backs of the infantrymen ahead of the guns rather than onto the enemy.

Rarely would it be mentioned in the tavern stories of the survivors, for it was indelicate, but the dragon Freezing manifested himself most cruelly when a soldier relieved himself. Then the layers of protective cloth had to be stripped away and bunched under protesting knee joints. A man sat hunched in the wind while the dragon chewed on his naked buttocks. To be constipated was to invite disaster.

Robertson slowed, letting the column catch up to him. Soon they went up a rise, then down into a bowl. In the center of the depression, Robertson halted and studied it. The edge of the bowl would keep at bay anything more hostile than the cold air. He decided they could safely rest there awhile.

"Let's take a break. Good a place as any."

The men sat down and lit cigarettes. Even Zuckerman took one. Still they did not converse. It was as it had been on the day of the lepers, Robertson saw. Each man wanted solitude for his own thinking, needing that to come to terms with his experience.

Because no one had wanted to walk near him, Klineschmidt had brought up the rear. No one looked at him when he came up. He sat sullenly on the fringe for several minutes, glaring at them. Then he turned on Sam Dougherty.

"Dougherty, everybody knows you're an ex-convict. Why try to hide it?"

This unexpected assault shocked everyone. Klineschmidt had violated the stiffest of Korean War infantry rules. The rule was simple: never throw social dirt in the face of a man who might be called upon to throw cemetery dirt in yours. This was why the white infantry units in Korea accepted blacks with scarcely a murmur, although a few generals had assured the Congress they would mutiny.

Robertson lifted his helmet with a finger. He saw that Klineschmidt still smarted from the rejections of the afternoon. He glanced at Dougherty, having decided instantly to let him get in a few good licks before he broke it up.

But Dougherty only smiled. "Gather round," Dougherty said cheerfully. "Good a time to deal with it as any."

Robertson caught Dougherty's eye and shook his head firmly. Dougherty smiled pleasantly and went on.

"In '47, when I was with the American constabulary in Germany, I took up with a *schatzi* named Marlena. Quite a girl—widow of a Werhmacht lieutenant who didn't get back from Stalingrad. Face of an angel, appetite of a mink, the kind of thing any trooper looks for. Anyway, I found out you didn't keep a trinket like Marlena on an SFC's pay, at least not when the SFC has an allotment going home to a wife and kid."

As if he waited for them to digest the preface, Dougherty paused. Then he said abruptly, "The army had a lot of stuff laying around and Germany had a good black market going. I swiped stuff and I sold it."

At first, no one responded, but at last someone broke the silence with, "Is that all? Only *that?* God, the army's got a million tons of stuff it don't need. We throw it away over here like there was no tomorrow."

"It was enough," Dougherty replied thoughtfully. "A general court-martial gave me four years hard labor, broke me, and laid a dishonorable discharge on me. Ellen, my wife, divorced me while I was in jail."

The voices all began at once, awed, incredulous. "Sam, that ain't fair at all." "Sam, you didn't have a kick like that coming just for taking up with a playmate on foreign station." "Damn, the army is stupid. Can you imagine giving a guy four years and a DD just for putting to good use some crap it didn't want anyway?" "No, Sam, it wasn't fair."

Dougherty stood erect and smiled down. "It was fair. I was guilty as sin. In fact, as near as I could understand the other cons during my ride in Leavenworth, I was the only guilty guy in the entire joint. Anyway, I laid out two years of my sentence and jumped at the chance to get paroled over here to the line infantry."

"Will you get a pardon for serving in Korea?" Zuckerman asked.

Dougherty shrugged and went off to stand by himself. Robertson saw that he stood proud and erect, and said under his breath, "By God, stand tall. You've just gotten your pardon."

Zuckerman, who rarely joined in the squad's hearty profanity, turned to Klineschmidt. "Kraut, you're a first-class asshole." Then he got up and handed his rifle to Choi Min-soo.

He had almost reached Klineschmidt when Robertson checked him with, "That's enough, Solly. You've made your point. It's too cold to fistfight."

Klineschmidt's shoulders slumped.

Robertson spoke loudly. "As long as we're reading each other's service records, I have something to add. When Sam gets to put on a dress uniform again, he'll put up a Silver Star, a Bronze Star with two *V*'s, and a Purple Heart. Not a man in this regiment is fit to shine his boots for him."

Zuckerman, fists still clenched, called to Dougherty, "Sam, if it's worth anything to you, I'd soldier under you in any army in the world."

Johnson jumped up. "That's double for me. I'd reenlist to do it, and I hate the fucking army worse than chancres."

They began to laugh and to roughhouse each other. Catlin made a snowball and hit Choi with it. It smashed against his helmet and cascaded snow down his face.

At first Choi seemed piqued, as if his Tungusic dignity had been ruffled. But then he laughed, as no one had ever heard him laugh before. So rare was it that it stunned.

Between shrill Asian guffaws, Choi got out, "Lieutenant Robbie-san, one has been challenged to a contest of puerility. One begs your permission to respond."

Robertson caught Dougherty's eye a moment, drawing him over, then turned to Carver. "Sergeant Carver, you choose and then I'll choose. One at a time. Snowballs at twenty paces. No truces for casualty removal."

"You are *on*, Lieutenant, sir."

Carver shot a scowl at Klineschmidt and deliberately chose Dougherty. Robertson chose Choi Min-soo. Carver chose Catlin. Robertson pointed to Zuckerman.

In the end, two menacing lines had formed, facing each other. Klineschmidt had gotten to his feet, clearly hoping to be chosen, but he had not been.

Robertson let the men stare at the downcast Klineschmidt for several meaningful seconds before saying to Carver, "Your turn to choose. Kraut hasn't been chosen."

"I don't want him," Carver said stiffly. "You can have him."

"We'd outnumber you by two men. And I'm a tactically qualified U.S. government-issue junior-grade officer."

"I don't care. I'd sooner be outnumbered and fight against a tactically qualified U.S. government-issue junior-grade officer than have Kraut on my side."

Robertson nodded thoughtfully, then turned to Klineschmidt. The man-chant stilled, as if they waited to hear what Robertson would say.

Klineschmidt fidgeted under Robertson's gaze. At last the lieutenant spoke. "Kraut, I want you to think about why the army issues pencils that have erasers on them. While you're thinking on that, I'd like to have you on my side."

Kraut whooped and ran to stand at Robertson's left shoulder.

They threw snowballs for almost twenty minutes, whooping gleefully. At the end, Robertson's side rushed the enemy and easily threw it into the snow.

Then they rested in the moonpath and threw up cigarette smoke and warm human steam. At one point, Choi Min-soo broke the pensive silence. "We are intertwined," he said, seemingly apropos of nothing. He paused and smiled at Zuckerman, adding, "My dear father—he is dead now—was a man of much sentiment. He once explained to me that the human heart weaves the threads of fortune into snares to catch and intertwine other hearts."

Robertson got up abruptly and struck off toward the tents of the Kumwha Reserve. The others followed. Now they chattered and walked together. Klineschmidt insisted that he walk beside Dougherty. Zuckerman, after maintaining a deferential few steps behind them, went to walk beside Robertson and Choi Min-soo.

Then suddenly, the inchoate idea that had nagged Robertson for several hours blossomed into full awareness.

But, before he let himself entertain the idea, he reached into his breast pocket and removed the hachimaki Choi had made for him. He lifted the folded cloth to his nose.

He smelled Korean blood and American gunpowder and his own sweat. Then he put the cloth away and let his eyes take in the men he had led for so long. He saw them as a single entity, harmonious and complete, and he knew that he had breathed into that entity all that he had left to give.

Then he admitted his idea to his conscious mind. Today, in the worst of places, he had been privileged, as few were privileged, to see the best in men.

He hoped that the pleasure they had shared back in the bowl of snow would linger with them after he left them, which he had to do, sooner rather than later. The pencil he had been issued that night in Chunchon had no eraser.

21

Christmas came and went, then 1952 came. George Company, sometime during that period, went from reserve to Sniper Ridge, taking over prepared positions there. A tedium gripped the war, a feeling of futility. The infantry companies rotated, going up onto the line to get chilled and exhausted, coming off to get chilled and rested, going back up to get refrozen. The rotations became so routine that General Van Fleet could have put a time clock at the bases of the ridges.

"How did it go on your shift?" inquired Puncher-in.

"So-so, for infantry work; mostly mortar fire; nine hit, two KIA. Watch out down on that finger ahead of the wire, the gooks like to snipe at anything moving out there," answered Puncher-out. "We're leaving our mortar ammunition for you; don't want to carry the shit out. We wanted to fire it at the gooks, but the Old Man said you guys might better use it."

"Did you clean up the bunkers for us?"

"Well, you know how it goes—the less a man has to do the less he does. Any women back there?"

"If there are, they hid out from us."

"Good luck."

"See you around."

The outfit G Company relieved had been energetic. Many of the positions had crude bunks and the bunk builders also had been excellent at contriving stovepipes from patiently stitched-together C-ration cans. But the bunkers stank of unwashed strangers and closely compressed trench winter, the latter a damp, sour, icy, almost crushing odor, tinged with urine and feces and sweat. From somewhere, the relieved company had acquired some crude flooring, but the walls of the bunkers were painted with a patina of frost.

As if the NKA commander understood he had new neighbors, he began at once to mortar a greeting—a two-hundred-gun salute for Hartung and his people—the Korean War version of an international welcome wagon.

The company tightened its collective sphincters and cursed frigidly and returned the courtesy. By noon of the second day, a rumor flew through the company that the Panmunjom negotiators had agreed to agree and they'd all be home by Easter. By evening, a second rumor ran from lip to lip that the first rumor had been a lie and that the company would mount out an attack frontally across the valley. That rumor was, within hours, replaced by another rumor which insisted the Koreans were employing suicide squads to come at night carrying explosives on their backs. By morning that rumor had transmogrified; now the suiciders were trained chimpanzees.

Sergeant Carver put a stop to the rumors at that point. "If they are chimpanzees, I hope to God they're romantically inclined female chimpanzees. Maybe we can get lucky and catch one."

Interspersed with the rumors came the mortar rounds.

Too real ever to be the grist for the rumor mill, mortaring is never taken lightly. Howitzers are honest monsters that announce themselves boldly. Mortars, on the other hand, are spiteful little bastards, whirring over before the mind really gets set up to deal with them. The Korean War infantry detested mortars, which killed thousands and maimed thousands more.

After seven days on the line, Captain Hartung and his officers discussed the willingness of the people across the valley to expend copious quantities of mortar ammunition. The enemy mortarmen had rested for three peaceful days, but in the night had resumed the racket with new vigor.

Lieutenant Shapiro remarked that the other side obviously had a three-day ammunition resupply format, which was better than that of the American army. Lieutenant Noume, such a plump open-faced Hawaiian everyone wanted to like him, bitched modestly about the inability of the expensive air force to interdict enemy supply lines.

"You just can't hit a chogie-bearer at night with a five-hundred-pound high-explosive bomb dropped from twenty thousand feet," Noume observed.

"Works as well as strafing fortified positions with a five-hundred-mile-an-hour airplane," Shapiro retorted.

Hartung held up a staying hand. "Let's not derogate a sister service. Some of us might have sisters in the air force."

Robertson himself had put his finger on the problem. Although he was by many months the junior of the platoon officers, and a mustang at that, it was understood that he spoke for them. "Unless he wants to risk the gully down on Second Platoon right flank, Captain, there isn't much else he can do but mortar us," Robertson said.

The officers nodded agreement with that obvious statement. The George Company position, which sprawled atop a steep-faced but rounded hill in about the middle of the battalion sector, which included other hills and ridge lines, was wired and mined to unapproachability. Only a line into Robertson's outpost position, which commanded a knoll slightly west of the gully, offered the enemy a meaningful axis of attack. Any attack there required darkness and luck, since once the attacker left the protection of the unmined gully, he placed his force enfilade to killing fire from the platoon led by Lt. Hoxie Noume, an officer who didn't smile much but who thought a lot.

Lieutenant Brady, now company executive officer and a silver lieutenant, asked Robertson, "Why does he do it? What does he have in mind?"

Robertson thought a moment, then shrugged. "To keep us on edge, hopefully bleed us a little. He'll come over some night and tell us why."

A moment of collective silence followed that remark. Then Captain Hartung announced that the officers were to inspect all the primacord in the company and that the time in grade from private to private first class had been reduced from sixty to thirty days. Robertson seized on the subject of promotions to recommend Zuckerman for sergeant and Dougherty for corporal. The other officers chimed in, soon posting about twenty promotions to cheer an otherwise cheerless day. Hartung agreed to them all, adding two of his own. The first sergeant winced at the work involved.

And the day was bleak. A winter sun spun around the southern sky, aloof, disinterested, denying the comfort that normally comes in daylight when a unit is closely gripped by a nocturnal enemy. The day was not overcast, but it also was not not-overcast. The ground was white; the sky was less white.

The day's only hot meal came up late, toward noon, inserting itself into lazy affairs of watching and dozing. Robertson told Carver, who was now platoon sergeant, to release the men in serial to go back and eat the powdered eggs and greasy bacon. Jorgensen dawdled with something and was many yards behind the others trudging rearward when the first flight of mortars came in. The rounds impacted to the right of Robertson and nearly on the crest of the ridge, above and to the left of Jorgensen. Jorgensen froze.

In the time required to readjust some knobs and drop missiles into the tubes and fly them across the valley, a second salvo impacted farther down the slope. The gunners had shifted right a few mils. They had a bracket on Jorgensen, but had missed the others.

Jorgensen did nothing. Robertson pumped himself across the space, struggling in the snow, shouting, "Get the hell out of there, Jorgensen! He's observing us and he'll fire again!"

Jorgensen was a frail, smallish man who scoffingly compared Korean winter to the winters of northern Minnesota. Robertson had several yards to close when the killing salvo came. The mortar rounds fell in a line. Jorgensen was obliterated into a snorting smoky blob of dirty snow and human limbs.

The deep snow under Robertson cushioned the blast and absorbed much of the metal. One large chunk caught him on an ammunition clip. He crumpled into the snow like a discarded rag doll.

Klineschmidt screamed, "It's Lieutenant Robertson! They got Lieutenant Robertson!"

Choi and Dougherty and several others came running. They dragged what was left of Jorgensen and the thrashing Robertson to the communications trench nearby and threw them in. The mortaring stopped, as suddenly as it had started.

Klineschmidt rubbed Robertson and patted his back. "Are you hurt, sir? Where are you hurt? What can I do?"

Robertson got up on his hands and knees, then straightened his back. Mouth agape, he drew in air. Already the puny 60s of the weapons platoon were answering the mail. "I'll be okay when I get my breath," he said finally. "See to Jorgensen."

But Jorgensen's jaw had been torn away and his skull oozed bloody brain. His eyes stared, as if he still saw the ultimate explosion of his war.

Late in the afternoon, after the talk of the noon event had rippled out and the westering sun sent its vague shadows across the snowscape, a grim-faced Robertson appeared to stand over the head of Pfc. Alton, who sat in a trench smoking a cigarette while Corporal Tatum stared northward with his nose above the parapet.

"Give me your sniper rifle," Robertson commanded. He wore his hachimaki. By now, most of the company understood that Robertson's Korean had made the hachimaki, and had grasped that when Robertson put it on, it was analogous to snapping a rifle off safety or arming a hand grenade.

Alton and Tatum stared suspiciously at the hachimaki, no doubt hoping it did not involve them. Alton did not want to give up his rifle, a bolt-action Springfield with an expensive telescopic sight. He spent hours peering through the scope at the North Korean ridge, sometimes firing. But as far as anyone knew, he never hit anything. Robertson suspected that was because Alton did not understand windage.

"You won't hurt it, will you, sir?" Alton asked.

"I'll get it back to you," Robertson promised.

"It's a good sniper rifle," Alton said. "I think I hit one the other day."

Robertson had removed his parka. He filled the pockets of his field jacket with ammunition and cradled the rifle across his arm.

Many watched, for an erect man in daylight was a rarity. Robertson's trajectory was clearly forward. Carver stopped him before he had reached Shapiro's wire. "Wait one, Lieutenant. I'll get my shooter and a couple of volunteers and go with you."

"Thanks for the offer," the lieutenant said pleasantly. "But no. I'm just going out to adjust Alton's scope for him. He's going to put a round over into Easy Company one of these days."

Choi Min-soo turned his head away and did not acknowledge that anything was happening. Klineschmidt came running. "Can I go, sir?"

Robertson smiled and shook his head. When Klineschmidt lowered his eyes in disappointment, Robertson said, "Kraut, did I ever tell you about the cowboy out in Kansas where I grew up who broke his leg on a horse? Guy was a hardcase, like you."

"No, sir. I never heard that story. You don't tell many stories. You always seem to be kind of sad about something."

Robertson grinned. "Horse wrapped him up in a five-strand barbed-wire fence and rolled on him. Bad compound fracture. Doc Feener decided he had to amputate, but the old cowboy—his name was Hank—was so tough the chloroform wouldn't put him under. Finally, Doc Feener sent down to the bootlegger for a pint of hundred-eighty-proof grain alcohol. That did the trick. When Hank woke up, Doc Feener asked him how he felt about losing his leg. Hank wiped his mouth and said, 'Great, Doc. Send down to the bootlegger for another pint of one-eighty and you can cut the other son of a bitch off.' "

"That ain't true, sir."

"Well, it's true enough to tell when you're in high spirits and good humor, Kraut." With that Robertson stalked on through Shapiro's wire and down the faint patrol path there. The novelty of this, added to the novelty of being so blatantly aboveground as Robertson had been, was sufficient to bring men running to watch.

Robertson angled down and across a swale and up onto the finger that protruded toward the North Korean rifle line, about five hundred yards away from that point. As the men who had binoculars to capture the details watched, he removed his helmet and upended it in the snow, disgorging from his pocket and into the helmet the loose ammunition he had brought.

Casually, he sat down beside the helmet and began to fire at the enemy positions, barely discernible, but definitely there, as several patrol leaders had learned.

Lieutenant Noume whispered huskily to Lieutenant Shapiro. "Send your runner for the captain. Tell him we need him here."

Shapiro dispatched a shaken runner and returned to the wire, next to Noume. "What on earth is Robertson doing? They'll kill him out there."

Watchers with naked eyes could see the snorts of snow that erupted around Robertson as the opposite ridge returned his insult. Captain Hartung came, breathless, followed by Shapiro's runner. "What the god-damned hell?" was about all the captain could get out. He lifted his binoculars, watching with the others as Robertson loaded and fired, loaded and fired, sitting in the snow as if he were on the five-hundred-yard target range.

"Insane!" someone cried.

No one answered. Breaths were checked.

No man could have counted either the rounds or the seconds, but the duel endured about ten minutes.

Robertson stood up. Casually, it seemed to watchers, he dumped the shell casings from his helmet. Then he seemed to search his pockets for more ammunition.

Choi Min-soo and Solomon Zuckerman watched the hardest, but said the least.

Then the enemy firing stopped. The air grew still and stiff, expectant.

Robertson waved toward the North Koreans and turned back up the finger. He walked slowly, holding Alton's rifle by the barrel, across his shoulder. As the finger rejoined the parent ridge, Robertson was silhouetted. No one breathed. Many closed their eyes.

But nothing was fired.

When Robertson was close enough for the men near the wire to see his expression, Zuckerman said to Choi, "He always gets that look, like he's disappointed. Why?"

Choi said nothing.

Robertson was now close enough to touch. Klineschmidt put out a hand, almost fearfully, as if the hand wanted reassurance it would be afraid to believe. Robertson started, as if he had been a man only minutes asleep, called to relieve a sentinel.

Everything stopped; the sky hovered. As Robertson came on up, followed by Klineschmidt, the men parted, standing aside, just looking at the lieutenant, eyes going from his face to the hachimaki. It was said that the soldiers stared at General Grant that way as he went through his investment line at Vicksburg, and at Patton when he inspected his tanks.

Suddenly, although it was expressly forbidden in the American army to cheer an officer, someone cheered. Then all the men began to cheer. The chorus rose, to become a rude mantra, a sneering chant conducted out of all the wearisome frustrations of the winter line. No syllables, no syntax, just a roaring chorus of male sounds thrust out of excited chests and throats.

The cheering rolled across the valley. The rigidly organized echelons of G Company disintegrated into a noisy mob. Many men ran down to the wire to shorten the range. The cheering then became jeering, and several men danced around Lieutenant Shapiro's apron wire, like Comanche warriors daring their enemies to attack. Several men pointed their middle fingers, shouting, "Up yours, you slant-eyed bastards. You couldn't hit Lieutenant Robertson if you had him tied to a stake."

Then, strangely, for there had only been apparitions at the other end of the mortar rounds, the shouting was answered by the enemy. A knot of them gathered on a knoll on their side of the valley; with binoculars, a man could have made out the faces. It became a new duel; each side brought up reinforcements to join in the shouting.

"That's too goddamned good a target to pass up." Hartung spoke some orders into Shapiro's telephone. The G Company mortarmen fired. Down the line a .50-caliber air-cooled machine gun began to chatter. The Koreans were swept from the knoll.

Within seconds, several counterbattery mortar rounds came over to burst in Shapiro's wire. The G Company weapons platoon shouted gleefully, dropped rounds in the tubes, held their ears, and for many minutes the sound of mortar fire drowned out the screaming. Nothing was aimed well; it was man-play.

Zuckerman shouted to Choi Min-soo, "What was he trying to do? I just don't understand it."

Choi did not answer at once. Then he answered cryptically, "You are not meant to understand it, Corporal Solly. He is alone in his cold embrace. That is the meaning of his hachimaki." With that, he walked away and was seen no more that afternoon.

Captain Hartung said to his executive officer, "Chew him out. Tell him to commit suicide on his own goddamned time, not on mine."

"*You* chew him out, Captain. I'm afraid of him."

"Well, don't chew him out then. He must know what he's doing. Best goddamned officer I got. What is that stupid thing he wears on his head? The army doesn't issue anything like that."

No one answered, because only Choi Min-soo knew fully, and he was no longer there. Robertson removed the hachimaki from his head and folded it, placing it in his pocket. He smiled at Hartung. "Good afternoon, Captain. I was test-firing Alton's sniper rifle."

He looked around until his eyes found Alton. He beckoned and Alton came to take the weapon.

"This thing is way off, Alton. Shoots low and to the left. I'd have the supply people take a look at it."

His tone smacking of exasperation, Captain Hartung said to Robertson, "If and when I get loose from that crazy North Korean bastard across the valley, Lieutenant, your ass is going to Japan on R and R. And I won't let you refuse again."

Robertson lifted and dropped his shoulders.

Hartung added, "And quit wearing that goddamned thing you wear on your head. You're terrifying my people with it."

"It's a personal matter, Captain," Robertson answered quietly.

Hartung stared helplessly a moment, then walked away, signaling the incident was closed. The sergeants and lieutenants put the sobering men back into their holes.

Two nights later on George Three, Platoon Sgt. Tommy Carver shook Robertson's shoulder and trench-whispered, "Wake up, Lieutenant! George One thinks they're going to hit us!"

That marked the beginning of the end.

PART

THREE

22

REST AND RECUPERATION CENTER, NARA, JAPAN, MARCH 5, 1952

Sgt. Solomon Zuckerman wiped the residue of the obligatory chocolate malted from his lips with a paper napkin and looked around. He sensed excitement. The soldiers sat at tables of four—eyes never far from the giggling Japanese mess-hall girls who served them— dining on beefsteaks and green peas and vanilla cake. Overhead, high on the wall above the steam tables, a sprightly sign welcomed the R and R personnel into the caring embrace of the Japan Logistical Command.

R and R, the enlisted men named it "I and I," for Intoxication and Intercourse, never wanting to call a thing what the officers called it, constituted a hundred-twenty-hour respite from Korea. Each man got it once. For five magic days an infantryman lived free of steel helmet and rifle, with the treasures of relatively Occidentalized Japan at his feet.

At the end of the five days' leave, an air force troop carrier airplane rushed him back, as it had wafted him over. Many returning R-and-Rs had barely slept for five days; many carried the worst hangover of their lives. Nevertheless, in the strange way of healthy soldiers, they were rested. This was the point of R and R.

R and R was an interlude, a personal regroupment, and Zuckerman felt suspended. He picked at his dessert, slowly closing as many doors on Korea as the freshness of Japan would permit. He wore ODs; Nara could be chilly in late March. The uniform tickled with clean crispness. Under the Combat Infantryman's Badge and Purple Heart over his left pocket, a fresh scar arose under the nipple, lancing downward and backward. The medic that night in January had given him a choice. "I can clean this up, sew in a few tucks, remind you that your ribs will be sore as hell for a few days, and send you back to your company, soldier, or I can give you a week or so at a MASH. You choose; I'm tired."

"I'll go back. But thanks for the choice."

Zuckerman had refused evacuation beyond the aid station mainly because of the exchange with Choi Min-soo, as they stood on the shambles on George Three after the hammering blast of the artillery Lieutenant Robertson had called down on their heads to end the fight. He and Choi met face-to-face while Zuckerman waited, under the hovering concern of Captain Hartung, for the platoon medic to take him to the battalion facility back off the ridge, about a mile down the road.

Choi, driven into something dark, had been taciturn and gruff.

Senses reeling, ears ringing, floundering for comprehension, Zuckerman had complained to him. "Lieutenant Robertson should have let me come out with you unwounded guys. I'm not hit that bad."

Choi had replied angrily, "Such a statement does not honor you, Solly Zuckerman. Those whom your officer placed in the bunker he desired most to exempt." Then Choi had walked away to stand near the silent prone ponchos that shrouded Sam Dougherty and Terry Cole.

Now, in the mess hall in Camp Nara, Zuckerman sat alone, thinking about Rachel Kahan. Suddenly, engagements to Fordham coeds were as irrelevant as yesterday's patrol. On that thought, Zuckerman had the stabbing sensation that he was like a man in a foundering ship; even the things he clung to were sinking.

One of the Seventh Division men who had flown across with him that morning came past the table. "Want to join us, Sarge? We aim to go out and terrorize and plunder before all the mooses and whiskey are used up."

Zuckerman smiled thanks and declined. He dawdled over his cake, then joined the last of the men to leave the mess hall. These were the older men, most of them senior NCOs, those Zuckerman was sure thought in that moment of another land, one in Korean War jargon variously identified as the States, the ZI, Land of the Round-eyed Women, the Land of the Big PX, or simply, Home.

After making his bunk in the squad room he had been assigned, reveling in the touch of clean white sheets and soft OD blankets, he sat down to write Rachel Kahan. An hour and several crumpled sheets of paper later, he had captured only part of what he wished to say, and that only poorly. The principal idea lay in two paragraphs that obtruded after a long preamble.

He wrote:

Korea has been a test for me, like the exams you take in college and write me about. And I don't think I have done very well. The others, even Johnson, the guy from Missouri I have mentioned before, deal with it. Each time it arises, I make myself promise to perform as the others do, but each time I fail myself. Even as a squad leader I fail, because the others know.

My father has always known. That is why he will never acknowledge me as a man. I'd not be good for you, Rachel. You deserve better. I wish I could find a softer way to say it, but there is none.

Knowing what logically would follow his last sentence, Zuckerman quit writing. He put the document under his pillow, where soldiers kept wallets and unfinished letters. He lay back on his bunk and listened to the sounds that echoed in the hollowness of the near-empty barracks. The barracks was no different from the barracks at Fort Ord, but somehow the very air in it suggested he was in a different land. He sniffed, smelling Japan, wondering what it had been like for the occupation troops, now so many of them, like Luke Plumber, sacrificed to their initial unpreparedness for Korea. They had not been a good army, Zuckerman knew, but that had not been their fault. A soldier is what he is asked to be. Captain Hartung had said it well: "We went into Korea with a bad army and we'll come out with a good one. It's natural selection."

Sleep eluded him. Zuckerman arose, put on his necktie, and went out, wanting to walk with himself through the mysterious ambience he had sniffed in the barracks.

The streets of Nara, a small town near Osaka, which graces one of Honshu's loveliest bays, led the soldiers from the R-and-R center into flesh and alcohol, in 1952 one of Japan's largest war industries. Vital Japan threatened to blossom, despite that tawdriness. The Japanese had learned well what Winston Churchill had learned too late. Often, it is better to import conquerors than to export victors.

After long minutes of listening to the ticking of his own heart and the tocking of his juices, as he strolled the dark streets, Zuckerman drifted into the neon and went into a dimly lit shanty of a bar that seemed to be named "Welcome GI All R and R." He found a booth and ordered an Asahi beer. He sipped and thought about the letter he had written. Rachel Kahan would go to her father; her father would go to his father. How would he deal with that?

A liquid belligerent voice came through the tobacco smoke and music and poked him. "Ain't you Zuckerman, the Jew guy?"

Sensing trouble, or at the least intrusion, Zuckerman looked up into the leering stubbled face of a Pfc. he did not immediately recognize. "I'm Zuckerman," he said cautiously.

The Pfc.'s uniform jacket was unbuttoned and his tie hung loose at the throat of a filthy khaki shirt.

"I knew you at Ord. I'm Clemerts."

Then Zuckerman recalled a scene, as much as he recalled a personality. Clemerts, one of the faces in the company in California, had once savagely beaten a much smaller man over a gambling dispute. He used words like "nigger" and "spick" and "Jew," all with identical ugliness.

"Hello, Clemerts. How have you been?"

Clemerts slumped into the booth. A Japanese girl who had been hiding behind him slid in beside him, looking down. She was small, in a red dress, and her long black hair was tied into a long ponytail with a jade-studded band.

"My R-and-R moose," Clemerts grunted, indicating the Japanese girl with a massive hand, adding offhandedly, "Pretty good fuck for a Nip."

Zuckerman winced and nodded to the girl, feeling trapped. He beckoned the waitress and ordered Clemerts an Asahi. "And bring the lady whatever she wants," he added.

Clemerts raised a hand to protest. "She don't need nothing; she's a whore. She'll order sugar water and the Nips'll rap you a couple hundred yen for it."

Zuckerman repeated to the waitress, "Bring her what she wants."

The waitress returned with two bottles of beer, a glass for Clemerts, and an orange drink. She slipped a brass token under the hand of the small girl who sat in Clemerts's shadow.

Clemerts drank long and put down his glass. He wiped his mouth on the back of his hand. Staring at the girl, he muttered, "Well, I wouldn't have bought her nothing, but they pay buck sergeants better than they pay Pfc.'s. You been lucky, Zuckerman. Can't make no rank where I am. Rank goes to the niggers, although the officers all know I can do their fucking jobs better than they can."

Zuckerman closed his ears and said nothing, staring at the girl, who continued to look down. Clemerts drank again and said, "I'm in the motor pool of a signal company at Wonju. Wouldn't want to be on the fucking line like you where the gooks lean on a guy's ass. You got to know how to work the system." He reached across the girl's shoulder and pulled her to him roughly. "Ain't that right, Moosie?"

The girl's head shot up. Zuckerman looked into brown almonds that pleaded.

Clemerts's hand had gone into the neck of the red dress. He grinned maliciously at Zuckerman. The girl cried out. Zuckerman realized Clemerts had pinched her.

In that instant, the noises in Zuckerman's head were those of Robertson and Dougherty, the squad-room social music of the Regular Army, where a man avenged his insults or hung his head in the chow line.

Alarmed at his own words, realizing at once it was how Robertson would have said it, he heard himself saying, with that same menace, "Knock it off. You're embarrassing and hurting her."

Clemerts sneered. "Fuck you, buddy. I bought and paid for this moose. If I want to pinch her tit, I'll pinch."

Zuckerman got out of the booth and stood up. He leaned his right leg against the wood and warned, "I won't ask you a second time." He assessed Clemerts, remembering the incident at Fort Ord. Surely he'd spot the big Pfc. thirty pounds.

Clemerts's face was locked up in malice. He began to whine. "I never heard of no real American taking sides with a Nip whore. You goddamned Jews—"

Zuckerman's arm flashed, an openhanded slap, surprising him as much as it clearly surprised Clemerts and the girl. Clemerts cringed in the corner of the booth and mouthed threats. Zuckerman stood, hearing his own pulse, certain he'd get beaten badly. He said nothing, waiting, as he had learned to wait during ambush patrols.

Then Clemerts pushed the girl out and got up. He was several inches taller than Zuckerman. Zuckerman backed up a step, but thrust his body forward, balancing on the balls of his feet.

Clemerts said nothing. He reached for the girl's arm. Seeing she resisted, Zuckerman shook his head firmly, as Dougherty sometimes shook his head.

"I got this Nip bitch until I ship out at midnight," Clemerts complained. "I paid her for five days."

"How much?" Zuckerman said quietly, reaching for his wallet.

Clemerts wiped his mouth nervously. "I still got about ten bucks' worth of her coming," he grated.

Zuckerman put a ten on the table and backed up again.

Clemerts snatched the bill, muttering, "Lucky for you I don't want shit with the MPs."

"Thanks for the ride," Zuckerman said quietly, almost as if Sam Dougherty had said it.

Clemerts staggered to the door and out. The smoke and music wafted over to the booth to fill the void he left there.

When Zuckerman sat down again, the girl looked up and said,

"Clemerts go back Nara now. R and R all done." She frowned in the direction of the door and added vigorously, "Yoshiko no rike. Number fucking ten GI."

Zuckerman studied her, startled by her English and the army's all-purpose word. It came from a mouth that was heavily lipsticked, now somewhat smeared. But it was a nice mouth, housing nice teeth behind lips much thinner than the red they carried. Merry brown eyes under dark brows contrasted against alabaster skin. He smelled lilac on a spring morning, he thought. Her eyes held him, and she spoke again. He had never met a prostitute before, although he had heard the profession much discussed. He tried to imagine what she was thinking, but images refused to come.

"Sergeant GI hava-yes girl?"

He shook his head negatively. After Rachel got his letter, that would certainly be true.

The girl smiled. Her slender fingers played with the untouched glass of orange drink. Zuckerman saw there something lovely and gentle. He studied her face again, aware that it was difficult to determine where the girl ended and the environment began. He thought this was a case of protective coloration, like the pattern on the wings of a butterfly or the unobtrusive color of an autumn flower.

She asked pointedly, "Hava R and R, ne?"

Zuckerman pondered her words. Then he said, "Have R and R yes." He held up an open hand and splayed all five digits. His legs under the table had stopped shaking from the aftermath of his confrontation with Clemerts.

He pointed to her. "Yoshiko?" She had called herself that.

She giggled. "Yoshiko. Number-one girl. GI come house of Yoshiko?"

Zuckerman took a deep breath and held it. He was on the line again, about to face himself. Finally, he sighed, for it was no more than he had faintly promised himself. "Sure. Why not?"

He saw she had beautiful ears, each wearing a small pearl earring. He fought against an urge to touch her. She smiled shyly and said, very quietly, as if she wanted to pretend she hadn't said it, "Yoshiko working girl. Sergeant GI prease give thirty dorru."

Zuckerman pretended to himself he wasn't paying. The money went into the pocket of her red dress. She stood and took Zuckerman's hand, tugging toward the door. Her touch was moist and alien and threatened to sear him. He had felt nothing like it since he had said good-bye to Rachel Kahan in New York twelve months earlier.

Yoshiko indicated they would walk. Once away from the bars, they drifted together across the night of a quiet world. Except for the smell of Japan, a gentle smell compounded of ancient time and rice straw, they could have been on any planet in the universe. Yoshiko brushed his hand. He caught her fingers and she pulled them free, scolding, "MP GI no rike hold hands on street. Sergeant GI wait for house of Yoshiko."

Zuckerman walked beside her through the darkness. He looked once into himself and realized he walked calmly, as if through a vaporous time, through novelty toward mystery. It was a good feeling, and he knew he'd never have able to feel this way before he came to Korea. He turned this idea over and studied the back door of it. He smiled for himself. Korea had taught him to separate imagined dangers from real dangers. It was not so much that he trusted her—and certainly Avram Zuckerman had cautioned his son to shun the carnal dangers of professional women—as that there was little the new situation could do to an experienced combat soldier unless it owned 7.62-mm PPSh-41 submachine guns and Tokarev rifles. This awareness pleased him.

Several minutes later, Yoshiko turned him down a somber narrow street. She stopped on the veranda of a low house and motioned for him to remove his boots.

Boots in hand, he followed her in. The house was large but narrow, and so angular it seemed to have sixteen corners. They went silently into a room at the rear of it. When Yoshiko switched on a light, Zuckerman confronted a hybrid; Japanese walls and mat floor, but an Occidental bed with a large recessed headboard. She had also a low table and a vanity. She fumbled with a minuscule record player. Zuckerman recognized the music, for it had gone to Korea from Japan with the occupation troops.

" 'China Night,' " he said.

Yoshiko beamed. "GI know song! Number-one song, ne?"

Zuckerman nodded his pleasure. Fowlkes had once told him that "China Night" was tears from the heart of a lonely Japanese soldier afloat in a ship. "That Nip feller sang about his geishy-gal," Fowlkes insisted. Zuckerman doubted that Fowlkes would know. But it gave the haunting syllables meaning.

Yoshiko disappeared for an instant and reappeared with a bottle of warm Asahi. Then she excused herself.

When she returned in about fifteen minutes, she had removed her makeup. She wore a bright kimono of reds and blacks. A yellow obi bound her narrow waist. Zuckerman savored her; she was Asian beautiful, he was sure of that, almost an exotic beauty, beauty reminiscent of the first glimpse of the islands of Japan he had caught from the damp morning deck of the

USNS *Pope* months earlier—mist-shrouded exotic, lovely, yet foreboding, suggestive of so much he could not then grasp.

She sat on the bed beside him and asked his name.

Before he answered, he let his nose taste her. She had bathed, washing away Clemerts. He gave her his full name.

She tried twice to say Solomon Zuckerman. Zoromun Zuzermun clearly would not do. He tried Solly; that came out of her mouth as Sorry. He scratched his head while Yoshiko giggled and made faces. He decided to retrench and went back to Solomon. After several tries, she rolled her eyes and got out "Solomon-san," making a fair "l." He trapped the merry eyes then and touched her cheek tenderly, just wanting to experience her. At that soft touch, he felt as if his life had never held a finer moment.

He had not touched the beer. She pointed to it and frowned. "Solomon-san no rike?"

"I don't like to drink very much," he answered.

Yoshiko's eyes widened over a puzzled smile. "American GI drink *takusan.*"

"No, not all." Both Robertson and Dougherty had been light drinkers, as if each feared it.

Yoshiko evaporated from the bed and rematerialized at her vanity. As he watched she did woman-things, the like of which Zuckerman had never seen. She creamed and perfumed and powdered and lipsticked. She let go her ponytail and brushed long slow strokes that made the black strands shimmer. She turned once and asked, in great seriousness, "Solomon-san rike Yoshiko, ne?"

"Yes, very much." She was color and animation and soft alabaster curves that tossed the light playfully.

As she worked on herself, she talked. "Solomon-san infantry?"

"Yes. That."

"Too bad."

He reflected a second. "Not so bad," he said. "You know other branches?"

Yoshiko turned her head. Zuckerman fingered the crossed muskets of his infantry insignia.

Yoshiko understood. Her face opened up. "Many GI. Artirery. Signer. Transportation." Yoshiko put down her brush and made the sounds of a cannon, a truck, and a telephone. Zuckerman wished he had not asked.

She resumed. When she stood up and turned away from her mirror, she had become a Western girl again. Absent the kimono, he'd have not been surprised to see such a face amid the throngs of students issuing from

Fordham or NYU. She was older in the West than in the East; he guessed
her at twenty in the former, eighteen or so in the latter.

A warmth radiated from the mat floor. Yoshiko glided across to her
record player and put on something Western and muted, turning that down
until it became a soft aura of sound, an anonymous melody calling to human
passion.

Yoshiko came to the bed and stood before him. Her hands acted on the
obi and the kimono.

She was the first naked adult woman Zuckerman had ever seen. It
shocked, as ambush fire shocks.

The reproving face of Avram Zuckerman rushed to his mind. He
flinched, but then reminded himself that the hulking Clemerts had folded
easily under a decisive blow. Instantly, he slapped his father's face and
sent him away. As instantly, he felt he had severed a bond, although the
things that swelled up in him pushed that out of mind.

He examined her. Yoshiko did not blush. Under the inviting smile he
saw breasts that were high and small, with defiant nipples. The pubic hair
at the base of her tight belly was lightly brown and supplied a seductive
counterpoint to her short legs. The legs tapered into slim ankles and pretty
feet with painted nails.

She brushed his lips with hers, bringing under swift sails something
awesome he had never before experienced. "GI and Yoshiko maku rove
now," she said softly, switching off the light as she spoke.

He undressed with virgin clumsiness and it was over in seconds. He
rolled away, not daring to touch her, wanting only to hide up against the
dark ceiling. His new failure was worse than his failure of the night he
rebelled against Lieutenant Robertson's order to get into the bunker with
the other wounded.

After a while she touched him, rubbing a caressing finger across his
chest, finding there the scar where the battalion medic had stitched. Her
finger explored knowingly. She whispered in the night, "War maku GI
much tired. Maku number-one rove tomorrow."

Yoshiko's softness was like a mild drug. He held her and fell into his
first unguarded sleep in months. He did not dream, but in the night he
woke once to smell her again, and slowly to touch her.

Her working surname was Yamada, as he was to learn, not realizing
Yamada was the Japanese equivalent of the Smith that so often went onto
motel registers after midnight.

By noon the following day, after a breakfast of overdone eggs and
stringy unidentifiable meat, Zuckerman had also learned that Yoshiko

owned not a lot of English. She had some nouns in her head and a few verbs, for the latter of which she indicated a weak sense of English tenses. A pixie in a ponytail needs no pronouns; she eschewed possessives, preferring instead the third person subject pronoun. And Zuckerman had more Japanese than he realized. Japanese words had infected Korean War argot. The densest of the Americans had *takusan* and *sukoshi* for "large" and "small"; the densest Japanese understood the gist of "number one" and "number ten." When Yoshiko wished to designate something grossly bad, she referred to it as "Number fucking ten, GI!"

Under her heavenly bed, Yoshiko kept her principal treasures, a stack of American movie fan magazines, a well-thumbed Sears catalog, and an English-Japanese dictionary.

With these artifacts, and with gestures, soft glances, smiles, tosses of the ponytail, rolling eyes, frowns, and clumsy clauses, they communicated. Zuckerman was beginning to realize that not a lot needs to be exchanged between locomotives going in the same direction along the same track.

Yoshiko was patently excited when Zuckerman demanded her antecedents, he probably being the first American soldier ever to ask her if she had lived a life before she became a working girl. The seaside village where the uniformed schoolgirl stared with horrified eyes at incendiary clusters spitting from the shiny bellies of B-29 bombers translated more easily into her English than the idea of the Bronx translated into his Japanese. Yoshiko well understood Avram Zuckerman, who was discussed for almost thirty minutes. "Father rike Japanese father," she admitted. Under hard probing, she confessed that her own father had not returned from New Guinea.

Yoshiko forced Zuckerman to study her many pictures of Elizabeth Taylor. "Miss Tayror number one," she insisted.

"Number one, Yoshiko." Zuckerman lied about Miss Tayror; personally, he regarded her as a spoiled brat and a mediocre actress, but he could never have translated such complicated concepts.

"Changu namu," Yoshiko said wistfully. "Be Erizabet, rike Miss Tayror."

Zuckerman kissed her neck. "Never do that," he pleaded softly. "Yoshiko is a perfect name."

"GI rike?"

"GI like. Number one."

Yoshiko sighed heavily and kissed him. There is less to romance than meets the eye: they built on what they had. They ambushed the words that ran through their time, each word prisoner of a new victory. Zuckerman's ear supplied the necessary intonations and rhythm; he transformed Yoshi-ko's *r*'s into *l*'s. His quickening heart supplied all the rest.

One principal error in Yoshiko had suggested itself the previous night. She wore brightly colored Western-style panties, on which the day of the week was inscribed above where the elastic cut a thin pink line into the velvet of her left thigh. Last night's lavender panty had proclaimed "Tues-day," which was the day of the week in New York. In Japan it had been Wednesday, a result of the International Date Line, which ran from ice to ice, cleaving the world into an east half and a west half. Today, lounging in wispy brassiere and panties, she seemed to insist it was Wednesday, when actually it was Thursday. When Zuckerman pointed out the error, Yoshiko shrugged. After a lengthy bout with the dictionary, she had gotten him to grasp that her chartreuse panty, unfortunately, represented a series of seven which could not be recycled. When all this was explained, Zucker-man regretted having wasted time on the issue. As Choi Min-soo would have explained, even the reality of colored panties is a swift river.

In the first of their precious hours, because Yoshiko frequently ex-pressed the idea of "many GIs," Zuckerman was sure he came to her from an undifferentiated mass, passing through her life like oily bilge passes an overboard pump. Soon enough he'd put the last of his hundred and twenty hours on the counter and return to "Campu Nara," which could have been an antediluvian monster that ate him whole, for all she would care. That saddened him, beyond measure.

At noon of the first day, Yoshiko led them out into the streets to set the pattern of their splendid days. She reveled in the shops, in 1952 already foreshadowing what a renascent Japan would do to an unsuspecting world. He made Yoshiko pose for a portrait and bought her a pearl necklace that cost him a week's pay. She spent five hundred yen on an identification bracelet with Zuckerman's divisional insignia on it. Zuckerman detested the jackets with maps of Korea or large tigers with tanks in their mouths embroidered across the back. They ate pastry and fish and much of the oversweet candy Yoshiko loved.

Excepting the merchants, the Japanese they brushed against frowned and looked away. "Japanese people no rike working girls," Yoshiko ex-plained sadly.

"That's too damned bad," Zuckerman said angrily.

They spent only five minutes visiting the Great Buddha of Nara. "He looks like a fat Choi Min-soo," Zuckerman said. When he explained Choi Min-soo, Yoshiko broke his heart by frowning and saying, "Korea man number ten."

Zuckerman angrily defended his comrade-in-arms.

Yoshiko rooted herself in the street near the Great Buddha and pouted until Zuckerman pulled her arms and made her laugh.

When they returned to the room in the rear of the angular house, Zuckerman yielded to her. She was adept, even professional, but for Zuckerman it went no better than it had gone the night before.

Yoshiko got up on her knees in the bed, folded her arms across her naked breasts, and studied the problem. "Come," she commanded, "Yoshiko and Solomon-san take bath."

The staved tub, located at the end of a dark corridor, obviously had already been heated by the other ghost figures who lived there, but who kept themselves isolated from, and unremarked by, Yoshiko. The tub could launder a squad, even if one of them was Luke Plumber.

Yoshiko slipped out of her kimono and tugged at the brown one she had lent Zuckerman. The heavy steam rising above the sunken tub was daunting, and Zuckerman balked.

Yoshiko got in and dragged him in behind her. The water scalded. Yoshiko giggled. Within a couple of minutes, however, Zuckerman adjusted. Super-hot Japanese baths are like firefights, worse in the contemplation than in the action, and delightful at the successful conclusion. He reached for Yoshiko. She pushed him away. Her frown spoke volumes; baths were for bathing, not some silly Western idea of play.

Afterward, Yoshiko slid open the wall of her room and shoved Zuckerman out into a tiny garden. It was a warm spring day. Zuckerman drifted in time, sensing that Yoshiko was beautifying herself at her vanity. After several minutes, she called to him and he went in.

A nude Yoshiko lay on the bed, black hair floating free against the pillow. Her right leg was drawn up slightly, aligning her body with the west light from the open wall. The light softened as it entered the shadowed room and ricocheted from Yoshiko's moistness and into Zuckerman's mind. In the bath she had been an houri, at the vanity a mystery, now she was quintessential woman. He fell upon her.

They made long kisses and she spurred him with sound and drove him with stroking featherlets of fingers, silkening his passion and firing his loins. They seemed to climb a mountain, each step a victory, as if the world subsided even as they mounted. No faked whore's moan came out of her. She thrust to meet him with quivering sounds. She shivered then, and sighed into his ear.

They did not go out again that day. At sunset, the light came in a different color and revealed her anew. She lay naked, her toes twitching as she dreamed the dreams that danced in the heads of poor Japanese girls in 1952. Zuckerman awoke and turned to her, seeing her not so much as a soldier examines his whore but as a sculptor contemplates his model. He viewed her in sections, from the feet to the ankles to the calves to the thighs to the belly to her breasts to her neck to the tip of her head and back again, ending on the painted toes that twitched out her vitality.

In the strange fading light of a Japanese day, Zuckerman studied his own naked body—hair and hollows, scars and lumps. He compared that to the unblemished loveliness beside him. In one of those exciting moments in which understanding is yielded whole, he seized on an alpha and a beta. For the first time in his life he understood adult maleness as his culture demanded adult maleness. Immediately his mind flew to Robertson and the dead Dougherty, and to what his experiences with them had been trying to tell him. He pictured them in his new understanding. He saw it! Solomon Zuckerman could look into himself and see what they had given to him. And they had given him a model—maleness, shorn of pretense, reduced to its elements, pristine in its fierceness.

Then, for a long moment, because he had to dig the memory out from under many layers, Zuckerman evaluated the man he had bayoneted to death on Heartbreak Ridge. He wished now that he had talked to Robertson or Dougherty about him. Suddenly, almost breathlessly, he realized he no longer was afraid of his dead man. Now he saw the Korean as he was sure *they* would have seen him—such a thing was something for the private mind to contemplate over a lifetime, a personal secret, one that molded its owner, an event with a thousand faces, none of them ever definitive.

A man had to live with that: to live with it was to be a man.

Zuckerman put all this away for important future reference and resumed his analysis of Yoshiko. He wanted to memorize each crevice of her flesh, each curve, how her hair looked where it joined her brow, her teeth, and how her ankle was proportioned to her foot. If he branded these things into his brain, and should he lose her, he could buy silk and satin and fragrance and sculpt her anew. That was pure desire. And no one in the world, certainly not Avram Zuckerman, any longer possessed the right to deny him his own desires.

The light fell into the sea far to the west of Korea. Yoshiko awoke and he took her in his arms, sealing her lips with a finger to trap unneeded words.

Much later, when his arms ached from holding her, he freed one and reached into the darkness above him to ambush with his trigger hand the seconds that patrolled past there. He wanted to catch one, as they ambushed the words, and make it captive; then he could use it over and over again, forever.

But the seconds escaped easily, and became platoons that formed minutes and battalions that formed hours and regiments that would form days.

When the seconds got away from him, Zuckerman ran to flank them with new ideas. It had been a day of heartfelt words, and he had stolen *kekkon* from Yoshiko's dictionary. He inserted *kekkon* into some other words to try the fit and came up finally with a question. He rolled the idea around in his head, as if buffing the words smooth. *"Watakushi, anata, gozaimusu kekkon?"* probably made execrable Japanese. But the words were so lovely.

He knew it was insane. Avram Zuckerman would die a little death if such a thing as his new question begged should transpire. But he no longer feared either fire or fathers.

Besides, wise black Thomas Carver, hooked into the tubes of the battalion aid station that bitter night and waiting for the surgeon to tape his gut, had told him something.

Zuckerman had lowered his eyes. Seeing Carver lived, he had said, "What Lieutenant Robertson did tonight was insane."

Carver had pushed a hint of smile through his pain. "All combat leaders are crazy, Solly. We have to be. Remember that. You'll get the squad now."

Three days from now, Zuckerman decided, he's ask his insane *kekkon* question.

Days two, three, and four were blurred, whirled like the frosting on a wedding cake, platinum hours of golden minutes, during which Zuckerman felt all the excited happiness of a new puppy.

On the eve of day five he had asked his question. He pointed to himself, said *"Watakushi,"* to Yoshiko and said *"Anata"* and then, pronouns out of the way, he offered *"Goziamusu kekkon."*

They were sitting in Yoshiko's minuscule garden doing what the Japanese love to do: watching a beautiful sunset from a terrace. Yoshiko's legs were tucked under, as Japanese women sit; Zuckerman sat on his rump.

Yoshiko's forthright eyes went from puzzlement through fright to anger. She exploded out of trembling lips, "Whatsamatter crazy GI! Working girl no can marry crazy GI and go stateside!"

"I don't see why not," Zuckerman said carefully, fighting a sense of alarm.

Yoshiko hunted up a word. "American people make much prejudiced to Japanese working girl."

"I'm a Jew. I know all about prejudice," Zuckerman reassured. "Let's get married."

Yoshiko offered a dozen definitive reasons why she couldn't. He offered a dozen countervailing reasons why she could.

Then Yoshiko began to cry. Zuckerman slid over to her. She put her forehead on his shoulder and quit sobbing when he patted her back.

"*Kudasai*, Yoshiko. Please think on it."

In the night some thick clouds came up from the East China Sea and drove down rain onto Yoshiko's house. They lay in her bed and listened to the drumming rain. Like a bundling board, the question lay between them. The earth turned, dragging through the ether its cold moon and its troubled children.

The dreary wet morning that followed had for Zuckerman all the passion of an early commuter train. The world was sick with fog and mists. At noon, Yoshiko sent him down to the corner to get pastry from the stall tended by a wizened little man with two missing fingers. He returned to a new vision.

Yoshiko bowed deeply and said, "*Ohayo goziamusu, Sergeant-san.*" She had put her hair into a huge bun with a long slender needle stuck through it, laying bare the neck, a part of the body considered highly erotic in Japan. White powder covered her face, contrasting with the severe black kimono she wore. Her eyes were pale and unshadowed, for the first time presenting a pronounced slant. All in all, he saw clearly, Yoshiko no longer aped a Fordham coed; now she was a samurai's mistress, Mount Fuji in a sere autumn, done in pastels.

Before he could react, Yoshiko dragged him to the dripping garden. In the lee of the overhang from the main house, she had set up a low table, although it was far too cool for an American to enjoy alfresco dining. When he sat on his rump, she spewed Japanese, gesturing to him to sit on folded legs. She served the pastry with a dish of pickled vegetables and pressed squid.

The food tasted vile to Zuckerman. He frowned. Yoshiko bowed away and returned with raw fish and sauce.

"Eat with me as we always do," Zuckerman pleaded.

Yoshiko kneeled carefully to his side, but not close enough to the table to share the meal. After pouring green tea into tiny blue porcelain cups, she chatted gaily in Japanese, punctuating her words with sharp "ne's" and "hai's." Her hands were folded on her knees and her head was down. She probably discussed the rain, or perhaps the goldfish she kept in her tiny pond, a body of water off the terrace about the size of a washtub.

Hoping to extricate himself from wherever he was, Zuckerman asked for some music. Yoshiko arose and glided away, using the secret muscles dainty Japanese women seem to have. The record player spun up a *plink, plank, plonk* and a vocal accompaniment that sounded to Zuckerman like a drunken Eskimo keening the loss of a sled dog. Zuckerman had never heard the samisen; he likened it to a broken banjo.

"Number-one song," Yoshiko said.

Zuckerman exploded. "Damn it, Yoshiko, what's going on? Why won't you eat with me?"

Yoshiko's eyes went down demurely. "Japanese woman no eat with Japanese man."

"American women eat with American men!"

Yoshiko answered sweetly, "Sergeant-san not in America. Sergeant-san in Japan."

All the obviousness of it fell into place. Zuckerman sighed. "You're right, Yoshiko." He realized he had gotten his answer to *kekkon*, served up with pressed squid and an ancient ballad.

Yoshiko giggled and tossed her head playfully.

In the final afternoon they did boy-and-girl things with dictionaries and beds and touches and liftings of the eyes. Yoshiko wiped away the white powder, but otherwise she remained carefully in the East.

The rain ended in early evening. Zuckerman lay on the bed shirtless, holding her. She touched the scar under his nipple, cut when the missile had glanced from his rib cage. A concerned, tentative, small finger traced it. "Solomon-san much frightened in war-ru?" a tender voice inquired, emphasizing the emotion with liquid brown eyes.

He thought a moment before shaking his head slowly in the negative. Then he asked, "What will the working girls do when all the GIs go stateside?"

Yoshiko clammed up, but soon spoke. "Be rich. Buy much land. Japan be rich rike America. Many PX. Ne?"

He caught a tear on his finger and tasted it. "Sure, Yoshiko. You deserve all of Honshu."

Later, she glanced at his watch, smiled sadly, and slid out of bed. She sat at her vanity, bare to her waist, pert nipples thrust toward what she did there.

Puzzled, Zuckerman could see she worked at writing. Consulting her dictionary, she created long columns of Japanese characters, editing as she wrote, once killing two entire columns with a slash of her pencil. After about ten minutes of this she put her paper aside and began to work on herself.

Off came the Orient; she crossed an invisible dateline and on went the West. Her satin hair came out of the bun and went again into the ponytail, caught there with the tiny band studded with jade.

Now in her other world, Yoshiko raced through her dictionary and snared words to write in English. Finished writing, she practiced silently about five minutes moving the words through her lips, watching herself in the mirror.

"What did you write?" Zuckerman asked. To translate, he held out his left palm and pretended to hold a moving pen with his right hand.

Yoshiko nodded her understanding. "Make-u words, Solomon-san. Number-one words, ne?"

Not knowing what the words were, he shrugged and smiled helplessly. She stood up clad only in a lemon weekie that was erroneously labeled Sunday. Zuckerman made a face. Yoshiko stared thoughtfully a moment, then rummaged in a drawer and came up with a bright orange panty. When she changed, Zuckerman smiled; the orange weekie had "Monday" printed near the crotch. Now the world of infantry sergeants and prostitutes was back in temporal sync.

On went the red dress and black pumps of the first evening. For his last R-and-R chore, Zuckerman fastened the clasp of the dainty pearl necklace he had bought her.

"Time go Campu Nara."

"Yes. It's time."

Yoshiko made the bus halt several long blocks from the cantonment. They lingered through a soft spring night, holding hands in defiance of the stern Japan Logistical Command directive against public displays of affection between American personnel and indigenous females. When they neared the gate, Yoshiko pulled Zuckerman off to the side near a high wall, into a black refuge lighted only faintly by the remainder of the world. Standing on tiptoe, pulling down his face with both hands, she kissed him.

Hardly was it a whore's kiss. Call it a long hungry gift, a fusion that admitted no barrier.

She stepped back, held both his hands, and spoke her sentence. Although she had labored hard for it, the phrases came out slightly stilted. Notwithstanding, the syllables were round and honest, with proper *l*'s. "Solomon Zuckerman, I love you with all my sad heart on this night of our parting and I envy with fierceness the fortunate woman who someday will possess you."

She brushed his lips and melted into the night. He thought he heard a stifled sob and waited. Perhaps she was merely caught in some perverse time warp that would disappear and restore her to him, returning to them the platinum hours.

But she was gone. One night had given her, another had taken her, leaving him only her memory. Like the thrush before Konsi, he had tried to touch loveliness and it had flown away.

That, too, was a man's lot.

23

RETURN FROM NARA, MARCH 11, 1952

The camouflage-drab C-54 banked lazily into the north for about three minutes. Then, the radar identification completed and the codes radioed, it banked left, as lazily as before, and resumed a heading of west by north, now with some assurance the antiaircraft of the United Nations would not blast it from the sky. An aircraft suspended in a cobalt yellow dawn over an azure sea defies the sense of motion, but the trooplift C-54 actually churned along at about a hundred and sixty knots. Perhaps it was capable of another fifteen knots, but the pilots this morning flew under curbed throttles; the Korean War effort in 1952 wanted endurance more than speed.

Misty Japan fell away behind the tail; misty Korea crept up over the nose.

In the drafty fuselage, Sgt. Solomon Zuckerman twisted on the hard bucket seat, dug a parachute strap out of his crotch, and turned to study the disheveled and sleepy men who rode with him. A fellow sergeant had yanked them out of bed at Camp Nara about 0300, ignoring one man's loud protest that nobody was up at 0300 except burglars and bad women. Zuckerman was nailed as NCO-in-charge. They breakfasted on cold cereal and lukewarm coffee and rode a bus to the airfield. Marching them from the bus to the terminal, Zuckerman had a new insight. In ranks, they were mindless; he could have marched them across Cathay to the frozen Gobi and they'd never have questioned his orders. Only out of ranks did men have individual accountability and purpose. He tucked that knowledge away with the other things he had learned in Japan.

A man with a huge nose over a handlebar mustache sat next to him. He shouted across the noise to a friend: "I'm going back there someday."

The friend frowned out of a hangover. "I ain't. I bet that old gal had clap."

Zuckerman fondled the manila envelope in his lap—it contained the letter he had started to Rachel Kahan and the picture of Yoshiko Yamada—and anchored the contradictions on each corner of his mind while he reviewed his own R and R, which had expired in the cheerless squad room at Camp Nara seven hours earlier. He sighed, then put his mind to Korea.

He thought about it differently now. In the early days of his tour, he had armored himself in the ignorant supposition that since he had never been killed before, he would not get killed in the Korean War infantry: KIA happened to the other guy. But, at some point—maybe it was the day he had cringed under the lash of Heartbreak Ridge—he had surrendered that armor, putting on thin sackcloth instead, yielding himself to the unthinkable, just wondering how it would happen, as it had happened for Kang and Fowlkes and Plumber and Dougherty and Cole and the nameless others in the company. It amused him that he could have thought about it either of those two ways. For the first time, he forced himself to view the reality of it. Unless he made an egregious error or drew a wrong card from the dealer named Luck, he'd survive, as most of them would survive. He had some control over error; he had none over luck. He'd concentrate upon what he could control.

The cheerful man with the handlebar mustache poked Zuckerman in the ribs. "What outfit?" he asked.

Zuckerman named his company and regiment.

The poker grinned. "Isn't that the regiment where that nutty lieutenant a couple of months ago called the 105s down on his own ass? Must put something in your coffee in that outfit."

Zuckerman smiled patiently. "Saltpeter," he said. "They put so much saltpeter in our coffee the married men begin letters to their wives with 'Dear Friend.' "

"The hell you say? Never heard that one." He shouted it across the aisle and his hungover friend threw up his hands in disgust. "Poor sick bastard's got no sense of humor this morning," said the man with the mustache.

When Zuckerman got back on the hill, he reported to First Sergeant Tatum, a cadaverous man who had replaced Manston. Tatum greeted, "Sergeant Zuckerman I presume. We missed you. How was R and R?"

Something warm in Tatum's manner struck Zuckerman. Then, although he barely knew Tatum, he felt the warm glow of homecoming. And there was something else, subtle to be sure, but as important. Tatum, who had surely served thirty years, greeted him as a fellow NCO, according him by tone and gesture full respect in the fraternity of sergeants. It was almost dizzying.

"Nipland was still afloat when I left it," Zuckerman answered. "How did it go here?"

"Swimmingly, Sergeant, for infantry work. Want to sleep it off or want to soldier today?"

Zuckerman grinned. "I'll soldier, Top. But thanks for the option."

"My pleasure."

Zuckerman hesitated a moment before asking, "My squad?"

Tatum smiled. "Your men are like you left them—on line, dirty, horny, and dumb."

Two days later, Zuckerman tore up the disengagement letter he had started to Rachel Kahan. He made the pieces so small that the wind snatched them away easily, blowing them east along the line, which now and then fitfully spat out mortar rounds and small-arms fire. Then, in the mood for correspondence, he wrote a long letter to his father. The gist of it was in the opening sentence. "I have been lying to you about where I'm serving." About midway through, the letter rounded a corner into "I'm sorry if my deceit hurts you and Mother, but at the time that's how I saw it. Before you blow up at me, I want to remind you that I am now as old as you were when you married Mother." The letter ended with a long description of the men of First Squad, living, wounded, and dead, although Zuckerman did not mention their particular statuses.

That evening, on cue from the CP, he led half his squad back to the kitchen bunker near the dirt road at the base of the hill to stand in line for Salisbury steak and powdered potatoes. At Zuckerman's order, the men stood a mortar-interval apart, to reduce the heartache should the Chinese get lucky.

But Klineschmidt had crowded up against Johnson. Zuckerman anchored the end of the line, as Robertson and Carver had done before him. His thoughts lagged behind his whereabouts. He only half realized that Kraut Klineschmidt was playing with a fragmentation grenade.

The game was for a man to unpin a grenade and press it up against another man's belly, saying something like, "I've had it, old buddy. Let's go out together." The butt of this evening's joke was John NMI Johnson.

Zuckerman heard someone shout, "Loose grenade!" and heard Klineschmidt answer, "Where? Where is a loose grenade?"

"On you, you fucking moron!"

Apparently startled, Klineschmidt dropped the grenade. It spun in the dirt, hissing as the powder train, no longer sleeping under the thumb of the butterfly safety, sizzled down toward the igniter. Everyone but Zuckerman, Klineschmidt, and Johnson scattered headlong. Klineschmidt and Johnson stood rooted, apparently staring down into the face of disaster.

Stepping forward instantly, Zuckerman snatched up the grenade, feeling it vibrate in his hand. He used a second of fuse time taking a deep breath, and another demonstrative second holding the grenade under Klineschmidt's nose. Then he shouted a playful "Fire in the hole!" and lobbed the grenade across the road in a casual underhand pitch.

The ridges echoed with the blast. Captain Hartung came down on the final echo, surrounded by blue air. "What the goddamned hell is going on here, you men? Who exploded a goddamned hand grenade?"

"I exploded the hand grenade, Captain," Zuckerman admitted.

"Why did you explode a hand grenade? Hand grenades cost money. You are not supposed to be exploding goddamned hand grenades now; you are supposed to be eating Salisbury steak and potatoes."

Zuckerman said, "I wanted to get rid of it; it was hot."

The white-faced men had reassembled. Several explained at once, fingering an ashen Klineschmidt.

Hartung snarled to Zuckerman, "Take the hand grenades away from this man and punish him. Give them *all* a lecture on weapons safety." He glanced around, shook his head sadly, and said quietly to Zuckerman, "Thank you, Sergeant. Takes a whole bunch of balls to scoop up a live hand grenade. If I didn't have good NCOs, I wouldn't have a soldier left."

The company commander went off to his command post, chuffing remarks about "goddamned kids and their goddamned toys" and "I only have one week to go and I have to put up with crap like this."

Klineschmidt shouldered his way through the other men and ran up the hill toward the perimeter. Johnson sat down shakily.

Zuckerman watched Klineschmidt's back until it disappeared, then went to the head of the chow line, past nervous men. One muttered, "Bastard Zuckerman's pulling rank on line. Just because he saved a couple of guys' lives, he wants to eat first."

Zuckerman spun slowly to stifle the mutterer with his newly acquired sergeant's hauteur, waiting hands on hips until the chow line settled. Then he turned to the cook. "I need two sandwiches. Make them good ones."

"I only got bread and margarine," the cook replied sourly. "This ain't the Waldorf."

Zuckerman smiled firmly and the cook built the sandwiches.

Several mortar rounds came in, impacting across the road. The men ducked, several spilling their mess trays. Zuckerman stood calmly, showing only casual interest, even when a second flight crawled a few yards closer to the road, but still far out of deadly range. Zuckerman knew the Chinese could not observe them there; it was as safe to stand one place as another. The others would learn.

One man, who had lost his tray, shouted angrily, "If those Chinks want to come over here and eat this stuff, I'll gladly go over there and fire their damned mortars for them while they eat."

Zuckerman took his sandwiches and started for the hill; life had returned to normal.

A dejected Klineschmidt sat in a sandbagged hole, head in his hands. The dirt on his cheek had been smudged by fingers wiping at his eyes.

"Brought you some chow," Zuckerman said gently. "Don't pass up hot chow. We don't know what the night will bring." He forced Klineschmidt to take the sandwiches.

"Christ, Solly. I almost killed Johnson with my stupid farting around. I wouldn't hurt Johnson for a million bucks."

"He knows that. Eat."

About midway through the first sandwich, Klineschmidt raised his head. He wiped a crumb from the corner of his stubbled lip and asked, "How are you going to punish me? Whatever it is, I got it coming."

"I'm punishing you now."

"How are you doing that? You seem to be being nice to me."

"Think on it," Zuckerman suggested quietly.

Klineschmidt chewed thoughtfully. Between sandwiches, he said, "Christ, if I didn't know you was Solly Zuckerman, I'd think you were Robertson. That's how he did it. He could ream your ass with one eye and make you feel good with the other one. Like you're doing now."

"No. I'm Zuckerman. But thanks for the compliment. If I had to be somebody else, I'd want to be Don Robertson."

"I don't know. He had a lot on his mind, and I ain't sure all of it was healthy for him. Wonder if he's still in Seoul? Captain Hartung said they had sent him back there from the MASH."

"Hundred and Seventh Evac," Zuckerman answered. "He'll surely be sent to the States from there."

After a moment, Klineschmidt asked, "Will we ever see him again?"

Zuckerman shook his head. He smiled. "The personnel clerks giveth and the personnel clerks taketh away."

Restored to humor, Klineschmidt laughed. "What do they giveth?

They ain't done nothing for me but assign me to the leg infantry and ship my butt to Frozen Chosen here."

After a long hesitation, Zuckerman answered, "They give us friends. Better than friends . . . they give us brothers."

A flight of artillery whistled overhead.

"Incoming?" Klineschmidt asked casually.

"Outbound."

The shells burst in the distance, spitting up light, then hollow sound. Zuckerman caught Klineschmidt's eye. He realized that they were sharing a moment of awareness. They laughed together.

"A few months ago we'd have been running for cover," Zuckerman noted.

"Ain't that the truth!"

The artillerymen did not fire again. Zuckerman surmised that they simply did not want to clean the tubes that night.

He took out his bayonet and played with it. He stuck it in the ground, pulled it back, then reinserted it, repeating the movement, deeper each time, unconsciously dealing with himself and the event in his life called Korea.

Finally, he stood and put the bayonet back into its scabbard. Before he could speak, Klineschmidt lifted a hand to gesture west. "Suppose we ought to write a letter to Lieutenant Robertson?"

"No. He'd not want that." A flurry of rifle fire erupted east of them. Zuckerman listened and heard no return fire. "Green men," he said absently. "They're firing at their own imaginations."

Klineschmidt nodded, then asked, "Why wouldn't Lieutenant Robertson want to hear from us?"

Zuckerman didn't answer that. Instead, he handed Klineschmidt the two hand grenades he had brought up along with the sandwiches. "Here, hang on to these. You're the only man in my squad who knows what to do with a grenade."

"You *really* mean that, Solly?"

"I mean it. The men will rag you about it a few days, then they'll forget it. Captain Hartung has forgotten it already."

Klineschmidt hesitated, wanting to upend something. Finally he touched Zuckerman's boot. "Would you please stay just a minute longer, Solly? I don't want to be alone."

Suddenly Zuckerman had a new insight. The army endowed officers with vast privilege to keep them aloof from the men, on the theory that privilege and aloofness bred awe, which engendered obedience. Then the sergeants, who lived so intimately with the men they could smell their very souls, carried out the war. There was no grander appointment, anywhere, than infantry sergeant on a combat line.

Zuckerman ran through his head a litany of night duties, the ever-pressing chores from which no trench infantry sergeant escaped. Things needed inspecting; weapons needed checking. He'd insist the men settle down with water, flares, and ammunition, lest they wander around in the night. He had a sign and countersign to learn and pass along. He needed to touch shoulders and pat fannies, to encourage, to correct. He'd ask casually about whether weapons had been cleaned and oiled, as though merely making conversation. He'd remind soldiers that only one man of a pair could sleep, and order that sleeping bags could not be drawn up further than the sentinel's waist. He'd have three men on a listening post down the hill. He'd not sleep, because they'd not sleep. He'd evaluate the orders he got and relate them to First Squad, Second Platoon, as Hartung evaluated the battalion orders and related them to the company. He'd listen to complaints and correct what he could, trying to explain what he could not.

For the fiftieth time he'd scrutinize fields of fire and approach axes, seeing in his mind barbed wire and land mines and machine-gun barrels, considering how the individuals under his orders would respond to this or that eventuality. He'd use what he had learned and guess at the rest of it, hoping he was correct. Then, if the Chinese came in the night, he'd swallow his own fear and try his best to keep his men alive.

Klineschmidt repeated, "Will you stay with me a few minutes?"

"Sure. If it's important to you, I can stay a moment. I have nothing else to do."

24

SEOUL, SOUTH KOREA, FEBRUARY 15, 1952

Lt. Vivian Hardiman swept into Robertson's room at the 107th Evacuation Hospital shortly after 0800 hours. The nurse walked head erect, smiling, heels clacking briskly on the hardwood floor. She carried herself the way a high-fashion model carries herself down a fashion show runway.

Robertson saw she dressed in what he assumed was Nurses' Class B—skirt, neat olive green blouse, hose, and heels. He knew it was not the uniform of the day. Marian, the friendly day nurse who had brought him breakfast, a chipper wake-up, and a thoroughgoing inquiry into vital signs, had worn fatigues, as had Mildred Baumiller the night before.

Then Robertson groaned inwardly. He remembered she had told him a general was coming.

Vivian entered grandly, as if on a cloud of perfumed loveliness, trailing two subservient hospital corpsmen and an elderly Korean who toted barber utensils. She went directly to Robertson's window and threw it open, despite the winter cold.

"Good morning, Lieutenant Robertson!" she chirped. "You have very distinguished visitors coming at 1100 hours. I must get you ready." Vivian's obvious good humor made her lovely soprano come across like crushed ice falling into a crystal glass.

Robertson sighed. The older of the two corpsmen smiled sympathetically. "I had forgotten all about that," he lied.

Vivian shushed him playfully. "You don't forget a visit from a three-star general. You're just too modest. General Holloway will bring the press . . . and our commander, Colonel Williams." She let that sink in and added, "It will be exciting for us, Lieutenant Robertson. You just wait and see."

Vivian waved a commanding hand and the Korean barber snipped at Robertson's hair. The two corpsmen stood, satellites to Vivian's sun, but got no immediate orders. No one spoke until Vivian was satisfied with the hair. She had wanted some more off over the right ear, but smiled when the elderly Korean parted it neatly.

She told Robertson he was quite a hero and that the general was really coming to show him off. She ordered the Korean to shave Robertson. The Korean produced a long straight razor and smiled deferentially.

"Show me off?" Robertson asked.

"Of course," Vivian replied. "What else would you do with a hero?"

Robertson groaned, blushing because the two corpsmen seemed enthralled by the silly exchange.

"You're our resident hero, Robertson. The general is coming to give you your Silver Star. Soon you will have your Medal of Honor."

Robertson felt well enough to scoff. "When the army gives you a medal, it just lets you knock off for an hour or two and sends you down to headquarters."

"Well," Vivian retorted cheerily, "the general is coming; that's what's important to us." She smiled down. "General officers certainly don't tell army nurses what they have in mind." Vivian said the latter as if she disapproved of it. The barber finished and wiped Robertson's face with a towel. The lotion from the black bottle he carried reeked.

Vivian backed up a pace. She put a hand to her lovely chin and studied Robertson. "That's the best I can do," she said absently. She snapped her fingers and the room emptied of corpsmen and barbers.

Robertson realized the corpsmen had done nothing except provide an entourage.

"You're going to freeze us to death," Robertson said to Vivian.

"Let it air out a few more minutes. We don't want a hospital odor that . . . well . . . that suggests you are infirm." She added, her voice scolding, "You're moderately handsome, Robertson. You've got to learn to use that."

Robertson groaned again. Sam Dougherty was the only man he had ever perceived in the context of masculine handsomeness. He decided to get off the subject. "I met Mildred Baumiller," he said tentatively.

"Mouse? She stood by for Marian yesterday. She normally has the night assignment. She's very junior."

"I don't think Lieutenant Baumiller likes the name Mouse."

"Why ever not? It fits her perfectly."

Robertson spoke sternly. "If it fits her, it's a bad nickname. Then it mocks the obvious."

Vivian had been about to turn away from the bed. Her face froze; the smile replaced by something hard and hostile. But in an instant that, too, was gone. "I'm sure I don't understand you," she said levelly. "If the name fits her, that is her fault. I can't change what she is."

Robertson saw that Vivian Hardiman, like most beautiful women, conceded nothing. She smiled once more, closed the window, and went out of the room.

Hospital minutes sigh; hospital hours weep. Robertson studied his lofty ceiling. He reviewed what he knew of generals. He had spoken to only one of them. It was not their rarity so much as their aloofness that had impressed him.

The one occasion had been at Fort Riley, about Robertson's ninth week of basic training, almost six years earlier. The training officer had ordered him back to the cantonment from a field exercise to attend one of the innumerable administrative matters that plague khaki men. "How will I get there, sir?" Robertson had asked.

"It's only five miles, soldier. Walk. You have ninety minutes and it's only *five* miles."

Robertson had put himself on the gravel toward the fort, accompanied only by a sense of urgency and a critical review of army personnel practices. After about two miles he heard a car brake a few feet behind him. He heard the horn, one commanding blast. He turned to confront a Plymouth staff car bearing for license plate a red square embossed with a single gold star. His heart pounded.

The black driver signaled through the windshield that Robertson was to present himself. He saluted the gold star and went to confront the driver.

The driver was a master sergeant. "Get in, soldier," he whispered. "General Knudson wants to give you a lift."

Unthinking, Robertson reached for the handle of the left rear door.

The black driver's eyes scolded majestically. "In the front with me," he hissed.

Robertson reddened and walked around the rear of the car to reach for the handle of the right front door. He felt overpowered; a soldier in basic training dwells in a world in which a corporal sits on the right hand of God.

The stiff white-haired figure in the rear seat cleared his throat loudly. Robertson froze, door half open.

The sergeant said, "The general wants to say something to you, soldier."

But the general wished to speak to his sergeant.

"The soldier can sit in the rear with me," the general said.

"He wants you to sit in the rear with him," the driver explained pleasantly.

Robertson closed the door gently and went around the rear of the car again to slide in on the left side of the general. The brigadier wore an Eisenhower jacket and three rows of ribbons. The sergeant engaged the clutch and drove. Robertson sat pressed against the door. He applied pressure on his knees to keep his feet from dancing on the general's beige carpet. Among other things, Robertson saw that the black master sergeant had a mole under his left ear, that the Plymouth had 17,654 miles on the odometer, and that the engine temperature and oil pressure were normal.

Several gravelly minutes tinged up under the fenders of the Plymouth. The general cleared his throat again.

"The general wants to speak," the driver explained, speaking over his shoulder.

Robertson licked his dry lips, but could say nothing.

"The general wants to speak," the sergeant reminded firmly.

Robertson panicked. He struggled to understand how he kept a general officer from speaking in the rear seat of his own Plymouth staff car. He managed a shaky "Yes, sir."

"What outfit are you with, soldier?" the general demanded in a paternal voice.

"B Company, sir. B Company."

"Good outfit?"

"Yes, sir. Very good outfit."

"Good."

The staff car passed two trucks towing trailers before General Knudson cleared his throat to indicate he wished to speak again.

Robertson had heartened. He did not wait for the general to invoke the black driver. "Yes, sir."

"B Company feeding you all right?"

"Yes, sir. The B Company food is very good, sir."

"That's good. Are they teaching you how to shoot?"

"Yes, sir. They issued me a new rifle. I like it very much, sir."

"That's good. A soldier should like his rifle." General Knudson said nothing more. The car went several long blocks beyond Robertson's destination before Robertson worked up the courage to clear his own throat. General Knudson cleared his throat. The car stopped at once, in a street between rows of barracks, near a company mess hall.

Robertson got out and stood next to a smelly garbage can. He came to attention and saluted gravely. He got back a half salute and a comradely smile. The driver nodded and the Plymouth pulled away. Robertson gazed at the red license tag with its single gold star until it turned the corner and disappeared.

So much for general officers. They cleared their throats a lot and they were interested in what people ate and whether or not people were learning to shoot.

Robertson was recalled from his reverie by the official flurry that exploded into his room. A thin colonel of medicine led an assault team that included a freshly lipsticked Vivian Hardiman, an Adjutant General Corps first lieutenant, and three individuals in civilianish ODs. The early-comers lined up in two files, leaving an aisle between them. Soon Gen. Milton Holloway breezed down the human corridor, smiling warmly.

General Holloway was younger than the elderly brigadier who had rescued Robertson from the gravel miles that day at Fort Riley. About sixty, he exuded an air of generous confidence that made Robertson want to like him, general officer notwithstanding. Robertson knew well that after Van Fleet, Holloway was considered the top soldier in Korea.

Vivian came to the head of the bed, smiled reassuringly for Robertson, placed her hand on his shoulder, and turned to face the three civilians, two of whom carried impressive press graphic cameras.

General Holloway extended his right hand.

Vivian was on her toes. "His right arm is immobile, General."

The general was momentarily flustered, then laughed. "Then by God we'll shake southpaw, Lieutenant Robertson."

Robertson got out his left hand. The general's grasp was dry and firm.

After the handshake, the AGC lieutenant stepped forward and handed the general a small, narrow blue box. The general opened it and withdrew a medal.

"Your Silver Star," he said, holding it up for the three civilians to see. The ribbon was red, white, and blue, suspending a star on a wreath on a star.

The AGC officer produced a citation and read aloud an improved version of what Captain Hartung had written a hundred and twenty days earlier. Even for decorations, the mill ground fine.

When he finished the recitation, the lieutenant glanced at General Holloway, who nodded for him to go on. "Lieutenant Robertson was an enlisted man then," the lieutenant explained to the three civilians. "His decorations have not been able to keep up with his promotions."

One of the correspondents, a sallow man reeking of self-importance, raised a hand. "I thought he was to receive the Congressional Medal of Honor?"

General Holloway spoke. "That's no secret. But the CMH is awarded by Congress, and normally is presented by the commander in chief. Lieutenant Robertson will receive that honor when he returns to the ZI."

Holloway put the medal on Robertson's blanket over his left breast and stepped back.

Two press graphics raised and pointed at Robertson. He felt Vivian's hand clutch his shoulder. The flashbulbs blinded. He felt Vivian's hand depart. He knew she would be smiling seductively; everyone except General Holloway and Colonel Williams stared over his head, obviously at Vivian. Colonel Williams gazed fondly on the general. The general smiled down at Robertson.

The scene continued. Robertson thought that the giving of medals must explain why French generals kissed their soldiers. You just can't put a Silver Star on a man's breast and walk away. The AGC officer—Robertson had guessed the man was a press relations officer, one of a corps of thousands busily engaged in selling the American people an army they had already bought—riffled through some releases.

"Here's something I prepared on Lieutenant Robertson's background," he told the three civilians, who just as obviously were the press to whom he related. "You can see that he's from Kansas." The PRO turned to Robertson. "You are from Kansas, aren't you?"

"Yes," Robertson said.

"Kansas," the PRO lieutenant repeated, his tone suggesting he had not expected the admission.

General Holloway rescued them. "Lieutenant Robertson is a very special soldier now. We want him to get well so he will be of use to us." The general fixed Colonel Williams in a firm do-you-understand gaze. Colonel Williams nodded vigorously.

The sallow correspondent came closer to the bed. Robertson met his eyes. The man reeked of arrogance, which Robertson suspected came with press credentials. War correspondents dressed like soldiers—they were granted a courtesy rank of major—to gain entrée, but were enough unlike soldiers to avoid combat. Robertson had heard about the regimental commander the previous spring who had been called a "little chicken colonel" by an insulted correspondent, apparently because the colonel was too busy fighting to host him. It was known widely among working soldiers that the little chicken colonel had personally thrown the war correspondent out of the command post on his well-credentialed butt.

The sallow correspondent about to interrogate Robertson was named Merriman. "Do you miss home?" he asked.

Robertson winced. Home had been the Tanner root cellar. But he lied, as regulations no doubt required. "Yes, sir. I miss home." Then he sighed heavily. Home was also the men he had left at George Company.

The scene still continued while Merriman wrote something on his pad. Robertson felt Vivian's hand again. The flashbulbs popped. Vivian's hand left his shoulder.

General Holloway cleared his throat loudly. The AGC PRO began to clear the room. Vivian frowned at Robertson, as if it had been he who excluded her, but she trailed Colonel Williams meekly enough.

After they were alone, General Holloway motioned to Robertson's bed. "May I sit down? Corps commanders are supposed to stand around and be stuffy, but we've had enough of that this morning."

Robertson knew his earlier favorable judgment of the general had been correct. He slid his legs over to make room.

The general offered Robertson a Lucky Strike and lit it for him. They smoked in silence a few moments. "Thank you, Lieutenant, and that's personal. Byron Thompson has told me about your record. You earned the Silver Star and the CMH. I'm proud to have you in my corps." General Holloway waved a hand in the direction of the EUSAK main line of resistance many miles north and added, "Colonel Thompson is also very proud of you. In many ways that's a higher honor than your medals. Byron Thompson is one of the finest officers in the American army."

"Others were involved, sir. Will they get medals?"

"I'm certain Colonel Thompson has his people busy on that," General Holloway said. He hesitated, inviting Robertson to speak.

Robertson saw an opportunity to say something that had been on his mind. He hesitated, gauging the moment carefully before saying, "There is one man, sir." He told the general about Dougherty, ending with, "When I left him out there, I . . . both of us . . . knew he wouldn't get out." He turned his head. Almost a minute elapsed before he said quietly, "That was my worst mistake, sir. I should have ordered them all out."

Holloway spoke as quietly. "Never hindsight a combat order, Lieutenant. No one but you can judge your decisions that night. And don't be hard on yourself. Whatever the Koreans had in mind, you and your man Dougherty put finis to it."

"Isn't there such a thing as a posthumous pardon, sir? He's earned that more than I've earned medals."

General Holloway frowned. "I'm sure that is possible. I'll have my senior aide look into it."

"And his rank, sir. He was a sergeant first class before . . . well, before his trouble."

"I'll have my staff look into that, too."

"Thank you, sir."

General Holloway asked a few innocuous questions, then asked, "How are you feeling?"

"Very good, sir."

General Holloway grinned. "I'll let you work me for decorations for your men, Lieutenant. But I will not let you bullshit an old soldier about gunshot wounds."

Robertson looked at the rows of ribbons on the general's chest. He saw a Purple Heart with two gold stars, indicating three wounds.

"You were an infantryman, sir?"

"Yes, I was, and I tried to be a damned good one. Regiment in the ETO and a division over here in 1950."

"I feel I'm getting stronger every day. I think I'll be able to return to the regiment in a few days."

General Holloway stood up and turned to catch Robertson's eyes. "How well do you know Colonel Thompson?" he asked abruptly.

"Not well, sir. What I know of him I admire."

"He drove down to corps headquarters a few days ago and had lunch with me. We had a long talk. Among other things, he feels he is responsible for your current wounds. He told me that when he commissioned you, he gave you some nonsense about an officer protecting his men with the armor of his thin khaki shirt."

"That wasn't nonsense, sir," Robertson protested.

"No, I suppose not." General Holloway put his hands out, as if to end that portion of the conversation. "Do you know why Colonel Thompson didn't come to the MASH to see you?"

Robertson hadn't thought about it. "I suppose he's busy. He's a regimental commander."

"He doesn't want to face you right now. He feels he made an error in judgment and he thinks now he should have sent you home instead of commissioning you. I'll give it to you in his words—he told me he didn't realize you were suicidally brave. . . ." The general went on quickly, obviously speaking now from a prepared agenda. "You badgered your physician at the 1037th to remain in Korea, and now you're badgering here. Do you think that wise?"

"I want to remain in Korea, sir," Robertson said firmly.

"Why? I admire a tiger, but you've had enough. Take your honors and go home. You've done your share. You have a fine career ahead of you. Byron Thompson will get a star when he leaves Korea. He'll ask for you—that's how you pull along in the army."

Robertson blurted, "Let me stay here, sir. You have the authority to order it."

"You haven't told me why I should. Your commander asked me to order you home. You're going against his wishes."

Robertson's eyes pleaded. The general looked away again.

The nurse Marian came in. She saw the general, mumbled an apology, and backed away.

General Holloway smiled toward Marian and she closed the door quietly but firmly. He fished two small objects from his shirt pocket. "Byron Thompson asked me to give these to you."

Holloway placed a pair of well-worn colonel's collar insignias in Robertson's left hand. Before Robertson could react, he produced a folded note. "This note is to accompany the eagles."

The regimental commander had written in longhand.

I've asked General Holloway to be my emissary with the eagles. About twenty years from now I want you to put them on your tunic and remember who gave them to you. I also want you to know that the most difficult order I've ever given—and I've given some difficult ones—is the order I gave Redman to fire your mission on the night of 4 January.

Robertson folded the note and looked up to meet Holloway's gaze. "Why give eagles to me? I can't honor them."

"Byron Thompson thinks you'll be chief of staff someday." Holding up his hand to stem protest, Holloway added, "I've known Colonel Thompson since he was a shavetail and I was the army's senior captain. He has excellent judgment. If he gives a lieutenant a colonel's insignia, I have no doubt he merely anticipates the promotion board by a few years."

Robertson suddenly felt drained. He clenched the insignias, then relaxed his hand and looked away.

Holloway stood erect. "I have deputies who can hand out Silver Stars, Lieutenant Robertson. I wanted to come here today to test my own judgment. I permitted the 1037th to send you here because I didn't know for certain what to do with you. Now I will tell you why I'm not certain." Holloway went to the window, speaking now over his shoulder. His voice had lowered and Robertson detected anguish there.

The general went on. "I persuaded my son to follow me into this business. Against his mother's wishes, he followed me into the infantry, then to Korea. Carl, that was his name, went missing during the Naktong defense. That's it—he just disappeared. Not a trace. Nothing."

Robertson winced inwardly. "It's natural that a son would want to go into his father's profession, sir," he said weakly.

Holloway turned. "Thank you. Everyone reassures me about that. Carl, like you, was a second lieutenant and a platoon leader. When I look at you, I suppose I'm seeing him. In any event, I don't want to make an error in judgment that hurts another fine young officer."

The general lowered his eyes and added, "I've got a dozen friends with enough metal on their shoulders to have kept Carl out of combat. That offer was made to me, and it was made directly to Carl—"

Sensing that the admission pained Holloway, Robertson interrupted. "I'm certain he refused it, sir."

Holloway started. "Why would you say that, Lieutenant? Anyone else not knowing the facts would assume it the other way. The army is nine parts politics."

"I've met his father," Robertson said simply.

Holloway beamed. "Now you've given *me* an award. And you're correct. Carl refused vehemently. It made him so furious he demanded immediate assignment to a rifle company."

"Perhaps he isn't dead, General. The NKA must have taken a lot of American prisoners on the Naktong."

Holloway shook his head thoughtfully before saying, "He's dead. They'd have let us know if they had a general officer's son. They'd glory in it."

Robertson started to speak, but fell silent.

"You wanted to add something?"

"I guess not, sir. I can't lecture you."

Holloway snorted, saying, "I think the standard army expression is 'man-to-man.' "

Robertson smiled, thinking how often he had heard that term used when the often clumsy protocols of rank got in the way of communication. "I have a Korean friend." Robertson went on to tell Holloway about Choi Min-soo, explaining some of what Choi had taught him about Korean culture. "I think Choi might see it exactly the opposite of what we Americans would expect, sir. He'd probably argue that if the North Koreans had a general's son, they'd keep quiet about it."

"But why? What would they gain?"

"You are their bitter enemy. They'd not comfort you."

Holloway stared. "I see it, a little. No one ever thought of that." The general smiled, but it quickly faded. "It's a chance in a million."

Robertson sagged visibly. Holloway rushed over. "Damn! I'm running

on about my own problems and I'm getting in the way of your recuperation."
He started to leave.

"Please consider my request to return to the regiment, sir." Robertson
caught Holloway's eyes firmly.

The general stared back, frowning lightly. "I am considering it, or you
would already be on your way home." Then he grinned, with genuine
affection. "That's how you make general, Lieutenant Robertson. Always
defer decision on the tough ones."

25

107TH EVACUATION HOSPITAL, MARCH 3, 1952

When an entire medical team came into his room, Robertson knew he was lying—they had let him stand only a few times in past days—on the threshold of something momentous. Not only was it a team, but it was a team headed by Maj. Walter Kerns. Robertson had learned that Kerns was to the physicians of the 107th what General Holloway was to the officers of the corps. Clearly, the 107th had drafted its assault plan, and now it had mounted out under a strong leader.

The major stood at the foot of Robertson's bed. He cupped his left elbow in his right palm and scratched his dimpled chin with his left forefinger. Then, apparently having reached his decision, he nodded to himself. He spoke to Robertson. "I think Jesus always told the sick man to pick up his pallet and walk. I'll play the role of Jesus if you want to play the sick man."

When Robertson made an immediate show of getting out of bed, the major rushed around to check him, "Not immediately, Lieutenant. In medicine we never do anything immediately."

Then, as if it were a regulation medical-corps apology, Kerns gave Robertson and the corpsmen and Vivian and Marian a detailed lecture on why Robertson had been at the mercy of the bedpan for so long. Robertson listened, understanding little of it, but feeling a rising sense of excitement.

Vivian smiled down as Kerns concluded with, "Someday, someone in military medicine is going to realize that it is counterproductive to immobilize a patient as long as Lieutenant Robertson has been immobile. He should have been walking as soon as he could tolerate function." Kerns grinned at Robertson, adding, "After all, he *is* an infantryman."

Robertson nodded his appreciation of the major's medical opinions.

Vivian suggested that Robertson's right arm be supported. A quick irritation flitted across Kerns's face, to be replaced immediately by a smile. Robertson surmised that if Marian Dawson had interfered in it that way, she'd have lost a head. Vivian Hardiman merely dispatched a chubby corpsman for an arm sling and smiled patronizingly at the major.

They got Robertson up. Three supported him. Vivian brushed deliberately against him. But as quickly as the sensation of her came to Robertson, it was quashed, as a large water pail would drown a small fire.

Robertson took a few creaky steps. He saw that walking, after a hiatus of weeks, was like Capt. James A. Hartung—it had more to it than people realized. Soon, Robertson dropped free of the supporting hands and went on his own. His right leg screamed, but he steeled himself against that.

After all too few minutes, Major Kerns halted the excursion. "That's enough for now. You'll have to readapt yourself to some things in the locomotor area. You may have the limits of the ward. Later, when you're stronger, you can expand on that." The major inclined his head to the nurses and corpsmen and led them out.

Alone now, Robertson got immediately out of bed and tottered toward his window. He tried to walk without limping, but realized that would take some work. The right leg was his own medical secret. He could not see the scar on his shoulder, but he could see the grimaces of those who looked at it. The medical people had concentrated their efforts on this part of his body, thereby unwittingly giving him a tactical diversion. But he had known almost from the first that the leg defined the mountain he had to climb. And he understood, because he could see his leg, that the deceptiveness of the wound lay in the cleanness of the healing scar, which concealed the fire smoldering beneath it. That was to the good. What he had set himself to do required two functional legs. A stiff shoulder was irrelevant.

It was about 1600 hours in the afternoon. He was at first disappointed when he looked out of his window. Seoul was to the east, under a gray dome that seemed to press it down rather than lift it up, as he supposed sunshine would have done. He could see the gate of the hospital with its sentry box and barber-pole barricade. A low wall, in places reinforced with wire netting, ran from both sides of the gate. To his left he could see a corner where the wall turned. To his right the wall crawled down behind a green Quonset building and disappeared from view.

Beyond, on the street, he could see busy military traffic. This dominated his view, but when he got his eye and his envy free of the American vehicles, he saw a few Koreans scurrying. Koreans always scurried. He thought about Choi Min-soo for a long time, with the aching that a soldier feels for absent comrades. This, coupled with the sight of the Korean pedestrians on the street below him, set him to thinking about the general condition of Korean-ness. He remembered that Choi, on the day he had given the hachimaki and the haiku, had asked him if he thought Asiatics even capable of romance.

Now, for a brief moment, he was able to accomplish a strange intellectual feat. He could picture the Koreans in the street the way Choi must sense that Americans pictured them. For that fleeting second Robertson was able to divide himself, letting his brain witness a Korean brain monitor an American brain that factored in American visions of Koreans. He shook his head back together; it was too confusing.

He whispered to the world outside his window, only loudly enough for himself to hear. "You're wrong in my case, Choi. If no other American knows it, I know it. Your countrymen have skin that bleeds and eyes that weep. Anything capable of those things is capable of everything."

He pounded his fist on the windowsill. "Believe me, Choi. I know."

Robertson turned away from the window. He remembered another comrade then. Sam Dougherty had told him, one still, intimate night on the line months earlier, how he had survived the Leavenworth cell. "You pace," he had said. "At lockup you start pacing and you pace until you're exhausted. Then you nap away an hour of your four years and you get up and pace some more."

On the wings of that idea, Robertson began to pace his prison. He shut out all thought. He soon arrived at the disciplined monotonous rhythm Dougherty had described. Back against the inner wall, eleven paces . . . no sensation of the outer wall, which was as Dougherty said it was for him in the cell . . . about-face and eleven paces, no sensation of the inner wall . . . about-face, eleven paces . . . about-face . . .

When his right leg threatened mutiny, he ordered it to shape up and pay attention to drill. Eleven paces . . . about-face . . . Ignore the pain . . . eleven paces.

Mildred Baumiller came into his room that night, as she did routinely most of the nights. She had kept at a shy distance during the past two weeks—even her occasional boldness smacked of timidity. As she always did on her first visit of the night, she had a stethoscope around her neck and a sphygmomanometer dangled from her hand.

She was clumsy, and before he could catch himself, Robertson was gruff. "I won't bite, Lieutenant Baumiller."

Mildred blushed scarlet. Instantly, Robertson corrected himself. "I'm sorry. That was rude of me."

"It's just a thing people say, sir," Mildred said so quietly Robertson barely heard it.

Robertson cast around for a way out of the mine field. Finally, he said, "A horse named Buck bit *me* once." Mildred paused with the stethoscope against Robertson's chest, looking up with a flicker of interest. She puzzled a moment. "I didn't realize horses would bite. But I grew up in a small city. I don't know anything about horses."

"They bite. I had my back to him getting the saddle down to put him to work and it was a hot Kansas day." Robertson laughed softly at himself. He recalled how his rump had felt against the saddle leather after he had gotten Buck rigged.

Mildred blushed again. "What amuses you, sir. Am I doing something wrong?"

"Of course not," Robertson responded quickly. "I was thinking of *where* old Buck bit me."

"You said that was in Kansas, sir. Is Kansas that funny? Must not be different from South Dakota."

Robertson suppressed a groan and studied her. She had a timid smile. He was sure of it. She was teasing him.

"Never mind. You came on duty early today."

Mildred nodded as she fixed the pressure cuff around his arm. "Marian has a date. She went into Seoul with Captain Blainey."

Robertson waited until Mildred got the stethoscope out of her ear and asked casually, "Do you have a Captain Blainey?"

"There is only one Captain Blainey, sir. He's our EENT man."

"I mean: do you ever go into Seoul on dates like Lieutenant Dawson does?"

Mildred shook her head. "No, sir. No one ever asks me to go."

Robertson saw the admission pained her. He said quickly, "Well, I suppose medical people are busy."

"Oh no, sir. We aren't that busy. We rarely have a full patient census."

She had blushed again. Robertson sighed inwardly. "Do I make you uneasy? I don't mean to do that."

"That's just the way I am, sir," Mildred said matter-of-factly.

Suddenly, he realized that of all the 107th staff who paraded through his room, only with Mildred was he truly comfortable, and he wanted her on his unwounded side. On his left he was uncrippled.

"Come around to my left," he ordered firmly.

Mildred frowned, but went around to the other side of the bed. "Is this what you wanted, sir?"

Robertson nodded, studying her intently, shunting aside the aware-ness that it made her flinch. Mildred was very feminine, with her fine-ly drawn face and honest blue eyes. Her cheekbones were Scandi-navian looking, high and prominent, almost hidden under hair that was so blonde it begged to be touched. Her breasts were small and her stomach flat. Likely the stomach was carried by trim legs, although her fatigues, unlike those of Marian and Vivian, were shelf-issue and untai-lored and hid any suggestion that something interesting might lurk under them.

He knew nothing about women, but at first Robertson thought she needed cosmetics, the kind Vivian wore. Then he saw that this was not so. Mildred needed to generate color from within herself.

Without warning, he heard himself say, "You're very pretty."

Mildred gasped and stepped back. "No one ever said that to me before, sir."

"That doesn't make it any the less true."

"Thank you, sir. It was nice of you to say it." Mildred pondered a moment, then added another careful "sir."

Robertson laughed, not gleefully, but suitably enough to a sickroom setting.

"Why are you laughing, sir?"

"You say 'sir' as though you mean it. I was thinking of an army story. An old first sergeant was briefing a young, new company commander. He said, 'The men will address you as sir, Captain, and I will address you as sir. But the men will mean it.' "

Mildred puzzled, and did not laugh. "I *do* mean it, sir. You are an officer and a valiant hero that everyone admires. I'm only an unimportant person."

"Don't talk like that," Robertson snapped. "I'm no more a hero than you're an unimportant person. Everybody counts one on the morning report."

Seeing that his words frightened her, Robertson sought to change the subject. "What is your date of rank?"

"Twenty-three August 1951, sir."

"There it is, then. You rank me. You do not have to address me as sir, and I have to address you as ma'am." Robertson smiled to show her he teased, and added, "Ma'am."

Mildred laughed at that, coloring her cheeks. "That sounds dangerous. I used to call my Grandmother Johansen in South Dakota that when I wanted something I knew she didn't want me to have."

The earlier pacing had left Robertson tired, but he didn't want her to go. "Tell me about Grandmother Johansen. Tell me about all your family."

Mildred started. "Really, sir? You'd like to know?"

"Yes, I would. Very much. I've lost touch with my family. Let me borrow your family. I guess I've even forgotten there is a world beyond Korea." He patted the bed beside his left leg. "And sit here."

Mildred approached warily, then caught at something within herself and froze. "I can't do that, sir. Army nurses are forbidden ever to sit on a patient's bed."

Robertson snorted. "I'll be Donald and you be Mildred. I want to hear about the Baumillers and Johansens."

Mildred sat down and rambled on for almost twenty lighthearted minutes about South Dakota. Robertson saw that talking this way brought color and vivacity to her again, and he felt very good for the first time in weeks. Animated, Mildred was lovely to behold.

Her account of herself was disorganized, but in it Robertson saw a timid girl who viewed herself plain, and who had only reluctantly left her safe, out-of-the-way place to confront the demands of the world. How differently he had fled the Tanners!

Slowly, he began to realize that Mildred was in one way like Solomon Zuckerman; they both were adrift and needed to find their own dimensions. On that thought, Robertson gave himself the answer to a question he had often mulled during the black nights of recent weeks. Why had he ordered Zuckerman, who was only slightly wounded and thus was far from being ineffective, into the bunker on George Three?

The answer was utterly simple, no matter that it had long eluded him. He had put Solomon Zuckerman into the bunker because he had wanted to conserve for the world something that was unquestionably decent. He sighed audibly. Although he had at the outset assured the First Squad of the Second Platoon that they were all equal, in the end they had not been equal after all. He felt no guilt for that deceit. Unfair as it was, it could have been no other way.

When she finished, Mildred wanted to know about Kansas. She was buoyant now, and he had to return something. He talked long about the quick horse Buck and made Tanner appear to be someone avuncular.

At last Mildred got up to go out. "Thank you, Donald. No one ever cared before who I was." She added carefully, "I'll come back to look in on you before I go off shift."

Robertson turned his face away. Mildred resumed her duties, which were those of evening nurse of the 107th Evacuation Hospital noncritical ward, caring for the sick, lame, and halt of the Seoul-Inchon base area.

When she was gone, Robertson got up and began the pacing again. Eleven paces, about-face, eleven paces . . .

He paced so long he lost track of time, which was the point of it. Later, when his right leg would accept no more, he leaned against the window, looking out, craning his neck to see into the lights of sleeping Seoul, the capital of his war.

Because he had permitted himself to think about Choi Min-soo and Solomon Zuckerman and Sam Dougherty, he now permitted himself to think of Braxton Fowlkes. The scene he recalled was bathed in the bright moon of Arkansas. They were going down the hot street away from the hotel where they had caroused with the whores, having gone there to squander the pass the first sergeant had given them for helping the paratrooper clean the .30-caliber machine guns. They were feeling lazy and were broke, drained of libido, sobering.

Robertson had also been feeling mildly remorseful about what they had done with a good pass and a month's pay. Then Fowlkes had reassured him, as if he, too, had been thinking about it. "Robbie, them old whores are good enough for common fellers like us soldiers." He pronounced the word "hoo-ers."

The memory saddened Robertson. He realized that never before had he experienced a moment like the one he had shared this evening with Mildred Baumiller. He also realized that had it ever happened before, he would not be where he was.

So it was not surprising that when Mildred returned to the room near the end of her shift, as she had promised, she found him still at the window. Nor was it surprising when he beckoned for her and drew her close to him, so close he could sense her flesh against his.

"Tell me what you've been thinking about here at your window."

He concealed the prostitutes and the gunshots, but he gave her Braxton Fowlkes.

"You must love him. You speak of him in the past tense. When did he rotate?"

Robertson shook his head.

Mildred gave out a little quick cry and put her hand to her mouth. "I'm terribly sorry for him."

"Don't be. Sorrow is dark poetry. Brax wouldn't want that. Even in the worst of it for him, my—" Robertson lifted his head for her, in need of a word. He found one, and completed his thought. "My *brother* Braxton Fowlkes was sunshine."

Nothing more needed saying that night. Mildred stood there silently with him in space and time and they were silhouetted against the sadness that was called Korea by Americans. On no other place on earth, at no other time, could it have happened.

After the shy nurse had gone away, Robertson resumed pacing.

26

107TH EVACUATION HOSPITAL, APRIL 4, 1952

Robertson had firefights with the hours. Except for long innocuous conversations with Mildred Baumiller, he had no distractions. Nevertheless, on this particular Friday, he realized he had killed the hours of an entire month the way an old woman in her garden kills a snake with a stick, thin blow by thin blow, until the month, like the snake, just gave up and died. Meanwhile, as they had done now for eight months, the armistice negotiators beat on their snake at Panmunjom.

His leg healed. This brought puzzled approval from the medical people who regulated his life. Major Kerns himself had noted on Tuesday, "You are incredibly resilient, Lieutenant Robertson. I'd have predicted you'd walk with a cane for the rest of your life."

The chief residual issue at Panmunjom was that of prisoner-of-war repatriation. Since the line of contact had fallen inextricably into trenches on the mountains, the sides had little to fire at each other except the prisoners—vacant-eyed victims who stared across the barbed wire.

Robertson read the *Stars and Stripes* avidly, and Lieutenant Elwood frequently wanted to discuss the war. Robertson knew what everyone knew. Recent events on Koje-do island, the mammoth UN POW enclosure off Pusan, had indicated the Communists took the prisoner-of-war issue seriously. Incredibly, the North Koreans had deliberately surrendered political cadres into captivity, no doubt losing many of them to edgy UN outposts. On Koje-do, these cadres fomented riots and demonstrations, aimed not at escape, but at changing a silly entity called world opinion.

Since neither the Americans nor the Chinese, the principal players in Korea, wanted territory, "Korea" was truly an ideological war. Recognizing this, each side harangued its captives with childish political lectures. Each side hoped to produce a magical world in which the POWs would either refuse to repatriate or, better, would go home to proclaim: "Hey, look at me! Not only have I repudiated us, but I have embraced them."

Eventually, forty thousand Orientals would do the first of those, as would a handful of United Nations soldiers. But the principal thousands just went home, changed clothes, and went to work. They were patently more interested in making babies than in making politics.

As he reviewed the POW problem, Robertson began to nurse a new guilt. He realized that he alone prayed the war would not end before he rejoined it.

Robertson had learned to keep a few neurons on sentry as he paced his cell. He did not want the medical people to catch him. He halted and waited when he heard footsteps this morning.

The courier who came into his room after a polite rapping was a master sergeant from corps headquarters.

"General Holloway hisself sent me, sir."

Robertson accepted a note and large brown package, thanked the master sergeant, and the man went away.

Fearing the note contained bad news, Robertson opened the package first. He was puzzled to discover that corps headquarters had sent him three square bottles of sourmash whiskey. That boded either good or bad, so he sat on his bed and read the quasi-official note from General Holloway.

> I called in a few markers I had outstanding, Lieutenant Robertson. The gist of what the markers did for us is that Silverwood, Oregon, is going to have an *SFC* Samuel Dougherty Day. Commanding General Sixth Army will be there to present Dougherty's son (and I presume his wife?) with Dougherty's second award of the Silver Star. It is little enough, but it will give his son something. The Jack Daniel's whiskey is for you, courtesy of our mess. In a few weeks, this will also be your mess. I will let you remain in Korea, but on these terms: one, you serve on my headquarters staff; two, no combat. Not even a sniff. To set the wheels in motion, I have suggested, although you understand I have absolutely no legal authority there, that Colonel Williams place you on light-duty status if you are ready for that. When you have learned how to soldier again, he is to send you to me. From what I saw at the 107th when I was there, they could use an infantry officer for a few days. Go easy on them.

The note was signed, simply, "Milt Holloway." Robertson still basked in the glow of it when Major Kerns, eyes glinting, came stiffly into the room. Robertson looked up.

"I don't practice infantry, Lieutenant Robertson, and I don't like to have infantry officers, even when they have three stars on their shoulder, practice medicine for me."

"Yes, sir."

"You are on light-duty status, as of now, as a resident outpatient. Report to Lieutenant Colonel Bladenburg on Monday morning. He'll put your feet under some of his adjutant work." Kerns surveyed the room. "Might as well quarter you here—good a place as we have."

Robertson's gratitude was so apparent that Kerns softened. He smiled. "Maybe General Holloway's suggestion is a wise one. We all need work."

Robertson glanced to his window and drew a breath. "And until Monday morning?"

Kerns shrugged. "Get out into the sun. Go see Seoul. Stinks almost as much as South Chicago, but it's a whole lot safer."

Vivian Hardiman swept into the room without knocking virtually the second Kerns left. Robertson had taken a USAFI course in Greek mythology: he understood in a flash what Ulysses must have felt when he heard the Sirens on their rock.

Vivian said pointedly, "Colonel Williams forbids personal relationships between nurses and patients, Robertson—" she interrupted herself to say nastily, "That is a policy which Mouse—"

Now Robertson interrupted. "Her name is Mildred Baumiller."

Vivian's eyes narrowed. "All right, Robertson . . . that is a policy which *Lieutenant Baumiller* apparently does not understand."

Robertson glared, but said nothing.

Vivian ignored the reproof and went on. "But you technically are not in that category now."

Robertson shrugged, bringing instant fire.

"Men never, *ever*, dismiss me that way, Robertson."

Robertson shook his head. "I'm new to the officer business, Lieutenant Hardiman, but I think this room is now a bachelor officer's quarters. I'm going to request that people knock for permission to enter it."

Vivian pouted a moment, then smiled. Her eyes went to the three bottles of whiskey on Robertson's bureau. "You can contribute these to our little informal officers' club, Robertson. You will escort me there tomorrow evening."

Before Robertson could say yea or nay, Vivian eyed him and said forcefully, "You are about Captain D'Arcy's size."

She swept out. The ward Robertson could hear beyond his door hushed its collective voice and—he did not doubt—raised its eyes.

27

STREETS OF SEOUL,
APRIL 5, 1952

Saturday . . . the holiday of the rural Kansas week . . .
On Saturday a farmer of Robertson's era shucked off his dirty overalls and
in clean overalls drove his pickup into the society of the town. It had not
been so long ago that they drove champing teams that pulled freight wagons
or buckboards. Even these teams—prairie-bred and rarely matched—were
excited on Saturday mornings. In town, the horses stood quietly in the dusty
street with the people while the women jawed and the men gossiped about
things at the statehouse and, if the scolding Baptists weren't looking, snuck
into the Prairie Belle for a dew-beaded glass of beer.

In this spirit, Robertson, in clean fatigues and glistening boots,
returned the salute of the bored sentry at the gate he had eyed so longingly
from his window and went into the streets of Seoul.

He tired quickly. Several long blocks from the hospital he had to find
a low wall along the sidewalk. He sat there. He studied what he saw and
banged the heels of his boots against the stones. Two young Korean girls
came along just as he was about to light a cigarette. They bubbled, wrapped
in themselves, scarcely glancing at him.

The girls had pigtailed hair and rouged lips. Something in their simple
appearance seized him. Realizing he had bitten the end off his cigarette, he
spat out the bitter tobacco and cleansed his tongue with his fingers, making
faces at himself. He looked away from the backs of the girls.

He watched a jangling trolley for a few seconds, wondering if the
Koreans who clung to the sides ever fell off to be crushed under the wheels.

He was swimming in his own aimless thoughts when a new thing,
evoking something old in him, stole into his awareness. He saw a horse,

a gelding, yellow gray like Buck, although possibly more dun than buck-skin. With three black pasterns, he was small, barely larger than a pony, much too small for the heavy two-wheeled cart to which he was shackled. The cart rolled on heavy truck tires, creaking sourly as it swayed to the exhausted rhythms of the horse's bony flanks under the baton of the driver's long whip, one blow per step.

Squadrons of flies escorted the cart, one similar to thousands of others in Korea. Occidentals called them honeywagons; they freighted human excrement from the toilets of the city to fertilize the grain and legume fields of the country.

Without really thinking, Robertson rushed into the street. He grabbed the headstall and spoke a gentle, "Whoa, horse . . . whoa now." The cart horse halted in its tracks, sagging, not looking, as if waiting patiently for the next discomfort. The cart man's face contorted. He shouted, startled and angry, and thrust the whip toward Robertson.

Robertson shot back a warning frown, freezing the whip in mid air, and examined the horse, stroking and talking in a gentle, concerned voice. "Your ribs are showing, fellow. And this rope harness has worn the hair off your withers." Robertson turned his head to the driver. "This is no god-damned way to hitch a horse. Your poles are making sores on him. And he's too small for this load."

The driver lifted the whip high over his head, poised to strike. His goatee bobbled when he talked, as had that of the hermit Robertson had met in the mountains. Robertson shook his head menacingly. The whip lowered. The driver got down from his seat on the honeywagon and stepped warily to Robertson, grabbing at his hand. Robertson put out his palm and pushed him back. The event on the Korean street slid into another stale-mate. Robertson stroked the horse's sweat, thinking guiltily that the horse was probably no poorer than its angry owner.

Several Koreans came. The driver gestured violently toward Robertson and spoke excited words to them. The Koreans murmured accusingly at first, but fell silent as a uniformed man with a large club on his waist threaded through them. The policeman reached for Robertson's hand on the headstall, but hesitated when Robertson turned to him and scowled. The Koreans surged in again, leaving a careful yard or two of space around Robertson and the emaciated cart horse. The traffic snarled behind the cart began to honk and race engines. The policeman reddened in a Choi Min-soo loss-of-face blush.

When the Koreans resumed their indignant chatter, Robertson shrug-ged and fished out his wallet. He gestured with it, from the horse to the driver. At first the Koreans did not understand. Robertson took the bills out of the wallet and gestured with them. The other Koreans grinned and looked expectantly toward the driver. The policeman grinned with them and gestured between Robertson and the horse, speaking what clearly was the official position.

The goateed driver frowned a few careful moments, then opened his mouth to show some yellow teeth and black gums. The policeman took out a notebook and wrote on a page the symbol for won, the Korean monetary unit. He spoke briefly with the owner of the horse, then wrote an Arabic three appended by six zeros. Robertson did the arithmetic. It boiled down to about a hundred and twenty dollars. He counted out six twenties. The policeman re-counted. He looked sternly at Robertson. Robertson handed over a seventh twenty, military scrip. The policeman put that in his shirt pocket with the notebook and handed the other six to the cart man. Everyone smiled happily except Robertson, who was beginning to feel foolish.

Several Koreans shrugged at once, looking between Robertson, the horse, and the horse's former owner. Robertson studied the problem. He led the horse to the curb. An American truck crawled by, impatient to gather speed. The trucker shouted out, "Get those gooks off the street, you stupid bastard."

Robertson fingered his collar with its new brass bar and called back, "Stupid bastard, *sir,* to you, soldier."

"Yes, sir. Sorry. Didn't realize it was official business."

The helpful Koreans took the weight of the poles, showing by the strain on their faces that the cart's balance was ahead of its thick axle. Robertson freed the harness and tugged the horse from between the poles. All the Koreans let go at once. When gravity did its work, ringing the pavement with a thud, one of the poles broke. A jet of brown liquid spurted out of the flapping cover of the cart. The squadrons of flies swooped. Sighing over the broken cart pole, Robertson fished out another twenty.

Discarding all the harness except the headstall and a lead rope, Robertson left that part of Korea. About a mile down the street, which had now become a road guarded on both sides by low humble houses more suggestive of the countryside, a jeep with a pink-faced Quartermaster Corps lieutenant colonel in it eased to a stop. The colonel frowned heavily and beckoned to Robertson and the horse.

"What the hell have you got there, Lieutenant?"

"A buckskin horse," Robertson said blandly, adding, "he leans a little toward dun."

"I can see it's a damned horse!" said the light colonel, who reminded Robertson of a dressed-up Harvey Tanner.

Robertson smiled patiently. He said nothing, prompting the inquisitive colonel to demand, "Just who the hell are you, Lieutenant, that you think you can lead a damned horse down a public road in Korea?" The colonel turned and spoke to his chauffeur, a thin-lipped Chicano Pfc., muttering, "I've been in the army twenty-two years and I've never seen anything like this. You ever see anything like this?"

"No, sir," the driver replied agreeably. "But I've only been in the army a few months."

Robertson gave the colonel his name. The colonel's eyes widened. "*The* Lieutenant Robertson of . . ." And he named Robertson's regiment.

"Yes, sir," Robertson admitted, very warily puzzled that the colonel knew.

The colonel wanted to shake hands. Then he said, "If you want to lead a damned horse down a road, Lieutenant Robertson, it's okay by me." He turned to his driver. "No regulation against a second lieutenant leading a horse is there, Rodriguez?"

"Who knows, Colonel? The army's got regulations on almost everything. But I've learned not to be surprised at what officers do."

"Well, there's not," the colonel retorted testily. "I've been in the army twenty-two years and I can assure you both of that."

When the colonel nodded to the driver, Robertson checked him. "May I ask a favor of you, sir?"

"You damned well can, Robertson. Any man with your reputation can ask anything of me."

"Could I borrow your sidearm? Until tomorrow."

At first the colonel resisted, but after gazing into the open countryside to the southeast, toward which Robertson tended, he relented. "Sure. If you're going out there with that horse you might be wise to carry a weapon."

He unbuckled his pistol belt and gave it to Robertson. "How will you get it back to me?"

"I'm at the 107th Evac—"

"Damned good. I'll send a courier for it."

Robertson buckled on the .45, hitching the holster around to accommodate his hip. The colonel said, "I've never fired that thing, but I suppose you know all about it."

The driver grinned at Robertson. Robertson saluted the colonel and the driver saluted Robertson. The colonel gestured and the jeep growled into gear and pulled away.

Robertson led his horse farther away from the city. He had learned his new horse's best gait was a mechanical plod.

About an hour later, after Robertson had gone past the clustering houses and through the sparse houses into the world free of carpentry, he left the road and went into a narrow valley that lifted itself up between some low hills. The valley widened at its head into a meadow. Halting the horse there, Robertson stroked it while it rested. Once he opened its mouth and studied the teeth. He spoke. "You've got no cups left in your teeth; got to be more than twelve. And your hooves are worn down." The horse backed an eye and flicked an ear. Robertson pulled some tall grass and wiped the horse dry of its sweat, which was attracting biting flies. After pondering the problem a moment, he got out his pocket comb and curried, enjoying old memories as the horse responded to what was probably its first grooming. "Bet you don't even have a name," Robertson said softly. Then he removed the headstall and walked over to sit on a little hummock. He smoked and watched the horse graze, gauging the transit of the sun. His legs ached, reminding him he dreaded the miles back to the hospital.

After three cigarettes, he walked over to the horse. The horse shied tiredly, but settled when Robertson squeezed his neck. "I'll name you 'Korea Buck,' " he said. "It's no honor to you, but you're the only horse I'll ever own."

Korea Buck lifted his head when Robertson slid back the barrel of the pistol to insert a round. The .45 snapped into the cocked-and-ready position. The arming was as incisive as the fire of a falling star on a black night.

Backing up a step, facing the horse, Robertson put the pistol to the animal's forehead. The front sight lay between Korea Buck's ears and his eyes. His finger tensed on the trigger.

"Stand for it like a proud horse," he begged softly.

Korea Buck rolled his eyes forward to meet Robertson's. A huge fly had been teasing and the horse rippled his neck muscles to drive it away. Robertson heard the fly scold.

The man and the horse stood that way for maybe a minute, which is a long time to debate squeezing a trigger. Then Korea Buck whickered, as if he didn't understand.

Slowly, Robertson's shooting hand dropped. The weight of the pistol sagged the rest of his body. He spoke in a quiet barn whisper. "I can't make your decision for you, old horse. I've made mine, but you make your own."

The irony was not lost. He said aloud, "Korea Buck, in setting slave horses free I've only trapped myself."

The buckskin plodded off a few steps and began to graze again. Robertson pointed the pistol at the innocent sky and pulled the trigger until all the ammunition was spent. "Flee!" The hills of Korea echoed with the anger of all that but the horse barely heeded. Robertson retreated. After several yards, he halted and turned back. He stood unmoving for a while, then called to the horse, "Keep away from Koreans or they'll hitch you to another cart. Get your strength and run." He remembered the old thing again, and added, "Run free in the wind and never let them catch you."

Korea Buck looked up briefly, then lowered his head to nip the lush grass. Robertson turned and walked away, slowly, accompanied only by his thoughts. He knew Korea would take up the horse someday; Korea would tolerate a loose horse no more than it would tolerate a loose man. Like the 107th Evacuation Hospital for him, the meadow would be only an interlude for Korea Buck.

In his room when he returned to the hospital, just after supper, a Class-A officer's uniform lay across the bed, CIB and ribbons in place, with a folded note pinned to the right pocket of the tunic. He examined the ribbons, quickly realizing that Vivian had read his service record.

Mildred Baumiller came in, armed with three yellow flowers still dripping water from their stems. She scolded tepidly, "Where have you been, Donald? You've missed your supper."

"Nobody ever died from missing an army supper," Robertson said. "I went out into the country. I got a ride back with an MP sergeant or I'd have missed breakfast."

"What did you do in the country? I never go there," Mildred said.

"Nothing," Robertson answered quickly. "Your flowers are pretty."

Mildred put the flowers on the bureau next to the Jack Daniel's bottles that General Holloway had sent. She went to the bed and pointed to the uniform. "Why do you have a dress uniform? That seems strange."

Robertson shrugged. "I assume it belongs to Captain D'Arcy."

Puzzled, Mildred reached for the note pinned to the lapel of the uniform. She handed it to Robertson. Her stare demanded that he read it. He read silently, then gave the note back.

Vivian Hardiman had written: "Pick me up at 2030 hours at my quarters. Bring the whiskey you promised to contribute to the mess."

Mildred read the note and blanched. At last she said, with the first anger Robertson had seen in her, "Lieutenant Hardiman has a nickname with the men." Robertson raised an eyebrow and she added fiercely, "Candy Tits. They call her Candy Tits."

"Well, I don't need D'Arcy's uniform. I'm damned well not going to an officers' club."

But the customary Mildred came back and shook her head. "You'd better go as she wants you to, Donald. She'll punish us if you don't." Then she put her hand to her bloodless lips and ran out of the room.

The awareness was as fleeting as a bullet ricocheting off granite, but Robertson saw he had another shy horse and another Tanner.

28

They walked through the warm spring evening toward the mess, which on Saturday night became the officers' club. Never having dated, in the more or less formal 1950s' sense of dating, Robertson felt he trod strange ground, although he had crossed that particular pavement before.

He had realized the discomfort of it during the twenty-minute wait in Vivian's Quonset, where, with Vivian's roommate, a captain of nurses, he had compared the weather of southwestern Kansas with that of Upper Michigan.

"It gets so cold in Upper Michigan the houses crack," the roommate had offered.

Robertson's necktie was too tight and he fidgeted uncomfortably in D'Arcy's uniform. Gazing around the room, his eyes caught on the beige cloth of a low table, where several photographs of smiling men inscribed to Vivian Hardiman stood. The photographs were arranged in ranks with several bottles and vials of what Robertson had been sure made Vivian the lovely artifact she was. He had the feeling he gazed upon the equivalent of guns and trophies of the hunt.

The door behind Robertson opened and a perfumed flurry announced Vivian Hardiman. He stood. She wore a black dinner dress with a low neckline and a hem that struck at midcalf. Below the hem, Robertson saw tanned, nylon-sheathed curves and black sling pumps. As the first rush of air had foreshadowed, Vivian smelled gorgeous. She looked even better. Robertson reflected that she taxed only the eyes and the nose; the other senses could idle.

"Ready at *last*," she trilled. She turned to her roommate, winked for Robertson to see, and said, "Don't wait up, Martha. Isn't Robertson handsome in a dress uniform?" Martha's eyes had lit up. Before she could reply, however, Vivian twirled to address Robertson. "Oh, Robertson, we'll absolutely knock them out!"

Robertson carried two of the bottles of Jack Daniel's across the dark compound. Vivian carried the third, cradling it against something Robertson would have wagered a month's pay that half the staff, and all the patients, of the 107th would have killed to kiss. Vivian walked closely to him, pressing him with her thigh. Unconsciously, Robertson skipped a foot to get in step with her.

The seductive notes of "Embraceable You" greeted them as they neared the officers' mess. Robertson's sense of impending ambush, an instinct highly honed in Korean War infantrymen, was strong. He stopped in his tracks, as Korea Buck had done this morning when he had grasped the headstall. "I don't know how to dance, Vivian," he said, flustered. "I've never been to a dance."

He had stopped Vivian so suddenly she almost fell off her three-inch heels. "I can't believe that," she said. "Everyone knows how to dance."

"You'll believe it if I try it," Robertson promised.

She ignored this. "There'll be plenty of men to dance with me. If I get time, I'll teach you."

Although Congress vaguely disapproved of officers' clubs in Korea, they might as well have forbidden diarrhea; two officers on a desert island with a single bottle of beer between them will organize an officers' club. The senior of them will drink the beer, which the junior of them will serve.

Vivian paused just outside the door of the mess. At the exact instant the music stopped, she made an entrance. Robertson's sense of ambush had not misled him. Of all the women present, Vivian alone wore a civilian dinner dress; the others wore duty fatigues. Of the men, he alone wore anything remotely like a dress uniform, although Major Kerns wore khaki. The major did not join the contingent of officers who rushed over to relieve Vivian of the heavy burden of the Jack Daniel's.

Vivian beamed and announced, "I brought Lieutenant Robertson; he's on our staff now."

Robertson blushed when Captain D'Arcy eyed the uniform. D'Arcy smiled apologetically.

While Vivian was enthusiastically making the necessary introductions, a lieutenant colonel shouldered in through the officers around Vivian to glare at Robertson. "This is Colonel Armitage," Vivian said gaily.

"He was to be my escort this evening, but he bowed out when I told him you needed a change of routine." She turned to Armitage. "That was so sweet of you, Kenneth." She rubbed a lovely knuckle across the colonel's cheek, seeming to heal him enough that he lifted his glare from Robertson. When the record player began to play "Deep Purple," Armitage tugged Vivian's arm.

She ordered, "Get me a drink, Robertson. Whiskey and soda; make it a single. We have a long evening." Armitage led her toward the dancing couples.

The bar was a piece of plywood laid across a steam table. The choice of beverages was limited. A black enlisted man in a white hospital jacket fixed Robertson a Jack Daniel's and water and Vivian's whiskey and soda. Vivian twirled by in the arms of the colonel. "That's our table, in the center," she called out to Robertson.

At the change of records, Colonel Williams, the hospital commander, claimed Vivian on the floor. Lieutenant Colonel Armitage stood on the edge of the dancing area, near a jumble of pushed-together tables, glancing sourly between Williams and the seated Robertson. Robertson gave him a brother-officer nod, but Armitage did not acknowledge it.

A brave major cut in on Colonel Williams, who yielded graciously. Within moments, a second major cut in on the first major. Robertson began to study the officers' mess. His spirits lifted when he saw Mildred Baumiller sitting at a table along the far side of the room, where she normally ate. Robertson recognized her companion as Lieutenant Erdman, who sometimes came into the ward to chat. The table was behind a four-by-six column that supported the wide roof trusses. Robertson lifted an arm. Mildred smiled timidly and waved back.

The music had stopped. Robertson glanced up to see the second major and Vivian, who stared pointedly at her chair. Fumbling, Robertson got up to help her. She said nothing until she tasted her drink. She made a face. "Get me a fresh one, like a dear, Robertson. I detest stale soda." The new record spun up "Tuxedo Junction" and a throng of officers rushed to the table. Colonel Armitage beat back the assault with a steely frown. Dutifully, although fighting down a sense of the ridiculous, Robertson went to the bar for a fresh drink. When the colonel returned Vivian to the table after the dance, Robertson stood to help her with the chair. Armitage uttered a stiff "At ease, Lieutenant!" and did the honors himself.

Vivian gushed, "Aren't we having fun, Robertson?"

Robertson did not reply. He turned in his chair and caught Mildred's gaze from across the room. Vivian speared Robertson's hand, gouging him with her nail. "You aren't paying attention to me, Robertson," she said stiffly.

Robertson muttered a "Sorry." Vivian darted a glance toward Mildred and Lieutenant Erdman. "You were paying attention to that damned Mouse in the wallflower chorus over there. Why can't you pay attention to me?"

The music began again. Wordlessly, Robertson stood. Vivian rose half out of her chair. She gasped audibly when Robertson spun and stepped across to Mildred.

Mildred blanched and stood as he approached.

"Would you like to dance?" he asked.

Mildred hesitated, but let him have her hand. His wounded right shoulder joint felt as if it was being ground on glass-shard bearings when Mildred came into his arms, but Robertson set his jaw against the pain. He whispered into her hair, "What do I do now? I never danced in my life."

"Never?"

"Never."

"Follow me," Mildred suggested. "Just let the music tell you what to do. Everyone has a different style."

Shortly, Robertson had the rhythm. He recalled that Sam Dougherty, who had been both handsome and socially adept, had once claimed that a lame elephant on crutches could learn ballroom dancing. Kraut Klineschmidt had raised the subject while recounting an obviously fabricated sexual-conquest yarn. Then, aware his thoughts strayed, and needing vaguely to pay off a debt to Mildred, Robertson forced the regiment out of his mind. At first, they danced at about the same distance from each other as the hospital commander had danced with Vivian earlier. But after Robertson had mastered the basic steps, he pulled her closer. He began to lead and Mildred began to follow.

Dropping his face into her hair, he smelled shampoo. Slightly uncomfortable with what he was feeling, he nevertheless gave himself to Mildred, molding himself to her, anticipating her movements even as she anticipated his. For a moment they became almost one entity, afloat on the muted music.

She put her lips to his ear. "You're dancing well. What are you thinking about?"

"I'm thinking I'd rather be here right now than anywhere else in the world."

"But this is just the mess hall, Donald. You'll be here for all your meals now."

He put his lips to her ear. "I mean with you, like this. We—" He would have sworn to it; he felt fire come into her cheeks. She missed a step and he drew back to look into her face. He had been right; what Mildred needed most was her own color. With spirit in her eye and flame on her high cheekbones, Mildred Baumiller was beautiful.

Another couple jostled them, so rudely it smacked of intention. Robertson lifted his eyes and met a full-battery glower from Vivian and an I-rank-you sneer from Kenneth Armitage. He whispered a question for Mildred. "Who is Colonel Armitage?"

"He's our cardiologist," Mildred explained. She put her lips to Robertson's ear and breathed, "He's married."

Robertson had witnessed things more scandalous and had participated in some of them. He changed the subject. "Doesn't Lieutenant Erdman dance?"

Mildred replied, "No one except Major Kerns and Colonel Williams ever asks us to dance. Sometimes we dance together—girls do that—but usually we don't come."

"Then why did you come tonight?"

Mildred stiffened in his arms, but said nothing.

When the record ended, Robertson led Mildred to her table and thanked her. Mildred smiled gratefully and nodded toward the center tables, where Vivian sat alone. "You had better go, Donald. Lieutenant Hardiman is furious at us. She brought you here to show you off and you haven't danced with her."

Vivian attacked before Robertson was seated. "You didn't ask *me* to dance."

"I explained that," Robertson offered lamely. "I don't know how to dance."

"You danced okay with that damned Mouse."

Robertson glared. "Her name is Mildred. She showed me how to dance; it was easier than I thought."

Vivian sniffed haughtily. "If you didn't know how to dance, why did you go over there in the first place?"

"Mildred is a friend. I like her."

"Shit!" Vivian lighted a Pall Mall and blew smoke at Robertson. She accused, "You lied about not dancing to embarrass me."

Robertson suppressed a growing anger. "I'm sorry if I offended you, Vivian. I didn't mean to."

Vivian's neck stiffened. She turned deliberately to Robertson. "Offend me? You can't offend me, Robertson. You embarrassed me. There's a difference, Robertson, a big difference."

"Well, it's done. Mildred was not dancing and you had a long line waiting to dance with you." Robertson's own jaw firmed. "You're still in the oak leaves, Vivian. Then you have the captains and the first lieutenants. I'm sure junior second lieutenants are at the bottom of the evening."

"You surely can't prefer that mousy bitch to me?" Vivian shot back.

Robertson stood, bumping the table hard enough to rattle the glasses. "That will do, Vivian. I've had enough for one night." His tone was the one he used when he corrected major indisciplines back in the regiment. He turned to leave. Vivian grasped his arm, shouting, "You're right, Robertson, *plenty* of damned men here want to dance with me. I don't need *you!* I don't care how many damned medals you have."

Conscious of the stares of many officers, Robertson went deliberately to Mildred. "Would you like to dance again?"

"Should we, Donald? We will only make Lieutenant Hardiman angrier. You're supposed to remain at her table and be punished."

"So I gather. She'll get over it." He led Mildred to the precise center of the floor and they danced a few moments. Colonel Armitage had reclaimed Vivian. Her glass was empty; her red-tipped Pall Mall smoldered in the ashtray. Robertson asked, "Would you like to get out of here for some fresh air?"

Mildred stopped in midstep. "Please, I'd like that."

He led her to the ward. Mildred chatted with Marian Dawson while he shucked Captain D'Arcy's uniform. After arranging it carefully on a hanger, he took the uniform to Sergeant Darrow, the senior of the night corpsmen. "Can you get this cleaned for me?"

"No trouble, Lieutenant."

"And see that it is returned to Captain D'Arcy. With my thanks."

"No sweat."

The night beckoned them, offering escape. Outside the gate, Robertson took Mildred's hand. They walked down the cobblestones of a soft night. The street life was sparse and only a few dim lights intruded onto the sidewalk. No words were spoken. Soon they reached the wall where Robertson had seen the cart horse of the morning. They sat there. "I was here today," he said. It seemed like such a long time ago.

"What did you do here?"

Struck again with the literal Mildred, Robertson sighed. He started to say "nothing." Instead, he told her about Korea Buck and how he had set the dun gelding free.

"Just like you did in Kansas," Mildred observed dreamily, after pausing to digest the strange account.

"Something like that."

"Why? Why did you spend all that money on a horse just to turn him loose? You could have arranged with the Koreans to keep him somehow."

"I never thought of it."

"But why did you do it?"

"I wanted him to be free of the things that tortured him," Robertson said simply. He sensed that Mildred waited for more, but he did not offer it.

They held hands and talked. He told her of the men at the regiment. He made them real for her, whole and entire, recounting for Mildred only the laughter, not the tears. After telling her about the snowball fight the night they walked through the moonpath away from the hermit on the mountain, he dwelt long on Choi Min-soo. Mildred listened thoughtfully, almost enviously, often squeezing his hand. Soon their communication dispensed with words and became the gentle sounds, the soft parry and thrust of beating hearts.

Toward midnight, the nurse in Mildred surfaced. "We had better go back, Donald. You've had a long day and you'll exhaust yourself."

At her prefab, Mildred pulled him off into the darker shadows. When she lifted her face, he kissed her. She said a whispered, "Thank you" as if he had done her a favor.

"Good night, Mildred. I've had a nice time with you."

Mildred lingered. She asked then, "Will you go walking with me tomorrow, Donald? I have a day off coming."

Robertson's ambush sense surged, but the warning went unheeded. After a moment, unable to comprehend what he felt, he replied, "Sure. Why not?"

Robertson closed the door to his room and undressed to his olive-drab boxer shorts. The room was warm from being shut up and he lay on the cover of his bed, staring at the ceiling.

His ear caught a stealthy noise. The door opened, letting in a splash of the ward's pale light, then closed. Robertson heard the bolt slide into the lock. He tensed and waited, knowing neither who had entered nor what was wanted. His mind flashed a recollection of a thief in a long-ago squad room.

The shade was down and the room black. Robertson heard the soft rustle and labored breathing of someone undressing. He checked his breath and poised himself for what was to come, dreading it.

He sensed movement toward him and called out softly, "Mildred?"

"Mildred? *Mildred.* You idiot!" Suddenly the light switched on. It struck Robertson's pupils with the suddenness of a Chinese night attack.

The intruder stood before him, naked. The light made her nudity garish and she weaved unsteadily as she stepped toward the bed. Her lipstick was smeared.

At first, feeling nothing but shock, Robertson stared at her. He had not seen a naked woman for almost a year, and few of them before that. Something instinctual flared in him, but died at once, leaving him quivering and empty.

"I want you," she announced huskily.

"No, Vivian, you're making a mistake."

He got off the bed and stood warily. In his shorts, he felt as naked as she. When she came against him, her intention burned into him.

She crushed her mouth to his and he felt her tongue.

The taste of her was bitter. He freed himself and pushed her away.

She recoiled instantly and renewed her assault. This time he imprisoned her with one of his arms and forced back her head with the other. With her head tilted that way, she was more stunningly dangerous to him than before. Her lips parted to smile seductively.

"Make love to me, Robertson."

"I can't do that, Vivian."

"Any *normal* man could."

When Robertson did not answer, Vivian wrenched an arm free and reached for his groin. Her hand groped there, then she hissed, "I can't believe you, Robertson."

He froze. In his mind he reexperienced the room he had entered in Chunchon the night he had pulled his world down around his own ears—all the flesh, all the odors of loveless passion. On that, he pleaded, "I can't do what you want me to do, Vivian."

The hand that had fondled him slid around his hip and up his back. The fingers began to feel for the surgical scar on his right shoulder and, finding it, poised there threateningly. Vivian pressed her breasts against his naked chest. He flinched.

Then Vivian exploded. He felt her clawing and pounding on the scar. She grated out, "You bastard, Robertson. You're not a man. Something's wrong with you."

Robertson fought down what boiled up in him and gritted his teeth. Soon Vivian began to sob helplessly and the hand on his shoulder became tender and caressing. He eased free of her and reached for his robe, putting it on her and making her sit on the bed.

When he saw she had surrendered it, he said softly, "You are a desirable woman, Vivian. A year ago I'd have welcomed you here."

"Why not now?"

Robertson shook his head. Vivian Hardiman had never had the slightest claim on knowing what had happened to him. Of them all, Fowlkes should have been told, and Sam Dougherty certainly, if the fight on Sniper Ridge had permitted him the time, and if the half-understood anticipation he so often entertained found a pretext, perhaps Mildred Baumiller. But never someone so alien to it as Vivian.

"You'd not understand it, Vivian. Let it go at that."

Slowly, Vivian recovered herself. "I had better go," she said. "Can I get out of here without anyone seeing me?" A little bit of her drunkenness returned and she giggled. "I suppose we *are* engaged in conduct unbecoming of officers."

They dressed and Robertson went to the door. When he saw that no eyes from the ward intersected their line of escape, he beckoned for Vivian.

Near Vivian's quarters, he halted her and turned to her. Her head was down, and he lifted it gently with a finger under her chin.

"Good night, Lieutenant Hardiman. We'll both forget."

Vivian nodded. As gently as a feather strokes satin, she brushed his lips with hers. "I want you to know two things, Lieutenant Robertson. You're the only one I ever wanted . . . and I want you to be the first to know that when Kenneth Armitage divorces his wife, I'm going to marry him." She added forcefully, "Soon Armitage will be a full colonel."

"I'm sure a full colonel will make an excellent husband for you, Lieutenant Hardiman."

Back in his room, still fully dressed, Robertson began to pace. Eleven paces, the unsensed wall, eleven paces. He speculated as he paced. How would he have reacted if the intruder had been Mildred Baumiller? That made him uncomfortable and he speeded up his pacing. Then a figure came to pace with him. He was aware of the figure for a long time before he admitted he was. Even then, he didn't speak to it. Instead, needing help, he conjured up a memory of Choi Min-soo, on the day Choi had said to him that life in Korea was a house of many doors. "Open any one of them," he had explained, "and a dragon might wait across the threshold."

Robertson had opened a door that night in the sleeping city of Chunchon, as lightheartedly as he had gone over the fence into the forbidden world. A dragon had waited.

Exhausted, he ceased that night's pacing and lay down on his bed. The bed whirled, as if he were in some centrifuge. Whirling, he was as defenseless as Vivian had been without proper lipstick.

The figure that had paced with him for almost two hours leaped naked into his mind. In his torture, he thought he saw it clearly. Vivian Hardiman had been sent by one of Korea's unforgiving gods to take off her clothes and to press her naked femininity against him. Now, no longer, as he had for months, could he fend off his phantom. Her name was Soon Lee, a name he had given her sometime in the course of it, naming her that after Soon Ok, the washerwoman, because he did not even know how Korean women were named and Soon Ok had been sent to him as Vivian had been sent.

Soon Lee's eyes accused him and her fantasy mouth spoke the indictment: *"Seikse! Seikse! Seikse!"* Her savagery made Vivian's pummeling of the aching shoulder seem like nothing.

Suddenly he leaped out of his bed and ran to his window, throwing it open. He knotted his fists and shouted into the night, "Damn you, Korea! Damn you. I never asked to come here."

But then, he realized, neither had any of them.

29

STREETS OF SEOUL,
APRIL 6, 1952

L ook, Donald! Look up there."

So high overhead the airplanes that made them were hidden from the eye of the ground, four contrails roped white. "Sabrejets," Robertson said. "Going up to duel the MiGs. That's about all the air force has to do now."

He knew why Mildred had demanded he look up. She had wanted to point out that the gray overcast that had oppressed them when they met in the mess for breakfast had relented. Now they had a brilliant yellow sun, all the more welcome for its lateness in arriving.

Wherever she led was her secret. "I want to surprise you," she had said over powdered eggs and hotcakes.

Robertson thought about the war as they walked. On line to the north of them pulsed King of the Hill. Infantrymen marched up and marched down, burning up gunpowder. The UN Sabres flew north daily. Keeping wing tips diplomatically south of the Yalu, the pilots sassed the Chinese and North Korean–flown but Russian-built MIGs on the airfields north of the river until the MIGs came up. Then the jets looped and swooped and burned up kerosene, later to return to base for whiskey and soda or tea and rice cakes.

At sea, burning up navy special fuel oil, the gray vessels steamed. In them gray sailors stared into surface-search radars. Every four hours, except for the two-hour dog watches, the officer of the deck wrote his log. The more common entry might read, "Steaming as before." Once each day the log would record a sprightly, "Wound and compared ship's chronometers."

Mildred was as splendid as the sun. She had cheeks as colorful as the early-blossoming flora. She wore a fatigue uniform, and Robertson had noticed in the mess that it was new, and that she had engaged a seamstress for it.

Some chattering Koreans in ceremonial dress—bird-cage hats and white flowing robes for the men, high-bodiced dresses and lavish color for the women—met them on the street. As they always did for American officers, and usually did for American enlisted men, the Koreans hushed and stood aside.

Clearly this simple courtesy disturbed Robertson, who had been silent since they had watched the contrails together.

Just as clearly, Mildred detected his unease. "You have strong feelings about Koreans?" she accused.

He shrugged helplessly and she added, "I see how you treat the Koreans who come into the hospital. You're the only one of us who treats them as . . ." Mildred searched for a word, then found "equals."

Robertson stopped walking. "How do *you* regard them, Mildred?"

The question had a barb in it, and she flinched, flustering a moment before smiling. "Kyoung-hee has a crush on you. I can see that, too."

Kyoung-hee was the Korean girl, about fifteen, all sparkling black eyes and agreeable smiles, who assisted the American nurses at the 107th.

"How do you know?" he demanded. "I can assure you that Korean girls are not that way."

Mildred blanched. "That upsets you, too. I should think it would please you. You know how young girls are. Koreans know about you. Kyoung-hee wants to be like Americans. She—oh, please, Donald, don't be angry at me."

At once, Robertson said, "I'm sorry, Mildred. Today I'm being what Braxton Fowlkes called a bear with a sore ba—foot. Tell Kyoung-hee I am honored and that I will try to be worthy of her."

Restored, Mildred pulled them on with a firm air of purpose. Soon, the buildings on the narrow streets along which they wended their way became houses set back from broad streets. Mildred tugged him around a corner and led him along a cobbled walk that brought them to a high stone wall. She took his hand and squeezed it excitedly when they reached a weathered wooden gate.

The gate creaked to Mildred's push. Inside, Robertson saw a grand house and a garden.

"Syngman Rhee has invited us to lunch," he remarked.

Mildred chided playfully, "*That's* not my house!" She took his other hand so that she could tug on them both. Skipping backward along a path through the greening foliage, she drew him to a small cottage that shared its south exterior with the stone wall.

Robertson saw that the house Mildred claimed crouched shyly under a slate roof, as if little time had been spent building it after the grand house had been built. He had to label it for it to make sense, so he decided some Koreans had gardeners and this was a gardener's cottage.

Mildred sat down on the low terrace of the house and began to unlace her boots. Watching her do that, Robertson froze.

Mildred looked up. "You don't have to remove your boots, Donald. I do it because it makes my house like a real Korean house. Koreans don't wear street shoes in their houses. This house belongs to Kyoung-hee's grandparents. I rent it from them. It's small, but it's a nice house. It was cold and damp last winter. I'm hoping it will be more pleasant now. Some mice were here, but I chased them out."

Robertson had learned that an alarmed Mildred fired sentences like a machine gun fires belted cartridges. Knowing he caused her discomfort, he sat down and untied the lace of his left boot. "It's just that an old infantryman hates to surrender his boots," he explained lamely.

The house had two small rooms. One obviously was for cooking; one obviously was for eating and sleeping and sitting.

"Do you like my house?" Mildred wanted to know.

"It's a nice house. Do you come here often?"

"Yes, when I want to be alone I come here."

"You aren't alone today."

"Today is different."

He studied the spotless house again. Everything was Oriental, but everything had Mildred's imprint on it. Each thing had an assigned place and had been put neatly in that place. The main room had a small closet set into the wall; he assumed that, too, contained neat things in proper places.

Mildred said happily, "Koreans serve tea. Would you like some tea?" She lowered her eyes sheepishly. "I swipe the tea from the mess when the cooks aren't looking."

Robertson said "yes, thank you" and added the observation, "It's difficult for me to see Mildred Baumiller of South Dakota in the act of swiping."

Mildred grinned impishly. "I swipe. That's how timid people have to acquire things."

Mildred put Robertson at a low table and went to light the charcoal in her minuscule black stove. It was cozy, and she flew on, talking about people they knew at the hospital, about her house, about little events and the general significance of ordinary things.

As they drank the stolen tea, Mildred sat ever closer and made sounds in a language Robertson had to translate. When he realized what she was doing, he was too committed to retreat with honor. She made love banter, and he could but borrow on her mood. Then Mildred was a candle and he a moth, circling about her, desirous but daunted.

Later, Mildred washed and put away her tiny, blue porcelain tea dishes. She returned to the table and sat beside him. She pressed her thigh against his.

"Well, you swiped some excellent tea. If I get detailed to sit on your court-martial, I'll consider your good taste as a mitigating factor. Maybe I can get the charge reduced from larceny to conduct unbecoming an officer and a gentleman. I don't know which article of the Manual for Courts-Martial covers larceny, but conduct unbecoming is Article 133."

Mildred feigned horror. "How on earth do you know so much about that stupid book? They read the punitive articles to us right after the army adopted it and I was too frightened to sleep for a week. The army can punish you for everything."

Robertson tensed, as would a man who had let a secret escape. He replied carefully, "Our platoon leader when I was an enlisted man knew it by heart. He threatened us with it so often I borrowed the manual from the company clerk one day and looked at it myself." He appended offhandedly, "It's the code soldiers live by."

Mildred wanted to know about Blackthorne. When Robertson finished, she put her lips to his ear and whispered, "Sounds like he is a complete . . . you know what . . . Sergeant Darrow calls people that. . . ."

Robertson puzzled and she whispered, "Asshole."

Robertson laughed. Mildred was delighted. "Oh, it's wonderful to have you laugh, Donald! You almost never laugh." She screwed up her face and said, "Grandmother Johansen would wash my mouth out with lye soap if she ever heard me say something like that. But if it made you laugh, I'm glad I said it."

"And I'm glad you said it. You're absolutely correct about him."

Without further warning, Mildred threw her arm around Robertson's neck and kissed him hungrily. When they drew back from the kiss, she stared at him a moment, then dropped her eyes. It had been an exploratory kiss, the breathtaking opening of the door.

Robertson sensed that Mildred expected something of him now, but he knew he must wait and let her declare it.

She floundered and made machine-gun sentences. She ran out of ammunition and fell silent, eyes lowered again. Helplessly, Robertson watched her. At last, as if she had found her resolve, she lifted her head. Her lips trembled before she formed words. The new words came dressed in a timid whisper.

"Shouldn't we do it now, Donald?"

Robertson stiffened. The most obvious "it" was out of Mildred's character to suggest. He decided again to wait her out.

More fire was in her eyes than he had ever seen there. "Don't make the woman beg, Donald. I've never asked before. I . . . I've never done it before. But I want to. With you. Oh, Donald . . ."

He took her into his arms and held her, resting his nose in her hair as he had done at the dance.

She touched his buttons pointedly, then got up and out of his arms and went to her closet. She returned with a quilted sleeping mat. She got down on her knees and unrolled the mat, efficiently, but more pleasurably than a nurse might make up a patient's bed.

"Here," she commanded. "Please."

Mildred stood. At first she turned her back to him, but after a hesitation, she turned and smiled prettily, head tilted. As she began to unbutton her fatigue jacket, she said softly, "We must not be afraid to see each other, Donald. Not now."

It was so Mildred Baumiller–honest that he knew he must not flinch. He saw that she wore plain white undergarments, which he assumed were the standard wear of standard girls. When her fatigues were a heap on the floor, she reached behind for the hooks of her brassiere. She blushed perceptibly, but whisked off the brassiere. "Now you," she said.

More hesitantly than Mildred, Robertson undressed. In seconds they lay on the mat, an uncertain union of confused passions.

Her mouth quested and he stroked her body. For a few seconds, his fingers tingled with electricity, but then came the specter who paced with him in his hospital room. He begged his specter to go away, although he knew it could not. The specter looked down upon him and accused. Then, as if the dynamo had exploded, the electricity vanished.

But Mildred pressed on and he entwined his hand in her hair and gently pulled back her head so that he could look into her face. She was stunning. No pale mouse lived there. Her lips were moist and parted, under eyes which even partly closed were shining with desire. She resonated, and to things he had never experienced before. Robertson knew he had never gazed into such a lovely flame.

Sweat began to bead his upper lip.

Slowly, as if she fought against it, her face changed. Now understanding flooded across it. Her eyes opened fully once, then closed with resignation. They sat up and she put her lips to his ear.

"Am I so ugly to you?"

Robertson choked back before he replied. He kissed her first, not the passionate mouth-wrestling of the heady outset, but tenderly and longingly, as a soldier kisses in the station when the beckoning train whistles.

"You are beautiful to me, Mildred. I have never seen a thing so beautiful as you. Please know that."

Mildred began to cry. He kissed her under the eye, needing to taste her. He could only say, "I'm sorry, Mildred. I'm so terribly sorry I hurt you."

"Just hold me. I want that now. I—"

Although Robertson was left-handed, it was with the right hand that he reached to seal her lips. It was as if the left, which was guilty of so much, was unworthy to touch her. They lay back on the mat. He wrapped his body around her protectively and they hid in sleep from their enemies.

After silent hours had paraded through the little garden cottage, they stirred. They covered their nakedness and then tacitly sat down together again.

It had not been resolved.

Robertson smiled helplessly. "I'll be leaving soon. I have to report to corps headquarters. When I get there, I'm going to ask General Holloway to return me to my regiment."

"But you'll be marked for noncombat duty. Major Kerns says that."

"You'll never see me again, Mildred. Find someone else to share your house."

Mildred blanched. "Of course I'll see you again. Korea is not all that large. If you stay in Korea, I'm going to ask to have my tour extended. They'll permit that."

"Go home. You'll meet someone who can give you what I obviously can't give you."

Mildred sniffed. "Marian Dawson says the two most overrated things in the world are sexual intercourse and medical doctors. You're recovering from wounds. It will change. We can talk to Major Kerns. Major Kerns is very wise. He can help us. I'll extend. I'll wait for you. I—"

He shook his head. "Nothing can come of it."

"Why, Donald? Tell me why?"

He looked up and shook his head again. "I'm sorry."

Mildred wiped the corner of her eye. Then her eye followed his finger as he traced circles on the low table. "I have a right to know. I have more right than anyone else in the world."

Robertson's finger halted in midcircle. "Why do you claim such a right?" When she gasped, he realized too late what he had said.

Mildred's chin jutted. "Because I *have* to know, Donald. I love you."

They finished dressing and went back to the hospital. Alone in his room, Robertson resumed his pacing. Always now he was accompanied. When she slowed, he slowed his pacing so that she could catch up with him.

30

107TH EVACUATION HOSPITAL, JULY 13, 1952

From somewhere off to his right, Robertson could hear the generator that supplied auxiliary current to the hospital when the uncertain powerhouses of Korea stumbled, which was often. The generator building, he reasoned, must be on the periphery of the 107th, against the wall. This was in deference to the subtle vibrations that came through the stones at his back. If he sensed it carefully, he found a certainty there, as if the generator itself said to Korea, "No sweat! Let me show you how reliably Americans make electricity."

But the generator was easily shut out. Robertson shortened the range of his ears and concentrated on what was visual. This, except for Major Kerns's office light, was as subtle as the generator noise. The world was misty. A warm wind came up from the harbor at Inchon, only a few miles away, and the wind bore the breath of the warmer sea across the cooling land. Robertson concentrated on that and realized that soon, when the greater system that drove the onshore wind tired, things would change, and the hot summer breeze would go from the land to the sea.

Choi Min-soo had always observed: Politics are as the wind, first from the land, then from the sea.

Nevertheless, as he stared at Major Kerns's light, Robertson knew the mists this night would not evaporate for him. In that mood, needing action, he removed from his pocket the eagle insignias that his regimental commander had sent him via the corps commander. He squeezed these in his right hand. One of the insignias' fastening pin had come unsecured. When this pricked him, he squeezed harder, savoring the minor pain.

He stared at the light, a diffuse square about twenty feet up in the black mist. Major Kerns that morning had promised to burn the light.

Robertson had been sitting across the major's desk. He had known why Kerns had sent for him, and as he listened to the major, Robertson unconsciously took up a number-two yellow pencil from the desk. He held this in his hands, his thumbs together in the middle of it, cupped fingers around the ends.

"I'd like to send you home," Kerns said.

"But General Holloway promised I could go to his staff."

"Well . . ."

"I've been doing administrative work for Colonel Bladenburg," Robertson pointed out. "If I can do work at the hospital here, I can do work at corps headquarters."

Kerns had been watching the pencil. He nodded toward it. "A thing can be bent only so far before it breaks, Lieutenant Robertson. That's as true of men as it is true of pencils."

Robertson frowned guiltily and relaxed the pressure of his thumbs. "As an assistant adjutant I should know to be more careful of army pencils," he muttered sheepishly.

Kerns smiled with a marked fondness. "The army has an endless supply of pencils, Lieutenant Robertson. And right now in Korea, I rather imagine it has a superfluity of second lieutenants. That's why I would like to send you home."

Robertson compressed his lips and said nothing. The knuckles of his thumbs whitened as he reassaulted the yellow pencil.

Kerns sighed and shifted his eyes to Robertson's personnel record on the corner of his desk. "I'm a one-man physical evaluation board this morning," he said. "Dr. Palmer and Dr. Alberts asked me to resolve it. I think they are a little bit afraid of you."

"Why would they be afraid of me? In a hospital, doctors have all the power. I'm merely Colonel Bladenburg's dog robber, and attached in light-duty status at that. Take my stapler away from me and I'm unarmed."

"It's a bit more than that, Lieutenant Robertson, but it is not relevant to us right now. What is relevant are your options. You have three, as I see it. First, I can give you a medical pension and send you stateside from here. You can go home and finish the degree you have started with USAFI, and the world is at your feet. I'd recommend something such as business administration for you. You have a control over other men few officers have. Even in this setting I see that." Kerns grinned. "Keep away from medical school or you'll wind up sitting in an uncomfortable chair like the one under me at the moment, trying to tell another man what is good for him."

"And the other options, sir?" Robertson asked immediately.

"Those are the khaki options. I can give you a permanent light-duty medical profile and send you to the States. The army would keep you around, but in a noncombatant assignment."

The pencil under Robertson's thumb broke.

Wordlessly, Kerns reached into his upper-left desk drawer and fished out another yellow pencil. He handed this to Robertson. "As I indicated, the army has many pencils."

"My third option, sir?"

Kerns sighed visibly. "I can send you to General Holloway. I'd have to falsify my opinion of your medical condition to do that."

"How is that?" Robertson demanded.

Kerns, as he always did when others intruded in medical matters, showed a quick flash of irritation, but one he suppressed quickly. He stared over Robertson's head at his window and lectured. "Gunshot wounds have no consequences only in the western movies. In real life, any severe wound—and you had several of them when you came in here—is a serious health matter. Your leg is a miracle, but you can't deceive me about your shoulder. You will never have full movement of it. Unless I slept through a few lectures in medical school, it will worsen as you age."

After a long silence, Robertson pleaded, "Have I any say in it, Major?"

Kerns nodded honestly. "I'm afraid so. Or else I'd have decided it for you before you even came in here."

"Then I want to go to General Holloway, sir. I can work on getting back to my regiment from there. I'd be dealing with soldiers again. . . ." Robertson caught himself, adding a low, "I'm sorry, sir. No offense meant."

"No offense taken, but that medically is the poorest option. I admit it shows only on your medical records, but you're a one-armed man."

Robertson drilled Kerns with his eyes. "Please, sir."

Kerns filled a pipe with London Dock smoking tobacco. He rummaged several moments in his middle desk drawer before he found a match. After the pipe was lighted, he reached pointedly and moved Robertson's records into the middle of his desk. Deliberately, he shoved everything else on the desk out to the rim, leaving the manila folders front and center. When he looked up from that work, his eyes had hardened into blue flints.

"I'm going to take the position that the American army owes an officer like you something, Lieutenant Robertson, even if that something is against the judgment of a crusty medical major. I'll request that Colonel Bladenburg cut orders to send you to corps headquarters, effective midnight tonight." Kerns's eyes relented then, and he smiled warmly. "Let's do it this way. I'm duty medical officer tonight and I'll be in my office unless one of the logistics commandos from the Seoul base area comes in with an emergency head cold. I want you to think about what we've discussed. If you wish, at any time between now and then, to change your mind, just come in here and blink an eye. Then I'll change the orders for you and send you stateside to a fine civilian career or a fine army career. Just blink an eye, Lieutenant. One eye. Then I'll make your decision for you."

"That's generous, sir. But I want to remain in Korea."

Kerns's eyes flinted again. He put both hands, palms flat, on his desk. "That finishes our medical business. I've done something for you and I want you to do something for me."

Robertson cocked his head. "That is?"

"Mildred Baumiller is everyone's little sister here. If you elect not to blink, I want you to let my little sister down as gently as you can." Kerns got out of his chair, still palms on the desk, and fixed Robertson's eyes. "She came here yesterday in tears and begged me to give you the first or second of your options. She loves you, Robertson, and that is a factor you must consider."

Robertson broke the second pencil and stood up.

"I don't know what drives you, Robertson. But for God's sake, think about it and come in here sometime before midnight and blink that eye."

The generator Robertson had been heeding as he mulled over his conversation with the major overspeeded and tripped its regulating governor. The light in Kerns's office blinked, as if to remind Robertson that the issue still lay on the major's desk.

Beside Robertson at the wall, Mildred stirred from the long morose silence that had held her for minutes. The generating rhythm of the world was restored, and Major Kerns's light was restored, a beacon in the mist of Korea.

Mildred spoke. "I can ask to have my tour extended. Then I'll be here when you come to Seoul from corps headquarters. Many corps officers come here. I checked on that."

Robertson squeezed the eagle insignias in his hand, enjoying the new pain. "You must forget me, Mildred. I can be nothing for you. I—"

"I'll never give you up." Mildred shook her head vehemently.

Robertson winced from the force of it. He had prepared his lines all day, planning, discarding, and redrafting. Yet still his dialogue was as weak as the tea talk of a second-rate drawing-room comedy.

He had brought her here to the angle in the hospital wall, sensing from the outset that this was both secluded ground and neutral ground. The night was warm and as soft as the mists.

They had, figuratively speaking, spent their coins. He realized painfully that Mildred had spent hers in a niggardly way, forcing each one to pass through her heart. But he had spent recklessly, like a ranch hand at a traveling carnival. The coin had been spent in the streets of Seoul. They had not gone again to the house under the wall. One day they went down Yulgong-no Street to inspect the Chongmyo Shrine. On another they walked rapidly up Sejong-no Street—rapidly so he could show Mildred his limp was almost gone—and gawked for hours at the Kyongbok Palace. They broke the EUSAK rules and ate Korean food. They broke EUSAK custom and smiled at the Korean fellow human beings.

Now the coin was gone. When first they had reached the wall, Mildred had sobbed quietly but then had lapsed into the sad silence.

"Please, Mildred. Forget me. I'm trouble for you."

Mildred put her arms around his neck, shyly, as she had continued in shyness since the day in the house. She whispered, "Say you love me. Even if it's a lie, I want to hear it from you once. You've never said it."

Robertson tensed and shut his eyes.

He recalled the gray day, now it seemed like a century ago, when Tanner had renewed the brand on the quick horse Buck. Tanner had thrown Buck and had heated the iron before the horse's terrified eyes—eyes that had experienced this pain once before. Then, although Robertson had walked away from it, with guilt tears on his face and lead in his heart, he had heard behind him the bite of the red-hot iron and Buck's answering scream. Now, as he had felt the scorch of Tanner's branding iron that day, Mildred's tears seared his cheek. And, if he just walked away from her tonight, he would hear again the anguished scream of betrayal realized.

Feeling cruel and guilty, he floundered. "There are things about me you don't know," he offered weakly.

Then Mildred sighed out the question he knew had waited just behind her lips for weeks. "Is there someone else, Donald? I have to ask you that now."

On that, he reached for the most vicious of the scripts he had planned. He began, "Yes, Mildred, there is someone else. Her name is Soon Lee. At least that is the name I gave her when I realized she had to have a name. I am going to tell you about her. When I am finished, you will hate me. Then it will be easier for you because you will *want* me to go away from you."

Robertson had gone into Chunchon thirteen months earlier, down by courier jeep from G Company on the Kumwha line, to answer one of several essay questions for the United States Armed Forces Institute: "Compare and contrast the poetry of A. E. Housman with that of William Butler Yeats."

Riding in the jeep that morning, he realized he was exhausted, but that was the normal condition of the line infantry, as familiar now as the steel that was a daily part of his life—steel rifle, steel bayonet, steel helmet—implements for shooting and clubbing and stabbing and for blunting other shootings and clubbings and stabbings. But he had his face in a clean wind, and quickly was able to shift his thoughts to poetry and college credits. He thought wryly that there was hope for a world that would excuse a soldier from combat so he could go to the division rear and discuss Yeats.

Chunchon, properly Ch'unch'on, lay crippled at the intersection of two main Korean roads, Routes 17 and 29, and the railroad that came up from Seoul to debouch the matériel of the war. The ROK Sixth Division had made one of the better stands of summer 1950 there, against the NKPA Second Division. Now, in June 1951, the city was recuperating from this, plus the other wounds inflicted on it as the war had twice surged through it.

That night, Robertson went over the fence of the replacement depot, certain he had written a good examination, as happy as—certainly that is how Private Klineschmidt, the replacement he would meet the next day, would have put it—a nymphomaniac invited to a battalion short-arm inspection. Chunchon excited him at once. Like all the infantry replacements of spring 1951, he, along with Braxton Fowlkes, had been rushed from the troopship to the line. Chunchon was the first Korean city Robertson had experienced.

But, even looking through Robertson's happy, excited eyes, only a demented poet would have found radiance in Chunchon that night. It had rained and the war debris of the city lay in foul-smelling mud, fog rising over that, smearing the lights of the dim oil lamps of the few street stalls whose proprietors still hoped for trade at this hour. The city was wounded, and it seemed to Robertson that its eyes had been poked out with a sharp stick.

In the muggy air that night, the characteristic odor of Korea threatened to overwhelm him. His uninitiated olfactory sense was savaged by the bouquet of traditional Tungusic poverty, a blend of unrefrigerated food, stale rice straw, and decaying human excrement, the latter the material generations of Koreans had worked into their tired soil to make the poor substance of their lives fertile. It clung to the American spirit like a leper's cloak. In the early part of his adventure there, before he dutifully numbed himself, Robertson had reflected that all else could be removed, all the trucks and all the cannons, all the wailing Koreans and all the cursing Americans, the very earth itself, and the odor would remain, durable enough to provide the Korean War a field of maneuver.

But Robertson found he could turn off his nose. He was more interested in the girl he followed. Once he had found her, losing the MPs who chased him down the narrow alleys of Chunchon had been child's play. The MPs had idled off in their jeep, head lamps delving tunnels in the murk, knowing, no doubt, they could catch a hundred divisional AWOLs like Robertson if they wished. Robertson bade them happy farewell. "Good-bye, MP-sans, to you and to the roan horses you rode up on."

Robertson followed the girl. Twice he stopped to take long drinks from the bottle of whiskey he carried. It was Suntory, illicit, bought from a wizened old *yangban* in a bird-cage hat for fifteen dollars. The whiskey went down easily now, not bitterly as it had gone down two hours earlier, to renew the glow of lighthearted intoxication. Drunkenness was a matter of military duty. Once having gone AWOL—and any Regular Army line soldier given a serendipitous night in Chunchon would have done that—drunkenness was a certainty.

He staggered slightly, but he easily kept pace with the girl while he debated with himself what to do about her.

He stopped again and looked around. The oily lights seemed conspiratorial and nodded to him in the Korean darkness, which had a way to Caucasians of being darker than the night-street darkness of their own cities. Something in it all seemed to say, "Take her. I will hide you while you do it."

It was a macabre euphoria that decided him to round out his AWOL by sleeping with the girl. He had not seen her face yet, but that did not matter. Brax Fowlkes always said, "Be a tit-and-leg feller, Robbie, then it don't count a fart to a hurricane if they have an ugly face."

Robertson knew the first question Fowlkes would ask him when he returned to the company the next day would be "Did you get any in Chunchon?" It would disappoint everyone if he had to answer no.

The girl slowed and turned toward him a moment. That closed the range and he called out, "Pretty girl! Wait for the poor drunken trooper."

She spun and walked on, more rapidly now. He easily caught up, closing the last of the yards that separated them. He caught her wrist and studied her. She was small and birdlike, in a short white jacket and the high dress he had seen other women wearing in the city.

"Girl-san make short-time with GI?" he asked.

She spoke forcefully. *"Seikse!"*

When he threw back his head and laughed because they were making language together, she cringed. He thought, because the word comes that way into American ears, that she had said that she was sexy.

Now more timidly, she uttered her word again. She pulled free and hurried off into the night. Puzzled, he followed, but now with the nagging, eerie sense that he was stalking her. He could not have explained that to himself. But it was there, as strong as the odor of Korea.

The street gave up all dimension, becoming narrow or broad and awash in oozing blackness. He sobered enough to sense what so many Americans would come home to describe, the nocturnal streets of the war-torn cities, when an American stood uncomprehending and naked in a world so alien the very stones cried anathema against him. He drank again, to drown that, the way Harvey Tanner drowned unwanted kittens.

She led him to a house, really more a hovel, for the Koreans had put tin over its shattered roof, and the overhang of the narrow porch slanted shamefully. She removed her shoes and went in, sliding the door behind her.

Robertson did not understand the custom and did not remove his muddy boots. When he tested the door, it resisted only slightly. He released a grenade burst of gleeful laughter.

Inside, it was hot, as if the hovel had been shut up against this moment. But it was lighted and the girl he had pursued waited there. Her head was down. Robertson lurched over to her.

She gasped when he reached for her. Eyes wide, she looked up at him. "*Seikse!*" she said again.

"I know. You are damned sexy," he lied gallantly. "We will make short-time."

He pulled her to him in order to sample what he was about to purchase. Her head reached only to the level of his nipples. Straight black hair framed high cheekbones and hooded brown eyes. Her skin was amber, but almost a jaundiced amber. He thought her mildly pretty, although Plumber had always insisted the girls of Japan were far prettier than those of Korea. Plumber called them "mooses," from the Japanese *musame.*

The lamp in the room flickered and cast long shadows to dance on the dark walls. The air seemed to become suspicious, as if there were something in the room he did not understand. But wasn't it merely the weary transaction between soldiers and whores, as old as the war club? If a soldier in a strange land needed it, he either bought it or raped it.

Suddenly he didn't want her so much as he didn't want to not have her.

The others back in the company would demand that he account for a few illicit hours in a city.

She stared down at his muddy boots. He reached for her jacket and tugged. Trembling, he thought, she undressed for him. Her garments were cotton and dingy, bereft of the erotic.

Robertson put down his Suntory whiskey and unbuckled his belt. Then his trousers were down around his ankles, shackling him to what he proposed to do.

He looked up to see her nakedness. If her wrist had been thin, her body was fleshless. She seemed leached. Small boylike breasts peeped from her chest. Robertson dismissed her nakedness at once as peach tits and a pitiful Asian straggle of coarse pubic hair, shadowing low, between stark hips.

After the girl undressed, she did nothing. Always before, the whore had lain down and had opened for him. Silly as it was, he advised her, "You'll have to lie down, girl-san."

"*Seikse.*" She lifted a hand to her mouth and waved it rapidly. "*Seikse. Seikse.*"

He pushed against her breast. She recoiled but stood erect again.

Then he pushed harder. To show her what was wanting, he clumsily put his trouser-shackled foot behind her to trip her back.

The birdlike girl fell. At first she resisted and tried to regain her feet, but then she seemed to give up to it, and fell rapidly with a stiffened body.

When her head struck the low chest that was near the wall, the sound was wet, like that an overripe melon makes when it is discarded from the truck onto the hard pavement.

Robertson dropped onto his knees, then over her. He felt resistance. He pulled away immediately. His penis was speckled pale red. Drunkenly, puzzled now more than ever, he wiped himself.

His mind reached to understand. Why had she entered into a contract she so obviously could not fulfill?

Now on his knees again, he leaned over her. She seemed to sleep. He seized her chin and rocked her head.

She moaned "*seikse,*" and then was silent. Now the word was shorn of romance. If anything, it came out of her like a dying declaration of her own inviolability.

Then, somehow, he knew the girl was dying.

Robertson sobered instantly. Suddenly he was frightened and alone, so far from his own familiar world that he was without defenses. His mouth was dry and his tongue was puffy.

Understanding struck with the force of the shrapnel that had torn his face only weeks earlier. When it came, it seized him in talon clutches. He was no stranger to what he saw. In 1951, on the hills of Korea, death by head injury was as common as the mud on his boots that had soiled her house.

He lifted his left hand to protest, and the hand hovered. Then, committed that deeply, it went hesitantly to the skin between her breasts. For several minutes he joined to her that way. Unconsciously, he pressed down on her, then lifted his hand, hoping her vitality would follow. Over and over, staring down in horror.

But that did no good. The girl's breaths flagged. At some point, under his hand, they ceased.

He sat with his hand on her for minutes longer, eyes closed, numbly begging that it was just a drunken delusion and that she would sit up and laugh at him.

A muscle in her relaxed and she gave out a little twitch. His heart leaped hopefully. But then he reminded himself he had seen that before also. Death's little joke.

At the last of it, he touched her face. When he did, the face flopped into the light. The head was bruised where she had struck her furniture. The eyes were open and they accused. He saw she had been young, surely no more than eighteen, maybe less.

He hitched up his trousers and ran out of the house and into the streets. At first the streets were narrow and serpentine and the phantom houses were closed in and seemed to strike at him with clawed hands. He shrank from them and sought broader streets, where the houses were set further back.

When he was fully captured by panic, he ran blindly, heart pounding and sides aching. Finally, he reached the crossroads, cornered all around with dwellings. Lost to himself, he halted and looked. To the east of Chunchon, a faintness revealed that dawn was imminent. He ran again then, for the day would bring back the world's lines and angles, sharp shadows somehow more moral and condemning than the soft dimensions of night. Realizing that this must explain why crimes were committed in darkness, he ran harder than he had ever run before.

It seemed hours, but at last out of the brown earth that glistened from the rain of the previous afternoon emerged the olive green tents of the replacement depot. He slowed.

The sentry challenged. Robertson froze. In Korea a sentry would shoot. Robertson straightened his clothing before stepping into the sentry's light. He blinked like a man coming up from a cave. With ashes in his mouth, he conjured up an unmistakable Americanism. "It's Tonto, buddy. Come in to join the Lone Ranger."

The sentry's laughter was mellow and safe. "Advance your American ass to be recognized, Mr. Tonto."

The sentry was huge and black and Alabaman. Clearly glad for company, he offered a Camel cigarette. They smoked together in silence.

Finally, feeling the stickiness on his groin, Robertson flipped away his cigarette. "Did they miss me?" he asked.

"Naw. Least if they did, they didn't say nothing about it to me. Get any?"

Realizing sickeningly that it was the first of the lies, Robertson answered in the negative.

In the tent he snitched the first towel and water canteen his hands came to and went out and between the tents. He dropped his trousers and scrubbed. Although the coarse towel blotted away the blood, it was futile.

Mildred heard it out. She had been leaning ever further away from him and now she fully was erect.

Insanely, she giggled, so hard she had to put a hand to her mouth. When she recovered, she said shakily, "It was only an accident. No one will blame you."

Robertson had known that would come. "No. It was no accident. I hunted her down."

"Well, you didn't rape her. She wanted you to follow her."

"If I am to believe I didn't rape her, Mildred, I must believe that a Korean virgin in her menstrual period would entertain the prospect of coitus with a drunken American soldier who tracked mud into her house."

"But no one else will ever know. It has been more than a year and you haven't been . . . been found out."

"I *know*, Mildred. And now you know. Even if we could live with it, we'd be living with a wall between us."

Mildred said nothing for long seconds, then she raised her head. "All right, Donald. We'll go see Major Kerns right now." She gestured toward the light in the window. "Major Kerns is very wise and he can help us. You can confess it and the army will scold you like it scolds about everything and that will be all of it."

"It can't be 'all of it,' Mildred. I told you a little lie a few weeks ago. I said I read the Manual for Courts-Martial because of Lieutenant Blackthorne. I read the manual because of Robertson. I want you to hear from it now."

"No, Donald. I don't want to hear any more."

Robertson took her wrists and held them firmly. "You must. Article 120 of the Uniform Code of Military Justice: 'Any person who commits an act of sexual intercourse with a female not his wife, by force and without her consent, is guilty of rape. Penetration, however slight, is sufficient to constitute the offense.' Article 118: 'Any person subject to this code who unlawfully kills a human being when engaged in rape is guilty of murder and shall suffer such punishment as a court-martial may direct.' " He forced Mildred to look into his face and added, "For murder committed during rape, the court-martial may direct hanging or shooting."

"No!"

"Yes, Mildred. That is the reality of it."

Throwing her arms around his neck, Mildred pleaded, "The army is not that savage. You might have to be in prison a few years, but I'd wait for you. I don't care what you've done—"

"That's out for me," Robertson interrupted quietly. "I'd be back in the root cellar, and even if I ever got out, I'd have to get down on my knees and pull Tanner's weeds again."

Mildred could only cling now. Robertson lifted his eyes to Kerns's light and studied it. Slowly a thought formed. He began to have a fantasy. He saw in the mist a house in some vague place where perhaps no one else would come. Mildred was there, chattering from the kitchen as she had chattered that day in the garden cottage. He was surrounded by books and he had the sensation that he could sleep soon against Mildred's untainted flesh and awake in the morning whole and clean. Who would come there to such a house and point a finger and cry out at him, "Murderer! Rapist!"?

He opened his mouth to explain his new thoughts. He got as far as "Mildred, maybe I'm seeing it wrong. Perhaps we could—" before Mildred interrupted.

She lifted her chin and said shrilly, "Of course you're wrong. *She was only a gook.*" Then she giggled.

The generator stumbled as it had earlier. The major's light blinked in that weak second.

Robertson stared at the light. He did not blink. He could never blink now.

The generator caught and ran on strongly.

He stood. "Good-bye, Mildred."

Mildred sobbed harshly. She reached into her breast pocket and removed a cloth, placing it in Robertson's left hand. "This is yours," she said quietly. "Sergeant Darrow took it from your things when you first came here, and I swiped it from him." She sniffed. "I told you timid people have to swipe."

Now he held the eagle insignias in one hand and the hachimaki in the other. He dropped the insignias and stepped off into the darkness, clutching the hachimaki.

After a few paces, he halted and turned. He could sense Mildred was still there where they had sat by the wall. He admitted to himself what he had known for weeks. He loved her. But he dare not say that aloud.

He put the hachimaki in his breast pocket and went on toward the orders that would send him to corps headquarters. There, he would deal again with soldiers.

31

107TH EVACUATION HOSPITAL,
OCTOBER 18, 1952

To the northeast roared the events of the final autumn. Still deadlocked over the issue of prisoner-of-war repatriation, the sides struggled, on mountains such as Old Baldy and White Horse and Iron Horse and Arrowhead Ridge, and, in Panmunjom, at the long conference tables. From time to time, the sides gave up temporarily, insulted each other, and walked out. The only strategy then simply was to convince the other side your side could die as well as his side could die.

For the infantrymen on the line, the military routine hardened. The rifleman's combat tour became as rigid as reveille and retreat and taps. Few alluded to it, but the war, seen through the rear peepsight of a Garand rifle, had become a stalemate. The bunkers took on the character of permanent dwellings, with stoves and makeshift bunks and even surfaced floors. On the turn of a duty roster, as formal as the guard mount, a man went forward to the outposts or joined a patrol. If he survived, which he did not always do, it was the next man's turn. Casualty attrition on many days approached the figure of one thousand.

Now with a silver bar on her collar, Mildred Baumiller wept often in the days following Robertson's departure, but they were tears without hope and they left her aching and unfulfilled. As she expected, he had not written. In the early days, she inquired eagerly of anyone remotely associated with General Holloway's headquarters. At first, she took heart, because the answer she got was always the same. "Robertson? He's a first lieutenant now. Damned good man. Keeps to himself."

Then one day she gave that up. Someday, she knew, she surely would get a different answer.

Tonight, Mildred realized she had been staring at the door to Robertson's room. He had been its only occupant, since VIP patients normally went to Japan. She now guarded the key, and tacitly the others accepted that. Major Kerns appeared and stood over her a moment. He smiled sadly for her, patted her shoulder, and went away silently.

After the major's departure, Sergeant Darrow came over. He sat on the corner of Mildred's desk and crossed his legs. Darrow was a shifty little man with a pencil-line mustache. Customarily, he passed the shift by regaling the corpsmen with kiss-and-tell stories and not-at-all-subtle assaults on Mildred's shyness. Tonight he caught her attention. "Mouse, when you give up on your hero, I might be able to find some time for you."

Mildred leaped to her feet and ran to the door of the VIP room. She unlocked it with fumbling fingers and went in, closing the door and leaning her back against it to shut out the ward. She trembled and fought against tears.

The room was neat and clean, although Mildred had not been in there since Robertson's departure. It seemed hollow now and markedly different than she remembered it. Then she realized that light slanted across the floor as it had not done when he slept there. She nodded to herself. A soldier had been killed on the street near the gate and Colonel Williams had ordered a security light placed on a pole near the wall.

Then it caught her. Seen in the new light was a line along the oak planks of the floor. So sure was she of this that she stepped over and went down on her knees. Slowly she let her hand brush the floor, seeking to convince herself that she felt a groove there.

She rocked back on her folded legs and put her hands to her face. She pictured Robertson, pacing to the wall, turning, pacing to the other wall. She cried easily, for the first time. "Oh, Donald! Did we do that to you? I saw that once. The snow leopard in the zoo in St. Louis when I went to visit my cousins. He was beautiful and he paced like that. And I knew he would continue pacing until he either escaped his cage or died. Nothing I could ever do or say would change that for him."

After about five minutes, Mildred got up and rubbed her eyes. She carefully renewed the hospital corners of the sheet on Robertson's bed, glanced around the room once, and went out. She beckoned at once to Sergeant Darrow.

"I'm going to my quarters a moment, Sergeant. I want right now for you to order the men to stop playing cribbage during their duty hours on the ward."

"We always play cribbage, Mouse. You know that."

Mildred didn't answer.

She returned in about twenty minutes. She had put on makeup and brushed her hair. She had changed from the fatigues she had worn earlier. Now, she wore an olive skirt and green blouse, hosiery and high heels, the uniform Vivian Hardiman often wore into the ward. Mildred also carried a book, morocco-bound and official looking.

Darrow rushed over at once. After a lecherous survey, he whistled. "Where have you been, Mouse? You're not all that bad looking a broad when you put your mind to it."

Mildred took a deep breath and counted to five. Then she lifted the book into Darrow's face. "Have you ever seen this book, Sergeant Darrow?"

Puzzled, Darrow got out, "Sure, Mouse. That's the army's Manual for Courts-Martial. Who are we going to hang?"

Mildred smiled. "Good, Sergeant Darrow. Are you also familiar with Article 89 of this book?"

"Can't say I am," Darrow replied carefully.

"No matter. I shall read it to you." Mildred had marked the page and she turned to it at once. "Article 89, disrespect toward superior officer. Any person subject to this code who behaves with disrespect toward his superior officer shall be punished as a court-martial may direct. . . ."

The sergeant squirmed and said quietly, "Yes, I've heard of that." When Mildred glared, he added a louder, "Ma'am."

Mildred put down the manual and stepped closer to Darrow. Her face was turned up under Darrow's chin. "Don't you agree that the word 'Mouse,' either applied directly to me, or used within my hearing, constitutes disrespect as described by that article, Sergeant Darrow?"

Darrow fidgeted and nodded glumly.

Mildred backed away, smiling warmly. "My name is Baumiller. You may, however, address me by my first name."

Darrow brightened. "Yes, ma'am. By your first name."

"And my first name is 'Lieutenant'!" Mildred said firmly.

"Yes, Lieutenant, ma'am."

Mildred put on an orange-red smile again and said, "Thank you for the compliment. Now have the men put away the cribbage board as I ordered and let's get about the business of the army medical corps."

After he had set the corpsmen to work, Darrow sidled over to Mildred again. "Lieutenant Baumiller, I'd like to apologize."

Mildred lifted her jaw prettily. "No apologies needed, Sergeant Darrow. We are just going to go on until the army rotates us from Korea. No matter what happens to a person, a person has to go on."

32

NEAR BIG NORI HILL, NORTH KOREA,
JULY 27, 1953

President-elect and General of the Army Dwight D. Eisenhower came to Korea in December of 1952 and looked around, high over the heads of the fawning lesser star men. At last the Korean War could be viewed simultaneously by a soldier and a politician. If Eisenhower talked to himself, he said, "Enough of this nonsense is enough."

Likely even the Communist side understood that the end was imminent. Imminent, in international affairs, means about six months, more or less.

But it was not over. First came the fierce, frigid hill battles of the final winter. The names loomed up red out of the white snow and vibrated along the tired newswires. The Hook, Gibraltar Hill, Big Nori, and Little Nori. One thoughtful man noted that when the Brits lost a pipe major in the winter scuffles, they blamed their colonel. "Easier by far to get hold of a colonel than a bloody good pipe major," the Tommies said.

For the third season, Siberian winds howled across the outposts ahead of the trenches. For the newcomers, and they were mostly new and drafted, the message was "Don't freeze. Try not to get hit and wait it out. Nine months. Survive them." Then the months with thirty-one days in them became another enemy.

The hagglers returned to their table. It was cold there, too. They stretched weary shoulders and drank bitter coffee while they struggled for a way to please General Eisenhower. Virtually everything had been agreed to except the final details of the POWs, the hanging tree of so many long weeks.

Finally, the tall turbaned Sikhs of India, beautiful men wearing

British-style uniforms and right minds, suggested an answer. "Look, you white guys and yellow guys are so pissed at each other, you'll never swap your prisoners and go home. Why not let us brown guys do it for you? We'll be absolutely impartial: we don't like either of you a whole hell of a lot."

Not being liked in Korea was the order of the day, and the Sikhs made sense. By March of 1953, the Communist side agreed in principle to the mechanics of the POW exchange, if not to the spirit of it. In fact, in a few weeks the world would learn that the Chinese and North Koreans would not account for thirty-five hundred captives. The victims would quickly be forgotten by a world that wanted Korea to be history.

But in March, this sad fact was in the future. The UN heaved a collective sigh of relief and began packing.

The packing was premature. New names were spat up for the cables— Dale Outpost, Eerie Hill, Pork Chop Hill. The awesome Arsenal and a dozen forgotten others. The Chinese slashed with a sharp sword. The North Koreans held their coats and cheered them on. Again, the UN wastage approached a thousand men per combat day.

In late April, the two sides met in stone-faced enmity to exchange a few sick and emaciated prisoners. The pillars of the world did not collapse. During spring break, the students of America, about the same age as the soldiers of Korea, invaded the beaches of south Florida. The number of recently deflowered virgins may have approached a thousand per combat day. The students were too elated at having escaped Korea to name their hills or count their casualties.

Already a Korean War soldier could limp with a U.S. government— issue cane down a street in Rapid City or Des Moines and have someone say: "Oh, where have you been? I see you've hurt your foot. Think it will rain?"

In May, in Korea, the fighting resumed with new vigor while the cease-fire terms were being typed up at Panmunjom. The next month, the Communists agreed to a hostile truce. Then it remained only for iron-skinned Syngman Rhee to agree to what had been agreed. The old patriot did not act impulsively. America tweaked its money machine and finally Rhee agreed. The prisoners could come home, then a few of the line infantrymen.

The POWs were preceded by a careful list, drawn by the Sikhs. General Holloway's son's name was included neither among the sick nor among the not-so-sick. Watching it at corps headquarters, Robertson saw hope vanish from the general. He sorrowed for him, but neither man remarked it.

But the fuse yet fizzled. At the penultimate moment, generally ignoring the Americans, the Chinese hurled a massive assault against the hill positions of the Republic of Korea army. They staggered the ROKs and overran them, sweeping into the support echelons where white-lipped Americans stood at the guns. Those Americans died with blasphemy on their lips. "Jesus God. Why now?"

The answer was obvious. Capt. Choi Min-soo of the 12th ROK, formerly on detached service with the American army as an enlisted man, explained it early in the morning to Colonel Min. The struggle for Choi's hill had abated, but the sniper fire falling onto the hill indicated it would resume.

"My dear colonel," Choi said very formally, "our Chinese cousins wish merely to remind us that they will remain in Asia when our American friends have gone home."

"You are familiar with Americans. *Will* the Americans go home?"

Choi replied thoughtfully, "Perhaps your great-grandchild will see that, Colonel."

Colonel Min looked out through the firing slits in Choi's command-post sandbags. "The fire on your flank is increasing, Captain. Perhaps we should discuss it."

Choi smiled and waited. Colonel Min was a fair soldier, but he suffered from indecisiveness.

Colonel Min pounded his fist into his palm. "On the one hand, one thinks you should . . . but on the other hand." The colonel frowned at himself and started to leave the command post. "I shall tell you of my decision, Captain. We must act either to evacuate or to hold."

Choi bowed slightly. He knew he would be frozen to the telephone now. Colonel Min would return to his own headquarters and drink green tea until he decided. Choi said, "One of course will await your orders."

Colonel Min went out. Choi sighed. He speculated that Min would do both: he would order the flank held, then he would order it evacuated.

He reached into his field pack and took out his last packet of Chesterfield cigarettes. Twenty, he thought. I shall give two each to my lieutenants and smoke the remaining twelve myself.

When Choi was well into his second cigarette, a runner came into the command post. His report was excited, and Choi had to settle him down. With the runner's information, Choi took a party of four, along with Lieutenant Duk, and went down to his flank. Three dead men lay outside the machine-gun position, but Choi reorganized the survivors and ordered that Lieutenant Duk hold until the colonel decided what they should do there. He went back to the command post, with several fewer men to command than he had had when he went out.

Artillery impacts had coalesced into one huge shout, but the killing area was to Choi's left, closer to the Nori hill mass. He smiled wryly. Here the enemy gripped him so closely their associates could not support them with artillery fire. Each nuisance had its own advantages. Choi's telephone jingled. Colonel Min's adjutant informed him that the colonel was deciding.

Another breathless runner came up from the flank to report that Lieutenant Duk was dead and that the remaining survivors of the earlier engagements had pulled back a few hundred feet. Angrily, Choi went down again. Sharp words and several blows reinspirited his command. The machine-gun position was retaken. Wearily, he climbed the hill once more. He was down to eight Chesterfields and two lieutenants.

During the late morning, an American first lieutenant sauntered into Choi's sandbagged bunker. Choi had heard the commotion of the officer's coming, and waited, face a mask.

"One would under other circumstances be elated that you have come, Lieutenant Robertson."

Donald Robertson smiled cheerfully. "It was a long walk up your ridge, Captain. And it was not easy to find you." He offered his hand. "You don't seem very surprised to see an old friend."

"One is not surprised, Robbie-san. Your inquiries of yesterday afternoon reached me here. I have been expecting you." Choi shook hands, only slowly permitting himself a formal smile.

Robertson looked through the command-post viewing slit and remarked, "Sounds to me like you have a little fight on your hands, Captain. As I walked up I saw that your valley flank hung in the air. They'll try to pick at it until it buckles, unless they've changed tactics since I last played ball with them."

Choi frowned and said nothing.

Robertson turned. "If you knew I was in the area, why didn't you make it easier to find you? I got the royal runaround from the ROK army all yesterday afternoon."

Choi gestured toward the battle sounds, clearly evading Robertson's question. "The final fight will be here, on these ridges. They will tire of it soon. Their support artillery is fixed and they cannot advance beyond the range of those heavy guns." Choi added sadly, "Even China forgets that in the end it will be North Korea and South Korea. And both"—he hesitated before continuing, as if the subject were distasteful to him—"both nations are much stronger now than in 1950." The Korean rubbed his stubbled cheek, wiped some matter from the lashes of his left eye, and sagged visibly.

"You've had a hard night," Robertson said. "Can I help?"

"This is an affair for Orientals."

Robertson nodded. Choi shared a long silence with him before saying, "The Korean intelligence apparatus watches the Americans as closely as it watches the enemy. I have been informed of your affairs. I must congratulate you on your promotion to senior lieutenant."

"I'd better congratulate *you* on your promotions, Captain. I'm glad to see the ROK command structure finally came to its senses."

Choi shrugged it off. "Now you must tell me how you came here."

Robertson waved a hand toward the south, not immediately replying in words. He turned and listened to the intermittent firefight downslope, easily sorting out the Garands and the .30-caliber machine gun from the rapid-fire Chinese weapons. Visualizing the action, he judged it a stalemate. He spoke over his shoulder. "General Holloway was feeling good about something and relented enough to let me come up and see you."

The corps commander had sent for Robertson the previous morning. Robertson went in apprehensive, the way an assistant intelligence officer would respond to a summons from a three-star general who was rumored to be in line for a fourth one. Colonel Whitehead, the energetic chief of staff, was in Holloway's office. A bottle of Old Crow and several glasses sat among the papers on the general's desk.

General Holloway returned Robertson's salute and beamed to Colonel Whitehead. "Here is the man of the hour in this headquarters, Johnny." The general turned, threw back his head, and launched another huge smile at Robertson.

"Did you ever get drunk with a lieutenant general?"

"No, sir," Robertson replied. "But I got a noseful with a master sergeant once."

Holloway chuckled and poured half a glass of Old Crow. He pushed the glass across the desk to Robertson. "It's time we promoted you to dissipating yourself with the loftier classes."

Robertson sipped his whiskey and asked, "What are we celebrating, sir?"

General Holloway frowned. "As an intelligence officer, you *must* know?"

Colonel Whitehead stepped forward to speak, but a quick lift of Holloway's hand stayed him. Robertson said, "I know that the cease-fire will be signed tomorrow, sir. General Harrison will meet with Nam-il at Panmunjom at 1000 hours."

Holloway drummed his fingers on the TWX message which lay face down in the middle of the desk. "You *don't* know about my son Carl?"

Robertson hesitated before answering sympathetically, "I know your son's name was not on the prisoner exchange list, sir. I read the list twice, hoping it would be misspelled or mislisted." He added, "I'm sorry, sir. I had hoped to find his name there, along with some others which I didn't find either."

The general spun to Colonel Whitehead, who obviously had been waiting to speak. "Robertson doesn't know yet! And he has more right to know than any man in this command except me. He gave me hope when I had given it up myself."

"The message was 'eyes only' for you, sir," Whitehead said quickly.

The general laughed. "Best damned chief of staff I've ever had and you fail me in my finest hour, Johnny." The laughter geared down to a warm grin. "Well, maybe that's for the better. I can tell Robertson myself, the way I should have done two hours ago."

Holloway handed Robertson the TWX message he had been drumming.

Robertson skipped the laborious date-and-time group and the encripting codes and read the plain language. The message was from a brigadier he recognized as being on General Harrison's negotiating staff at Panmunjom. "Eyes Only to Gen. M. Holloway: Amended prisoner exchange list contains name Holloway, Carl H., 2Lt, Inf. Date of Birth 4Jan28. Health reported as Fair. Release scheduled 14 days."

Feeling better than he had felt in a year, Robertson smiled. "I'm happy for you, sir."

The general lifted his glass. "Let's drink to that, and to this damned mess being over."

After the toast, Holloway told Whitehead about the conversation in Robertson's room at the 107th on the day of the Silver Star presentation. Then he turned to Robertson again. "What do I owe you?"

"You owe me nothing, sir. I should never have intruded my opinion in a personal matter that way."

Holloway gestured to his chief of staff. "What do you think about it, Johnny?"

"I concur, sir. We owe Lieutenant Robertson."

Holloway turned to Robertson. "Name it. I'll grant it. But you needn't ask for your captaincy or for a commendation medal. I've already given orders on those two. And I've also given orders to send you stateside. General Thompson, your old regimental commander, has a fine command in Europe and he reminds me I've kept you here long enough."

When Robertson hesitated, Holloway added, "I also kept my promise to you, as you kept your promise to me."

Holloway spoke to Whitehead again. "I demanded that Lieutenant Robertson promise me that if I let him stay in Korea, he'd keep his nose out of combat. I know that wasn't easy for him. The junior officers tell me Robertson is a floor pacer. When a young officer paces the floor of his quarters at night, you know he is a man restive in an unwanted assignment."

Robertson made a motion to leave but Holloway stopped him with the warm smile again. "You apologized for putting your opinion into my private affairs. With an advance apology to you, I am going to tell you that I, too, am capable of a little intelligence work. A certain young nurse you kept company with at the 107th is now at Fort Sam Houston. You have enough accrued leave to get down to San Antonio after General—that is, President Eisenhower pins the Congressional Medal of Honor on you, and do most anything you want—"

Robertson took a deep breath and interrupted. "May I go up and say good-bye to an old friend, sir?"

The general frowned. He stared at Whitehead until the chief of staff broke the heavy silence with, "All American units are on easy alert, sir. The ROKs are engaged, but likely the Chinese will break contact any moment now."

Holloway drummed his fingers suspiciously, staring at Robertson, then at Whitehead. Slowly, the general's face relaxed, the way a face does when its owner has reassured himself. "Why the hell not? I said I'd grant his request, and that's his request. I'd have asked for more if I were in his boots." He grinned at Robertson. "I'd have asked for a voluptuous WAC, a private shack, and a new jeep with a top on it."

All three men laughed at the American soldier's hallowed wish list. They drank again and Holloway said, "Here are your terms, Lieutenant. Letter authority over my signature to go anywhere you wish. Two days. Than back here . . ." He turned once more to his chief of staff. "I want you to hurry those promotion orders for Robertson. Before I kick him out of here I want to put captain's tracks on his shoulders so he can afford to keep a wife."

At noon Robertson rattled down onto the division landing strip in the rear seat of an L-19. General Holloway's magic letter quickly produced a jeep and driver to take him to the ridge occupied by the Third Battalion of the 12th Regiment of the Republic of Korea army.

There, Robertson's intelligence work with the corps' Korean liaison officers had informed him that he would find Capt. Choi Min-soo commanding a company of riflemen.

Choi's telephone jangled again. Robertson and the three Koreans with Choi listened to Choi's side of what obviously was a rapid-fire exchange on tactical procedure. When he was finished, Choi put the telephone down and turned to his men. A sharp order removed them from the command post.

"My colonel is deciding," Choi said, smiling apologetically to Robertson. "He is of Taegu and is a man of great indecision." He frowned. "The man needs three hands, Robbie-san. On the one hand . . . then on the other hand . . . then again." He threw up his own hands in mock disgust.

Robertson smiled understandingly.

Choi's eyes narrowed. He lit two cigarettes and handed one to Robertson—the old gesture. "You came to me in haste, as would a man who fears an affair will expire before he is able to join it. I tried to delay you."

Robertson said nothing and Choi demanded, "Since I am your unwilling agent, you must at least explain to me how you now conceive it."

Robertson went to the firing slit again. The fight on Choi's right flank went through a brief flare of violence, then resumed the steady drumfire of the standoff. After listening to it a few moments, he turned and stared at Choi's telephone while he spoke.

"You have a right to know all of it, Choi."

The story of the *seikse* in Chunchon was easier to tell to Choi Min-soo than it had been to tell Mildred Baumiller. In the second telling, Robertson was able to discard the irrelevant details. If anything, that pointed and sharpened what remained.

Choi sighed heavily. "Then my comrade, too, has the severed head of a Corporal Saito at his feet."

"I'm afraid that is true, Choi."

Choi glanced pointedly at his telephone. "Colonel Min soon will have consumed his green tea."

The old shrapnel scar under Robertson's eye twitched, but he said nothing.

Choi's face hardened. "You Americans are romantics. A man dead is a man who is dead. That is all."

Robertson smiled faintly. "But it was you who told me about *ji-jin*, and you also explained that what is applauded in Seoul will be scorned in Washington. It is the other way around, too."

Choi hastened to say softly, "One does not scorn you."

The telephone rang. Choi listened in silence, then put the instrument into its receiver. He laughed bitterly. "Colonel Min has gone to relieve his bowels. He promises to inform me of his decision when he has accomplished that."

Robertson laughed. "Well, I am in high spirits and good humor. We can permit your colonel to be human."

Without warning, Choi reached brusquely for Robertson's arm. "Tell me, Robbie-san: that night in Chunchon, when you, as you define it, stalked the *seikse* you named Soon Lee, did you see Soon Lee as a gook?"

"Yes. I am sorry for that, but I did."

Choi nodded knowingly. After a moment he squeezed Robertson's arm and said, "Fortune is a ginner of vicissitudes and a weaver of snares. She weaved a snare and drew you to an alien land and set you down on a dark street and pointed to a small girl with her horrible finger. 'Go and take her. That is permissible because she is a gook and you are an American.' "

Robertson started to protest, but Choi silenced him and went on. "I have explained to you that 'gook' is simply our scurrilous Korean term *migook,* which means 'foreigner,' corrupted and turned back upon us, as we deserve." Choi went on rapidly now, his eyes fixed on the telephone. "I have also explained to you that politics are as the wind, now blowing from the land, now blowing from the sea. Someday, fortune will weave a snare for another peasant boy. She will draw him to a dark night street in America and point with her finger again. 'Take her,' she will hiss. 'She is a *migook* and you are a Korean.' "

When the telephone rang, Robertson's upper lip began to bead with sweat, a trait Solomon Zuckerman had several times noticed.

Choi listened in silence again, barking out only a sharp "Hai!"

He revolved slowly until he faced Robertson. "One is heartily sorry. The colonel's bowels are relieved."

Lt. Gen. William K. Harrison, for the UN, and the hard-faced North Korean Nam-il, for the Communist belligerents, had in stony silence inked the documents that would settle nothing at 1000 hours that Monday morning of 27 July 1953. A young American MP stood at parade rest behind General Harrison's table and a North Korean soldier stood at attention behind that of Nam-il. Early in the negotiations tables and chairs had been important. The Communists owned the hall and they had sawn the legs off the Americans' chairs. This was done to convince the attending world that defeated Americans looked up in supplication to victorious Orientals.

Notwithstanding the new amity of the equalized chair legs at Panmunjom, the Chinese and the 12th ROKs and their American guest on Choi's hill near Big Nori fought most of the afternoon. Because the firefight was as indecisive as Choi's Colonel Min, it dragged on, like the war of which it was a part, between killing lethargy and killing vigor.

Robertson had borrowed an M-1. Helmetless except for the hachimaki Choi Min-soo had made for him, he fought in the most exposed area of Choi's right-flank perimeter, often standing erect, firing as calmly as he would have fired on the three-hundred-yard target range. When his rifle seized with heat, he took another from one of Choi's casualties. The casualty had been hit in the head and slumped against the sandbags by Robertson's right foot, arms strangely folded in his lap. After a while, Robertson had put down the rifle to turn the Korean's face away, not wanting to have dead eyes staring at him any longer.

Since neither side could intervene with artillery fire, Choi's fight was an affair of rifles and grenades, a dust-shrouded effort reminiscent of Cemetery Ridge or the Reno fight on the ridge above Little Bighorn during the Custer battle.

As on Little Bighorn in 1876, it became punishingly hot in the early afternoon. Heads began to ache from the constant hammer of ordnance. When the canteens dried up, lips chapped and tongues thickened. The wounded began to cry out for water. Choi's Koreans twice tried to get water onto the position. Both times the galling Chinese fire interdicted.

Once the Chinese surged up through the plum trees to within grenade range. Robertson stood on the sandbags, silhouetted against the sky, throwing down the grenades Choi passed up to him.

By 1600 hours, Choi was out of machine-gun ammunition. Within minutes, as if they had been informed of it, the Chinese shortened the range. Now, from the shelter of trees, they sniped away and Choi's worst casualty attrition began. Soon he was reduced to nineteen men and Robertson. Choi dispatched two men for machine-gun ammunition. The Chinese cut them down before they had gone a hundred feet. Then Choi had seventeen men and Robertson.

The fight lulled, and a Korean pointed up the slope, shouting excitedly.

They watched the Chinese fire prick up dust at the feet of the runner who weaved down toward them. As he ran, the man lost his helmet. Where the band had been was a white strip of wet flesh. The face the runner put to

Choi's was contorted and grimed. Choi listened to him, then turned to Robertson.

"Colonel Min has found his other hand. Now I am no longer to hold this position."

Robertson set his lips. "Take your men and get out, Choi. I'll stay. You need someone to cover your disengagement."

"One can leave a countryman. Come with me. I beg you."

Robertson hesitated. Then he brushed the hachimaki with his fingers and said, "No, Choi. You know I can't."

They stared at each other. Choi's eyes slitted as they did when he debated himself, but he said nothing.

Three brown-clad riflemen stood up in the plum trees down below them and began firing. The rounds passed overhead. Robertson shouted, "Now, Choi!" and leaped over the sandbags to stand between the Koreans and the Chinese. He fired rapidly and Choi flushed his men. Not looking back, the Koreans fled up the hill, dragging their wounded, leaving the machine gun and the ROK corpses.

Choi followed a few paces, but stopped when heavy fire broke out back at the position. Robertson was down on his knees now, but still fighting. He paused to reload, and the three Chinese he had held at bay advanced several paces, firing as they walked. Robertson reeled back on his heels, then tried to stand. A Chinese fired a long burst and he fell.

Choi screamed, "No! No, Robbie-san!"

He ran back. He had discarded his own rifle.

The three Chinese stood staring as Choi reached Robertson's side. Back to them, as Robertson's back had been to the enemy that day on Konsi, Choi took Robertson into his arms, as Robertson had taken Fowlkes.

In all the armies, in all the world, there is no other way to console a dying comrade.

Robertson's eyes opened once, as if he recognized Choi. Then they closed. Blood seeped through the hachimaki and ran down his face. But the face was in peace. All the world pain had gone out of it.

Choi sat stiffly, head bowed, cradling Robertson, heedless of the men at his back. Somewhere down below the leafless plum trees a whistle blew, three sharp longs and one short, as the grim-faced infantrymen of the American divisions had heard the shrill, eerie Chinese communications whistles in 1950. Choi lifted his head and turned to confront his enemies.

His eyes selected the taller of the three Chinese infantrymen. Choi spoke in Mandarin, a language he had learned when he had been a young officer serving the Imperial Japanese Army in China.

"Your mother," Choi said forcefully, "is a promiscuous harlot."

Turning back, Choi could see the sun, now falling downward, arcing lovely and orange against the mountains of the austerely beautiful land of the ancient Tungusic people. That sun sang sweetly to him, as it had sung sweetly that day in Okinawa when he first had put eyes to the lovely Kyoko in her gay kimono and getas. But he closed his eyes from it. He took a deep breath, savoring that instead.

The tall Chinese lifted his burp gun. "Such an insult cannot be accepted," he said to Choi's back. "It must be avenged. But I shall offer you a moment."

Choi whispered to Robertson, in Japanese, to keep it private for them. "You are my second chrysanthemum, but no less radiant for that."

Eyes yet closed firmly, although the sunlight got in through the lids, Choi lifted his head and thrust out his chin.

The tall Chinese fired.

The whistle blew again. The three Chinese riflemen backed up a few paces, then turned and went sliding down the hill, leaving a trail of red dust behind them. The fight on the anonymous height near Big Nori ridge was over.

And, at 2200 hours that evening, three years, one month, two days, and two million human lives after it began that rainy Sabbath day in June 1950, the first gunpowder phase of the Korean War was over.

EPILOGUE

Fort Hood, Texas,
August 20, 1953

In a column of twos, the platoon marched down the boulevard between the white barracks. There was something elegant about the marching men in their uniforms, an image of order imposed onto a disorderly world.

The recruits wore shiny fatigues over new, but dusty boots. They slung M-1 rifles. The web belts around their damp waists bristled with bayonet, canteen, first-aid packet, and although it had scarcely rained on Fort Hood all that Spartan summer of 1953, each soldier had a folded poncho bumping on his backside.

Sgt. Solomon Zuckerman marched on the street side of the column. Head erect, he carried the cadreman's ubiquitous clipboard in his cupped left hand, against his wrist. He swung the clipboard. Several automobiles followed the column, observing the iron rule of military posts: marchers first, vehicles second.

Bronze-tanned, muscular, the sergeant wore an infantry blue helmet liner to set himself apart from his charges. His fatigues were gray with a hundred starchings, creased sharply even in that late afternoon of a day on the blistering training range. On his left breast, Zuckerman wore the Combat Infantryman's Badge, a musket on a blue background, superimposed on a silver wreath. In 1953, that was not a trinket given for having had lunch with an infantry officer.

Overhead, the sky reached to the end of the universe. The summer sun lazed, now somewhat down, angling toward its own retreat in the sanded nothingness west of Fort Hood. Beyond the sand lay the Pacific, then a few rocks, then the peninsula that still occupied the thoughts of khaki men.

His platoon was obviously tired. The men had dark circles under their armpits. Here and there a heavy face dripped sweat, for Zuckerman had double-timed them for almost all of the first mile. The formation was an olive green centipede, with a hundred pounding feet. It approached the intersection of the broad boulevard and the narrower blacktop street that led to the company area. Zuckerman turned his head and barked, "Road guards out right and left! Ho!" He glanced to see that his two men had gone out to stand at parade rest in the face of the oncoming traffic, halting it for the marchers. He added automatically, "Pick up the step!" That was unnecessary. He had drilled them well, not a man put down his right when he should have put down his left.

Beyond the intersection, the sergeant called in his guards. He began the mindless, "Your left, your left, your left right left. Hup twop threep fourp, your left . . ." He fell silent. The column passed A Company mess hall. Two KPs looked up from scrubbing the garbage cans and he gave them a thin sympathetic smile. Beyond the one-story frame building that housed A Company supply room and its dayroom, he ordered a column right, then a halt, then a left face. He kept them at attention a moment, as if he did not want to let them go. But then he called, "Platoon! Fall out."

Instantly, the taut ranks dissolved into a mob, talkative as novices released from a long vespers.

Before the men had evaporated, as if he had forgotten something, Zuckerman shouted, "Fall in!"

A soldier cried out, "Shit, no. Not again?"

Zuckerman shook his head. He smiled sadly but said loudly, "Yes, Private Billings, if it would not be too inconvenient for you at this moment, it would be very pleasing to me if you gentlemen would reassemble in our little military formation."

A few of the men snickered. One goosed Billings with the barrel of his rifle. The men re-formed too slowly. Zuckerman shouted fiercely, "Fall in! Goddamn it. I've seen better drill at the old soldiers' home."

The men murmured and hastily completed the formation. They jostled and nudged to get their intervals. "Fall in at attention!" Zuckerman reminded, as he always did.

The eyes went front, staring, half-fearful in the face of this unexpected behavior.

Zuckerman grinned. "I'm going to the separation center in the morning. I forgot to say good-bye to you."

Billings called out of ranks, "How many days, Sarge?"

"Five," he said. "Takes half a day to get in the army; takes ten half days to get out of it." His grin broadened. "Five days," he repeated. "Four more taps then one glorious reveille."

The men snickered jealously.

The sergeant grew serious. "You troopers might make passable infantry soldiers if the horned lizards don't eat your toes off when you go out on bivouac next week. Sergeant Danbury takes over tomorrow. He's Third Division out of Korea and he knows where the bear hides in the woods. Soldier for him as well as you've soldiered for me, and if he's in a good mood, he'll teach you how to keep from getting your asses shot off."

First Sergeant Wherron, a heavy, muscular man in his forties, came out of the side door of the supply room and stood watching. Zuckerman grinned affectionately in his direction and said to his formation, but clearly for Wherron's benefit, "Love and respect the First Shirt here, but don't believe a damned word he tells you. He's World War II–issue and he thinks we still use smooth-bore muskets." Dropping his voice, he added, "You'll train for Korea, and you well might get to go there. If you do, I hope you get an NCO like the one I drew when I went."

The first sergeant laughed and gestured to the men. "You've lathered them enough for today, Sergeant Zuckerman. The Old Man wants to see you in his office."

Zuckerman studied his ranks a moment, then dismissed them. Several came to punch his shoulder for being wise enough to accept a discharge from the army. They bubbled a bit, then began to drift toward the barracks and the waiting shower room. He watched them go.

He was more certain of it now than ever. In ranks, men were a soulless machine with a mindless purpose. Only out of ranks did men have individual purposes. He smiled. It would be up to them to learn what that meant.

Wherron led him into Captain Williams's office and closed the door firmly. Captain Williams looked up from his papers and said, "I'm supposed to give you a reenlistment speech."

Zuckerman smiled and said politely, "Yes, sir, I know that. And no, sir."

The captain nodded thoughtfully. "Thought so." He cupped his hand to his ear and spoke to the first sergeant. "Isn't that the retreat gun I hear?"

Wherron glanced at his watch. "No, sir. Can't be. It's only 1642."

Reaching into his desk drawer, Williams removed a fifth of Cutty Sark. Rummaging loudly, he came up with two small glasses and a coffee mug. He grinned at his first sergeant. "As between a commissioned officer and an enlisted man, First Sergeant, who is presumed to have the better ears."

"An officer, Captain. Must have been the retreat gun you heard."

"Never drink on the duty side of the retreat gun," the captain said solemnly. He poured them three large drinks and lifted his glass to Solomon Zuckerman. "You're a damned fine NCO. Thank you. Wish I had a dozen like you."

"A damned fine NCO taught me, sir."

"Whoever he was, he taught you well."

They finished the drinks and shook hands.

"Good luck out there," the captain said.

Zuckerman went over to the mail room and caught the mail orderly just as he was locking the window.

"Three today," the orderly said. He held one of the letters to his nose and sniffed lasciviously. "Sugar report from Miss Kahan. Right on schedule."

Zuckerman walked slowly over to the barracks and went up to the second floor. The captain's farewell Scotch had warmed him and he felt suffused with the tired glow of a day's duty, well done. His day had begun at 0500.

He turned right at the head of the stairs and stood a moment before the door of his cadre room, one of three such rooms at the end of the troop bay. As he always did, with a glow of pride, he read the placard.

"S. Zuckerman, Platoon Sergeant, Third Platoon."

Inside, Zuckerman unlaced his trim jump boots, working with one hand while he studied the envelopes. Rachel's letter was on top, pink, perfumed stationery. It would be rife with wedding plans. He threw it onto his desk, on top of his clipboard. The second envelope was typed. That indicated Avram Zuckerman; the letter would be fat with admonitions and fatherly advice, done now with tactfulness that bordered on the clumsy. Zuckerman wriggled his grateful toes and put the typed letter on top of Rachel's.

The third letter was grubby and wrinkled. It bore no postage, simply marked "Free." The envelope carried an APO, San Francisco, return address, and the name Klineschmidt. Of the three, it called out loudest.

Klineschmidt had not written since he had volunteered ten months earlier to return to Korea. Zuckerman opened it greedily. Under dateline of 29 July 1953, Kraut had penciled:

What I'm writing about, Solly, is something that happened yesterday. I got sent with a detail over to the 12th ROK regiment on our flank to get the body of an American who was killed there. At least that's all I thought it was at first. Lieutenant Galt took us. All I knew when we hiked out was that the dead guy was a first lieutenant from corps headquarters. Figured it was some staff officer who wandered into the ROKs' fight and got it in the last hours. (The Chinks hit the ROKs like a ton of you-know-what on the last day, almost right up to the last minute.) Anyway, I guess I'm getting you confused. I'm not good at writing letters, Solly, but I'm trying to tell it to you the way it happened to me. And how it would have happened to you if you was here.

Klineschmidt had scratched out two sentences. Then he wrote:

I may as well tell you, Solly. The American was Robertson and he had got together with Choi somehow. He was with Choi down in a bunker. Choi must have lived for a while after they got hit and must have dragged Robertson in. There was a long trail of blood. It had to be Choi who died last, Solly—Lieutenant Robertson was hit bad, right in the head.

I wish I was there with you when you read this, Solly, to tell you how sorry I am. I know how you felt about Robertson and Choi.

Here, Klineschmidt had crossed out another sentence.

Zuckerman rubbed his hand quickly across his dry mouth and resumed reading.

Anyway, the ROKs hadn't moved the bodies. Guess they were afraid that we'd get pissed off that one of ours got hit in their area and didn't want responsibility for it. They might be right on that score. When I explained to Lieutenant Galt who Lieutenant Robertson was, he turned white as a sheep and said the corps commander would have somebody's ass over it. Don't know what that was all about.

They were down in a bunker like I said and Choi was holding Robertson in his arms like Robertson held Fowlkes on Konsi that day. Robertson wore that white cloth on his head like he used to and scare the s—t out of us.

After another obliterated sentence, Klineschmidt had written:

Choi had his lips on Robertson's forehead. Lieutenant Galt said it was accidental and called it a macabre kiss (another guy spelt that one for me) and said they just died and fell into that position. I set his ass straight on it. It was an intentional kiss, Solly, and we both know that.

Anyway, I wish again I could tell you in words how I felt about it. They was true friends to both of us, maybe you more than me. You've probably already done the counting, Solly, but I've done it, too. Of the original guys in summer '51, only me and you and Carver are left. Gives a guy a lot to think about.

It was over at 2200 hours on the twenty-seventh. Now everybody wants to go home, but I got news for them. We are going to be here for a while. The shooting stopped, but the war ain't stopped. Anyway, when we got the word, we fired up everything we had to celebrate.

Below his signature, Kraut had written a postscript. "I got to thinking about it just now. Americans and Koreans must have died together like Robertson and Choi in the first days."

Zuckerman folded the letter and put it on his desk. He lay back on his cot, arms behind his head, and stared at the brown pressboard ceiling. He idled in time, using up only space.

Later, a sergeant from the adjoining room opened the door and put his head in. "Want some chow? Meat loaf and mashed potatoes."

Zuckerman shook his head. After the man was gone he got up and locked his door. Sitting at his desk, he removed the picture of Yoshiko Yamada from his writing portfolio. He studied it, recalling effortlessly the day in Nara he had caused it to be made. Yoshiko posed in her red dress with his pearls at her neck. Her hair fell down in a ponytail and she smiled through lips made thick with red under the dark pixie eyes. Firmly, grim-lipped, bowing his head the way a man leans unconsciously into the fire of a frontal attack, he tore the picture into shreds, throwing it into his green wastebasket.

He lay down as before and let the darkness come in through the curtainless window and find him that way, staring at the ceiling. He had put Yoshiko Yamada down into some buttressed compartment of his to-be-remembered youth where she would be safe forever. He had turned his thoughts to Rachel Kahan, and college and law school, using the thought the way he once had used soil thrown up around his fighting hole.

He dozed lightly, still dressed. He awoke when taps sounded. The bugle notes rose and fell, tinny in the company public-address system. Within seconds, he heard beyond his door the thud of the charge of quarters' boots as he climbed the stairs for lights out.

The slot at the base of the door went black. The bunker on George Three had gone dark that way the night Robertson had sealed the opening with his own body.

Sleep denied itself to Zuckerman, leaving him a prisoner of his own troubled mind. He kept seeing an image, one he always had understood partially, but now completely for the first time. He saw the stretcher bearers carrying Lieutenant Robertson away from the bunker on George Three. He had seen men walk hurriedly with stretchers. He had seen men trot with stretchers. But only for Robertson did he ever see them run.

Something else struck. He reached across to his desk and switched on the light, groping for Klineschmidt's letter. When his eyes adjusted, he held the letter against the lamp. Now he could read the obliterated sentences. As he expected, one of the sentences Kraut had crossed out was, "You might think I'm Asiatic or something, but I loved Robertson like I loved all you guys."

Toward midnight, Zuckerman got up to stand at the window of his room, next to the tall brown locker that contained his uniforms and equipment. A small light wafted over the open assembly ground between the Second Platoon and the Third Platoon barracks and a breeze came down across there from the slot between the buildings. That ground was hard, worn grassless, packed by a thousand boots. Zuckerman rubbed his forehead with his hand and the hand came away wet.

The air temperature had sagged to its dew point. Vapors had formed a few feet above the earth to undulate on the breeze. Zuckerman stared a long time at the mist.

Then he was certain of it. Figures had come to dance there. At first they were phantasms, formless and sexless. Only when they turned their faces up to him did the mists assume meaning.

The figures laughed and they cried. They had laughed that way the day they ran down the hill to chase Robertson's errant helmet. They had cried that way the day they patrolled to the hut of the old Korean hermit and the dying North Korean soldier.

Zuckerman lifted a hand and waved. As his own platoon had done earlier in the day, the figures formed and, in unison, waved back. The leader smiled, but he did not beckon. Then the mists disintegrated and became merely Texas radiation fog again. It was as if the figures had crossed a river, out of sight, but, vehemently, never out of mind.

Zuckerman thought then about all of them who had gone to the war. Pliant, unquestioning children of the forties, they had gone without a parade to listen among the hostile rocks of Korea for the sound of tigers who wore tennis shoes and who beat cymbals and blew whistles. No parade greeted those who returned; perhaps no monuments would ever be built.

But they had kept the faith of their place and time. Even if history proved the Korean War only the morbid jest of an irresponsible god, that honor could not wilt.

In effect, they had paid a ransom. Zuckerman sighed when he realized that. A democracy had a right to be wrong, but it did not have the right to refuse to pay the blood price a violent world demanded it pay for its own maintenance.

They had gone. Often outnumbered by the tens to the one they had stood in the crushing heat of the Korean summer and in the brutal wind of the Korean winter, always fighting up onto higher ground.

And, strange as it may seem to those who had not gone, the Americans and Chinese had fought in Korea without personal hatred. Already, the Chinese told the world that the army the homebound Americans had scorned was the best of the many they had fought. American infantrymen returned the honor to the Chinese, doubled and in spades.

Zuckerman had not believed the stories until it happened to him. Late one night, when his pounding heart sucked his mouth dry, he had blundered a patrol into the muzzle of a Chinese machine gun. That night in Korea had been overcast, and at that moment the moon broke out. Zuckerman remembered he had motioned for his men to take cover, but that he himself had been able to stand, drawing the gunner's attention away from his men. He had held his breath, certain he was to die.

He could see it now, as he had recalled it a thousand times. He and the Chinese gunner had stared across the space that separated them. Zuckerman waited for the finger to flex on the trigger of the gun. But then, inexplicably, the gunner had stood, exposing his own body, and waved them on to safety.

It was strange even to him, and he'd never tell it to anyone else, but Zuckerman that night had walked erect away from the gunner, presenting the broadest back he could possibly have offered, although his reprieved men scrambled. He had not even drawn in his head. As accurately as Zuckerman had ever been able to explain it to himself, and he had thought about it more than a year, the Chinese, who was merely keeping his own faith, true to his own place and time, was entitled to change his mind.

And perhaps the mortal faith he and the Chinese shared in those few seconds was the best faith of them all.

As Choi Min-soo so often explained, politics are as the wind.

Now, at his window, Zuckerman made a vow. Someday—maybe he'd be old and the war forgotten—but someday he would ride another ship across the Pacific. He would revisit Korea, then go on to Peiping or Canton and stand in a street and demand to meet his enemy. They'd be old, too, but, as would he, they'd remember well the nights on the angry mountains.

"Come, brothers," he would say to them. "Let us break bread together."

Given sufficient time, and enough political wind, that could be done in Pyongyang.

Solomon Zuckerman felt rising in him the thing that had come as an infant that day when strong tortured Dougherty and strong sad Robertson buried the two dead North Koreans in their own fighting hole under the trees. That infant had grown, and it had become strong. He didn't know when the infant had matured, maybe in Nara, maybe later when he scooped up the hand grenade from under Kraut's feet, but it matured. No one would understand it who had not been there, but Zuckerman knew it now for what it was.

Zuckerman threw open his window and put his head out into the night. He whispered, for a whisper is as likely to cross a river as Choi's chrysanthemum was to reach the sea.

"We went and we did what had to be done. In the midst of that, despite them all, we loved each other. Let that be our monument."

ABOUT THE AUTHOR

James Hickey served as an infantryman and as a guard in a U.N. POW camp during the Korean War. Born in Kansas, Hickey has taught journalism and communications research at the University of Colorado and the University of Oklahoma. His published work in magazines includes several pieces on military history. This is his first novel.